Kristi Gold has always believed that love has remarkable healing powers and feels very fortunate to be able to weave stories of romance and commitment. As a best-selling author and a Romance Writers of America RITA® Award finalist, she's learned that although accolades are wonderful, the most cherished rewards come from personal stories shared by readers.

You can reach Kristi at KGOLDAUTHOR@aol.com, through her website at www.kristigold.com or snail-mail at PO Box 9070, Waco, Texas, 76714, USA. (Please include an SAE with return postage for a response.)

D0756134

A Royal Wager

KRISTI GOLD

MILLS & BOON

All rights reserved including the right of reproduction in whole or in part in any form. This edition is published by arrangement with Harlequin Books S.A.

This is a work of fiction. Names, characters, places, locations and incidents are purely fictional and bear no relationship to any real life individuals, living or dead, or to any actual places, business establishments, locations, events or incidents. Any resemblance is entirely coincidental.

This book is sold subject to the condition that it shall not, by way of trade or otherwise, be lent, resold, hired out or otherwise circulated without the prior consent of the publisher in any form of binding or cover other than that in which it is published and without a similar condition including this condition being imposed on the subsequent purchaser.

® and ™ are trademarks owned and used by the trademark owner and/or its licensee. Trademarks marked with ® are registered with the United Kingdom Patent Office and/or the Office for Harmonisation in the Internal Market and in other countries.

First Published in Great Britain 2018
by Mills & Boon, an imprint of HarperCollins*Publishers*
1 London Bridge Street, London, SE1 9GF

A ROYAL WAGER © 2018 Harlequin Books S. A.

Persuading the Playboy King © 2004 Kristi Goldberg
Unmasking the Maverick Prince © 2004 Kristi Goldberg
Daring the Dynamic Sheikh © 2004 Kristi Goldberg

ISBN: 978-0-263-26875-1

0818

MIX
Paper from
responsible sources
FSC™ C007454

This book is produced from independently certified FSC™ paper to ensure responsible forest management.

For more information visit: www.harpercollins.co.uk/green

Printed and bound in Spain
by CPI, Barcelona

PERSUADING THE PLAYBOY KING

KRISTI GOLD

To my incredible editor, Patience Smith,
for believing in this series.

Special acknowledgement goes to Geoffrey and
Lisa Buie-Collard for pushing me beyond high school
French. And to their niece, Dorian, for inspiring a
fantastical country.

Prologue

Prince Marcel Frederic DeLoria had a fondness for fast cars and the freedom he enjoyed while executing hairpin turns on winding roads. Yet his greatest pleasure came in the form of more dangerous curves, those that could be found on a woman. He appreciated every nuance of the opposite sex—the way they looked, the way they smelled, their innate intelligence and, admittedly, the challenges they could present when it came to the chase.

But as much as he loved women, he hated goodbyes and for that reason he'd avoided emotional entanglements. Still, tonight an inevitable parting hung over him like a guillotine, poised to sever ties four years in the making.

A few hours ago, Marc had taken his Harvard diploma and was now set to embrace his independence. However, he did not particularly look forward to saying goodbye to Sheikh Dharr Halim, in line to rule his country one day, and Mitchell Edward Warner III, the son of a United States senator and

American royalty in his own right. Three men bound by status, united by all that their legacies entailed, forever joined by a friendship that had grown and strengthened during their time together.

Noisy revelry filtered through the closed door from outside, a celebration signaling the end of an era, the end of their youth in a manner of speaking. The trio had opted to forgo the party and instead sequestered themselves in their shared apartment where they had formed their own fraternity of sorts, spending the past four years discussing culture, world events and their latest adventures skirting the ever-present paparazzi. And their favorite subject—women.

But tonight an uncharacteristic silence prevailed, as if the time-honored topics were inconsequential in light of what now awaited them—a future that no one could predict beyond their families' expectations.

Marc reclined on the black overstuffed chair, his heels propped on the table before him. Dharr sat regally in the tan leather lounger across from Marc, the traditional Arabian kaffiyeh no longer covering his head; yet he still gave the appearance of a born leader. Mitch had opted for his customary roost on the floor reclined against the wall, dressed in jeans and scuffed leather cowboy boots, apparel that stood out from the crowd like a crown on a pauper. But although they were all different, Marc acknowledged, they still shared notoriety, the reason behind their frequent gatherings, a means to cope with the pressures of celebrity.

Mitch tossed aside the magazine he'd been reading since their arrival and picked up the bottle of fine French champagne, compliments of Marc's brother, the king. "We've already toasted our success. Now I suggest we toast a long bachelorhood." He refilled his glass, then topped off Dharr's and Marc's.

Dharr raised his flute. "I would most definitely toast to that."

With champagne in hand, Marc paused to consider an idea—an appropriate send-off. One that would pique his friend's interests. "I prefer to propose a wager."

Dharr and Mitch glanced at one another then leveled their gazes on Marc. "What kind of wager, DeLoria?" Mitch asked.

"Well, since we've all agreed that we're not suited for marriage in the immediate future, if ever, I suggest we hold ourselves to those terms by wagering we'll all be unmarried on our tenth reunion."

"And if we are not?" Dharr asked.

Marc saw only one way to ensure the wager's success. "We'll be forced to give away our most prized possession."

"Give away my gelding?" Mitch grimaced as if he'd swallowed something foul. "That would be tough."

Dharr looked even less enthusiastic as his gaze fell on the abstract painting of a woman hanging above Mitch's head. "I suppose that would be my Modigliani original, and I must admit that giving away the nude would cause me great suffering."

"That's the point, gentlemen," Marc said. "The wager would mean nothing if the possessions were meaningless."

Mitch eyed him with suspicion. "Okay, DeLoria. What's it going to be for you?"

Marc thought only a moment before adding, "The Corvette."

"You'd give up the love mobile?" Mitch sounded incredulous.

"Of course not. I won't lose." And he wouldn't, because Marc DeLoria hated losing anything of worth.

"Nor will I," Dharr stated. "Ten years will be adequate before I am forced to adhere to an arranged marriage in order to produce an heir."

"No problem for me," Mitch said. "I'm going to avoid marriage at all costs."

Again Dharr held up his glass. "Then we are all agreed?"

Mitch touched his flute to Dharr's and Marc's. "Agreed."

Modern-day musketeers entering into an all-for-one pact.
Marc raised his glass. "Let the wager begin."

Marc had no qualms about the ante. He could most definitely resist the temptation of a woman bent on tying him to
an uneventful existence. He had no reason to marry, nor was
he bound by duty to do so. Only one thing would be as unappealing to Marc as marriage—leading his country. But thanks
to his birth order, Prince Marcel Frederic DeLoria would
never have to suffer the fate of becoming king.

One

Nine years later

Marcel Frederic DeLoria had become a king.

Kate Milner had known him only as Marc, a seriously charming young man. A seriously inept biology student by his own admission, the reason why Kate had tutored him their freshman year at Harvard. And now he was the ruler of Doriana, a small European country.

Incredible.

Of course, the fact that she was standing in a storybook castle thousands of miles from home, preparing to see him again almost a decade later, seemed highly improbable, too. That made Kate smile.

But her smile immediately dissolved when he appeared at the end of the ornate palace foyer, a starched and polished middle-aged gentleman at his side. The mirrored walls, reflecting bursts of light from the crystal chandeliers, seemed to shrink as he drew closer, his confidence and calculated control almost palpable, even at a distance. His hair was still the same golden brown, somewhat longer than before, Kate realized, the fine layers windswept away from his face. Although he stood only slightly over six feet tall, he seemed more imposing now than when she'd known him before, with a broader chest and equally broad shoulders encased in a short-sleeved, form-fitting navy knit shirt that enhanced the considerable bulk of his biceps. He also wore a pair of faded jeans that outlined his narrow hips and solid thighs—the kind of clothes he'd worn in college, much to Kate's surprise. He was, after all, nobility.

Good grief. Had she really expected him to be decked out in a jewel-encrusted crown and red velvet robe? That he would be clutching a scepter instead of a pair of sunglasses? Silly that she would even consider such a thing. But she'd expected he at least would be wearing an expensive suit, not attire that could be found in a chic women's magazine ad extolling the virtues of cosmopolitan casual on hard-body hunks. Not that she was complaining.

When he came to a stop a few feet away, Kate was suddenly gripped by the sheer power of his presence, her pulse accelerating in response. She clung tightly to her composure when she contacted his piercing cobalt blue eyes—eyes that no longer held the mirth she had often witnessed during their previous time together. She saw something there that she couldn't quite peg. She also sensed an edge about him, a definite change that went far beyond the physical aspects.

One thing Kate did know, he gave no indication whatsoever that he recognized her. But why should he? Kate had changed, too, hopefully for the better.

The attendant took a brusque step forward and executed a slight bow. "Dr. Milner, I am Bernard Nicholas, His Majesty's primary aide."

Kate had the illogical urge to salute—or curtsy. She opted for a smile. "A pleasure to meet you."

Mr. Nicholas turned his attention to the silent, stoic king. "Your Majesty, may I present Dr. Katherine Milner, our latest candidate for the hospital position."

Marc moved forward and extended his hand, which Kate took after a slight hesitation. "Welcome to Doriana, Dr. Milner, and please forgive my appearance. I wasn't given much notice in regard to your arrival."

His voice sounded much the way Kate remembered, European sophisticated and distinctly seductive, only deeper. Yet he didn't look at all pleased, didn't even hint at a smile. In fact, his courtesy seemed almost forced. Considering the early hour, and his unshaven face, she couldn't help but wonder if maybe he'd just left the company of a woman, quite possibly a woman's bed.

His extracurricular activities shouldn't concern her. Yet the feel of his large masculine fingers wrapped around hers brought about a keen sense of awareness, the kind of awareness that came when confronted with a man she had been far too fond of. But Marc DeLoria was no ordinary man; he never had been. And obviously he had no recollection of their time together.

Kate decided he simply needed a reminder. "It's very nice to see you again, *Your Majesty.*"

He released her hand and frowned, fine lines deepening at the corners of his eyes, but they didn't detract from his magnificent face. "Have we met before?"

"Actually, the last time we were together, we were dissecting a deceased frog."

Confusion worked its way into his sedate expression followed by a fleeting glimpse of the carefree charmer she had once known. "Katie? The tutor?"

Kate's gaze faltered for a brief moment as she became the circumspect girl again. She forced away that notion, forced herself to look at him straight on. "Yes, that's me. Katie, the tutor. But I prefer Kate now. Or Dr. Milner, if that's more acceptable considering your current circumstance."

"My current circumstance?"

He actually had to be reminded of that, too? "You're a king."

"Ah, yes. That circumstance." He stared at her for a long moment, as if he couldn't quite believe she was there. Kate couldn't quite believe it, either.

After a bout of awkward silence, she finally said, "It's been a while, hasn't it?"

"Yes, quite a while." Although his smile had yet to form, he at least looked a little less perplexed when he gestured to a nearby room. "Shall we conduct the interview in the library, Doctor?"

Obviously he had no intention of taking a walk down memory lane. "Of course."

When Marc stepped to one side of the room's entry, Kate passed by him and caught a whiff of fresh air and fragrant cologne—clean, expensive, heavenly. Even though she shouldn't react so strongly, he still made her breathless. She'd always been that way to some degree in his presence.

Gathering her wits, Kate slowly turned around to survey the mahogany shelves lining the room. "This is quite a collection of books."

"My mother's favorites." He indicated a small settee near the window. "Please, have a seat."

Kate slid onto the green brocade sofa while Marc took the burgundy wingback chair across from her. When Mr. Nicholas positioned himself near the now-closed door, Marc told him, "That will be all."

The man stood steadfastly in place like a sentry, shoulders square, feet slightly apart, hands behind his back. "Beg pardon, but I believe it would be best if I remained, considering our guest is a lady."

"This is not the eighteenth century, Mr. Nicholas. You are dismissed."

"The Queen Mother—"

"Would understand the need for privacy."

"But—"

"I assure you that Dr. Milner's virtue is not in peril." Marc turned his attention to Kate. "Would you prefer not to be alone with me?"

She shrugged. "I don't see it as a problem at all. It certainly wouldn't be the first time." She secretly hoped it wouldn't be the last.

Marc sent another warning look at the attendant. "Tell Madame Tourreau to bring Dr. Milner some refreshments."

"As you wish, Your Reverence," Mr. Nicholas said, then took his leave.

Kate turned her attention to Marc, who looked anything but pleased. "Your Reverence?"

"Please ignore Mr. Nicholas. He's been with the family for quite some time and he has a penchant for making up titles. You should be flattered, though. Normally he doesn't do this around strangers, unless he feels they might appreciate his extremely dry and somewhat annoying British sense of humor."

"Oh, I see. It's sort of a game between you two."

"One game I would prefer not to play."

Kate could only imagine the games he did like to play—sensual games—and she really wouldn't mind playing them with him.

Business, Kate. No games, just business.

Marc crossed his legs at the ankles, his elbows resting on the chair's arms, hands clasped across his midsection. "So tell me, Dr. Milner, how did you discover we're seeking physicians in Doriana?"

Kate toyed with her hem, surprisingly drawing Marc's gaze. Considering her disheveled state, he probably wondered if the royal cat had dragged her across the regal door-step. Her lavender silk suit showed creases resulting from hours of travel. Her hair had lost every bit of its curl and now hung down in board-straight strands to her shoulders. When his gaze came to rest on her mouth, she assumed she had a pink lipstick smear across her teeth.

Kate resisted the urge to run a finger over her incisors. "I saw the story in the alumni newsletter, right after your coronation," she said, pulling his attention back to her eyes. "You mentioned that your first order of business involved recruiting doctors, so I contacted the hospital, and now here I am. By the way, I was very sorry to hear about your brother's car accident."

She saw a flash of sadness in his eyes before it vanished as quickly as it had come. "Did you attend medical school at Harvard?"

Considering his swift change of subject, Kate made a mental note not to bring up his brother's death again. "Actually, I returned home to Tennessee and went to Vanderbilt. I needed to be close to my family."

"Was someone ill?" he asked with concern.

"Not really." Only needy, and very overprotective as always, which was one of the reasons why Kate had decided to apply for the position—the other was sitting before her. She'd grown tired of being the perfect, reliable daughter—the person both her parents depended upon for everything. She loved them dearly, but at times she wished she'd had siblings to ease some of her burden.

Marc crossed his arms over his chest, looking commanding and no less sexy. "You say you needed to be close to your family yet you have traveled thousands of miles away to work in our hospital?"

"I've been looking for a change of pace." A change of scenery. A change in her life.

"What is your medical specialty?" he asked in an all-business tone, confirming that he was only interested in the interview.

"Family practice," she said. "But I enjoy treating children the most. I've always loved children."

"They're our hope for future generations," he replied. "We've made some strides in pediatric health care, but not enough for my satisfaction."

"I'd enjoy that challenge, Marc. I mean, Your Highness." Her first breach of royal protocol, and probably not her last. "I'm sorry."

"No apology necessary, Dr. Milner."

"I really prefer you call me Kate. I'm just a simple kind of person."

"But you're also a physician," he said. "Not many can lay claim to that."

Kate felt the bloom of a blush on her cheeks. She'd never been well versed in accepting flattery graciously, but then compliments hadn't been a common occurrence in her life. "Speaking of doctors, how soon do you plan to reach a decision on who you'll be hiring?"

"The decision will come when we find the right candidate. And on that thought, could you tell me about your experience?"

"Exactly what experience are you referring to?" How could she have asked such a stupid question? Easy. The man was sucking her brain dry of lucid thought with his high-powered aura.

She noted a spark of amusement in his eyes and the first signs of a smile, but not enough to reveal the dimples framing his mouth. "Medical experience, of course. Unless you have other experience that you believe might interest me."

If only that were true. "Medically speaking, I've only recently completed my residency. I haven't been in private practice at all."

His dark gaze pinned her in place, even though she wanted to fidget. "I assume you've been adequately trained."

She lifted her chin a notch. "In one of the top programs in the country."

"Then I would say you could handle our hospital clinic."

"I'm sure I could." Now for the nitty-gritty. "And the pay?"

Marc leaned forward, bringing with him another trace scent of cologne. "If we come to an agreement, I would be willing to match whatever salary you were making in the States."

"Believe me, my salary barely enabled me to make ends meet. Long hours, low pay. I still have some student loans to take care of."

"I could at least double it," he said. "More if necessary."

This deal was getting sweeter by the minute. "Why would you do that?"

"Because we are in need of good doctors. And after all, we're old friends."

"Lab partners," she corrected. "I never really considered us friends."

He leaned back, but kept his eyes fixed on hers. "Why is that, Kate?"

"That's fairly obvious, considering you're a king and I'm, well, me."

"But when we knew each other before, I wasn't a king."

And she'd been far removed from royalty. She still was. "No, you were a prince. I was never all that comfortable around you because of that."

"Do I still make you uncomfortable?" he asked in a deep, deadly voice that held both challenge and temptation.

Very. "Not really. I've had interviews before. I consider this opportunity an adventure."

"Then I'm to assume you're looking for adventure?"

"And a job."

"We have the job covered. So what type of adventure are you looking for, aside from your career?"

The question hung in the air for a time until she finally said, "I'm not sure. Do you have any suggestions?"

The dark look he sent her said he probably had plenty. "Unfortunately, Doriana is a rather sedate place in July. But if you're here during the winter season, you could take advantage of our ski resorts. We have some challenging slopes, if you're not afraid to attempt something that could be deemed dangerous."

Now why had that sounded like an invitation to sin? "I've never tried skiing, but it sounds like fun."

"I wouldn't object to teaching you as repayment for what you taught me. I doubt I would have passed biology had it not been for you."

She certainly wouldn't object to anything he wanted to teach her. "Are you good?" *Great, Kate.* "At skiing, I mean."

His eyes seemed to grow even darker, effectively dispensing the last of Kate's calm. "Yes."

"I imagine you're probably very good at everything you do." Imagined it in great detail, she did. "Aside from biology, that is."

"I would imagine the same applies to you, Kate, considering how well you handled me during that first year."

She made a shaky one-handed sweep through her hair. "Funny, I don't remember handling you at all."

He assumed an almost insolent posture, his gaze now centered on her lap where she ran her fingertips up and down her purse strap. "Well, if you had *literally* handled me, I would not have forgotten, I assure you."

If he only knew how many times she'd imagined "handling" him in her wildest fantasies. How many times she had imagined this moment when they were again face-to-face. How strongly she was reacting to him on a very primal level.

Following a brief span of tense silence, reality finally drilled its way into Kate's psyche. She could not let him get to her again. Not this time. All those years ago, she had fallen hopelessly in love with him, knowing he could never feel the same—a mistake she didn't dare repeat.

But that was then, and this was now. She had matured beyond the point of having puppy-love crushes on unattainable men. She had only fond feelings for Marc DeLoria.

Okay, maybe fond wasn't a good assessment. She was unequivocally ready to jump his aristocratic bones. But she wouldn't.

Marc DeLoria was a dynamic king, a magnetic man. And from all news accounts, he was also a rounder, a rogue and one of the world's most notorious playboys. She needed to remember that—even if she was still seriously attracted to him, whether she wanted to be or not.

Kate tried to appear nonchalant when her overheated body was anything but unfazed by his continued perusal. "Anything else you need to know about me?"

"There is something I would like to do with you, if you're not too tired from your trip."

Her heart rate did double time. "What would that be?"

"Show you the hospital, as soon as I change into something more appropriate."

Darn. For a split second, Kate had hoped he was going to propose something more exciting. "I would really like to see the facilities."

"And I see no reason why the position could not be yours if you so choose."

She frowned. "Just like that?"

He rubbed a hand along his shaded jaw. "Frankly, you've already been highly recommended by the hospital's administrator. Our meeting is only a formality."

"I'll definitely consider your offer," she said. "But first I'd like to take a look around and make sure it's the right place for me."

"Speaking of that, do you have a place to stay?"

"I have a room at the St. Simone Inn."

"You should stay at the palace as our guest. You would be much more comfortable here."

No, she wouldn't. Not with him occupying the same castle, even if it did have a hundred rooms, which she suspected it did. "I appreciate your hospitality, but I would prefer the inn."

"Please let me know if you change your mind." His voice had the appeal of hot buttered rum, rich and warm going down.

"I sure will." Her voice sounded a little too down-home with a too-high pitch.

After a brief knock, a stout, gray-haired woman breezed into the room with a tray of tea and cookies. She kept her eyes averted as she served Kate first.

Marc declined the tea, but after the woman retreated, he took one of the treats and held it to her lips. "Try the *rollitos*. They're Spanish cookies, one of my two favorite indulgences."

She wasn't sure she could swallow. "Really? What would the other be?"

Marc's smile arrived slowly but it quickly impacted Kate's control at the first sign of his deep dimples. "A person should be allowed to have a few secrets, Kate. Even a king."

Kate bit into the cookie but she didn't taste a thing. Considering Marc's overt sensuality, she suspected he had a lot of secrets. She also suspected his other favorite indulgence had nothing to do with food and everything to do with his desires as a man. A man who was much too tempting for his own good. For Kate's own good.

Since his days at Harvard, Marcel DeLoria had spent almost eight years seeing the world and its wonders. For the past nine months, he had seen what it was like to have every molecule of his character examined as if he'd been placed under a high-powered microscope, not on the proverbial throne. But in all his experiences, he had never seen anything quite as surprising as the woman sitting across from him in the back seat of the Rolls-Royce.

Years before, he'd known her as a shy, intelligent student who had hidden behind too-big clothing and owl-like glasses, not the confident, stylish woman she had become. He admired her self-assurance as much as her physical conversion. And he definitely needed to quit admiring her altogether lest she catch him in the act.

As they continued through St. Simone en route to the hospital, Marc turned his attention to the quaint, colorful shops lining the cobblestoned streets. Streets practically void of automobile traffic, yet heavy with tourists and locals who had stopped to watch the motorcade pass. Would he ever grow accustomed to such spectacle? Probably not.

At times, he longed to walk among the villagers as an ordinary man, stop by the bakery and pick up his second-favorite indulgence—in terms of food—éclairs. At times, he craved putting on his old college sweatshirt and jeans to join in a game of rugby with the local team. At times, he wished he had never been born into royalty.

"This town is incredible, Your Highness."

The soft lilt of Kate's voice brought his attention back to her, brought to mind more of Marc's recollections of their time together. He remembered being enamored of its quiet charm—a southern accent, she had once told him. But he had never viewed her as more than a friend. And somewhat of a savior. Had it not been for her, he might never have finished that first grueling year at Harvard.

She pointed out the window. "What's that building over there?"

Against his better judgment, Marc moved to the seat beside her, maintaining a somewhat comfortable distance. "That is St. Simone Cathedral. My parents were married there."

She turned her incredible green eyes on his. "It's beautiful, all that stained glass."

"I tend to take the village for granted," he told her, striving for casual conversation when what he wanted to do with his mouth had nothing to do with talking.

"I guess that's understandable," she said. "Beauty is easy to overlook if you face it on a daily basis."

When she turned back to the window, Marc decided she was very beautiful as well. He supposed many would view her as merely cute, with her upturned nose, graced with a slight spattering of freckles, her rounded face, not the more striking, sharper features common among what some considered the world's greatest beauties. But her large eyes—a near match in color to the pines blanketing the Pyrenees—and her chestnut hair falling about her shoulders, were very pleasing attributes, in his opinion.

Although he tried to tear his gaze away from her, Marc found himself taking another visual excursion. The tailored lavender silk suit she wore fit her to prime perfection, showcasing a pair of elegant legs that would garner any man's attention. She was relatively small—small hands, small feet and best he could tell, not endowed with ample curves or breasts. But he'd always believed that some of the best things in life came in small parcels. He imagined Kate was no exception.

Even though he shouldn't, he saw her as attractive woman that he would like to know much better. Perhaps eventually in the tangle of warm satin sheets—not in the cold confines of a college laboratory. But that was impossible.

As much as the man in Marc desired Kate Milner, the king that he had become prevented him from acting on that desire. He must remain strong in light of his need to be taken seriously as his country's leader.

Still, it would be very easy to press the button on the console, raise the windowed partition separating them from the

driver and Nicholas, and allow some privacy away from prying eyes.

A fantasy assaulted him then, sharp as shattered glass—images of sliding his mouth up her delicate throat, working his way
to her lips and engaging her in a provocative kiss. In his mind,
Kate would be receptive to his affections, encouraging him on-
ward as he slipped his hand beneath the hem of her skirt, moving up, up until he touched her, first through damp silk, then
beneath the barrier so he could experience her heat. He would
tempt her with his fingers, tantalize her with his mouth and endeavor to make her moan, make her want him inside her. He
would gladly comply without regard to who he was or where he
was. Without consideration of the consequences. He would make
love to her until they were both sated, if only temporarily…

The vehicle came to an abrupt halt, effectively splintering
the images but not the results of Marc's journey into a wicked
fantasy. He was hard as slate below his belt and could do nothing to hide his predicament short of grabbing a handful of ice
from the built-in bar and shoving it into his lap. He only
hoped that Kate would not notice before he had a chance to
compose himself, and that his dress coat would amply conceal his sins once they exited the car.

Marc straightened his shoulders and assumed his royal demeanor while continuing to battle a strong desire for Kate
Milner that made absolutely no sense. He wrote the libidinous
stirrings off to a lengthy celibacy—a situation born out of necessity due to his brother's tragic death that had thrust Marc
into the role of reluctant ruler.

He adjusted his tie, tugged at his collar and sent Kate a polite smile. "It seems we have reached our destination." And
not a moment too soon. Otherwise, he might have forgotten
who he was and what he lacked—a life he could call his own.
A life that had no room for courting women, stealing kisses
and touches or forbidden fantasies.

Seeming not to notice his discomfort, Kate glanced out the window at the simple two-story building. "It's a very nice hospital."

Marc detected a hint of disappointment in her tone, aiding somewhat in his body's return to decency. "It's very small and admittedly somewhat lacking in modern equipment. But I'm determined to remedy that soon."

Health care was of the utmost importance, not only to Marc but also to his people. Doriana needed better facilities, more doctors. Had the hospital been modernized, Philippe might still be alive, and Marc would still be feeding his wanderlust instead of attempting to prove himself.

Kate offered an understanding smile. "These things take time."

Marc couldn't agree more, but he felt as if he were running out of time.

When Nicholas opened the door, Marc took Kate's hand and helped her from the car. Her slender fingers cradled in his palm spurred another random fantasy that involved another pleasurable touch. How could he continue to be around her and still maintain control?

On sheer willpower alone.

But after Kate slid from the limo and his hand came to rest on her lower back, contacting the delicate dip of her spine encased in silk, Marc's willpower went the way of the wind, replaced by an instantaneous shock to his senses—one that he had to disregard in order to save face.

He focused on the substantial crowd that had gathered, held at bay by a contingent of bodyguards. As always, he was forced to play the royal role with a regal facade and an official smile. Kate paused at his side when he stopped to shake the hands of a few subjects. The crowd voiced their pleasure with applause and several women pointed, but not at him. They were pointing at Kate, whispering behind their hands.

Marc realized all too late that they mistakenly believed Kate to be his current paramour, understandable since he again had his palm firmly planted on her back.

Marc took a much-needed step away from Kate, but not before he was joined by Dr. Jonathan Renault—resident hospital irritant—who had worked his way through the chaos.

"Good day, Your Majesty," Renault said, his voice dripping with sarcasm.

Marc did not trust the man, and even less so when Renault blatantly assessed Kate from forehead to toes. "Good day, Dr. Renault," he said with strained civility.

When Marc tried to usher Kate away, Renault stopped him cold by saying, *"Je voudrais faire la connaissance de votre nouvelle petite amie."*

Petite amie. A direct intimation that Kate was Marc's mistress. And to add to his total lack of propriety, he'd had the nerve to request an introduction.

In another time, in another place, Marc would have gladly punished the bastard with a slam of a fist into Renault's prominent jaw. But Marc's title prevented what would be considered a crude, common act. Crude, yes. Common, yes. Unjustified? Not in Marc's opinion.

"For your information, Dr. Renault," Marc began, an intentional trace of venom in his tone, "this is Dr. Katherine Milner. She is a very skilled physician, and quite capable of managing the entire clinic by herself."

Although Kate looked somewhat confused, Renault didn't appear at all affected by the pointed comment. Instead, he sent Kate a seamy smile and took her hand. *"Enchanté,* Dr. Milner. I would be happy to have you join my staff."

Kate quickly pulled out of his grasp, giving Marc great satisfaction. Obviously she recognized the lecher beneath the lab coat. "Nice to meet you, Doctor," she said with little enthusiasm.

Renault winked. "And I will look forward to seeing you again."

With that, he strode away with a self-important lift of his pointy chin and a swaggering gait.

Kate leaned over until her lips were practically resting on Marc's ear. "What did he say to you?"

"Keep walking." Marc took her by the elbow and continued on to the hospital entry. Once they were on the steps, he lowered his voice and said, "He suggested we are lovers. A totally absurd assumption, but then Renault is somewhat lacking in restraint."

Yet Marc wondered if something in his own demeanor, the way he had looked at Kate, the way he'd touched her so casually, had encouraged the speculation, not only in Renault but also in the minds of his people.

If that were the case, he would have to be more careful from this point forward. He could not allow anyone to believe that he had taken Kate Milner as his lover, even if he longed to do that very thing.

Two

An absurd assumption...

Up to that point, Kate had allowed herself to imagine she was a real, live, honest-to-goodness princess greeting royal subjects with her prince, who'd kept touching her as if he wanted everyone to know she was his.

King, she reminded herself. A man who was obviously the object of desire to women of all shapes and sizes. A man who could have his pick among any woman in this village, probably in the world. She would never be among them. This wasn't a fairy tale, and this particular monarch wasn't interested in common Kate Milner.

But Dr. Renault had certainly seemed interested, and that consideration made Kate cringe. The guy gave her the creeps.

None of that mattered. She was here on business, not to worry about some dubious doctor with "I want you" written all over his face. Not to get caught up in some overblown forever-after fantasy involving a king who thought the idea of being her lover was absurd.

Forcing herself into professional mode, Kate followed behind Marc as they made their way to the hospital's entrance where two guards remained posted. When they entered the building, she was pleasantly surprised by the modern interior. The practically deserted waiting room, filled with contemporary chairs and tables as well as a television suspended from a stand in the corner near the ceiling, was much larger than she'd expected.

A sign positioned near the elevator written in French and Spanish indicated the location to various units. She knew some Latin, a few basic words in Spanish and only enough French to inquire about restaurants and rest rooms. She had brought along some books and tapes to study. But when treating patients, communication was a must. Maybe she would be making a mistake if she accepted the position, something she would definitely have to consider.

Kate followed Marc to the reception desk, where he presented a polite smile to the pleasant-looking older woman seated behind a computer.

A few moments later, an elderly, distinguished man with thinning gray hair pushed through the double doors to the right of the waiting area. He approached them with a wide smile. "Ah, Doctor Milner, I presume. I am Dr. Louis Martine, chief of medicine. We spoke briefly on the phone when you inquired about the position."

Kate extended her hand. "A pleasure to finally meet you, Dr. Martine."

He inclined his head and looked at her quizzically. "You truly have a unique accent."

Obviously her Deep South roots were still firmly wrapped around her tongue. "It's southern United States."

Dr. Martine smiled. "*Très charmant* to suit a *belle femme.*"

"I'm sorry, I'm afraid I don't understand," Kate said.

"Very charming to suit a beautiful woman," Marc supplied, followed by an appreciative look that made Kate shiver.

She felt another blush spreading from her throat to her forehead and tried to will it away. Contacts instead of glasses, a new wardrobe and a good beautician might have changed her outward appearance, but it couldn't mask the plain, unassuming girl that lived inside. At times she still saw herself as too skinny, too short, too awkward, too lacking in social skills. So what was she doing here, in the presence of royalty?

Ludicrous. She was a doctor, and she'd worked too darned long to let insecurities derail her hard-earned self-confidence.

Marc made a sweeping gesture toward the double doors. "Shall we take the tour now?"

Kate followed Marc and Dr. Martine through a maze of hallways into a place resembling a clinic. This particular waiting room was full of mothers and fathers and children. When she detected the familiar sterile scents, she felt somewhat back in her element and relaxed.

They strode through another door where an attractive brunette nurse with huge blue eyes and large breasts eyed Marc as if he were today's special at Bennie's Diner. Marc ignored her furtive glances and guided Kate inside a small office.

"This would be your station should you decide to accept the position," Marc said.

Kate did a quick visual search and noticed the desk was cluttered with charts and coffee cups. "Whose office is this now?"

"Jonathan Renault, our current family practitioner," Dr. Martine said. "I'm afraid you will have to share the space with him until we can set up another office for you."

Oh, joy. Kate was not looking forward to that.

"And I assume you will be seeing to a private office for Dr. Milner immediately, Louis?" Marc stated in a firm tone.

"Of course, Your Highness," Martine replied. "It shouldn't

take more than a day or two should she decide to join our staff."

That remained to be seen. Kate had already come upon two very important challenges—the language barrier and the beast named Renault. Three if she considered her attraction to Marc.

Dr. Martine studied the stethoscope dangling from his neck. "Dr. Renault is a good *médecin,* but I am afraid he is not as interested in his practice and the patients as we would wish him to be."

Marc frowned. "I would say that is a grave understatement, Louis." He gave Kate a cynical look. "Renault is much more interested in the female staff. I have put him on notice that if I receive one more complaint, he will have to return to Paris."

"Oh," Kate said. "What hours does he work?" If luck prevailed, she could avoid him—if she decided to stay.

"Since the clinic is only open during the day, you would be working together," Martine said.

No luck there, Kate thought.

"If he becomes unmanageable, inform me," Marc added. "I will take care of him."

"I'm sure I can take care of myself," Kate insisted, mildly insulted that men tended to see women as the weaker sex. She might be small, but she knew where to thrust a knee on a strategic part of the male anatomy.

A rap came at the door and Nurse Lustful entered. She exchanged a few words with Dr. Martine, who then turned to Marc. "You have a call from the palace, Your Majesty. Line one."

After he uncovered the debris from the desk phone, Marc picked up the receiver. He again spoke words Kate couldn't begin to understand, but his distress was very apparent in his expression. Once he hung up, he turned to her and said, "We must return to the palace immediately. There's been an incident."

A serious incident, Kate presumed. "Should I stay here? Dr. Martine could show me around."

"I could possibly need your medical expertise."

Kate's concern increased. "Has someone been hurt?"

"Not exactly. But it does involve a child."

With Kate trailing behind him, Marc strode into the palace's formal parlor to find his mother seated on the settee, holding what appeared to be the reason for his urgent summons.

She nodded at the sleeping infant in her arms and said, "I do hope you can explain this to me, Marcel."

Explain? "It appears to be a child, Mother."

She rose with typical grace and laid the baby in Marc's arms, much to his dismay. "It appears to be your daughter, my son."

He heard the sound of Kate's sharp, indrawn breath from behind him. Unfortunately, Marc's respiration had halted altogether.

Once he'd recovered his voice, he said, "This is not my child."

The baby chose that moment to lift her head, turn an alarming shade of red and wail at the top of her lungs. Marc had no idea such a small creature could create such a furor. He also had no idea what to do when she began to writhe, except to hold on tightly lest he drop her. The tighter he held her, the more she wrestled and squirmed, arching her back against her confinement.

"Here, let me." Kate took the baby from him and positioned the child on her shoulder, patting her back. The infant immediately quieted, her sobs turning to sniffs.

Kate had rescued him once again, at least for now. He met his mother's disapproving expression. "Mother, I have no idea why you would believe this is my child."

She turned to her attendant, who stood in the corner looking as if she would greatly like to flee. "Beatrice, bring me the note."

The young woman hurried over and handed her a plain

piece of white paper. In turn, his mother handed it to him. "The baby was left at the gate in a pram with a bag full of clothing and bottles. We found this note inside."

Marc read it silently. The words were English, brief, but to the point.

"Her name is Cecile. She is a DeLoria."

Shoving the paper into his pocket, he said, "This does not prove a thing. It's obviously a ruse."

"Look at her, Marcel."

Marc turned to the baby now propped on Kate's hip, occupying herself with the button on Kate's jacket. True, she had his hair color and blue eyes, but that did not mean she was his. He had been careful to the extreme. He had not been involved with anyone since Elsa Sidleberg—an international supermodel who still graced renowned runways—and that had ended over a year ago. This made no sense whatsoever.

"Again, her appearance proves nothing," he insisted.

"Nor does it disprove anything," his mother replied.

Kate stepped forward. "Maybe I can help."

Marc realized that his mother and Kate had yet to be formally introduced. He supposed his lack of manners was understandable considering the circumstance. "Kate, I present to you the Queen Mother, Mary Elizabeth Darcy DeLoria. Mother, Dr. Kate Milner."

Kate smiled and held out her free hand. "It's very nice to meet you. I'm sorry, but how do I address you?"

She took Kate's hand for a brief shake. "I would prefer you call me Mary." She sent a sardonic glance at Marc. "Obviously, you now know the family secrets, so I believe first names are appropriate."

Marc clung to his last thin thread of control. "I have no secrets, Mother. And this is not my child."

Mary smoothed a hand over the baby's hair. "Then why

would anyone claim this precious girl is a DeLoria? What other possibilities are there?"

Marc knew of one, and he was taking great risk by mentioning it. But he felt he must. "Perhaps she is Philippe's child."

His mother sent him a startled look, as if he'd proclaimed that a deity had committed a mortal sin. "That would be impossible. Philippe has been gone for almost a year."

Marc turned to Kate. "How old do you think she is?"

Kate regarded the baby for a moment. "At least six months old, maybe a bit older if she's small for her age."

"It really doesn't matter," Marc said. "She could have been born before or shortly after Philippe's death. Definitely conceived while he was still alive."

"Philippe was engaged to marry Countess Jacqueline Trudeau for two years."

"Perhaps she is the mother, then."

"Nonsense. She married another man not long after Philippe's death."

Ah, true love, Marc thought cynically. "Then perhaps Philippe fathered a child with another woman."

"Philippe never would have denied his child," Mary said.

Anger welled inside Marc. "And I would?"

"As his mother, I would have known if he had been hiding something. He was never good at telling untruths. He lacked the cunning you have."

The woman who had always been Marc's champion had called him a practiced deceiver in front of Kate, a woman whose respect he greatly desired. "Are you saying I am prone to telling falsehoods?"

"I am saying you've always been more clever and not as easy to read."

"Of course. And Philippe was destined for sainthood." Marc could not keep the sarcasm and bitterness from his tone even though he, too, had admired his brother. But he had also lived in his shadow. He was still living in it.

His mother's expression softened. "My dear Marcel, we barely saw you over the past ten years, let alone knew with whom you were involved aside from what we read in the papers."

"And you knew of Philippe's comings and goings all the time, Mother? Might I remind you that no one knew where he was going or where he had been the night he died."

"I am deeply wounded by your suggestion that your brother was carrying on with someone I knew nothing about, much less had a child with that someone without my knowledge."

Kate watched the verbal volley as she continued to hold the baby on her hip, feeling totally like an outsider. The tension in the room was as thick as buttermilk and although she had no business getting involved, she had to do something. "There are ways to prove parentage," she offered.

Both Marc and his mother unlocked their gazes from each other and turned them to her.

"Perhaps a birthmark?" the queen mother asked in a hopeful voice. "Marc does have a very unusual one on his—"

"Mother, I believe Dr. Milner is referring to something more scientific."

Kate was, but she had to admit she was curious about Marc's royal birthmark and where it might be residing. "I'm referring to DNA, which is complicated if the testing can't be done here." Not to mention they would have to obtain some from the deceased brother, a fact she didn't dare bring up now.

Marc streaked a hand over his nape. "We are not up to speed with that yet. We would have to involve Paris."

"We cannot do that," the queen mother said, looking alarmed. "We must keep this concealed until we decide how to handle such a sensitive issue. The media would tear Marcel to shreds if they even suspected he had fathered a child out of wedlock. He would lose all respect in the eyes of our people."

Kate could understand that, and she was more than a bit concerned herself. "I could draw and type her blood but without knowing the mother's type, it might not tell us anything."

"My blood type is rare," Marc said. "Would that make a difference?"

"It could if she has it. That could prove she's a member of the family, but it still might not rule anyone out." She didn't want to ask, but she had to. "What about Philippe's type?"

"His was the same as Marc's," Mary said. "The night he died…" Mary's voice trailed off along with her gaze.

Marc released a gruff sigh. "My mother was about to say that the night he died, I was in Germany on a diplomatic mission. He suffered severe internal injuries in the car crash. He lost too much blood and I didn't arrive in time to give him some of my own."

Kate's heart went out to Marc in that moment. She couldn't think of anything to say to ease his guilt, so she said nothing.

"Dr. Martine can provide all the medical records since he's the royal physician," Mary said. "We can trust him to be discreet." She paused before adding, "And I assume we can trust you as well, Dr. Milner?"

Marc moved closer to Kate, a purely defensive gesture. "Mother, Kate is a physician. She is accustomed to confidentiality."

Mary arched a thin brow. "Kate? How well do you know each other?"

Oh, heavens. If she didn't set the record straight, the queen mother might assume she was Marc's lover. Worse, she might believe Kate had parental ties to the child considering the timing. "Actually—"

"Kate, forgive my mother. She might be descended from genteel British aristocracy, but she has the bluntness of a barrister pleading a monumental case."

The queen mother patted his cheek, a true display of fondness that took Kate by surprise in light of their recent confrontation. "And so do you, *mon fiston*."

"In case you haven't noticed, Mother, I am no longer your little boy."

"Yes, you are a man now and clearly responsible for your actions."

"Kate and I knew each other at the university," Marc continued, obviously not willing to react to the innuendo, much to Kate's relief. "I assure you that we have not seen each other in years."

"We were college lab partners," Kate interjected. "Only friends."

Finally, Marc smiled. "And she's come to Doriana to join our hospital staff."

The baby wriggled and gave a whine of protest. Kate wanted to do the same since she hadn't exactly agreed to take the job. "I think we should wait until morning to do the tests. She's been through enough today." And so have I, Kate thought.

The queen mother patted her neat silver chignon, her features mellowing when she smiled at Kate. "Welcome, my dear. We are very pleased to have you."

Kate considered insisting that she hadn't made her final decision, but with the queen mother and king looking at her expectantly, she felt as if she had no choice.

She would agree to take the position—for the time being. If it got too hot in the castle kitchen, if it turned out the baby was Marc's and he'd left some woman high and dry, alone and pregnant, she would have to reconsider. She couldn't respect a man who would do that, even if she did crave his company.

"Thank you. I'm very glad to be here."

For now.

Marc spent the remainder of the afternoon making numerous queries, only to learn that no one seemed to know who had delivered the baby at the gates. He called Louis Martine and explained the situation, then arranged to meet him early in the morning at the hospital for Kate to run the tests. Louis had assured him that he would practice prudence when it came to gathering records and assisting in trying to determine the baby's parentage. Marc had no choice but to trust him. He could not say the same for the rest of the hospital staff, Renault particularly, so they would have to proceed with caution.

Frustrated and exhausted, Marc set off to locate his mother and Kate, who had insisted on staying to care for the baby. Beatrice directed him up the stairs to what was once his and Philippe's nursery, but which had long ago been transformed into a guestroom. He entered to find Kate sitting in a rocker, holding the sleeping child against her shoulder. She put a fingertip to her lips as she rose and laid the little girl in the nearby crib. The baby stirred a bit and Kate remained there for a while, patting the child's back and cooing like a dove. After a time, she turned away and signaled him to join her in the hall.

Once there, she shut the door behind them and sighed. "I think she's finally down for the count. It took a while. Apparently she's used to someone rocking her to sleep."

Marc rubbed his neck, trying to work away the tension coiled there, to no avail. "I suspect her mother had that duty, whoever she might be."

"I'm sure you're right. And obviously Cecile's been well cared for. She looks very healthy. I'll do a full exam tomorrow, just to be sure."

Marc glanced at the closed door. "I'm surprised at how quickly you've made the room into a nursery again."

Kate shrugged. "I didn't do anything but play with Cecile while the staff moved in the furniture."

"My mother must have called in all her favors to have a crib delivered so quickly."

"The crib was yours."

"I had no idea my mother kept it."

"She obviously cares a great deal for you," Kate said softly.

Marc acknowledged that his mother had always cared about him, but after the events of the day, he questioned whether she respected him. "By the way, where is she?"

"She had a terrible headache so I insisted she go to bed. I'm sure it's stress."

No doubt due to the situation, and him. "I hope we clear this up soon. She's been through quite a lot over the past year with Philippe's death. And now this."

He saw true sympathy in Kate's emerald eyes. "Yes, she has been through a lot, and so have you."

How unselfish for her to consider his feelings, Marc thought. A rare occurrence in the household. "I've adjusted." He'd been forced to adjust. No time to consider anything but duty. No time to really grieve.

"Are you sure you've adjusted?" she asked.

No, he wasn't, yet the time to assess his situation would probably continue to elude him. "Of course."

Kate hid a yawn behind her hand. "I'm so sorry."

Marc felt like a selfish fool. "No apology necessary. You must be exhausted from your trip."

Her ensuing smile tripped Marc's pulse into a frenzy. "Yes, I am tired. Beatrice has agreed to sleep in the room adjacent to the nursery in case Cecile wakes during the night. Do you think Mr. Nicholas could drive me back to the hotel?"

Marc wasn't ready for her to leave. He wanted to spend more time with her even knowing it was selfish on his part, and totally ill-advised. "Are you certain you wouldn't like to stay here considering the lateness of the hour?"

"My clothes are at the hotel and I really need a bath."

Marc did not need to imagine her in the bath, but he did— in great detail, right down to the curve of her hip, the shading between her thighs, the roundness of her breasts where his gaze now came to rest.

Kate pointed to a dark smudge above her right breast. "Strained peas. Little Cecile is a healthy eater but she loves to toss food. Her aim is pretty darned good."

Marc reached for a lock of Kate's dark hair. "Yes, I do believe I see a few remnants here."

As he twined the soft strands in his fingers, their gazes remained fixed as Kate said, "I'm only a phone call away if you need anything."

Marc needed something from her now—although he couldn't act on that need. He dropped his hand and stepped back. "I will personally see to your return. I'll drive you myself."

Her expression reflected wariness. "Are you sure? You look pretty beat."

"I promise I will stay awake long enough to make certain you are delivered safely to your room."

And he promised himself that he would leave her at the door because if he did not, he would find it very difficult to leave her at all tonight.

Three

A cool breeze whipped over Kate's face as they traveled the darkened streets of St. Simone in Marc's classic convertible chick magnet. No slick, mean, manly machine had ever turned her head. She preferred comfortable sedans and comfortable shoes, which reminded her of the less-than-comfortable pumps squeezing her feet like a sadistic vise. She was tempted to kick them off but thought it best to leave on all articles of clothing, in case Marc got the wrong idea.

Like she would really try to seduce him in her current state. Her suit was wrinkled, her hair was a mess and her bra cut into her like steel fingers. Whoever invented push-up braziers should be bound at the wrists and ankles by underwire for at least forty-eight hours.

And Marc, with his suave sophistication and the wind blowing his golden hair away from his face, could easily pass as a sexy super spy like James Bond. Kate could be his girl of the month and sidekick, Roadkill. Yeah, he would definitely be interested in *that* scenario.

Marc pulled up to the curb in front of the inn and put the car in park. They were immediately joined by two other black vehicles, one in front, one in back.

Marc glanced in the rearview mirror and muttered, "For once, I wish they would leave me the hell alone."

"I'm sure they're only concerned for your safety."

"I seriously doubt any dissidents are waiting inside the hotel on the off chance that I might pay a visit in the middle of the night. They seem to forget that for most of my adult life, I've seen to my own welfare."

"But that was before you were king."

"And that seems like decades ago." He shifted in the seat to face her. "I want to thank you again, Kate."

She dislodged the rest of her wind-blown hair from her face and stared at him. "You're welcome, but I didn't really do anything."

"Don't underestimate your assistance. I'm not certain my mother would have managed the situation quite as well had you not been there."

Kate noted the weariness in his tone and in his eyes. "What do you think will happen now? With the baby, I mean."

"Right now, I'm too bloody tired to worry about it." He brushed one stubborn strand of hair away from her face. "I'm sure you're exhausted, too, although you look very beautiful at the moment."

Kate's eyes widened. "You're kidding, right?"

"No. I'm very serious."

That dog don't hunt, Kate thought, her grandfather's favorite saying. She would do well to remember that Marc DeLoria was a master of seduction, and obviously desperate if he considered her beautiful when she was sporting the results of wind-wrecked hair and an infantile food fight.

Desperate? Ha! His little black book was probably as big as her *Physicians' Desk Reference*. In fact, he'd probably utilized this very hotel for clandestine affairs.

"I've never been at this inn before," he said, as if challenging her assumption.

Kate studied the red brick building's facade and the flower boxes framing the windows to avoid his continued scrutiny. "It has old-world charm, Your Highness." Marc wasn't suffering in the charm department, either.

"Kate, as long as we're in private, you may call me Marc."

Her gaze snapped from the building to him. "What if I slip up at some point in time?"

He grinned, revealing his drop-dead gorgeous dimples. "Then it's off with your head."

Kate circled her hands around her throat. "Maybe I should just stick to Your Highness. Hard to treat patients without a head."

He looked suddenly solemn. "Seriously, I would appreciate you calling me Marc. I could use a friend."

She could use some strength. "Okay, Marc. I'll be your friend."

"Thank you."

He looked so appreciative, so sincere, so darned sexy that Kate had the strongest urge to lean over and kiss him senseless.

Party's over.

Kate needed to go upstairs, take a bath and crawl into bed. Alone. Before she did something really stupid, like convince herself that he might actually find her desirable not only as a friend, but also as a lover. How absurd. "Thanks for the ride. I can manage from here."

"Nonsense." He moved with the speed of a cougar as he slid out of the car and rounded the hood before she even had a chance to draw a breath.

Kate stared at him when he opened her door, afraid to move, to speak.

"Well?" he asked. "What are you waiting for?"

Her pulse to return to normal. "Really, I can see myself in."

His grin outshone the moon. "And disobey the king?"

"Since you put it that way, I guess I'll have to submit or risk the gallows."

Obviously she had already lost her head for letting him escort her. Only to the lobby, she reminded herself. She would say goodbye then go upstairs alone.

Marc followed Kate into the red-carpeted vestibule absent of people except for the forty-something man sitting behind the registration desk, looking totally disinterested in the king and his entourage's sudden arrival. Had Marc told her the truth, or was his appearance at the inn a common occurrence?

She was too worn out to contemplate that now. She needed sleep. When she turned to dismiss Marc, he asked, "Do you have your room key?"

She fumbled in her bag, withdrew the key and held it up. "Right here, so I'm all set. I'll see you in the morning."

He took the key from her hand, easy as pie. "I'll see you to your room."

Of all the sneaky sovereigns. Maybe she should summon a bodyguard for her own protection. Not that Marc seemed like the kind to do her bodily harm. But he could certainly do things to her body that she'd never before experienced, that much she knew. He'd been doing it all day without even touching her.

"I can make it to my room just fine." Kate tried to recover the key but before she could, he quickly tucked it into his pants pocket. She didn't dare try to go after it, since rifling in the king's pocket would probably be the ultimate breach in etiquette. Mighty fun, though.

Taking her by the elbow, Marc guided Kate up the staircase. Once they reached the room, he faced her and said, "Are you afraid of me, Kate?"

"Of course not." She was more afraid of herself and her own vulnerability where he was concerned.

"You have no need to be." He held up his hands, palms forward. "I promise my intentions are honorable."

"That's too bad." Who said that? Surely not Kate the Crusader—able to thwart all come-ons with a single put-down. But he hadn't been coming on to her at all. Maybe subconsciously she was wishing he had. What else could explain her suggestive remark?

Leaning forward, closing the space between their faces, he said, "In what way would that be bad?"

"I was just spouting off, that's all."

"That's all?" he repeated in a rough, seductive whisper.

That wasn't all, Kate thought as he came closer and closer, in slow motion it seemed, his lips only inches from hers.

She wanted this so badly. Wanted to feel his mouth on hers, wanted to know that he did see her as more than a physician, more than a friend. Know that the thought of his being her lover wasn't absurd after all.

But instead of kissing her, Marc framed her face in his palms and tipped his forehead against hers. "We can't do this, Kate."

She glanced to her right to see one bodyguard positioned at the landing, facing the descending stairs. "I understand. We have an audience."

"It's not only that. Nothing can happen between us."

Kate lowered her eyes at the same moment her heart took a dive. "I know. I'm not exactly suitable."

"You're wrong." He tipped her chin up, forcing her to look at him. "You are a beautiful, remarkable woman, Kate. And it would be incredibly easy to kiss you right now, to back you into your room, remove all your clothing and make love with you all through the night. But because of who I am, I don't have that luxury. I still have too much to prove."

"What do you have to prove?"

"That I've not bedded every woman from Belize to Great Britain."

"You haven't?"

His smile was cynical. "No. I've escorted quite a few women in my time, and I've not been a long-term celibate, but there have not been as many lovers in my life as most have assumed."

Long-term celibate? She wanted to ask him how long had it been since he'd had a lover. But it really didn't matter. He couldn't be hers. "So you're saying that you can't be involved with anyone?"

"Not at this time. Not until I can establish myself as a serious leader, and then only when I'm ready to settle into a marriage. I doubt I will be ready for that for quite some time."

Kate stepped back and wrapped her arms around her middle to mask the sudden chills. "Well, thanks for letting me know." She hated the disappointment in her tone but had to admit she liked what he had said—that he did find her desirable. That he had actually had the same thoughts she'd had all day. But that didn't change the fact that their relationship would have to remain platonic. And she might as well accept it, beginning now, even if she didn't like it.

Again he touched her face. "Kate, it is as much for your sake as it is for mine. The people of Doriana are basically kind, but they can also be judgmental when it comes to their leaders. I wouldn't want you to get hurt."

Kate could certainly accept that, but she already did hurt a little knowing that she couldn't have him, not that she'd ever really believed she could.

After checking her watch, she tried to smile. "It's really late. Have a good night. I'll see you in the morning."

He took her palm and raised it to his lips for a gentle kiss. "Sleep well, Kate."

He brushed another kiss across her cheek, then turned and walked away, leaving Kate stunned into silence, tingling at the place where his lips had been.

Kate recognized that a secret part of her still loved the man buried beneath the facade—the carefree man who existed before the kingdom had carried away his freedom.

Even if she could only be Marc's friend, nothing could stop her from attempting to lighten his spirit, ease his burden, help him have a little fun, a little adventure.

After all, that's what friends were for.

The shrill of a phone had Kate bolting upright from deep sleep. Disoriented, she thought she was back in the hospital on-call room. She fumbled for the phone and answered with the habitual Dr. Milner, as if she were still a resident.

"I'm sorry to bother you so late, Kate, but I'm having a problem with Cecile."

Cecile? The baby. She wasn't at the hospital; she was in a foreign country. The man on the other end of the line wasn't someone on staff; he was the king. A distressed-sounding king at that.

Kate sat up and glanced at the bedside clock. Almost midnight. "What's wrong?"

"I'm not certain. Beatrice and I have tried everything to calm her before she wakes my mother, but I'm afraid we're failing miserably. Could you suggest anything?"

"She's had a bottle?"

"Several. The last one landed on my forehead."

Kate fought back laughter over the image of a six-month-old using a royal forehead as target practice. "Her diaper's dry?"

"Yes. Beatrice has changed her several times. All those bottles, you know."

"And rocking her—"

"Hasn't done any good. She's determined to protest, very loudly."

Oh, well. So much for sleep. "I'll come and see what I can do."

"Are you certain?"

"I'm sure."

"I'll send Nicholas right away."

"I'll be ready."

"And Kate, I truly appreciate this."

No problem, and it really wasn't. She'd grown accustomed to odd hours and very little sleep during medical school and residency. She'd also learned to dress quickly, which she did, in jeans, T-shirt and sneakers, sans bra. If she had to tend to a baby in the middle of the night, comfort would have to take precedence over class.

By the time she retrieved her standard black medical bag and hurried through the front door of the inn, Mr. Nicholas was waiting for her outside the limousine. He greeted her with a polite smile and, "Good evening, Dr. Milner. Quite a nice night for a drive."

Kate returned his smile. "A really nice night for sleep."

"I am sure the king will be very happy to see you," he said as he opened the back door.

Pausing with her hand on top of the car, Kate said, "He's having a tough time, huh?"

"I believe His Brilliance has been bested by a baby."

Kate chuckled at Nicholas as she climbed inside the Rolls. She'd seen true affection in the man's eyes when he'd delivered the dig at Marc's station.

They rode in silence as Nicholas wove the car along the winding roads leading to the palace. The route was illuminated by the moon, higher in the sky than it had been when she'd been with Marc earlier.

Marc.

She'd hoped to avoid him until morning. In reality, he'd been in her dreams—an odd, surreal dream where he was riding to her rescue on a massive white steed—totally naked. Such a shame that the phone had awakened her before she got to the good part. Now she really needed to get a grip.

On arrival at the palace, a very forlorn, disheveled Beatrice directed Kate to the nursery. She entered the room to find Marc wearing a gaping white dress shirt and navy pajama bottoms, sprawled out among the randomly discarded bottles and toys, his eyes closed and his head tipped back against the crib. Cecile sat in his lap, looking sassy and content as she chewed on a plastic duck, drooling like a leaky faucet.

A priceless picture. The portrait of father and daughter, and that thought gave Kate pause.

She couldn't think about that now. She had to consider the baby's well-being.

"Hey, little one," Kate said softly. "What are you doing up so late?"

"She's bent on torturing me." Marc spoke without opening his eyes, his voice gruff from frustration and probably lack of sleep.

Cecile smiled a toothless grin and squealed with glee. Totally smitten, Kate set down the bag and grabbed the baby into her arms. Only then did Marc come to his feet, giving Kate an up close and personal view of his bare chest—a really, really nice chest...

Examine the baby, Kate silently admonished. *You're here to see about the baby.*

Kate turned her attention to little Cecile, whose eyes looked clear, bright and alert. No signs of obvious illness. In fact, Cecile looked happier than she had all day.

Kate glanced at Marc over the top of the baby's head. "My

diagnosis is that little Cecile is suffering from separation anxiety."

"She's not the only one who's suffering," Marc said then moved to Kate's side to lay a gentle hand on Cecile's forehead, belying his annoyed tone. "Are you certain she doesn't have a fever?"

The parental concern in Marc's voice surprised Kate. "I take it you didn't check it."

He looked more than a little alarmed. "I would not even attempt such a delicate matter."

Kate rested her cheek against Cecile's and found it cool. "I'll take her temp but I imagine it's normal. She doesn't look at all feverish. She could be teething, though."

Marc held up his pointer. "I have no doubt about that since she has spent the past hour or so chewing my fingers until I located the duck."

Kate smiled. "If you don't mind, look in my bag and get me the thermometer."

Marc complied and held it up. "Is this it?"

"Yes. Bring it here."

He eyed the instrument with disdain. "Isn't this rather large for such a small child?"

"It's made for infants."

"I'll leave the room."

"Why? It's painless."

Marc shifted his weight from one leg to the other, looking uncomfortable. "That would be the opinion of one who did not have to suffer the indignity."

Kate realized Marc had never seen a digital thermometer before. Smiling, she slipped it in the baby's ear. After the beep sounded, she checked the reading. "Normal."

Marc's expression heralded his relief. "Now why in the devil didn't they have those when I was a boy and my mother thought that every sniff warranted a check?"

"The wonders of modern medicine." Kate glanced at the bag resting on the dressing table. "Are those her things?"

"Yes."

She strolled around the room, bouncing Cecile gently in hopes that she might become sleepy. "Look through it and see if you can find a security blanket or toy. She might need that to go to sleep."

Marc rifled through the contents and withdrew a clear plastic bag. "This is all I can find aside from her clothes."

Kate strolled to his side to examine the object—the probable answer to the sleep dilemma. A pacifier. "Take it out and wash it off with hot water, then bring it back to me."

Without a word, Marc went into the adjacent bathroom and then came out a few moments later, holding the pacifier by its pink plastic ring as if it were radioactive.

When Cecile caught sight of it, she whimpered and opened and closed her tiny fists as if to say, "Hand it over now, Buster!" Marc relinquished it to her and she popped it into her mouth, then laid her head against Kate's breast.

Kate paced the room a few moments longer as the baby's eyes grew heavy, then finally closed. Carefully she laid her in the crib, covered her with a blanket, and turned down the lamp, leaving the room in darkness except for a small nightlight near the door.

She turned to discover Marc had disappeared. Obviously he'd carted himself off to bed. Obviously she was wrong, she realized when she stepped into the corridor, closed the door and turned to find him standing there—right there—one shoulder cocked against the doorframe.

He sent her a sleepy and overtly sexy smile. "You're a genius, Kate."

She shrugged. "Not really. I used to baby-sit to earn extra money, so I've had some practice with the nighttime ritual. And pacifiers."

"Ah, so that explains why Cecile responds to you so well. Your skill with children is very apparent. You must be a remarkable doctor."

"Thank you. I think you handled the situation well. Not many men would've stayed up with a baby that wasn't theirs?" She hadn't meant to say that, much less end the sentence on a question.

"She's not mine, Kate," he said adamantly, then more gently, "but she is quite the charmer when she wants to be. She actually smiled at me a few times."

If only Kate could believe that Cecile was fathered by someone else. Hopefully they would soon learn the truth, if not through medical means, then through an investigation if the mother or father didn't come forward. And how could a mother give up such a beautiful child? Unless she didn't have the means to care for her. Marc definitely had the means.

"I do hope she stays asleep for a few hours," Marc added. "Oddly enough, I'm now quite awake."

So was Kate. Sleep was the last thing she wanted, with him staring at her expectantly.

Attempting to focus on something other than his alluring eyes, Kate's gaze dropped to the gaping shirt that revealed his naked chest, well-toned and tempting with its golden color and a patch of brown hair between his nipples. And below that she caught a glimpse of his navel and the stream of darker masculine hair leading downward, but no birthmark. Where in the heck was the birthmark? And where in the heck was her brain? This was no time to eyeball his very male anatomy. And it wasn't like she hadn't seen a naked man before. In fact, she'd seen several, but not many who looked as well developed as Marc DeLoria.

She forced her gaze up and blurted, "Thank goodness for those pacifiers."

"I find it amazing that a rubber nipple would be so appealing to a child." His grin deepened, showing off his dimples to full advantage. "As a man, I personally prefer something more natural."

Oh, no. Much too late at night for sexual innuendo. Kate pointed a finger at him. "You really are a rogue, King DeLoria."

"And that is your fault."

"My fault?"

"You bring out that side of me." He inched a little closer, seeming to steal the air from the atmosphere with the scent of soap that reminded Kate of spring, warm and wonderful. "I hope this doesn't mean you'll now refuse to be my friend." His voice was a low, deep hum—hypnotic, enticing.

Kate pretended to consider it while trying not to lose her bearings in the depths of his deep blue eyes. "I guess I'll cut you some slack this time. I'll still be your friend."

"Good. I have an idea how we can spend the rest of the evening together." He leaned forward and Kate's resolve melted completely when he murmured, "If you're interested in a little friendly late-night adventure."

Four

A midnight raid on the royal kitchen.

That was Marc DeLoria's idea of adventure—and Kate's biggest disappointment of the evening. She'd been hoping for a midnight swim in the moat, although, come to think of it, she hadn't seen a moat. At the very least, she'd been hoping for a walk in the palace gardens. She had seen those when she'd first arrived—beautifully manicured gardens with roses and topiaries and a fountain set in the middle of a reflecting pool.

But instead of taking a romantic stroll with the king, she was standing in the middle of a cavernous kitchen while Marc rummaged through a lower cabinet looking for heaven only knew what. However, he was bent over at the moment, giving Kate a really nice view of his bottom, sheathed in a thin pair of pajamas that showcased the finer points of his dignified derrière. She wondered if that was where the birthmark might be found. With just a few steps forward, and a quick tug, she could find out.

Not a good idea.

She could look all she wanted, but she couldn't touch. He'd made that quite clear outside her hotel room door. No touching allowed. No kissing. No covert rendezvous on the palace grounds, or any grounds, for that matter. But she could still fantasize about it—about him—and remember the words he had spoken earlier in a voice that had nearly brought her to her knees.

…it would be incredibly easy to kiss you right now, to back you into your room, remove all your clothing and make love with you all through the night.

It was definitely getting hot in the castle kitchen. Kate was practically going up in flames and Marc hadn't even turned on the stove.

"I've found it." Marc straightened and showed her a sauté pan along with his sexy and oh-so-charming smile.

Was he planning to make breakfast? Kate's belly roiled in protest. She didn't eat heavy meals in the middle of the night. "I'm not really fond of eggs."

"Nor am I. But I do have a fondness for crepes."

Kate leaned back against the spotless workstation centered in the room. "I know you didn't learn how to cook in the biology lab."

He set the pan on the stove and turned on the burner beneath it before facing her again. "Someone taught me how to make crepes."

Kate assumed the "someone" had been a woman. "I'm sure she got a kick out of teaching a king to cook."

"Yes, and she taught me many things."

Just as Kate had suspected. "Oh, really? Such as?"

"How to tie my shoes, how to read. Her name was Mrs. Perrine, my first nanny."

"Your nanny?"

"You thought I was referring to some nubile young woman.

I assure you Mrs. Perrine was anything but nubile or young. She was as tough as any headmaster, but she did have a way with crepes."

"I'm looking forward to sampling yours."

He sent her another killer grin. "My crepes?"

He pinned her in place with his blue eyes and suggestive tone. No touching, a little voice warned her. No nothing, just friendship. "Yes, I'm looking forward to trying your crepes, Your Highness. Or maybe I should say Your Chefness, since Mr. Nicholas isn't around."

"Marc will suffice," he said as he retreated to the monstrous refrigerator and rummaged around some more, withdrawing two covered bowls and a block of butter. He set the items on the counter next to Kate and opened the bowls. One held strawberries, the other a stack of what looked to be pancakes.

"Actually," he said, "the cook has already prepared the crepes, so I will only need to prepare the filling."

Kate crossed her arms over her middle. "Is there anything I can do to help?"

He gave her a visual once-over, pausing slightly when his gaze passed over her breasts. "You need only stand there and look beautiful, since you seem to do that very well."

Sheesh. Beautiful? She was bare-faced and bleary-eyed. "You are such a liar, Marc DeLoria."

His expression went stern. "I have never lied to you, Kate. I have no reason to lie."

Remorse brought heat of a different kind to Kate's face. Why couldn't she stop throwing around the "L" word? "I'm sorry, it's just that I'm not used to men saying those kinds of things to me."

Marc took a cutting board and knife from the counter and began slicing the strawberries, precisely, slowly. "I assure you, Kate, men have said you're beautiful, even if not to your face. Perhaps you give off signals that indicate you don't wish that kind of attention."

Kate frowned. "Do you really think…I mean…do I?"

He leveled his eyes on hers. "You do."

Kate had never considered that before, but maybe he was right. Maybe she had been too afraid to make herself that accessible for fear that she would be rejected. "Then you're saying I'm a snob?"

"No. You're friendly enough yet you still retain an aloofness, as if you are untouchable. Some men find that very intimidating."

She thought of her one medical school fling with Trevor Allen and how he'd often complained that she seemed to save all her emotions for her parents and her patients. "Do you find it intimidating?"

"No. I find it very appealing."

A network of chills slid down Kate's spine as Marc continued to look at her with eyes that could liquefy the stainless steel appliances. How many women had succumbed to his overt sexuality? Probably plenty. And she shouldn't want to be among them, but for some stupid reason, she did.

Glossing over the moment, Kate turned around and propped her elbows on the counter, her palms supporting her jaws. "Are you sure I can't help you with something? I feel so useless, just standing here looking *beautiful*."

His smile finally reappeared. "Can you melt butter?"

She was melting every time he flashed his dimples. "Yes, I can do that. How much?"

He took a large wooden spoon from a ceramic container, scooped a large chunk of butter from the block then handed it to Kate. "Put this in the pan and watch it for a moment to make sure it doesn't burn."

Kate took her place at the stove and slapped the butter into the already heated pan. It sizzled just like the blood in her veins when Marc came up behind her and added the strawberries and brown sugar, his solid arms forming a frame around her.

"Stir that, please." His warm breath caressed her neck.

"Stir it," she repeated as if the instructions might be too complex. How ridiculous was that? She'd been through med school, for heaven's sake. She could cook a few strawberries.

Marc went away for a time and she glanced at him now and then over her shoulder while he mixed whipped cream in a bowl. He returned to the stove with a ladle filled with a clear liquid. Some kind of liqueur, Kate presumed, considering the pungent aroma. Again he stood behind her as he heated the ladle over another burner for a few seconds before igniting it with a gold lighter. The flame rose from the ladle then spread over the strawberry mixture like a blue blanket as Marc poured it into the pan. The flame quietly died away, but the fire spreading through Kate when Marc's hand came to rest on her waist singed her through and through.

"Now what?" she asked, surprised she had recovered her voice.

"We wait until the alcohol burns for a while."

Marc's voice, the heat radiating from his body so close to hers, acted on Kate as if she'd consumed the entire bottle of liqueur. She leaned back against him for support and his arms came around her, strong and inviting. Then he slowly turned her around in those solid arms until she was facing him.

Again Kate witnessed the indecision warring in his eyes, but this time she also saw desire win out before he cradled her jaw in his palms, then touched his mouth to hers. Yet he only brushed her lips with tempered, chaste kisses, drawing back each time until she thought she might go crazy. She wasn't sure if it was uncertainty on Marc's part or if he was waiting for her to make the next move. The need to know how it would feel to have him kiss her completely drove Kate to clasp his nape and pull his mouth full against hers to finally have what she craved.

Although she had imagined Marc's kiss, although she'd

thought she was ready, Kate soon realized she'd been totally deceiving herself. Skill wasn't an adequate enough word to describe Marc DeLoria's expertise. Never before had she been kissed so softly yet so thoroughly. He used his tongue like a feather, invading her mouth with fine strokes without being at all intrusive. And Kate felt it down to her knees and lower.

He pulled her against him and slid his hand down her back to her hips. She realized the result of this spontaneous kiss when Marc pressed against her, showing Kate up front that he was very affected. And so was she.

After abruptly breaking the kiss, Marc took a step back, rubbed a hand over his jaw and exhaled a long breath. "My apologies, Kate. Something about you standing at the stove made me forget myself."

Kate wasn't sure whether to be flattered or insulted. She was, however, very winded and very warm. "Oh, so do you have one of those French maid fantasies or do you just prefer the domestic type?"

His expression turned serious. "I have to remember that nothing has changed since I left you at your hotel door. We really can't be doing this."

"We just did."

"I know, and it shouldn't happen again."

Kate couldn't stop her smile when she realized he sounded as if he were trying to convince himself it *wouldn't* happen again. "Then I guess we should avoid kitchens if seeing a woman standing at the stove turns you on."

He smiled reluctantly. "You're probably right, and I believe the strawberries are done now."

Obviously, so were they, Kate decided.

Marc assembled the crepes and placed them on plates while Kate looked on, still reeling from the kiss. She had to hand it to Marc, he had an iron will. Or maybe he was just being nice to her. But she hadn't seen *nice* in his expression when she'd been in his arms. She'd seen want, maybe even need. And her thoughts at that moment wouldn't qualify as nice, either. But from this point forward, she would probably have to settle for just that single memory.

They carried the dessert into a comfortable den with a cushy tweed couch and a fireplace in the corner. Marc set his plate on the coffee table in front of the sofa and settled beside Kate.

Kate waited for him to take the first bite, but instead he cut into one of her crepes and held it to her lips. "Your first sample."

She slid the crepe into her mouth and savored the flavors of strawberries, whipped cream and sugar; the delicate crepe practically dissolved in her mouth. "This is almost sinful."

His eyes held fast to hers. "That would depend on your definition of sin."

"Calories," she added after she swallowed another bite. "And carbs, especially when they take up residence on your thighs."

His gaze drifted to her thighs, then traveled slowly back up again to her face. "I doubt that you need to worry about that."

"From your mouth to my metabolism's ear."

"I hope you'll put away all your concerns and simply enjoy."

Kate did as Marc asked and ate every last bite of the crepes, all the while wondering if Marc's comment about sinful behavior went beyond indulging in dessert. But she didn't dare hope, didn't dare consider anything more than spending time with him as a friend.

After they both finished, Marc grabbed the remote control and snapped on the television positioned in the entertainment center. He flipped through the channels, pausing at one nature program heralding the mating habits of the mongoose. With a groan, he changed the channel to a French-speaking movie where two people seemed engaged in a battle of wills.

After tossing the remote back on the table, he leaned back

against the couch. "Not much variety this time of the night, so I suppose we'll have to settle for this. Unless you're ready for bed."

Kate assumed he'd meant alone and right now that didn't float her boat. "Funny, I'm not all that tired, although I probably should be."

"Then perhaps this movie will put you to sleep."

"It could, since I have no idea what they're saying."

Marc draped his arm over the back of the sofa, only a few inches separating their bodies. "The man's name is Jean-Michel and he's telling the woman, Genevieve, that he must leave her since he belongs to another."

"The cad. What did she say to that?"

"She says *Tu me veux. Je te défie de me dire que je me suis trompée.* She claims he wants her and she's daring him to deny it."

Hearing Marc speaking in French in a low, husky voice blanketed Kate in chills. She glanced at him and realized he'd moved much closer, rekindling the fire that had been smoldering deep within her all evening. "Is he denying it?"

Marc's gaze drifted to her mouth. "*C'est impossible.* It's impossible for him to deny that he wants her."

The conviction in Marc's voice, the heat in his eyes, fed Kate's optimism that he was speaking of his own desire—desire for her. Or maybe she simply wanted him so badly that she'd invented something that wasn't really there.

Turning her attention away from Marc and back to the movie, she got the full effect of Jean-Michel's weakness for Genevieve. Now tangled together in a passionate embrace, the lovers' actions spoke loud and clear in that age-old universal language of love. Kate twitched when the camera panned in for an up close and very personal shot of the actors' lips melded together, their hands roving over each other as if they couldn't quite touch enough to be satisfied. She squirmed some more when the couple tore at each other's clothing until they were completely, unabashedly naked.

"This must be a cable channel," she muttered, all too aware of how dumb and unsophisticated that must have sounded.

"Actually, no. Freedom of expression is highly regarded here. Nudity is considered natural and beautiful. So is lovemaking."

Kate's heart bounded into her throat when Marc's arm came to rest on her shoulder, his fingertips tracing slow, random circles on her upper arm as if drawing his name in the sand. Marking his territory so to speak, and making Kate mindful of how much the movie and his touch were affecting her.

"Maybe we should watch something else," she said.

Marc nuzzled his face in her hair, taking her by surprise and her senses by storm. "Does it make you uncomfortable?"

Kate bit her bottom lip, hard. "A little."

"In what way?"

"I don't know." She did know, and Marc probably knew, too. The uncensored sex on the screen, Marc's close proximity, was turning her on, turning her into a woman on the verge of asking him at the very least to kiss her again.

She didn't have to ask, and this time there was no reluctance in Marc's kiss, no hesitation. So focused was Kate on the welcome invasion of his tongue, the soft insistence of his lips, that she was only mildly aware of the lovers' soft moans coming from the TV, Marc's evening whiskers abrading her chin and his hand traveling up and down her side, grazing her breast with each pass.

Time seemed suspended and Kate acknowledged she could go on kissing him forever. But a girl could only be kissed this way for so long without other parts of her body becoming present and accounted for. Her nipples hardened against his chest. Fire spread through her belly and settled between her thighs in a dull throb.

As if some wild wanton creature had crawled beneath her

skin, Kate lifted her leg over Marc's thighs. He groaned against her mouth and took her down onto the couch, where he settled on top of her, his own leg dividing her legs. He momentarily broke the kiss to raise her shirt, untie his robe and push it open, before taking her mouth once more. But he didn't use his hand to tantalize her; he used his chest, lightly rubbing her bare breasts, drawing away slightly then rubbing again and again, in maddening circular motions. The fine veneer of chest hair tickled her nipples into hard, sensitive buds and sent a wash of dampness between her thighs.

Unraveled by his skill, his welcome weight and deep kisses, Kate tilted her hips up to feel him more, as if that might soothe the ache. And she did feel him, every solid inch of him, through the thin material of his pajamas.

As if he recognized her need, Marc slid his hand between them at her abdomen. The tug on the snap of her jeans only heightened Kate's excitement and spurred her anticipation.

Then suddenly, there was nothing. No kisses. No touches. No Marc.

Kate opened her eyes and looked up to find Marc standing several feet away, his back to her, both hands laced together behind his neck. And then came Kate's complete mortification in a few moments of silence that seemed to last hours.

"I'm sorry, Kate."

He was apologizing again, and Kate was without a doubt more embarrassed than she'd ever been her entire life. She pulled her shirt down, scooted to the edge of the sofa and clutched her disheveled hair by the roots. "I can't imagine what you must think of me right now."

He sat beside her, his expression remorseful as he took her hand into his. "Would you like to know what I think of you? I think you're the most incredible, sensual woman I've encountered in many years, if not ever. I think that if I hadn't remembered why we cannot do this, I would be inside of you at this moment and that would be wrong."

His words gave her a courage she'd never known before, at least where men were concerned. "Why would it be wrong, Marc? We're both adults. No one's around. No one would have to know."

He released a harsh sigh. "Because I could only offer you a casual affair, in secret. Because you're a good woman, Kate, and you deserve to be treated as such, not hidden away from the world."

Kate had always been the good girl. The good, reliable girl. She'd grown tired of bearing that label, weary of being that girl. Besides, she was a woman now, with a woman's desires and needs—and she was with a man who had the knowledge and the means to take her beyond the limit. But he wasn't willing to answer those needs, at least not now.

Kate wrenched her hand from his and crossed her arms over her chest thinking that might alleviate the sudden cold that had replaced the heat, a futile gesture. "I guess you're right, Marc. So let's just chalk up my total lack of restraint to my current state of jet lag. I should probably go back to the hotel now."

When Kate stood, Marc caught her wrist. "Stay here, tonight, Kate. With me. You need your rest. We can both sleep on the sofa."

"I'm not sure that's a good idea," Kate said, although regardless of her reckless behavior and his subsequent rejection, she would like nothing more than to wake in Marc's arms.

After gathering a throw from the opposite arm of the couch, Marc tied his robe, worked his way to the corner of the sofa and pulled her down into his arms. "Stretch out your legs and put your head on my chest. I promise to keep my hands to myself."

"Darn it."

He tossed the throw over them both. "Don't make this any

harder than it already is, fair lady, or I'm afraid I'll have to lock you in the dungeon."

Kate felt giddy and punch-drunk. "Exactly how hard is it?"

Marc cracked a crooked smile. "You could not begin to imagine."

Oh, but she didn't have to rely on her imagination. She'd gotten the extent of "it" a few moments before and in the kitchen. She doubted she would ever forget how he'd felt against her. But right now she should try to sleep. Morning would come all too soon, and her time alone with Marc would probably come to an end. After tonight, she had no doubt he would probably avoid her from here on out. And maybe that was best. After all, he was a king, she was a doctor, and he had something to prove—that he could resist her. That made Kate smile as she closed her eyes.

Imagine that. King Marcel DeLoria had found her irresistible.

"Marcel, wake up."

Marc forced his eyes open to find his mother standing before the sofa, Cecile propped on one hip, flailing her tiny arms about as if directing an orchestra. What in the devil was Mary doing up this time of the night and why was she fully dressed as if ready to hold court? Unless it was already morning. Surely not. No more than an hour had passed since he'd finally drifted off, or at least it seemed that way.

Every molecule of his body ached from the position he'd kept for the past few hours, one part in particular, thanks to the woman in his arms. Some time during the night, Kate had inadvertently landed her palm on his groin—and for some insane reason, he'd left it there. Luckily the throw and his robe covered his lower body, adequately concealing his predicament from his matriarch.

When Cecile squealed, Kate snapped up like a bedspring, tossed the cover aside and pushed her hair away from her face. "What time is it?"

Marc slid the throw back into his lap as nonchalantly as possible. "Very early," he said, his voice rough from lack of sleep, unanswered need and an abundance of annoyance.

Mary took a seat in the chair across from the sofa, Cecile in her lap happy as a lark. "It's not quite dawn. When Cecile awakened, I relieved Beatrice so she could have some sleep, since it seems our little one has her days and nights confused."

"At least someone's sleeping," Marc grumbled yet he couldn't help but smile at Cecile as she gummed his mother's favorite string of pearls hanging from Mary's throat. Only an innocent could get away with such anarchy.

When Mary surveyed Kate's disheveled appearance, Marc could almost hear the cogs turning in her mind. "I hadn't realized Kate had not returned to the hotel," she said.

Kate averted her eyes and tugged at her wrinkled T-shirt. "Actually, I did return to the hotel. Marc called and asked me to come and check on Cecile when she wouldn't sleep. He thought she was ill."

"She certainly seems well enough to me," Mary said as she brushed a kiss across the baby's cheek. Then she leveled her gaze on Marc. "I hope you didn't take advantage of Kate's courtesy, Marcel."

He glanced at Kate who was sporting a deep blush. "Mother, I assure you I did not take advantage of Kate. And if you're intimating that something sordid went on last night, you are wrong." Not that he hadn't considered it. "We were both very tired and we fell asleep during a movie."

"Of course I would not think such a thing, dear boy. Kate would never do something sordid."

He experienced a sudden surge of anger that effectively repressed any lingering effects of his desire for the doctor. "But I would?"

"I suppose not, since you appear to have on your robe, although it's difficult to tell with you clutching that throw as if you feared it might walk away."

Marc yanked the blanket aside. "Happy now, Mother? I have done nothing to compromise Kate's or my reputation." And not because he didn't want Kate; he did. Even now with her curled up on the couch, both her clothes and hair a mess, he still wanted her. Badly.

Mary sighed. "But you did leave quite a disaster in the kitchen. Cook is already grousing this morning."

"I'm afraid that's my fault," Kate said. "I meant to clean up before I fell asleep, since Marc did the cooking."

Mary sent Kate a kind look. "Nonsense, my dear. You are our guest. Marc could have cleaned up after himself, although I'm not certain he's learned the fine art of housekeeping."

His mother was obviously determined to ruin his day. "Don't you think I already have enough responsibilities, Mother?"

"Yes, dear, you do." She sent a pointed look at Cecile, causing Marc to grit his teeth.

After coming to her feet, Kate walked to the chair and said, "May I hold her?"

"Why, of course." Mary stood and relinquished Cecile to Kate.

Kate hugged the baby and kissed her cheek. "I hope you've gotten plenty of sleep, little one, since we have a busy morning ahead of us at the clinic."

Marc leaned his head against the sofa, all the energy seeming to drain from him at that moment. "I bloody well forgot about the damn test."

"Take care with your language, Marcel," Mary scolded. "You have two ladies present and one grandmother who will not tolerate disrespect."

"My apologies," Marc muttered, a long list of descriptive curses threatening to explode from his mouth. The queen mother was already laying claim to Cecile before proof of that fact existed.

"How is your headache, Mary?" Kate asked, looking uncomfortable over the exchange between mother and son.

Mary laid a hand on Kate's arm. "My dear, it is completely gone, thanks to you. That neck massage you gave me did the trick."

"It was no problem at all." She regarded Marc over her shoulder. "I learned some massage therapy while I was in med school. Pressure points, that sort of thing, to relieve tension."

Marc had a point of pressure he would greatly like Kate to relieve. Instead, his mother had received a massage and he'd only acquired a painful kink in his neck and a prominent swelling beneath his pajamas.

Kate handed the baby back to Mary and said, "Well, I guess I need to return to the hotel and freshen up before we go to the clinic."

"You must stay for breakfast, dear. Cook has begun the preparations."

Kate turned to Marc as if seeking reinforcement. "It might be better if I leave now. We need to get everything done before the clinic opens."

Marc stood. "I'll have Mr. Nicholas take you back to the hotel immediately."

"That's fine," Kate said, a hint of disappointment in her tone.

Marc had done nothing but disappoint her the past few hours; that much he knew. Last night, she had needed something from him, something he hadn't been able to give to her—and not because he hadn't wanted to. But if he'd touched her in the way that he'd wanted, he might not have been able to stop with only a touch. And if not careful, it would happen again…and again.

An hour later, Kate and Marc slipped through the clinic's back door with the baby in tow, fortunately finding the place totally deserted. In a small room at the far end of the corridor, Kate thoroughly examined Cecile, who remained content by chewing on the hem of her discarded cornflower blue dress while Marc looked on. Cecile seemed very healthy, only slightly below average in weight and height for a child of seven months, if, in fact, that was her age. Kate could only estimate unless the mother came forward. At least today they might learn more about the father, namely if he could possibly be Marc or Philippe.

With that thought, Kate took a lancet in hand to draw Cecile's blood. She hated this part the most—sticking an unsuspecting baby.

After returning to the table, she told Marc, "If you could just hold her a little, that would be a big help."

Marc frowned. "Will it hurt her very much?"

Kate smiled at the concern in his tone and expression. "Only a little finger prick, but she's not going to like it. That's why I need to make sure she doesn't move away."

Marc did as he was told, speaking to Cecile in a soothing tone while Kate applied the stick. Cecile looked surprised at first, then her tiny bottom lip quivered and she let out a wail when Kate began to knead her finger.

"That's it, sweetie," Kate said after she had enough of a sample on the glass slide. "All done here. I hope you don't hate me now."

Cecile buried her face against Marc's chest and released a few sniffles before turning back to Kate and holding out her arms.

"Obviously she doesn't hate you at all," Marc said as Kate took the baby.

Kate wondered if Marc hated her after their interlude last night. Maybe hate was too strong a word, but she doubted he was pleased by her behavior. She couldn't worry about that now. She had too much to do.

Kate swiped the downy blond hair away from Cecile's

forehead and planted a kiss there. "She's a very brave girl. Now I'll just get her dressed and you can take her home while I work on the test. Hopefully she'll be ready for a nap."

"I am most definitely ready for a nap," Marc said, his off-kilter smile reappearing. "I'm sure you are as well. We could crawl up on the sofa and see what we can find in the way of daytime programming."

Okay, so maybe she'd been wrong. Maybe he wasn't all that concerned about what had and hadn't happened last night. But it would be best for all concerned if they steered clear of that kind of situation from this point forward.

She sent him a cautioning glance. "I think we should avoid the TV at all costs."

He looked frustrated. "You're probably right. While you're dressing Cecile, I'm going to see if Dr. Martine has arrived yet. He's supposed to be on his way. I'll be back as soon as possible since it's getting late. Perhaps we'll be able to leave undetected."

"I'll see you in a while then."

Marc leaned over to kiss Cecile's cheek and for the briefest of moments, Kate thought he might kiss her, too. Instead, he turned away and quickly headed out the door.

Kate rummaged through the bag and withdrew a clean diaper to change Cecile, who wasn't altogether cooperative. Several times, Kate feared that the little girl might hurl herself off the table before Kate had the diaper secured. After success finally came, Kate pulled her up and began to dress her.

"I wish I had your energy, little one," she told her when Cecile immediately discarded the sock that Kate had just slipped on her foot. "I just know you're going to give Beatrice a run for her money today. That is, if I can get you to keep your clothes on." With effort, she finally managed to secure the rest of the buttons on Cecile's dress. "But I can't really blame you. Right now, I'd really like to get out of these slacks and shoes and take a long, hot bath."

"Do you need any assistance?"

The hairs on Kate's neck stood at attention when recognition dawned. She glanced over her shoulder to confirm her fears and found Renault leaning in the doorway with all the cockiness of a twenty-year-old jock—and only half the height and body. His sparse blond hair was slicked back, his beady brown eyes focused on the baby. So much for a quick getaway.

Kate lifted Cecile into her arms and faced the jerk, trying to affect calm when her mind was struggling to come up with an explanation. "Good morning, Dr. Renault. I wasn't expecting you so early."

"Nor I you." He moved closer and surveyed Cecile. "I've been told you would not assume your duties until tomorrow."

Evasion was probably her best line of defense, Kate decided. "That's correct."

"Yet you're examining this child."

"Yes."

"I did not see anyone in the waiting room. Does she have parents?"

"Of course she has parents. Didn't they teach you in medical school that those old folktales about storks and cabbage patches aren't true?"

Renault's smile was cynical. "I assure you, Dr. Milner, I know all the workings of procreation. You have still not answered my question. To whom does this child belong?"

Think quick, Kate. "Actually, she belongs to me."

Renault raised one bushy eyebrow. "Martine did not mention you have a child."

"Well, I do, and this is her. Cecile."

He stroked his pointy chin. "Ah, Cecile. A very fine French name. Is your husband French?"

"I don't have a husband." And that wasn't a lie.

"The baby's father, then?"

"He's not in the picture." An understatement in the first order.

Renault gave Kate a slimy visual once-over, fitting for a human slug. "I must say, you are in very fine shape given the age of this child. I admire you for that. In fact, I admire everything about you."

Kate resisted telling him where to stuff his admiration. "Thank you." She had to get away before he asked more questions. "I really need to get her home for her morning nap. But first, I have a few tests I need to run."

"Is she ill?"

"No. Just routine labs."

"I would be more than happy to assist you."

"I believe Dr. Milner is quite capable of working alone, Renault."

Kate turned to see Marc sporting a look that could wither the overhead light.

Renault didn't look the least bit concerned over Marc's presence or his sharp tone. "I am most certain, Your Highness, Dr. Milner is quite capable in all that she endeavors. I was simply trying to be accommodating."

Marc balled his hands into fists at his sides. "She doesn't need your assistance, I assure you."

Renault turned back to Kate, bowed slightly and kissed Cecile's hand. "You are a lovely girl, Cecile."

Kate wanted to cheer when Cecile pulled her hand away and hid her face against Kate's shoulder. Either she had stranger phobia or good instincts. Kate assumed the latter, considering she had taken to Kate, Marc and his mother without hesitation.

Before Renault passed Marc at the door, Marc told him, "You will practice the utmost in decorum where Dr. Milner is concerned or you will answer to me. Is that clear?"

Renault sent Kate a lecherous glance, then glared at Marc. "Quite clear, Your Majesty. I do not intend to tread on another man's territory."

With that, he was gone and Marc looked as if he could blow

a fuse when he faced Kate again. "Did he do anything inappropriate?" he demanded.

Kate considered telling him about Renault's intimations but decided to wait until later when she was assured they were alone. "His kind are a dime a dozen and I know how to handle them."

"And you will tell me if he is the least bit out of line." It wasn't a request.

"I promise I'll tell you if I have to hurt him." She handed Marc the baby and smiled. "Now you go with your…king, Cecile, and I'll be back later today." She kissed the baby's cheek one last time and reined in her urge to do the same to Marc. "Be a good girl, sweetie. I'll be back as soon as I can."

"I'm certain she'll look forward to your return." Marc leaned toward Kate's ear and whispered, "And so will I, so hurry."

Then Marc left the room, leaving Kate standing alone in a state of confusion. Couldn't Marc make up his mind? He was making her head spin with his no-we-can't and yes-we-will attitude. He did want her; that was becoming apparent to Kate each time they were together. Yet he kept saying he couldn't have her. But if Marc's resistance completely waned, how far would she allow things to go, since she recognized it wouldn't be more than a fling? Did she dare make love with him?

Yes. No question about it. She wasn't looking for a knight's rescue, only a night of incredible lovemaking. A little adventure. She wanted to experience true freedom in his arms without worrying about pleasing anyone aside from herself—and Marc DeLoria.

She shivered thinking about it, thinking about him, thinking about all the ways he could take her places she'd never been before.

Imagine that, making love with a king. Now if only the king would cooperate.

Five

After Kate conducted the lab tests, Dr. Martine asked if she could possibly see some patients—minor cases, most involving common colds and well-baby checks. She agreed and was accompanied by a very nice Australian-born nurse named Caroline, who aided Kate in interpreting conditions of those who spoke only French or Castilian, and there were more than a few.

By that afternoon, Kate was high on adrenaline but still concerned about the language barriers. She made a mental note to get out the tapes and books to study when she had a spare minute. If she ever had a spare minute. She also needed to call home soon. She hadn't spoken with her mother, hadn't even told her that she'd accepted the position. Kate refused to perceive that as a problem. It was high time for her family to learn to live without her constant attention.

Fortunately, Renault had been scarce during the day, which was probably the reason why the clinic had been running so far behind, not that Kate had minded his absence or treating his patients. She'd welcomed rejoining the world of medicine—and avoiding confronting Marc with the knowledge she now held—the test results.

After arriving back at the palace, she waited in Marc's private study with that knowledge while Mr. Nicholas summoned the king. It could be a while, Nicholas had told her, since Marc had gone out for a drive. Kate assumed this was Marc's only means to relax—or to escape. And when he found out that Cecile shared his rare blood type, he might climb back into his coveted car and keep driving.

Kate milled around the office, pulling various books from the shelves, mainly from nervousness instead of real interest. Most involved business acumen, as far as she could tell, since all were written in French. Except for one well-worn English volume of *Hamlet* that looked as though it had been handed down through the generations. Ironic, Kate decided, since to be or not to be was definitely the question of the moment in terms of Marc's possible parental ties to Cecile.

Yet he'd been so adamant he wasn't Cecile's father that Kate almost believed him. In some ways she still did, since she really had no reason not to take him at his word. She also knew that accidents happened, and unless Cecile's mother came forward, they might never know the truth.

When the phone shrilled, Kate nearly jumped out of her functional black shoes. She waited while the phone rang again for someone to answer. Maybe she should answer it. It could be Marc's private line and he might be calling her to say he'd been detained. If not, she would have to take a message.

But how should she answer? The DeLoria Residence? The King's Office?

On the fourth ring, Kate leaned over the desk, grabbed the receiver and settled for a simple, "Hello."

A long silence ensued until a breathy feminine voice asked, "Is this Marc's secretary?"

Kate was overcome with an insane spark of jealousy. "No, this is not Marc's secretary."

The woman released a grating laugh. "Then you must be my replacement. I do hope you are taking advantage of Marc's expertise. He is quite a skilled lover, isn't he? Has he taken you to the little mountain cabin yet?"

Kate had no desire to confirm or deny anything to this woman, especially since she appeared to be one of Marc's erstwhile lovers. "May I ask who's calling?"

"Why, darling, this is Elsa," she fairly purred.

As if that should mean something to Kate. "Well, Elsa, is there something I can do for you?" *Darling.*

"I am calling to see if Marc received the gift I had delivered to the palace."

Gift? Surely she didn't mean… "Does this gift happen to have blue eyes and blond hair?"

"Why yes, darling, it does. A little reminder of our time together. Tell Marc to enjoy."

The line went dead and Kate could only stare at the receiver before slamming the phone back on its cradle.

Obviously she had been wrong to believe Marc. Obviously this Elsa was Cecile's mother, if you could actually call her that. What kind of woman would just drop her baby off at a gate and then leave? A heartless, cruel woman who didn't have a maternal bone in her body.

Kate's heart felt weighted with the knowledge that her questions had now been answered. Marc had fathered a child by some flighty femme fatale who had no business being a parent. And Kate dared Marc to deny his daughter now.

Marc couldn't deny he was in a huge hurry to see Kate. He entered the palace through the back access at a fast clip, Nicholas dogging his every step. "Where is Dr. Milner now?"

"She is waiting in your study, Your Eagerness."

Marc muttered an oath. "This is no time to joke, Nicholas. Did she seem concerned about anything?"

"Actually, she did seem a bit on edge."

Striding down the corridor toward his office, Marc pulled his sunshades off his eyes and tossed them and his keys to Nicholas. "Have someone park the car, and make sure I am not disturbed until I say otherwise. Is that clear?"

Nicholas stopped outside the study and saluted. "I live to serve you."

After sending Nicholas a harsh look—which the man did not seem to heed—Marc opened his office door to find Kate leaning back against his desk, her arms stiff at her sides and her eyes reflecting displeasure. Obviously Renault had used his torrid tactics to try to bed her, or she had confirmed Cecile's blood type as his match and still believed he wasn't being truthful.

After closing the door behind him and tripping the lock, Marc decided to begin with his concerns over her colleague. "Did Renault do something to you?"

"I didn't see him again after your left. I did see a few patients after I typed Cecile's blood."

"Then you have the results?"

"Yes, and I also have a message for you." Her tone was clipped and cool, devoid of welcome.

"A message?"

"From Elsa, *darling.* She called a few minutes ago. I answered the phone because I thought it might be you."

Why in the devil was Elsa calling him? He'd made it quite clear that he wanted no contact from her, not that his demands had ever stopped her. "What did she want?"

Kate strolled around the room for a moment before facing him again. "She wanted to know if you received her gift, the one with blue eyes and blond hair. She had it delivered to the palace. So I suppose you could say the mystery of Cecile's mother is solved."

At first Marc was perplexed, until he realized what Elsa had been referring to. He couldn't stop the chuckle, not a good thing to do considering the acid look Kate sent him. If her eyes were dueling pistols, he'd be a dead man.

Marc pushed away from the door, crossed the room and reached behind the armoire to retrieve the "gift" in hopes of clearing up this whole misunderstanding.

Grabbing the edge of the frame, he withdrew the photograph and presented it to Kate. "This is Elsa's gift. An eleven-by-fourteen glossy from her recent photo shoot. You will note that she has blond hair and blue eyes." And practically no clothes on aside from a skimpy swimsuit.

Kate took the picture from him and stared at it for a time before bringing her gaze back to Marc. "She considers this a gift?"

"Elsa considers herself a gift to all mankind." He took the photo back and hid it away again behind the armoire before returning to Kate, maintaining some distance even though he wanted to kiss away her doubts. "She thought I would be interested enough to keep it as a reminder of our brief association. She was mistaken. I've meant to have Nicholas discard it, but I've not had the time with everything that's been happening of late."

"But you don't deny you were lovers."

"No, I cannot deny that." He also couldn't deny the jealousy in Kate's tone, nor could he deny that on some level that pleased him.

She narrowed her eyes. "And there's no way she could be Cecile's mother?"

"There is as much chance of Elsa being a mother as there is a chance that her breasts are real."

A hint of a smile teased at Kate's full lips, but it didn't quite form. "How can you be so sure?"

He offered his own smile, hoping to lighten the mood. "I happen to know when a woman has natural attributes."

She frowned. "I meant about her not being Cecile's mother."

So much for his attempt at humor. "If Elsa had been pregnant, she would not have abandoned the baby. That much I know."

"Then she's not just another pretty ego?"

"Elsa is very self-absorbed and she would not risk an end to her modeling career with an unplanned pregnancy. She made it quite clear she never wanted any children. And if by some chance she'd chosen to have a baby, she would have turned it into a publicity campaign, especially if that baby were mine."

Kate remained silent for a few moments as if attempting to digest the information. "Okay, I guess I believe you."

She might as well have slapped him. "You guess? Have I not given you enough proof?"

"You've provided proof that Elsa probably isn't Cecile's mother. But I have the proof that odds are Cecile is either yours or Philippe's child."

As he'd suspected. "Then she has our blood type."

"Yes. I confirmed the results with Dr. Martine."

He saw mistrust in Kate's eyes, and he hated that. "You must believe me when I tell you that Elsa was the last woman in my life for well over a year, and I have exercised the greatest care. The baby is not mine."

"It doesn't really matter what I believe."

"It does to me."

"Why?"

A difficult question, and one he had avoided asking himself. "Because you're a very special person, Kate. I need you to trust me. I know that you hold the truth in very high esteem."

Kate's gaze faltered. "I'm not beyond telling a lie, Marc. In fact, I told one today. A big one."

"You've lied to me?"

"Not you. Renault. When he came into the exam room, he started asking questions. I told him Cecile is my daughter."

He could not have asked for a better plan. "That's brilliant, Kate."

"It is?"

"Yes. Perhaps now there won't be any speculation in terms of Cecile's parentage until someone comes forward with the truth."

"*If* someone comes forward."

Marc did not foresee that happening, at least not soon. It would be up to him to clear his name. "I doubt that will be the case, but it's still imperative that we find out who the mother is. Chances are, my perfect brother was not so perfect after all."

She sent him a severe look. "Are you doing this for Cecile or for yourself? Do you want to prove that Philippe wasn't as innocent as he seemed? And if you do that, how will it affect your family?"

Kate's honesty threw Marc mentally off balance. He hadn't considered how the truth might affect his mother if they proved Philippe was Cecile's father. "I need to put this issue to bed once and for all, for everyone's sake. How I'll handle the rest remains to be seen. First, I must attempt to find out the mother's identity."

"And how do you propose to do that?"

He had no right to ask, but Kate was his only hope. "With your help."

"My help?"

"I'm only asking that you keep your ears open for any gossip. Perhaps search the hospital's records for any mysterious woman who gave birth six to eight months ago. The staff in the palace might be forthcoming with information about my brother since you're—"

"A commoner."

"Yes, in a manner of speaking."

"Then you're asking me to do a little investigating in my spare time."

"Only if you feel comfortable in doing so."

"As long as we've absolutely ruled out your lover."

He took a step forward. "*Former* lover. It's over between us, Kate."

She slowly ran a fingertip along the edge of the desk, fueling Marc's all-consuming desire for her. "Obviously you still have something she wants."

"She wants attention and not necessarily only from me."

Kate leaned back against the desk, using her arms as a brace, thrusting her breasts forward, driving Marc to distraction. "Are you sure about that? She's very vocal about your skills as a lover. So are you, Marc?"

A fool? A man too weak to resist her charms? "Am I what?"

"A skilled lover?"

Marc was only certain about one thing—he couldn't ignore Kate's query, asked in a sensual voice that threatened his control. Couldn't ignore her simple black slacks and plain white blouse that would be easy to remove. Couldn't ignore the tightness in his groin when she streaked her tongue over her lower lip.

"I do not make it a habit to speculate on my skill," he said, clinging to his last strand of restraint.

"Maybe I should judge for myself."

"You have no idea what you're asking, Kate." He did know all too well she recognized the power she had over him at that moment, and he found that incredibly hard to resist.

She swept her dark hair away from her face with one hand. "You're wrong, Marc. I know exactly what I'm asking, and so do you. Does your expertise live up to the hype? Are you a good lover?"

"Good is an interesting term. Good only comes when you do not aspire to be great."

"Do you aspire to be a great lover, Marc DeLoria?"

"I refuse to settle for mediocrity in any of my endeavors."

She challenged him with a look, dared him with a sultry smile, enticed him with words when she said, "Then prove it."

Marc was losing his tenuous hold on his common sense. He only knew that if he didn't get away from Kate now, he would kiss her—deeply and without reservation. Touch her without hesitation. Without consideration of the consequences. He had no call to want her as much as he did. He had too much to consider in light of his position and too little to offer her beyond mutual pleasure. But he did want her, and he'd be damned if he had her—or damned if he didn't.

Propelled by his weakness for this woman, Marc closed the distance between them in two strides and braced his palms on the desk on either side of her. He sought her mouth in a rush, as if he couldn't survive without exploring the territory once more. She opened to him, played her tongue against his, pushed him to a point where he could easily dispense with all formality and clothing to get inside her immediately. But he rejected that notion. If he could touch her, taste her, tempt her, then that would be enough. It would have to be enough.

After breaking the kiss, he settled his face in the hollow below her throat, pressing his lips there while inhaling her enticing fragrance.

"Marc, I thought you said we couldn't." Her voice was a teasing, breathy caress at his ear.

"Shouldn't," he murmured then slid his tongue down the cleft between her breasts, stopping where the opening of her blouse ended and buttons began, knowing he should not go any farther. But knowing what he shouldn't do did nothing to quell the urge to do what he wanted to do. To her, with her.

Kate threaded her hands through his hair, back and forth in long, torturous strokes. "Maybe we should go somewhere more private."

He straightened and slipped the first button on her blouse, ignoring the persistent voice telling him to stop. "I've locked the door." He released two more buttons, keeping his gaze fixed on Kate's eyes, searching for any sign of protest. He saw nothing but need. "I gave orders that we are not to be disturbed."

"Very resourceful," she said, followed by a shaky smile that indicated nervousness, but not reluctance.

Finally, Marc parted her blouse, exposing her bra, which he unhooked with a quick flip of one finger beneath the front closure before pushing it aside with both hands. His gaze roved over her breasts, round and pink tinged to match the flush on her face when he lifted her up and seated her on the desk's edge.

As he traced a path around one rosy tip with his finger, Kate watched his movements, her chest rising and falling in rapid succession. *"Tu es parfaite,"* he whispered. " Perfect."

Dipping his head, he drew one nipple into his mouth, relishing the feel of her against his tongue. He wanted more. He wanted it all. He wanted to undo her slacks, slip his hand inside, experience her wet heat. He wanted to open his own fly, give himself some blessed relief, and thrust inside her.

When Kate released a soft, sexual sound, reality forced its way into his psyche and he took a step back. "We have to stop this, Kate."

"Why?"

Marc had so many reasons, but he began with the most important. "I have nothing to protect you against pregnancy, and God knows I do not need another complication."

Kate's face fell as if it had the weight of the world attached. "Complication? So that's what I am to you?"

"No…that's not…" What in the hell could he say? Yes, she was a complication. His overwhelming desire was very complicated, as were his feelings for her that he did not dare examine. "Look, Kate, I've done what I said I would not do. I've proven my weakness for you against my better judgment."

"Weakness for me, or for women in general?"

That brought seething anger to the surface of Marc's attempts at a calm facade. "I've spent almost a year being celibate, and it was not due to a lack of propositions. I've met many women over that time, in many different places, and not one has tempted me the way that you do. Only you, Kate, and no one else."

She looked a bit more relaxed, if not totally pleased, as she redid her bra. "And what do you propose we do now? Ignore our attraction to each other?" She paused with a hand on the blouse and looked at him thoughtfully. "Or were you just trying to prove a point?"

"If that were true, Kate, I would not have stopped."

She sent a direct look at his distended fly. "Then you're determined to be the king of steel, is that correct?"

Steel would be a more-than-adequate description in terms of his erection, but not when it came to his strength as far as Kate was concerned. "I cannot make love to you Kate. If I do, then I am in danger of hurting you in the process."

"You can't hurt me, Marc. I know what this is all about. Chemistry. Attraction. Not ever-after."

"But you have no idea what my life is about. If anyone even suspects we're involved, you will suffer for it."

"I'm not a wilting flower. And as I told you before, I'm only looking for some adventure." She didn't sound all that convincing. "But I'm not going to force you to do anything you don't want to do."

Right then, he would have gladly taken her down to the floor and finished what they'd started—what he had started. Instead, he turned away and headed for the door.

He needed to remember who he was—a king with a consuming need to be accepted. But his need for Kate was beginning to overshadow everything else.

He could not let that happen. It might destroy everything

he had sought to accomplish in terms of his reputation. But worse, it could destroy her.

Without facing her again, he said, "I will see that Nicholas returns you safely to the hotel."

And then he would retire for the evening, alone, to chastise himself for his complete lack of control.

Even after Marc had been gone for several minutes, Kate could still feel his mouth and hands on her breasts, could still hear him say that he couldn't make love to her, that she was a complication. She refused to be a complication.

Probably just as well he'd stopped, Kate decided as she adjusted her clothing before leaving the office. And she was crazy to think that she didn't want him with every fiber of her being. She did take some comfort in knowing that he wanted her, too. At least from a physical standpoint. Unfortunately, she had tried to fool herself into thinking that she only wanted some adventure with Marc, a few goes at hot and fast lovemaking. In reality, she wanted to be more than his friend, more than his lover. Yet Marc wasn't the kind of man who required more than temporary affairs—without complications.

Kate's feelings for Marc were very complicated and she would have to analyze them later. Right now she needed to put aside her predicament, will away the shakes and see about Cecile. With that thought, she opened the door only to be met head-on by the queen mother.

"Hi, Mary," Kate said in a too-loud voice laden with fake cheerfulness.

"Hello, dear." Mary's gaze roamed over Kate from head to toe. "Have you seen my son?"

Oh, she'd seen him all right, and he had definitely seen her. "He left his office a few minutes ago. How's Cecile?"

"She's an angel and down for her afternoon nap."

Searching for a quick escape, Kate pointed toward the

back staircase leading to the nursery. "I think I'll go check on her now."

"I would prefer you take a walk with me."

Oh, boy. "Any place in particular?"

"The gardens. It's a beautiful day and a good opportunity for us to have a little talk."

Kate assumed her face probably flashed guilt like a billboard, triggering the queen mother's request. Mary most likely suspected something was brewing between Kate and the king. Kate saw no way out aside from running away, but that would further encourage the queen mother's suspicions.

When Kate said, "Lead the way," surprisingly Mary linked her arm with Kate's and guided her down the gilt and marble corridor, then through a pair of double French doors that led to the rear palace grounds.

They remained silent as they strolled along a rock path lined with rose bushes and neatly trimmed hedges. When they reached a stone bench, Mary sat and patted the place next to her. "Join me, Kate."

Kate complied, keeping her gaze trained on a tree where a bluebird flitted along the branches, wishing she could sprout some wings and fly away.

Mary's sigh floated over the gentle breeze. "I suppose you now have the results of Cecile's blood test."

At least she hadn't quizzed her about Marc, Kate thought. But she wasn't sure it was her place to deliver the news that would most likely be a reality jolt. However, she couldn't lie to this woman who had been nothing but kind to her since the beginning. "Yes, I have the results."

"Well?"

Kate shifted until she faced Mary, taking the woman's hand into hers. "Cecile has Philippe's and Marc's blood type."

Mary drew in a long breath and released it on a weary sigh. "Then she is most likely my grandchild."

"Unless there is someone else in the family that could be a possibility."

Mary shook her head. "No. The line ends with Marcel. His father had only one niece, his deceased sister's child, and she is in Canada, happily married with two children. I have no one else in my family."

Kate ached at the loneliness in Mary's voice and grasped for words that might ease her pain. "And now you have Cecile. And Marc."

Mary studied their joined hands. "Marcel has been a stranger to me for the past few years. He's always been searching for something, although heaven only knows what."

"Respect," Kate said with certainty.

"I suppose you're right about that." Mary lifted her gaze to Kate. "Do you believe Cecile is his child?"

"He's adamant that she isn't."

"But do *you* believe him?"

Kate wanted to, honestly she did. "What I think doesn't matter," she said, the same thing she'd told Marc earlier. "Cecile's well-being is important, though. She needs your love."

"She will have it," Mary stated. "I am more concerned with my son. He has much to bear as a king."

"I know, but he has broad shoulders." In both a literal and figurative sense.

"He also needs the love of a good woman."

Kate shrugged. "I'm sure there's a princess somewhere who would be more than willing to give him that."

Mary patted Kate's hand. "My dear, we are running relatively low on monarchs in this day and time. Marcel needs someone who understands him. Someone who can settle him down. A nice, educated woman would fit the bill."

The expectant look on Mary's face took Kate aback. "Again, I'm sure someone will turn his head."

"Someone already has, and that someone is you."

Kate's breath hitched hard in her chest. "Mary, I really don't think—"

"You need not think, Kate. You only need to be there for him. The rest will take care of itself. Unless you do not care for him."

Kate looked away, knowing the guilt had returned. "I'm very fond of Marc. I have been since the day I met him nine years ago."

"But can you love him?"

In many ways, Kate already did. In many ways, she always had. "Right now, Marc needs a friend, and I'm willing to be that to him."

"Friendship is a good place to begin." Mary stared off into space while the afternoon sun washed the gardens in a soft golden glow. "Marcel's father was my friend and my confidant. My lover. The love of my life, even though it was ordained that we marry."

"You mean some sort of arrangement?"

Mary smiled. "I know that must sound archaic to a modern young woman such as yourself. But I tend to believe that fate had a hand in our union. If only fate had not been so cruel as to take him from me much too soon."

The sorrow in Mary's voice, the mist of unshed tears in her eyes, caused a lump to lodge in Kate's throat. After fighting back her own tears, Kate said, "You're still young, Mary. You could find someone else."

"There is no one else for me, my dear. I've loved only one man in my life, a wonderful man, and he has no equal." She drew Kate into an unexpected embrace. "I wish for you that kind of rare and precious love, my dear Kate."

Kate desperately wanted to believe in its existence, but with Marc? Only if he was willing to return that love.

Once they parted, she told Mary, "Thank you. Your story inspires me."

Mary squeezed Kate's hands. "And your presence here is very welcome, which leads me to a request."

"Anything."

"I would like you to move into the palace, or I should say onto the palace grounds." She gestured beyond the path to a break in the hedge. "Over there, you will see a small cottage. Philippe used it as his own private retreat. We've removed his possessions, but it's still nicely furnished. It would afford you some seclusion."

Being so close to Marc both thrilled and concerned Kate. If he decided not pursue a relationship, then she would have to face him on a daily basis, and that could be very detrimental to her heart. "I'll think about it," she promised Mary, and she would think about it, probably most of the night. "In the meantime, I'll be happy to remain here for the next few days to help take care of Cecile."

"That's not necessary, Kate. Beatrice will serve as her nanny. Besides, you will have enough on your plate when you begin your work tomorrow."

"I don't mind missing some sleep where Cecile is involved," Kate insisted. Or where Marc was concerned. "She's such a joy to be around."

Mary stood and stared down at Kate with a knowing look, as if she could read Kate's thoughts. "She is very fond of you, too, Kate. And whether he cares to admit it or not, so is my son."

Six

Marc did not care to admit to himself that what he was feeling for Kate Milner went far beyond simple lust. He admired her conviction, reveled in her strength of will, her insight. Yet he couldn't deny that he longed to make love to her. He also couldn't deny that she was effectively breaking through the armor he had erected to protect his emotions. And he had no idea how he had allowed that to happen.

Yes, he did know. When he was with her, he didn't feel so alone.

But he was alone in his office now, trying to concentrate on work, yet he could only ponder his situation with Kate, memories of their earlier interlude in this very place battering his mind. He could not fall into that trap. Not now. Not with so much riding on his country's expectations of him as a leader. In less than six weeks, he would appear before the governing council to state his case. Doriana needed to move into the twenty-first century, and providing premium health care was of the utmost importance. He had to prove to the ruling body that he had his country's best interests at heart and he needed the funds to see his plans come to fruition.

Now nearing midnight, he tossed aside the proposals he'd been composing for some time and opted to retire to bed. On his way to his suite, he stopped at the nursery to look in on Cecile, hoping to find Kate so he could issue another apology since he had not joined her for dinner. But he only found Cecile, sleeping soundly in the dimly lit, deserted room.

Quietly he approached the crib and stared down at the infant lying on her belly, her knees tucked beneath her and her face turned toward him in profile. Marc watched her for several moments, trying to find something in her features that reminded him of Philippe. She could belong to either one of them based on looks alone. But Marc was very certain she was not his child, even though in many ways he felt responsible for her. After all, Philippe was gone, and she was all that remained of him—if, in fact, Cecile was his child. Deep down, Marc believed that to be the truth. If only he could prove it.

When Cecile released a soft whimper, Marc feared he had inadvertently roused her by his presence alone. He laid his palm on her tiny back and patted her a few moments, praying she would settle back into slumber before she roused Beatrice. Instead, she let go a cry, prompting Marc to pick her up. He walked her around the nursery, soothing her with soft whispers in order not to wake the household.

"You and I will be in a great deal of trouble if you make too much of a fuss," he told her as he retrieved the pacifier from the crib then placed it in her mouth. "Now be a good girl and go back to sleep."

She rubbed her eyes, reared her head back, poked her finger in his mouth then grinned as if to say, "Silly king, I have no intention of sleeping."

How could he resist such a captivating child? He couldn't,

and she knew it. This particular female was determined to wrap his heart around her finger and she was succeeding. So was Kate.

He brushed a kiss across her warm, downy-soft cheek. "Your mother must have held you often, if only we knew who she was."

Cecile yawned, then palmed his jaw as if fascinated by the feel of his whiskers. Without warning, she settled her head on his shoulder.

Marc experienced an unexpected swell of emotion and a fierce protectiveness as he relished her warmth against his heart. She was an innocent, and she deserved the best in life. Even if they never confirmed her parentage, Marc vowed to make certain she was safe, secure and well loved by the family. She would never know the misery of not being accepted.

When he felt she had sufficiently calmed, Marc laid her back in the crib and held his breath. Her eyes opened briefly and she raised her head and leveled her unfocused gaze on him. Then she turned her face away, laid her head back down and her respiration once more became steady and deep.

Marc was greatly satisfied that he had been able to calm her with little effort. If only something so simple could ease him into sleep. If only he had someone to comfort him, to reassure him at times that he wasn't totally floundering as a leader. If only he had Kate to talk to.

But Kate obviously had returned to the hotel, and he would have to face the night alone.

After retiring to his suite, Marc took a quick shower then slipped beneath the cool sheets without bothering to dress. He punched the pillows several times, but couldn't seem to settle down despite his exhaustion.

Turning onto his back, he stared at the ceiling and considered going for a drive. But even that held no real appeal. What he wanted most—what he needed most—was Kate. Odd that he'd spent years without needing anything or anyone, and now in two days' time, he missed her more than he'd missed any human being aside from his father and brother.

Yet he couldn't have a casual affair with Kate; it would have to be all or nothing. And he couldn't consider a serious relationship because, in all honesty, he'd never really had one before. Solid relationships took time to evolve, and at present he did not have an abundance of spare hours. Even though he was expected to marry one day—as Philippe had been expected to—Marc wasn't certain when he'd be ready for that day.

He recalled the wager he had made all those years ago and the reunion with Dharr and Mitch that would take place next spring. The bet had once been a reason to avoid marriage, but now he viewed it as ridiculous ramblings of youth. His reasons to avoid marriage now were much more compelling and complex. And he couldn't let his attraction to Kate sway him, for both her sake and his.

But he did have a yearning for the beautiful doctor that knew no true logic. The remembrance of her kiss, the flush of her breasts, the taste of her against his tongue stirred his body back to life. He rubbed a hand down his bare abdomen, imagining her hand there and much lower. He grew hard as a brick when he fantasized about having her in his bed, sliding into her body, holding her close in his arms. But as much as he desired her physically, he longed more for her trust and respect.

And that could prove to be the greatest challenge of all.

Kate entered the clinic the next morning prepared for her first official day at work. Or as prepared as she could be, considering she'd had relatively little sleep over the past three days. Last night was no exception, thanks to Cecile—and to Marc. But she couldn't be angry with either one of them, especially not after she'd observed Marc's late-night interaction with Cecile. She'd remained hidden in the doorway of the room adjacent to the nursery when she'd heard him come in and watched in fascination as he walked Cecile around the room, comforting her until the baby had finally gone back to sleep. And Marc had left the room not knowing Kate had been there witnessing his care and concern.

To Kate, Marc had seemed like a natural father comforting his daughter. Even if it turned out that he wasn't the father, at least Kate was assured that Marc would step into the role with little effort if necessary.

But right now she had to get her mind on to the business of healing.

After checking in with the clinic's receptionist, Kate was directed to follow Isabella, the nurse who had eyed Marc as if he were chateaubriand during their first meeting. After they entered a small lounge, she told Kate, "You may place your things in the locker," then immediately left, as if she couldn't quite take being in the same room with the new doctor. Maybe she viewed Kate as competition, a ridiculous assumption, Kate decided. She'd never been anyone's competition. And she also needed to remember that the woman's name was not Nurse Lustful so that she wouldn't accidentally slip up.

Kate settled into the routine without much trouble, considering she had acclimated herself to the surroundings the day before. The schedule again was hectic as Kate moved through the exams with Caroline, fueled solely by adrenaline, since she hadn't had the opportunity to have lunch. By the time the afternoon ended, she'd seen almost twenty patients but fortunately she hadn't seen Renault—until she kicked off her shoes and collapsed into the office chair with a cup of weak coffee and a headache that throbbed with each beat of her pulse.

Renault eyed her stocking-covered legs exposed by the skirt she wore, and her bare feet propped on the desk. His perusal made Kate feel as if she'd taken off all her clothes. "Is there something you need, Doctor?" She regretted the words the minute they left her mouth when he sent her a sleazy grin.

"You seem as if you have had a rough day. Perhaps I should ask if there's anything you need from me?"

Your absence. "I'm fine." Kate lowered her feet to the floor and slipped her shoes back on, but she still felt grossly naked due to his continued assessment. "I was just leaving for home."

"Where is home, Dr. Milner?"

How should she answer? She didn't like the thought of mentioning a hotel in the presence of a man who fancied himself a Don Juan. She wasn't too fond of mentioning the palace either, but at least he would realize she had guards at her disposal. Of course, she could say it was none of his business. She opted to affect courtesy and give him a partial truth. "I'm staying at the palace for the time being, until I can find a place of my own."

He took the chair across from her. "I believe there is a cottage available next door to my apartment. It is not far from the hospital."

Living on the other side of the continent from him would be too close for Kate. "Thanks for the suggestion."

"I also have a spare bedroom, if you are interested."

Not on your life. "I don't think that's a good idea."

He nailed her with his demonic eyes. "I believe it would be a very good idea. We could get to know each other better."

"I prefer to keep our relationship on a professional level."

"That is not as enjoyable, *ma chèrie*. But I assure you that my intentions are very honorable."

The scoundrel didn't know the first thing about honor. "Again, I appreciate the offer but I need extra room for myself and my daughter."

Kate picked up her bag and moved from behind the desk, ready for a quick exit until Renault came to his feet and asked, "How is your daughter? Did her laboratory tests turn out well?"

"She's fine. Very healthy. I'll see you tomorrow."

"I find it somewhat coincidental that she looks very much like the DeLoria family. Is there any relation?"

"Of course not," Kate snapped, probably to her own detriment. "Why would you think that?"

"I suppose you could say that I've noticed how the king looks at you. Are you lovers?"

Are you a jackass? "No, we're not lovers. We attended the same university in America. We're friends."

"Only friends?"

"Yes. I need to go."

He moved in closer like a snake in the grass. "First, I would like to say I am pleased you are working with me. Running this clinic can present quite a challenge. At times I wish that I had pursued my goal to become a surgeon."

No one wished that as much as Kate at the moment. "You would've made a good surgeon, I imagine."

"I am flattered, but why would you believe this about me since you have not seen me in action?"

Kate was going to enjoy the heck out of this. "Your hands are made for surgery. Small. Easy to fit into tight spots. And you know what they say about small hands and feet. Guess that's why you tend to overcompensate in other areas."

She headed out the door, smiling all the way down the hall as she reflected on the shock and chagrin on Renault's face.

Little man, big ego, bigger mouth.

After exiting through the service entrance, Kate was surprised to find Mr. Nicholas hadn't arrived to take her back to the palace. When she'd called a few minutes before, he'd said he was on his way. She decided to check the main entrance in case she'd misunderstood his instructions.

She crossed the hospital's vestibule and pushed through the double doors leading outside. Suddenly, hordes of reporters surrounded her, led by one balding, rotund gentleman holding a tape recorder. "Miss Milner, I have a few questions." His English was impeccable but his clothing was not. He looked as though he'd slept in his suit, but then Kate probably didn't look much better.

"*Doctor* Milner," she corrected, craning her neck in hopes of finding the Rolls waiting at the curb to rescue her, but it wasn't to be.

Cameras flashed and videotape rolled when the man said, "Could you please state your relationship with King DeLoria?"

Not again. Why couldn't everyone mind their own business? She had no idea how to handle this situation, but decided honesty would be her best course. After all, she had nothing to hide—except her feelings for the king. She hoped her face wouldn't give her away. "We're former university colleagues."

"Are you lovers?" another man asked.

First Renault, and now this. Where was Marc when she needed him? "We're friends and nothing more."

"Then you deny the rumor that your child was fathered by the king?" one woman shouted from the center of crowd.

Where had that come from? She suspected she already knew the answer. Dear Dr. Renault. "Yes, I deny that," she snapped, then added more sedately, "Before three days ago, when I arrived in Doriana to accept the hospital position, I had not seen King DeLoria in almost a decade."

The bald guy shoved the recorder close to her mouth. "But are you not staying at the palace with him?"

"I'm staying at the inn." Kate breathed a huge sigh of relief when she saw the Rolls pull up. "I have to go now."

She tried to shove her way through the crowd, which was larger now, since several villagers and tourists had stopped to check out the commotion. The crush of people seemed to close in on her with every step, threatening to steal her oxygen as she struggled to reach the bottom of the stairs. Then a hand grabbed her wrist and pulled her forward, while a contingent of bodyguards moved in and attempted to push the onlookers and press corps away.

Marc.

She'd never been so grateful to see anyone in her life. But she didn't reach the safety of the car before one man swung around to capture the king on film and, in doing so, whipped his video camera into Kate's forehead. Her head snapped to one side. Pain shot from the place of impact, bringing tears to her eyes and clouding her vision. Yet she could see well enough to witness Marc drawing back his fist and then landing a punch in the cameraman's nose, sending the man backward into the arms of two guards.

Marc wrapped his arm around Kate's shoulder and herded her through the stunned crowd toward the car where Nicholas stood by, holding open the door and sporting a satisfied smile. "Good show, Your Manliness."

A regular sideshow, Kate thought as Marc ushered her into the car. Only three days spent in this quaint country and she'd already started a riot. Well, she'd wanted some adventure and it looked like she'd gotten it.

Once they were settled into the seat side by side and the door had been closed, Marc leaned forward and told Nicholas, "Take the back route to the palace." Then he hit a button on the console that raised the smoky tinted glass, concealing the rear seat from the driver's view.

Marc turned to Kate, a mixture of anger and concern flaring in his cobalt blue eyes. "How badly are you hurt?"

Kate touched her fingertips to her forehead, right above her left eye. The spot was only slightly tender. "I'm okay. I'll probably just have a bruise for the next few days."

"I'll have Louis come to the palace to examine you."

"I'm a doctor, Marc. Nothing's cracked. No indentation. Just a bump. I have a very hard head."

"Obviously. I will have Dr. Martine examine you regardless," he repeated.

Kate was simply too tired and too rattled to argue. "Suit yourself."

He shifted in his seat and leveled a serious stare on her. "Why were you not waiting at the service entrance?"

Kate bristled at his severe tone. "I went there first. When I didn't find Mr. Nicholas, I decided to check the front in case I was wrong about the location. I had no idea I'd be bombarded with questions."

Marc sighed. "This is my life, Kate. Your connection with me opens you up to scrutiny. What did they ask?"

Kate didn't want to anger him more, but he deserved to know the truth, at least about the impromptu press conference. She would tell him about Renault's speculation later. Much later. "They asked about our relationship. Then they insinuated Cecile is our child, yours and mine, if you can believe that."

Marc reached into the briefcase resting at his side and withdrew a newspaper, then handed it to Kate. "This is where they came up with that theory."

Kate couldn't read a word of the print, but the somewhat blurry photograph of the king carrying a baby into the hospital, a woman by his side—in this case Kate—needed no interpretation.

She tossed the paper aside. "This doesn't prove anything."

Marc turned away and stared out the window. "It's enough to raise suspicions. And damn the vulture who took it."

Kate noticed Marc's hand resting between them, the bruised and puffy knuckles. She caught his wrist and worked his fingers back and forth, all the while watching Marc's face for any signs of pain. He just sat there staring straight ahead, his jaw clenched tight.

"You're going to have some swelling," she said. "But I don't think you've done too much damage. I'm not sure I can

say the same about the camera guy's nose, or your reputation."
She sent him a shaky smile. "I can see the headlines now—
King Saves Damsel in Distress."

"And hopefully will not be charged with assault."

"Can they do that?"

"I'll have my staff deal with it."

Kate allowed a few moments of silence before she said,
"I'm sorry, Marc. I should have been more careful."

He pulled his hand from hers as if he couldn't stand to
touch her. "This isn't your fault. It's mine. I should have prepared you for this."

"How would you do that? Teach me Camera Dodging, 101?"

For a moment she thought he might smile. Instead, he
streaked both hands down his face then his gaze came to rest
on her forehead. "Are you certain you're all right?"

"I'm positive. Promise."

Surprisingly, Marc moved closer and settled one arm along
the back of the seat. "I would not have forgiven myself, Kate,
if something more serious had happened to you. And what did
happen was bad enough."

"It was stupid for me to think that if someone suspected
we were more than friends, it wouldn't really matter."

He took her hand and twined their fingers together. "It
does matter, and I'm the foolish one, Kate."

"Why is that?"

"Because I have inadvertently involved you in this scandal." His intense eyes sent Kate's heart on a marathon. "Because I know I shouldn't do this, but I'll be damned if I can
help myself."

Inclining his head, Marc captured her bottom lip between
his lips before kissing her deeply, tenderly. His mouth melted
into hers like cinnamon candy, a taste she detected on his
tongue that played against hers so sweetly, softly.

For a fleeting moment, Kate rationalized that his kiss was

a result of his frustration and anger, the means to let off steam and the reason why it continued and grew more passionate with every ticking second. But when he slid his palm down her rib cage, to her hip and then back up again, she couldn't lay claim to any rationality for either of them. All she recognized at that moment was a heady warmth oozing from every pore and a desire for Marc DeLoria's full attention that knew no limits.

What else would explain her lack of resistance when he cupped her knee, which was exposed by her skirt that had ridden up to her thighs? What else except a total absence of common sense drove her legs to part in invitation while they were driving in a car? What else could have incited the low moan climbing her throat when he slid his palm beneath the hem of her skirt?

She was very aware of what Marc intended when he kept going until his fingertips hovered at the junction of her thighs. And when he fondled her through the nylon, all thoughts slipped away.

She was growing hotter by the minute, closer and closer to losing it as Marc increased the pressure, both with his mouth firmly joined with hers and his hand working wonders between her thighs. Feeling brazen and bold, she slid her palm up his thigh and to his groin where her fingers contacted the ridge beneath his slacks. She touched him the same way he now touched her, through fabric that created a frustrating obstacle but not enough to stop either one of them from the erotic, forbidden exploration. She didn't think anything could stop them.

"We're here, Your Highness."

The grating sound of Nicholas's voice filtering in from the overhead intercom broke the spell and the kiss. Marc pulled his hand away, slid to the other side of the car and leaned his head back against the seat, his chest rising and falling with his ragged respiration. Kate had trouble catching her breath as well. She already missed his touch, his heat, his mouth that had shown no mercy on her senses.

As they rode through the gates, Marc's rough sigh broke the silence. "My mother told me she offered you the guest-house. I'll see that your things are brought here."

At least this time he hadn't apologized for losing control since Kate wasn't the least bit sorry. "But won't that be worse, me staying on the grounds?"

"The press probably knows you're at the inn. You'll be afforded more protection here."

The media knew where she was staying because she'd told them, another huge mistake. "If you think that's best for the time being, then I don't have a problem with it."

Marc turned his head toward her. "But we still have one other problem."

"What's that?"

"I'm not strong enough to resist you."

That brought on Kate's smile. "I'll try to behave myself."

"I'm not concerned about your behavior. I am concerned about mine."

Kate was concerned most about her growing feelings for him. "Look, you just punched out a reporter. You can deal with me."

Marc returned her smile with one of his own—a smile that could move the mountains surrounding them. "That is the problem, Kate. I want to deal with you in a very intimate way, and that should be more than obvious to you now. If we had not arrived here when we did, I can promise you I would have done much more, regardless of the fact we were in a moving vehicle with only a glass separating us from prying eyes."

And Kate would have let him.

He leaned over and kissed her cheek immediately before

Nicholas opened the car door. "I'm not certain I will be able to overcome that problem."

Kate sincerely hoped he didn't.

In the middle of the night, after Cecile was tucked safely in bed, Marc escorted Kate to the inn to retrieve her belongings with a bevy of armed guards as their chaperones. Regardless, he'd done well to keep his hands off of her in the privacy of the car, but once they returned to the deserted guest cottage, he questioned how long he could maintain his resolve.

Marc considered leaving her alone, but he truly didn't want to leave, especially after Martine had told him that although Kate's wound didn't appear that serious, someone should watch her in case she showed signs of a concussion.

Presently, she showed Marc a pair of shapely legs encased in nylons as she strolled around the small living room to examine the odds and ends on the bookshelves in the corner. Those damn panty hose had saved him from doing something totally inadvisable earlier that day, before Nicholas had delivered his untimely interruption.

"Another great collection of books," she said, keeping her back to him. "Just wish I could read more French. But I am doing some studying."

Marc was doing some studying of his own—namely the curve of her buttocks and the dip of her waist—as she replaced one volume above her head.

"I could teach you a few words." The words running through his mind now would not be deemed appropriate for common usage. But in bed....

She smiled at him over one shoulder. "I'm doing better at the clinic, picking up a few phrases. I'm sure the more I'm exposed to the various languages, the more I'll learn."

Marc wanted to expose her to more than words. He wanted to expose her to his hands, to his mouth, to his body.

He tried to relax on the floral sofa that now felt as hard and uncompromising as his escalating erection. With every move Kate made, his muscles clenched with the effort to maintain control. But when she turned to him and began pulling the tails of her blouse from the skirt's waistband, he was as hard as he'd ever been in recent memory.

"I think I'll take a shower now," she said.

Marc thought he should show himself to the door before he showed her how much she was affecting him. "Are you feeling well enough to do that?"

"I feel fine."

How well he knew that. "Perhaps I should stand outside the bathroom door in case you should become dizzy."

She strolled to the sofa and stood above him. "Perhaps you should join me in the shower."

He groaned. "I thought you were going to behave."

"I thought you were going back to the palace."

"I am."

"What are you waiting for?"

He waited for his mind to commandeer his libido. Waited for her to toss him out. Waited for logic to come forth and issue a protest strong enough to stop the overpowering need to touch her.

When none of those things happened, Marc caught her wrist and pulled her forward between his parted legs. He slid his hands up her sides, relishing the feel of her curves against his palm, needing to feel more of her, and soon, duty be damned. His reputation be damned. They were alone, and no one would have to know. If he couldn't have all of her, he could at least give her what she needed. He could gain some satisfaction from satisfying her—if that was what she wanted—and he assumed it was, considering her eyes held the cast of desire.

He ran his palms up her thighs, this time beneath the skirt. "I believe I have some unfinished business."

She brushed his hair away from his forehead. "What unfinished business would that be?"

"What I started in the car."

She smiled. "Really? I thought you said—"

"I know what I said. I'm tired of fighting this."

"Then don't fight it."

Marc pulled her down on the sofa into his lap, effectively
cutting off all conversation with a kiss that was as intense as
the one they'd shared in the car. Kate released an unmistak-
ably sexual sound against his mouth that encouraged him to
keep going. She tightened her hold around his neck as he
nudged her legs apart and slid one hand along the inside of
her thighs, contacting the frustrating barrier bent on keeping
him from his goal. Whoever invented panty hose should be
bound and gagged with nylon for at least a week.

But that did not deter him. Barriers were made to be broken,
and he sufficiently broke through this one with a tug and tear
at the seam, revealing she wore nothing beneath them. Kate's
gasp didn't stop him either; the press of her hips toward his hand
indicated she wanted this as badly as he wanted to give it to her.

Her legs opened more, leaving her completely open to
him. Yet as he broke the kiss to watch her face, he considered
stopping. He had her at an unfair advantage, and she had him
at a crossroad where he greatly questioned his determination
not to take her completely, right there, on a sofa. But to stop
now would be unimaginable. Not until he gave her the release
she deserved, even if he could not have his own.

He found the small bud that blossomed beneath his touch
as he caressed her. "Does this feel good?"

Her eyes drifted closed. "It feels…great."

"I cannot argue that," he told her, even as a myriad of arguments against this very thing warred within his conscience.
He chose to ignore his concerns and focus only on Kate and
her pleasure.

Marc claimed her mouth again as he slid one finger inside her and stroked her, inside and out. He burned to know how it would feel to have her surrounding him when the orgasm claimed her. He settled for only imagining when she climaxed in strong, steady spasms much sooner than he'd expected. But why should that surprise him? They had engaged in enough foreplay to keep them both balanced on the brink of spontaneous combustion.

Had Marc not been resigned to giving Kate only this much, the feel of her might have been his undoing, literally, because in a matter of moments, he could have his slacks undone and his body seated deeply within her heat. His mind insisted he stop now, stop with just this prelude. Instead, he kept touching her, wringing out every last pulse of her climax as he considered giving her another, this time with his mouth…until she said, "I want you, Marc. All of you. Now."

His strength fractured in that moment, even as his mind warned him not to give in. His resistance evaporated completely when Kate moved to his side, released his belt, lowered his zipper, then pulled his slacks and briefs down his hips. She kissed him as she explored him, drove him to the edge with hands as fine as velvet. Marc needed to stop her, that much he knew. He needed to put an end to this madness before it was too late. Before they couldn't stop.

But it was already too late, so at the very least, he needed to make certain he protected Kate against pregnancy.

He caught her wrist and brought her hand up, temporarily ending the torture.

Her eyes narrowed with frustration. "I want this, Marc. So do you."

"We should go to the bedroom, Kate."

"I don't want to wait."

She wrested from his grasp and fumbled with the buttons on her blouse, then slipped it away along with her bra. Marc wasn't sure he would make it to the bedroom when Kate stripped out of her skirt and ruined panty hose, then tossed them away. Now she was beautifully naked, and completely his. After tearing off his own shirt and kicking off his slacks, he bent, reached into his pants' pocket and withdrew the condom he'd brought with him, knowing all along this would probably happen. Hoping all along that it would.

After he had the condom in place, Kate stretched out on the sofa and held out her arms to him. He gladly eased into her embrace, eased into her body and experienced a freedom he hadn't known in years. It had nothing to do with the length of time since he'd been in a woman's arms. It had everything to do with Kate Milner and the hold she had on him. For a moment, the guilt tried to come forth, but he pushed it aside as he put himself at the mercy of nature and his need for Kate.

Marc moved in a slow cadence at first until the chemistry that had been flowing between them exploded in a wild, reckless rhythm. He slid his hands over Kate's body as if he could not get enough of the feel of her. She raked her hands down his back and molded them to his buttocks as he drove harder, faster, losing all sense of time and place in pursuit of pleasure. When he felt the first ripples of Kate's climax, Marc drew one crested nipple into his mouth, sending her over the edge and drawing him farther into her body. Not long after, he joined her with a jolt and a shudder that he couldn't control any more than he could temper his pounding heart. He regretted it had happened too quickly, had been over too soon. Right now he felt too damn good to ruin the moment with any other regrets.

They remained twined together in a tangle of limbs, their bare flesh slick with their efforts and their breathing broken and heavy. Marc buried his face in Kate's hair and savored the feel of her hands stroking his back, their bodies still closely joined. He could stay this way forever and say to hell with the world, to his responsibilities and the problems facing him.

The shrill of the phone splintered the silence and sent Marc up and away from Kate as if he'd been caught red-handed by the royal court.

Kate leaned over him to grab the phone from the end table, rubbing her breasts across his chest, eliciting his groan.

She fumbled for the phone and answered with a breathless, "Hello," then sent Marc a forlorn look. "Hi, Mary. No, you didn't interrupt anything. I was just about to take a shower."

Marc mouthed, "Do not tell her I'm here," but realized it was too late when Kate said, "He's here. We've just returned from the inn with my things. He's about to leave."

Marc rose from the sofa, snatched his clothing from the floor and headed to bathroom while Kate told his mother, "If it's okay, I'm going to get dressed first and take a quick bath. I mean, undressed and take a bath, then I'll be up to see if I can get her to sleep."

Marc was quite up again and doubted he would be sleeping at all.

After dressing, he returned to Kate and found her wearing only her blouse that came to the tops of her thighs. "Nothing like a fussy baby to interrupt," she said, looking self-conscious.

Marc streaked a hand over his nape. "It was a timely interruption, otherwise we might have gone to your bed, and that would have been unwise, considering I only have one condom."

She walked to him and circled her arms around his waist. "It would have been wonderful, and the night isn't over yet, unless you don't have any more condoms in your room."

Held captive by her body molded to his, he slid his hands down her back and palmed her bare bottom. They came together in another earthshattering kiss until reality and regret tunneled their way into Marc's brain.

He pulled her arms away and stepped back. "I can't offer you anything beyond lovemaking, Kate. Not at this point in my life."

She lifted her chin a notch. "If you tell me that one more

time, I'm going to scream. I don't expect anything from you, Marc. And I don't believe you didn't want this to happen."

He'd definitely wanted it, more than he should. "I certainly didn't want to be king, but that decision has been forced upon me."

She looked despondent and Marc wished he could take back his thoughtless words. "Are you saying I forced you to do this?"

"Of course not, and you should realize that. My only regret involves the chaos my life has become. You do not deserve that."

Kate frowned. "Why don't you let me decide what I do and don't deserve. And as far as you being king, why don't you try and concentrate on the good you're doing?"

"Sometimes I wonder if I am doing anything right."

"You are." She touched his face with reverence, as if she believed in him. "I know firsthand what it's like to have people depending on you. My parents are very needy and I couldn't take it anymore. That's why I came here, to get away and make my own life."

He took her hand and kissed her palm before releasing it. "But I cannot walk away." At times, he wished he could.

"No, you can't, but you can focus on the positive aspects of your power and skills." She winked and grinned. "I've certainly experienced a few."

His body lurched back to life. "Kate, you have no idea what you do to me when you make those statements."

She ran a slow fingertip down the ridge beneath his fly. "Yes, I do." She returned to the couch, retrieved the panty hose, balled them up and then tossed them at Marc. "Here's a little souvenir of our night together, so you don't forget."

As if Marc could really forget something that had been so incredible.

With a wicked smile, Kate turned and walked down the

corridor leading to the bath, leaving Marc holding her ruined panty hose while he clung to his last vestiges of sanity. He recognized it was only a matter of time before they made love again, unless he developed a steel will. He did not foresee that happening, considering he now knew how good it had felt to be inside of her, to be totally lost in her.

Yet it was Kate's understanding of the man beneath the king that had begun to appeal to him on a deeper, distinct level beyond carnality. As a king, he feared disappointing his people—and as a man, he feared disappointing Kate. Not when it came to lovemaking; he had always been confident in that regard. They were good together. Damn good. But could he be the man that she needed, the one she would want for all time? And could he give all of himself to her, even the part he had kept hidden from the world? Kept hidden from himself?

If he made a commitment to explore more than their mutual desire, he would have to follow through, since Kate merited a man who would give her all his attention and consideration. While before he would have rejected that prospect, he was actually beginning to consider all the possibilities—and advantages—of having Kate Milner in his life.

Seven

Kate Milner had done the unthinkable. She'd fallen in love with Marc DeLoria all over again.

Oh, she'd tried to convince herself that all she'd wanted was a little adventure with Marc. For that reason, she'd been playing the primo seductress when, in fact, she wanted his heart as much as she wanted his body. And three nights ago, he'd proven to her that he was the consummate lover—and a man who had no designs on being tied to a serious relationship.

How many women had fallen hopelessly in love with him, only to be left behind? She couldn't begin to imagine, but she also wasn't ready to give up. Some day, someone was going to lay claim to his heart. Why not her?

Because the only commitment that interested Marc was his commitment to his kingdom. Kate was a diversion, someone to keep his mind off his troubles during a few stolen moments. Yes, he'd said he respected her, thought she was special, even beautiful, but he hadn't mentioned anything about his feelings for her beyond that. It was crazy for her to expect anything else, especially since she hadn't seen much of him at all for the past few days. Once more, he'd become the elusive king, choosing to keep himself secluded doing heaven only knew what. She only knew that it hadn't involved her.

She had to accept the realization that their one night together might be all that they would ever share. Had to accept she would probably be one of many women who had tried to win him over, without success.

At least her day at the clinic had been relatively successful, and somewhat quieter than the past few days. But unfortunately, that had allowed her time to think about Marc and worry about how long she would continue to hope that her relationship with him might evolve into more. That wouldn't happen if he continued to avoid her. At least his mother and Cecile had been great company. Although she'd enjoyed being with them, it wasn't the same thing as having time alone with Marc.

She was simply too tired to think about it at the moment. Now nearing 6:00 p.m., she'd seen her last patient an hour ago and had remained to catch up on some paperwork before she called Mr. Nicholas for her ride back to the guesthouse. One thing she did know—she would never, ever go near the front entrance again, even though Marc had ordered guards posted at every access. And she felt somewhat guilty that that had been necessary.

Kate charted the last of her notes at the desk in the small office Dr. Martine had arranged for her this morning. At least she was out of Renault's line of fire now, with the exception of passing him in the hall. And at least he hadn't tried to make a pass. Otherwise, she might have introduced her knee to his family jewels.

The sound of voices startled Kate, since she assumed she was alone in the clinic. A woman's voice and a man's voice—namely, the queen mother's and the king's.

Kate pushed back from the desk and opened the door to

find them standing outside the office, both looking extremely distressed.

Panic settled on Kate's chest. "Is something wrong with Cecile?"

Mary attempted a smile. "Oh, no, dear. Cecile is fine. She's with Beatrice."

"Then why are you here?"

"Because of this." Marc held up another newspaper. "Aside from my show of temper with the cameraman, it covers the 'palace baby' and cites an anonymous source who claims he or she has proof that the child is yours and mine."

Kate closed her eyes and pinched the bridge of her nose between her thumb and pointer finger. "I was afraid this might happen."

"This is not your fault, Kate," Mary said. "The media know no restraint where our family is concerned. Some people delight in creating false rumors to discredit us."

Kate looked up to see indisputable anger in Marc's expression and regretted not telling him about Jonathan's comments. "The source is probably Renault. He made the first insinuations three days ago."

Marc's eyes narrowed. "Why did you not tell me after this happened?"

"Because I didn't want to upset you further."

"You can bloody well believe I am upset."

"Settle down, Marcel," Mary scolded. "Kate does not deserve your anger. She was only doing what she thought was best for you."

Kate turned her attention to Mary because it was too painful to look at Marc. "Is there anything I can do? Maybe an interview?"

Mary gave her a sympathetic look. "No, my dear. We will have to allow this gossip to run its course until we can come up with our own retraction."

"Or the proof that Cecile is Philippe's child," Marc added.

"And what purpose would that serve?" Mary asked.

"To clear Kate's name. And mine."

Kate felt as if she were being pulled into a human tug-of-war. "Don't worry about me, Marc. I can cope with this."

He sent her a hard look. "Can you?"

Mary wrapped her arm around Kate's shoulder and gave her a squeeze. "She most certainly can, Marcel. Kate is a mature, strong woman. I have no doubt she will deal with the situation with grace."

Kate wished she had Mary's confidence. "I'll do whatever you instruct me to do. I promise I won't speak to anyone without consulting you first."

"Of course, dear. We trust you. We simply wanted to forewarn you and have Marcel escort you back to the palace." Mary dropped her arm from Kate's shoulder and stared at Marc. "And you will be courteous to the doctor. In the meantime, I will return home to check on our charge. I'm certain Beatrice would appreciate someone to relieve her."

Kate saw her chance to escape. She didn't want to talk to Marc until he'd had time to calm down. "Give me a minute and I'll be ready to go. I can help."

"I need to see you first. Alone."

Marc's command caused Kate to stiffen from the fury she sensed building just below the surface of his composed demeanor. She wasn't afraid of Marc; she was afraid she couldn't find the words to reason with him. But she had to try.

"Okay. I can do that," she said.

"Take your time," Mary said as she headed away. "I will tell the guards to remain posted outside and have Nicholas return for you after he has delivered me to the palace."

Once Mary was out of sight, Kate gestured toward the office. "Let's go in here so we can have some privacy."

Marc stepped inside the room and reclined against the

desk, arms folded across his chest. Kate closed the door and leaned back against it for support.

"You should have told me about Renault. We might have prevented the rumors from escalating, or at least been better prepared."

"The damage was already done by the time the press got to me," Kate said. "And again, I didn't say anything about Renault because I knew you had already reached the boiling point."

"It's been three days, Kate. You could have told me in that length of time."

Her own anger rose to the surface. "How was I supposed to do that? You haven't been around. It's hard to tell someone something when that someone refuses to talk."

"I've had a lot on my mind."

"So have I, Marc."

"I know. And that, too, is my fault." His anger melted into resignation. "I should probably claim Cecile is my child and allow the council to do as they see fit with me."

Kate was only now beginning to recognize that a scandal of this proportion—real or fabricated—could do irrevocable injury to Marc's standing as a leader. She should have realized that he was no different from any man in power, even if he had been born into the responsibility. "They can't oust you, can they?"

"No, but they can make it difficult for me to accomplish anything from this point forward. I rely on their complete support. Without it, I am only a figurehead."

"Then fight them."

"What would be the point?"

Kate sent him an incredulous look. "What would be the point? Because you're good at what you do. Because you want to make your country a better place. You care about your people. Everyone knows that."

"You're making a huge assumption."

Stubborn man. "I'm not illiterate, Marc. I read the papers. I've followed your rise to power. I know how much you've been admired in your diplomatic endeavors, and your recent reputation as a strong leader."

"You've forgotten my reputation of being a womanizer. That seems to have taken precedence in my adulthood."

"Until Philippe died. Since then, you've gained respect from world leaders."

"I've achieved nothing, Kate, at least in the eyes of my people. They will not forgive this."

Kate threw up her hands and released a frustrated sigh. "Okay, Marc. Give up, if that's what you want to do. I'm certainly not going to stop you. Just don't expect me to stand by and watch you self-destruct."

Though it was the hardest thing she'd ever done, Kate turned away from him. She saw no sense in trying to convince him to fight, not when he seemed so against undertaking the battle—one he would have to face alone, by his choice.

Kate only got as far as the door when Marc slammed his palm against the facing, preventing her from opening it. "I need you to understand, Kate."

She turned and saw a pain in his eyes that stole her breath. "I do understand, Marc, more than you give me credit for. I just can't stand the thought of you throwing in the towel. You can't back down now, not when you have so much to lose."

"Right now, I would gladly walk away, but you're right. I owe it to my country to fight. I owe it to Philippe's memory."

"You owe it to yourself, Marc. This is only a temporary situation. We'll get through it together. We're both strong enough, and we're a good team."

He touched her face with tenderness. "I don't know what I have done right in this lifetime to have you on my side, especially after the way I've treated you of late. And I am sorry for that."

"I know. I also know you're a good man with a huge burden to bear. And you'll be a good father to Cecile. She needs you, too, even if she's not your child."

"And I need you. More than you realize."

Kate waited to experience the suffocation, the resentment of someone needing her. It didn't come.

She doubted Marc was inclined to ask for help very often—partly from pride and partly from trying to prove he could go it alone. The admission seemed to be costing him a lot, evident in the uneasiness in his expression. And if she could help him, she would. She loved him that much.

"I'm here for you, Marc." At least for now. "But you have to let down your guard and let me in."

He tipped his forehead against hers. "You're the only sanity in my life, Kate, and I want you so badly at times it hurts. That's why I've avoided you, knowing that every time I look at you…touch you…every time…"

He kissed her then—a passionate kiss that exposed his desperation, his need, causing the carpeted floor to sway beneath Kate's feet. Without breaking the kiss, Marc spun her around and guided her back until she felt the desk nudge her bottom. He pressed against her, letting Kate know exactly how much he needed her, setting her senses on maximum alert and sending her pulse on a sprint. He slid his hands over her body, from shoulders to hips and then back up to fondle her breasts through her beige silk blouse.

He undid her slacks and slipped his hand inside, touching her as if starved for the intimate contact. He made her body weep with every caress of his fingertips, made her give everything over to the sensations he evoked so masterfully. Kate trembled from the onslaught of feelings, from the love she'd kept hidden from him and probably always would.

Before the climax completely took hold, Marc took his hand away yet kept his mouth mated firmly with hers. She didn't have to ask what he was doing when she heard the metallic sound of his belt buckle release and the track of his zipper.

They shouldn't do this, Kate thought. Not here, not now, not without…

Marc pushed her slacks and underwear to her thighs then pushed into her with a hard thrust. Her body responded with an all-consuming climax that nearly brought her to her knees, saved only by Marc's hold on her. Her mind now trapped in a carnal web, Kate could no longer think coherently as Marc set a frantic rhythm, his hands molded to her bottom, pulling her closer, moving in deeper and deeper.

He finally ended the kiss and brought his lip to her ear, whispering something in French…a low, deep declaration that set her imagination on fire.

His respiration increased and his heart pounded against her chest. With one last thrust, his frame went rigid in her arms and he shook with the explosive force of his own climax.

She kissed his face, stroked his hair, held him close as their breathing returned to normal. But the return of awareness of what had happened—and what they hadn't done—hit Kate with the force of an earthquake. She'd wanted to absorb his pain, escape their problems and make more memories—only to disregard the one thing that had been necessary to prevent creating more havoc in both their lives.

She knew the moment reality hit Marc when he muttered a harsh curse in English, one she had no trouble understanding. He braced his hands on the table on either side of her and kept his eyes lowered. "We didn't—"

"I know."

"Can you—"

"Get pregnant?" she finished for him. "Yes."

"Bloody hell."

Kate had mistakenly envisioned Marc's words of love, not words of regret, after the tender moments they'd shared before this uncontrolled act. How ridiculous of her to think such a thing. How stupid of her to be so careless. She was a doctor. She knew the possible consequences, but so did Marc.

His remorse became all too clear when he slipped from her body and turned his back on her. "I do not expect your forgiveness for my total disregard for caution," he said as he redid his slacks.

She couldn't disregard the emotional wall he had erected, his distant tone.

Kate adjusted her clothes with trembling hands, unable to shake the seriousness of the situation. She hoped an attempt at humor might defuse the situation. "Well, we can now add offices to our list of places to avoid, along with sofas and kitchens. Maybe if we just sleep together in a bed, we'll be able to control ourselves."

When he faced her again, Marc's stony expression told Kate her efforts hadn't worked. "It doesn't matter where we are, Kate. The only way we'll avoid losing control is by avoiding each other. I can only assure you that I've never been this irresponsible. Never. It seems all I do is create one problem after another."

Kate should be flattered by the fact that she'd driven him to such abandon, but she wasn't, considering what it might mean in the long term. Considering he saw her—their lovemaking—as a problem, when she considered it a gift. "Look, if I happen to be pregnant, I don't expect anything from you. But you have my guarantee I'll love any child that belongs to me, whether you choose to be involved in its life or not."

Anger turned his eyes as dark as moonless midnight. "Do you believe so little of me that you think I would abandon my own child? If that is so, then it would stand to reason that you don't believe my claims that Cecile is not my child."

Could things get any worse? "I do believe you, Marc. I just don't want you to feel obligated to do anything you don't want to do. And if you think we should avoid each other, then all you have to do is tell me. I won't bother you again."

"Kate, I want…" He hesitated then spun around and headed to the door. "Nicholas is probably waiting. I'll ride back with one of the guards. We can discuss this later."

Kate fought back a sudden rush of tears as she followed him into the hall. "Marc, we need to talk about this now. You can't just walk away."

"Are the king and his lady having a lovers' quarrel?"

Kate and Marc turned simultaneously toward the end of the corridor. Mortification set in when Kate realized the annoying voice belonged to none other than Jonathan Renault.

How could they deny his allegations now?

Marc chose not to fight the sudden fury welling within him. In fact, he welcomed the wrath that he now directed at Renault with an acrid look, his hands fisted at his sides itching to wipe the smug look off the doctor's face. "You are treading on dangerous ground, Renault. You have been since you made your erroneous assumptions known to the press."

Renault looked Kate up and down before centering on her flushed face and kiss-swollen lips. "It seems my assumptions have been correct, although I assure you I've said nothing to the press."

Marc took a menacing step forward. *"Menteur."*

"I am a liar? Forgive me, Your Highness, but are you not guilty of the same? You have lied about your relationship with Dr. Milner. Of course, I do understand your motivation. I cannot imagine the people of Doriana would accept that their king had taken a common *putain* as his lover."

No one called Kate a whore. No one. "You low-life bastard." Rage sent Marc forward but before he could land a fist on Renault's ugly face, Kate grabbed his arm. "No, Marc," she said. "This will only make matters worse."

"Listen to your lover, Your Highness," Renault said, cowering in the corner of the corridor. "I will press charges with the authorities if you lay one hand on me. I do not care if you are the king."

Marc derived some satisfaction in the terror calling out from Renault's eyes. "You're right. I am not above the law. But I am within my rights to dismiss you from your position. I expect you to vacate the premises tonight and not return. And if I see you again, I won't be so benevolent."

"Are you threatening me, King Marcel?"

"I am saying I will no longer tolerate your insolence, Renault."

"And I promise you will regret your decision."

After the doctor scurried away, Marc crouched in the hall and grabbed his nape with both hands. He couldn't remember feeling so drained and useless. He'd always shown great restraint when dealing with the likes of Renault and practicing care when it came to lovemaking. Tonight he had done neither.

He felt a gentle touch on his head. "Let's go home, Marc." Home.

Marc didn't feel as if he really had a home, a place where he truly belonged, at least not one where he was welcome...except when he'd been in Kate Milner's arms.

Two days had gone by since the clinic fiasco and Kate had barely seen Marc except in passing. Again. She'd occupied her time with work and searching hospital records for any mysterious women who'd given birth six to eight months before, as Marc had requested. Yet she hadn't come across any information that might lead to the identity of Cecile's mother. All the children had been accounted for through pediatric follow-ups except for one, and that had been a boy. Most likely that child's family had moved away, and it began to look as if Cecile had not been born at St. Simone's hospital after all, which greatly complicated the investigation.

Kate decided she would have to start questioning the staff, if she could even begin to concentrate on anything aside from Marc's troublesome, self-imposed withdrawal. Right now, she had to feed a very fussy Cecile.

"I am worried about my son."

Kate looked up and centered her gaze on Mary. Obviously his mother shared her concern. "Marc's worried about everything." She made silly airplane noises while trying to slip the spoon of strained carrots into Cecile's smiling mouth.

Mary reached over and swiped at the baby's face after Cecile blew a raspberry, sending the orange pureed food all over Kate's T-shirt. "He has much to be concerned about, but he will get through this with you by his side."

Kate sensed Marc wanted nothing to do with her now, and that made her hurt in the worst way, right in the area of her heart. "He'll get through it by himself. He's a very strong man."

Mary smiled a mother's smile. "A very strong man who is fighting falling in love every step of the way."

Kate spoke around her shock, with effort. "Mary, I hope you're not misunderstanding mine and Marc's relationship. We're just friends." Her declaration had a false ring to it, and she figured Mary had seen right through the pretense.

"I do not presume to know anything, Kate. However, when he looks at you, his heart shines from his eyes. Have you not noticed this?"

No, she hadn't. She'd only seen regret and anger. The past few days during their limited contact during dinner, she'd seen nothing at all. "He's mad at me. It doesn't have anything to do with love."

"He's angry at the world, Kate. He's in love with you."

Needing an escape, Kate rose from the table, cleaned Cecile's hands and face then slid her from the high chair. "I'm going to put this little one to bed after her bath."

"Beatrice can do that, dear. You look as though you might collapse from exhaustion."

True, every one of Kate's muscles protested the least bit of activity, but that had to do with some very strenuous love-making in some less-than-comfortable positions, even though it had been days since her last interlude with Marc.

Heat traveled up her throat to her face when the images came to mind. "I'll put the baby to bed. It will give Beatrice a break and me a chance to wind down after a long day."

Mary's grin was surprisingly wicked for a sophisticated queen mother. "I can think of other ways to do that."

Kate frowned. "I'm not sure what you mean."

"Yes you do, and so does my son. But if you prefer to play innocent, I'll certainly understand. One does not normally discuss matters of an intimate nature with one's future mother-in-law."

Kate's eyes opened wide and so did her mouth. "You're kidding, right?"

Mary rose with stately grace and patted Kate's cheek, then Cecile's. "I would never make light of something so important. And I have very good instincts about these things. I only hope that you do as well."

Mary sashayed away, her red silk caftan flowing behind her. She smiled at Kate over her shoulder before she disappeared out the door.

Kate took a moment to absorb Mary's outrageous assumptions. Wrong assumptions, at least about a marriage between her and Marc. But she hadn't been wrong about their relationship progressing beyond friendship, at least for Kate. Mary was mistaken to think that her son was at all interested in settling down, not with the weight of the kingdom resting on his shoulders.

"Isn't that a silly idea, Marc wanting to marry little old me?" Kate asked Cecile as she headed to the nursery.

Cecile blew a bubble and belly laughed.

Kate hugged her hard. "My sentiments exactly."

Again Marc found himself locked in his suite, attempting to lock out his problems. For the past few days, he'd met with advisers and his press aide to try to counteract the allegations. But the speculation involving his relationship with Kate and Cecile's parentage had already reached most of Europe. Nothing like a royal scandal to wake the world.

He'd also successfully pushed Kate away, and he regretted that decision even if it was best for them both. He had battled the urge to go to her, make love with her, lose himself in her and in doing so recapture some of his strength. Yet he couldn't keep relying on her to serve as his proverbial port in a storm. He'd never relied on anyone to see him through his problems. Except for Kate, he realized when he reflected on their first encounters, her assistance with his studies all those years ago. But since that time, he'd been on his own. He would continue to make it on his own. Alone.

But he had found some solace during a few late-night meetings with little Cecile. He could basically set his watch to the exact moment when she would wake and require soothing, half-past midnight. Several times he'd almost laughed when he'd heard Beatrice telling his mother that the baby was now sleeping through the night. But his laughter did not come easily these days.

He glanced at the bedside clock and realized the time for Cecile to rouse was upon him now. He might not be able to establish a solid role as a leader to suit everyone concerned, or give Kate all that she needed beyond physical pleasure, but he could at least play the part of white knight to an innocent child. A child who looked to him for nothing more than company, looked at him with admiration, without judgment, when he rescued her pacifier from the floor.

After shrugging on his robe, he walked quietly through the hallway to the nursery and opened the door. Instead of finding the room totally deserted, he discovered Cecile cradled in Kate's arms, both sound asleep in the rocker.

Marc leaned a shoulder against the door and watched them with a warmth that radiated from his soul and settled on his heart. Kate's face looked tranquil and beautiful in sleep. He wanted to put Cecile to bed, then carry Kate to his bedroom. He settled for staring a few more moments, then closed the door behind him.

He leaned back against the wall outside the room and stared at the ceiling. He could not fight his feelings for Kate any longer. He cared deeply for her, more than he had for any woman. And he wanted to be with her, regardless that he shouldn't.

Determination sent him back to his suite to plan. He would somehow make it up to Kate, do something to show her how much he did care.

If, in fact, she still wanted him.

Kate really wanted to holler like a maniac.

If one more person asked if she was the king's girlfriend, then she would let go a yell that would be heard across the ocean. Her mother had been the latest in the long line of inquiring minds during their recent conversation. Kate had told her that she and Marc were just friends, not exactly the truth but not really a lie, at least not now. They hadn't been much of anything for the past five days.

Kate needed a break from it all, from the gossip and innuendo and sideways glances. Today was Saturday, a much-needed day off, and she prepared to spend some of her time talking with the staff about Philippe DeLoria. If she happened to come upon any relevant information, then she would have an excuse to talk to Marc. Otherwise, she refused to invade his privacy since he seemed determined to steer clear of her. Eventually, she did intend to confront him, but not until she knew exactly what she would say.

Following a meager lunch, Kate made her way through the gardens and entered the palace through the kitchen, coming upon Beatrice preparing several of Cecile's bottles. A good place to start with her inquiry, Kate decided. After all, they'd become fast friends, and the nanny did speak decent English.

"Hi, Bea," Kate said, bringing forth the nanny's smile over the pet name Kate had given her.

Beatrice swiped a forearm across her forehead, where wayward tendrils of auburn hair rained down from her neat bun. "Hello, Dr. Kate. If you are looking for the baby, she is sleeping. The queen mother is also taking a nap."

Kate took a stool at the kitchen workstation across from Beatrice and immediately thought about the first time Marc had kissed her by the stove. They'd come a long way in a short time, and they still had far to go—if Kate had any say in the matter.

Pushing those thoughts aside, she said, "Actually, I wanted to talk with you, Bea. Did you know Philippe?"

Beatrice didn't look up from screwing the cap on to one of the bottles. "Yes, ma'am, I did know him."

"Then you worked here before he died?"

"Yes, ma'am."

"How well did you know him?"

Beatrice's gaze snapped up, her hazel eyes wide with horror. "I did not know him in *that* way, mademoiselle."

Her strong reaction made Kate question if the woman was telling the absolute truth, but then Beatrice was a year away from forty and didn't seem like the kind who would take a younger man as a lover. However, nothing would surprise

Kate these days. "I'm not saying you and King Philippe were close in that way. I'm just wondering if maybe he was involved with a woman. Someone the family might not have known about."

Beatrice fumbled with a bottle, barely saving it from a major formula spill. "He was engaged to marry Countess Trudeau."

Kate suspected the woman's nervousness could indicate knowledge of a secret tryst. She bent her elbow and leaned her cheek against her palm. "What was she like, the countess?"

"I have never met her."

"Then she wasn't around all that much."

"No." Beatrice picked up the bottles and put them in the refrigerator before coming back to Kate. "I must go and check on the baby."

Kate rested her hand on Beatrice's arm. "I know you probably don't want to answer my questions, Bea, but this is very important. You can trust that whatever you tell me will be protected."

"I do not understand what you are asking of me."

"I think you know something about Philippe DeLoria's love life. Did he have a secret lover?"

Beatrice twisted the white apron she wore over her plain gray shift. "I could not say… I should not…"

"I have to know, Bea. This could help us find Cecile's mother."

The nanny glanced around the room like a frightened doe, then turned her attention to back to Kate. "If I tell you, will you vow not to tell the queen mother the information came from me? I have been sworn to secrecy when it comes to the royal family's privacy."

Kate raised her hand in oath. "I promise."

After looking around the room once more, Beatrice leaned forward and whispered, "It was rumored he had a lover in one of the mountain villages, a peasant girl. I think I saw her once, in the guesthouse late at night. I was…" Her gaze faltered. "I was going for a walk with a friend in the gardens."

Kate was curious about Beatrice's little late-night rendezvous with the *friend,* but that wasn't the main issue. "Can you describe her to me?"

"I could not see her."

"Do you know her name? Even her first name would help."

"No. I heard him call her *mon amour.* My love. That was all."

And it was more information than they'd had to this point. Kate circled the counter and drew Beatrice into a quick hug. "Thank you, Bea. You're the best."

"And so are you, Dr. Kate. You bring joy to the household."

If only that were true, Kate thought. At least where Marc was concerned. "Have you seen King DeLoria?"

"Bernard…" Beatrice blushed like the devil. "I mean Mr. Nicholas said that the king would be gone most of the day."

Bernard and Beatrice. Maybe that mystery was solved. If only Kate could say the same for the mystery mother, and Marc's activities over the past few days. Maybe he had found a lover in a mountain village. Kate burned over that thought.

"Could you have Mr. Nicholas tell the King I need to see him, Bea? I'll be waiting in the guesthouse."

"As you wish, Doctor."

"Just Kate. I think we should be on a first-name basis now."

Beatrice beamed as if Kate had offered her the queen's palace suite. "I would like that very much, at least when we are in private. Otherwise, it would not be respectful."

Kate shrugged. "That's fine. I'll see you later. And thanks for everything."

With a newfound energy, Kate strode through the gardens, stopping to smell the roses lining the path. She skipped the last few yards like a schoolgirl and burst into the guesthouse, pulling up short when she found Marc sitting on the elegant wingback chair in the corner next to the white brick fireplace, looking dark and imposing against the pristine backdrop, and incredibly sexy in his faded jeans and black knit shirt.

"Where have you been?" His voice was low, demanding.

Kate refused to fall at his feet, although it was tempting. "What does it matter to you? You haven't been all that concerned over my whereabouts for the past week."

"I've been busy."

"So have I." She started to tell him about the conversation with Beatrice but words escaped her when he kept staring as if he really wanted to get her naked. And she really wanted to let him.

But first and foremost, she had to maintain some control in his presence. His recent rejection still stung and she needed to resist him.

"Why are you here?" Her timid voice betrayed her conviction.

"You need to accompany me on a drive," he said.

She snapped her fingers. "Just like that?"

"Yes."

"I'm supposed to drop everything?" Her clothes immediately came to mind.

"It would be in your best interest to accompany me."

Of all the arrogant kings. "And what if I don't?"

At least this time she sounded more confident. But Kate's confidence scattered when Marc came to his feet slowly, his eyes burning holes in her fake bravado. He stalked toward her until he stopped immediately in front of her, so close she could trace the outline of his Adam's apple. "Do you really wish me to show you what I'll do if you do not agree?"

Kate dared him with a look. "If you think you're man enough."

Proving he was very much a man—a Cro-Magnon man—Marc grabbed her and tossed her over his shoulder, then headed out the open door. He took away her breath when he set her in the all-terrain vehicle and slid his tongue across her lower lip. Then he took away her sight when he covered her eyes with a strip of white cloth, brushing one breast with a fingertip after he was done.

As ridiculous as it seemed, Kate didn't care what he did as long as he eventually removed the blindfold—and anything else he cared to remove.

So much for resisting him.

Eight

"**H**ow much farther?"

"It won't be long now."

Marc glanced at Kate, who seemed extremely sedate for someone wearing a blindfold. Although the pastoral terrain offered a panoramic view, the less she knew of their destination, the better. He wanted to save the full effect of the scenery for when she first encountered four thousand square feet of natural wood structure, set among ancient forests and majestic mountains, miles from any significant population, at least during the summer, before the arrival of snow.

He intended to use the remainder of the weekend to treat Kate as she deserved to be treated, to make love to her undisturbed in a real bed in the glow of firelight. To tell her what he was feeling. As far as Marc was concerned, his own private retreat would aid in accomplishing that goal, if Kate chose to cooperate.

After pulling into the narrow drive, Marc shut off the Hummer and opened his door. "We're here."

"Where is here?"

When Kate reached for the knot on the cloth, he told her, "Do not take that off yet."

She wrinkled her upturned nose. "Why not?"

He leaned over and whispered, "Because I want to remove it." He anticipated taking off more than the blindfold before evening's end.

After sliding from the seat, he rounded the vehicle then helped her out. The afternoon sun enhanced the chestnut highlights in her hair and, when he untied the cloth, illuminated her deep green eyes that revealed surprise and something he couldn't quite name, but it almost resembled anger.

Without speaking, she surveyed the pines surrounding the lodge for a few moments then climbed the steps leading to the porch that spanned the length of the building. She faced him again, her hands clasped behind her back as she rocked on her heels. "This must be the infamous cabin."

Infamous? Obviously the staff had been talking, Marc decided.

He passed by her and inserted the key into the lock, disappointed over her lack of enthusiasm. "I see that someone has ruined my surprise. Was it Nicholas?"

"Actually, it was Elsa."

Marc's hand froze on the doorknob. "Elsa?"

"During our phone conversation, she asked me if you'd taken me to the 'little' cabin yet, although I can't say that I agree with her definition of 'little.'"

Damn Elsa and her cavernous mouth. Marc would like to find a phone to give her a piece of his mind. But no phones were available here, a very good thing in his opinion. No phones, no interruptions. Unless Kate now demanded that he take her back to civilization. He planned to prevent that from happening, or at least try.

Marc pushed the door open, stepped to one side and considered Kate's entry into the cabin without coercion a small victory. Very small when he noted the continued absence of eagerness in her expression.

He decided the best course would be honesty when it came to his past. "I brought Elsa here only once. My mother was getting on her nerves, so I decided this would be a good place to escape. Elsa lasted less than an hour before she demanded to return to the palace after incessant complaining about the shortage of modern conveniences."

Kate ran her palm along the back of the brown suede sofa, stirring Marc's libido to life. "No indoor plumbing?"

Marc closed and locked the door behind him. "Not enough outlets in the bathroom for her appliances."

A smile played at the corners of her mouth. "I would think if you were here, she wouldn't need any appliances."

Her show of humor encouraged Marc somewhat. "Appliances as in hair dryers and myriad curling irons. Elsa spends hours in preparation from the minute she crawls out of bed."

Definitely the wrong thing to say, Marc realized when Kate's frown deepened. He made a mental note not to use "Elsa" and "bed" in the same sentence again. In fact, he vowed not to mention Elsa's name in any context unless absolutely necessary.

"Elsa's a real beauty queen, huh?" Kate asked wryly.

So much for that plan. "Elsa is high-maintenance. She makes a living from being—" Do not say beautiful, Marc. "From being presentable."

"Oh, I see. But I don't see how your mother could get on anyone's nerves. She's wonderful."

"Mother was not overly fond of Elsa. It was nothing like your relationship with her. I do believe she thinks you are responsible for the sunrise each morning."

"I like your mother, too, Marc. She's a great lady. And she loves you."

Sometimes Marc wondered, yet he didn't want to broach that subject now, or think about it, for that matter. "Would you like to see the rest of the place? Make certain you find it suitable for your needs?"

Kate shrugged. "I didn't bring any appliances, so I don't care about outlets. I also didn't bring any clothes and I assume that means we won't be here long."

Marc leveled his gaze on her. "You've assumed wrong. I plan to keep you here through the night, and you will not need any clothes."

She brushed her hair away from her face and tipped up her chin in defiance. "You are a very confident king."

"Only determined, Kate."

"Determined to do what?"

"To spend quality time with you. To make up for my disregard over the past few days. I've missed you."

She walked to the large window that faced the forest behind the cabin and pulled back the curtain, keeping her back to him. "I've missed you, too, but that doesn't mean I'm quite ready to forgive you for ignoring me for the past week."

Marc came up behind her and took a chance by circling his arms around her waist. "I will attempt to earn your forgiveness and alleviate your anger tonight."

When she started to turn, he commanded, "Don't."

"Why not?"

"I have something for you." He withdrew the necklace from his pocket and told her, "Hold up your hair." When she submitted, he kissed her neck and then clasped the chain, before taking her by the shoulders and turning her around. The delicate emerald necklace, surrounded by diamonds, rested between her breasts. Marc traced the oval with a fingertip. "As I predicted, it matches your eyes."

Kate lifted the stone and studied it with awe. "Oh, Marc, it's beautiful."

"And so are you."

He saw a glimpse of gratitude and pure pleasure in her gaze. He planned to see more of that tonight, especially the pleasure. "Why did you do this?" she asked.

"Let's just say it is a token of my appreciation, a peace offering of sorts. I know it's probably an inadequate gesture but—"

She placed a fingertip to his lips. "It's wonderful. No one's ever given me such an incredible gift."

Marc realized Kate had given much more than he'd warranted. "You deserve the best, Kate. I only wish my current problems did not involve you."

"Why don't we just forget about everything tonight? Let's just be together and not think about anything else."

"A very good idea. Then you forgive me?"

She toyed with the necklace. "I'm warming up to the idea."

He intended to do more than warm her up. He wanted to make her hot. But first things first. "Now I have something else to show you."

She sent him a sassy smile. "Is it in your pants, too?"

"I would be happy to allow you to do a full body search, but not now. What I want you to see is in another room."

He took her hand and led her into the great hall that held the massive dining-room table, now laid out with myriad canapés, cheeses, fruit, dishes and desserts for their evening meal.

Kate turned around the room and took in the various coats of arms hanging along the paneled walls and the twenty-foot, floor-to-ceiling russet stone fireplace. "This room is huge. Do you use it for entertaining dignitaries?"

Marc moved to the table and leaned against it. "Actually, I've rarely had any guests. It was originally a ski lodge and when the owners retired, I purchased the place as my own private haven." His place to escape.

Kate surveyed the banquet awaiting them. "Oh. I thought

maybe we're expecting the entire continent for dinner, considering all the food."

Marc had gone to a great deal of trouble having the meal prepared and delivered by the staff. It was excessive, but very impressive to the observer. "It's all for us."

She strolled along the table's edge, sampling a few items as she went. "I'm not sure I'm *that* hungry."

"We could wait until later, if you wish." He could think of other ways to spend the time.

She slid her fingertip through the chocolate mousse and licked it, sparking Marc's imagination. "Come to think of it, I could use some food." She claimed the high-back chair at the end of the table, farthest from the food, without taking a plate. "Okay, let's eat."

"Kate, there is no one here to serve us."

She rested her clasped hands in front of her. "You're here. If you want my forgiveness, then you're going to have to work for it."

Marc saw no problem with that. He predicted finding many ways to make it up to her with lovemaking she would not soon forget. Nor would he.

He took a plate and heaped it full of the fare, carefully selecting several baked oysters still housed in their shells. He had never proven or disproven their aphrodisiac qualities, but he assumed it could not hurt.

After filling his own plate and pouring two glasses of wine, he took the chair on the side of the table closest to her, expecting her to begin eating. Instead, she simply stared at him.

"Do you not find my choices satisfactory?" he asked.

"I'd like it better if you fed me."

Fed her? Kate, the confident doctor who had made it quite clear she disdained being helpless? Yet when he noted the fiery look in her eyes, he realized this could be her idea of foreplay. Obviously, he was losing his insight into the feminine mind. He would make it up to her with his knowledge of the feminine body.

He started with the oysters first, holding the fork to her lips and frankly expecting her to protest. Instead, she took the bite without any revulsion, a point in her favor. Many did not enjoy the delicacy as he did.

"I love these," she said after swallowing the bite.

"So do I." And he loved the way her lips looked at the moment, moist and pursed with pleasure. "What shall it be now?"

She nodded toward the fruit. "Grapes. I've always wanted someone to feed me grapes."

He complied, popping the fruit into her mouth. She chewed slowly, deliberately. And when she streaked her tongue across her bottom lip, Marc's jeans grew unbearably tight.

He picked up the glass of wine and offered it to her. "Would you care for something to drink now?"

She nodded and he held the glass to her lips and in his haste, inadvertently tipped it too far and missed the mark. The liquid ran down her chin and onto the front of her pale pink T-shirt. When he muttered an apology and reached for a napkin, she said, "Don't use that."

He dropped the napkin and locked into her gaze. "What would you wish me to use?"

"Your imagination, and if that doesn't work, your mouth will do."

Marc decided he could quite possibly lift the table with the strength of his erection when Kate crossed her arms over her chest then pulled her T-shirt over head, leaving her clad in only a white lace bra and jeans.

He stood, leaned over the table then slowly licked the scarlet path down her chin, her throat and on to the cleft of her breasts where he paused to outline the necklace with one fingertip. All the while, Kate kept her hands braced on the arms of the chair as if she might slide away. Marc would definitely not have that.

Once he was through with his thorough cleaning and re-settled into his chair, he expected Kate to suggest they forgo the meal and go to the bedroom. Instead, she rose, turned her back to the table and scooted onto the cloth-covered surface, leaning back until she was laid out before Marc like a center-fold. She rolled to her side and faced him, her bent arm and palm providing support for her cheek.

She nodded toward the trays. "You know, that quiche looked really good."

Marc wasn't too sure he could find the strength to leave her to get the damn quiche, considering the picture she now presented and his supreme state of arousal. But he forced himself to move back to the end of the table to retrieve a slice of the pie.

He came back to her and offered a heaping forkful. She wagged a finger at him. "This isn't for me, it's for you. Un-less, of course, you believe that old adage that real men don't eat quiche."

"Real men are up for any challenge." He was definitely up for it.

She sat up and released her bra, tossed it aside then dipped her finger in the filling to paint a design around and between her breasts.

Truthfully, Marc didn't care for the dish, but he would put aside his tastes for a taste of this woman who surprised him at every turn. After Kate lay back, he had no trouble remov-ing the quiche trail with his mouth, pausing to sample her nip-ples that peaked to perfection as he suckled them with a slow pull of his lips. He continued his course down her torso, think-ing the very best was yet to come.

When he stood and walked to the end of the table, Kate braced on her elbows and stared at him with dismay. "Is the party over?"

"It's only beginning. Sit up."

She did as he asked and he tugged her legs forward so he could reach the buttons on her jeans. He released them then pulled the denim down her legs until she was left wearing only white lace panties and a devilish smile.

"I personally favor the chocolate mousse," he said.

She swallowed hard. "I agree. It's very good."

"And I will endeavor to be very good, too, Kate." He went back to the spread of food and picked up the entire bowl of dessert. When he came back to Kate, he swirled his finger in the mousse then held it to her lips. She took his finger into her mouth and withdrew it slowly with an added flick of her tongue across the tip.

It was all Marc could do not to throw the bowl across the room and take her right there. Instead, he moved back to the end of the table and painted the inside of her legs with the chocolate dessert. He definitely preferred this to the quiche and after placing the bowl on the chair, he went to work enjoying every last bite.

He started at Kate's ankle, working his way up to her knee then on to the crease of her thigh. He moved to her other leg and did the same until all the dessert had disappeared.

He straightened to find Kate watching him, her breasts rising and falling with every ragged breath, her eyes clouded with need.

"What would you like me to sample now, Kate?"

"Anything that suits your fancy."

He took her hands and pulled her forward until her legs dangled completely over the edge of the table. "Anything?"

She sighed. "Anything."

He slid her panties away. "Are you certain?"

"Yes."

He started with her mouth, sweeping his tongue inside to savor the piquant taste of wine and the sweet taste of Kate. He moved to her breasts, feasting on one, then the other, while Kate firmly planted her hands on his head, following his movements. He ended by taking a seat in the chair Kate had occupied and centering his attention on the soft shading between her thighs, first testing the territory with his fingertips, then with his mouth. He had imagined doing this to her, only to hold back until he thought the time was right. The time was definitely right.

Kate thought she might totally fade away into a carnal void, or bolt off the table at the first sweep of Marc's tongue. She thought she might demand that he stop because it was almost too much to bear, the intensity of the sensations as he explored her with more finesse that she'd ever thought possible. She thought she might actually scream when he slipped a finger inside her, then two, while he continued working his magic with his incredible mouth.

This kind of intimacy made her feel so open, so vulnerable, yet in some ways so free. She simply gave in to the moment, gave herself over to the feelings, the building pleasure facilitated by Marc, who knew exactly what he was doing— and what he was doing to her. He was completely possessing her, and she willingly relinquished all control. She had no choice.

The orgasm hit her fast and furiously, sapping her strength, causing her to bow over and rest her head against Marc's. Never before had she reacted so strongly to a climax. Completely and utterly lost, she rode the waves of pleasure, her whole body trembling with the force of the release, until reality broke through the bliss.

This wild, decadent behavior was so out of character for normally cautious Kate, something she had dared to imagine only in her most secret fantasies. Now Marc DeLoria had brought those fantasies to life, and with that came a few revelations.

She understood all too well why women were drawn to him. He was the ultimate lover. But what she loved about

Marc went far beyond his sensual skills. She loved the man who resided beneath the exterior. She loved him with all of her heart and she would always love him, even if he didn't have a penny to his name or a place in a monarchy. Even if he never loved her.

Kate couldn't control the sob that escaped her mouth or the ensuing tears that she'd never wanted him to see. But he did see them as he raised his head, confusion and concern calling out from his endless dark blue eyes. Now she was totally open, body and soul, and she hated being that exposed.

He stood, wrapped his arms around her and held her for several moments until she regained some of her composure. Then he lifted her chin and thumbed away a tear.

"Kate," he said softly. "Did I hurt you?"

She shook her head. "No, not at all."

"Then what's wrong?"

"I don't know."

He brushed a kiss across her forehead and framed her face in his palms. "There is no shame in what we've done."

"I'm not ashamed," she said, followed by a sniff. "I'm just surprised by my behavior. I've never done anything like this before."

"Do you not think that I know that?"

"I don't know what you think. You're hard to read."

He sighed. "I care a great deal about you, Kate. I only want to give you pleasure and make you feel as good as you make me feel when I'm with you."

He *only* wanted to give her pleasure. She'd known this all along, his resistance to commitment. But it didn't make it any easier for Kate to accept. Regardless, she would take what time they had together and keep it close to her heart and her own feelings close to the vest. "I'm just a little overwhelmed."

"Are you certain that's all it is? You're not usually one to hide your feelings."

If he knew what she was hiding—that she was in love with him—he would have to make a retraction and probably run like the wind. "I'm okay now. Really."

"Do you want me to take you back to the palace?"

That was the last thing Kate wanted. These moments with Marc might never come again, and she intended to enjoy each one. "Actually, I want you to take me to bed and ravish me."

"You're positive that's what you want?"

She grinned despite the ache in her heart. "If you think you're man enough."

By the time Marc carried Kate into his bedroom, he wasn't certain he was man enough to give her everything she needed beyond the physical aspects. Her tears had taken him by surprise, caused him to assess where their relationship was leading. Yet with her standing before him bathed in firelight coming from the corner hearth, beautifully naked, he could not think beyond the moment, or consider anything but this time they had now.

He led her to the bed and nudged her onto the edge, then undressed while she watched. As ready as he was to make love to her, he thought it might be best to simply hold her for a time.

He tossed aside the covers and told her, "Climb in."

She did as he asked and he walked to the opposite side of the bed, then slid between the sheets. Kate settled her head against his shoulder and slid her fingers through the hair on his chest. She paused to stroke his nipples, then moved on to his abdomen, circling her finger in his navel.

This wouldn't do, Marc decided. Not if he wanted prove to her—and to himself—that he could be in bed with a woman without the sole intent of bedding a woman. "Turn to your side, away from me."

She raised her head, her hand poised immediately above dangerous ground. "What?"

"Right now I only want to hold you."

"Hold me?

"Yes. Is there something wrong with that?"

"No, not if that's what you really want." Her voice sounded tentative.

He brushed a kiss over her lips, keeping it chaste in order to keep his desire in check. "For now, that is what I really want."

She rolled to her side and he fitted himself to her back, gritting his teeth when she nestled her bottom against him. He draped one arm over her hip then slipped the other beneath his pillow, contacting the condom he'd put there in preparation for this moment. He drew back his hand as if he'd been bit.

"Are you comfortable?" he asked, his cheek resting against hers.

"I'm fine, Marc. You don't have to do this."

"I want to do this." And he did, more than he had realized to this point.

Tonight marked a milestone for Marc DeLoria. He had an incredible, sensual woman in his arms. A woman he wanted so much that he physically hurt from the intensity of his need. Yet he found a certain satisfaction in knowing he was stronger than he'd assumed, than anyone had assumed. And he had Kate to thank for that.

He wanted to tell her again how much she meant to him, this time with more conviction than before. But truthfully, he was almost afraid to tell her, for fear he might be forced to admit to himself that he was that defenseless.

Instead, he held her tighter and simply enjoyed the placid atmosphere—the fragrant floral scent of Kate's hair, the crackling logs in the fireplace, the cool breeze filtering in from the partially open window at his back.

Just when he felt his body starting to calm, Kate reached back and ran her palm down his hip and his thigh, then back up again. And when she rubbed her bottom against him, he again grew hard as granite. She turned her face toward him and Marc responded by kissing her. A long, deep kiss resurrecting the desire he had for Kate, crushing his determination to only hold her.

With his last ounce of strength, he broke the kiss and buried his face in her hair. "Kate, we—"

"Need to be closer," she said on a broken breath, then rolled onto her back. "I need to be close to you. I want you inside me."

Marc gave up his resistance, grabbed the condom from beneath his pillow and tore it open. He had it in place in a matter of moments and rose above Kate. When he guided himself inside her, he was overcome with the feeling of completion. He had insulated himself against this very thing for most of his life, and he wasn't prepared for what he felt at that moment.

He reined in those foreign emotions and kissed her again, holding her closely with his hands beneath her bottom, bringing her up to meet his thrusts.

Sheer pleasure, he thought. Mind-shattering, incredible pleasure.

"You feel so good," Kate whispered between kisses. "I can't believe how good."

"So do you, *mon amour*," he whispered.

My love. He had called her his love.

Marc was shaken to the core. He'd learned at a relatively early age how to please a woman, but he'd never resorted to professing love in the heat of the moment. Was this only the heat of the moment, or blind truth staring him in the face?

Kate's eyes reflected the glow of the firelight, and he saw something there that went beyond physical need. Perhaps she expected more declarations, more than he could give her.

With effort, he slipped from Kate's body, wanting it to last, to make it a memorable experience for Kate, or so he told himself, when he knew deep down that he was pulling away from the intimacy.

His actions immediately brought about Kate's protest. "Where are you going?"

"I'm going to make this better for you. For us."

She frowned. "I'm not sure I can stand much better."

"Roll back to your side, and trust me."

Kate did as he'd requested, and Marc once more fitted himself against her back, slid his arms around her and pulled her closer.

"Oh, yes," Kate murmured as he slipped into her welcoming heat again.

He caressed her breasts with one hand and divined the damp, smooth flesh between her thighs with the other, plying her with long, fluid strokes as he moved within her, with her. Marc slowed the pace to regain his bearings. He'd mistakenly believed that by not looking into her eyes, he could distance himself. Instead, he only felt closer to her, totally one with her. Maybe it was time he stop fighting this, fighting her. Fighting himself and his feelings.

Kate's body went rigid in his arms, but it wasn't from fulfillment, that much Marc realized when she abruptly raised her head. "Do you hear that?"

He couldn't hear much of anything aside from the pulse pounding in his ears. "Hear what?"

"Footsteps."

Marc clenched his jaw and stopped all motion to listen. "I imagine it's only the caretakers," he said, even though talking took great effort. "They've come to put away the food."

"Are you sure?" She sounded wary, something Marc decided to remedy by resuming his touch, more deliberately this time, until he felt her relax somewhat.

"Don't worry," he whispered. "They won't bother us."

Marc ran his tongue along the shell of Kate's ear and picked up the tempo of his thrusts. Then he discerned footfalls coming down the corridor, louder this time.

"They're…getting…closer," Kate said, but continued to be an active participant in their lovemaking, belying any real concern.

"They will not come in here," Marc assured her, although he briefly wondered why the caretaker or his wife would be seeking him out after he'd left instructions, in no uncertain terms, not to be disturbed.

"But what if…" She drew in a ragged breath. "What if they do come in?"

Right now Marc did not give a damn if every member of the council paid them a visit. He was on the verge of a searing climax, and so, he suspected, was Kate. "Let them, dammit. I can't stop."

The footsteps grew heavier, louder as Marc moved harder and deeper within Kate. The minute the rap came at the door, the orgasm claimed Kate and she cried out, in turn, bringing about Marc's own climax.

Marc drifted back to coherency, enough to realize another knock had sounded at the door, his euphoria now replaced by frustration and anger.

"Shouldn't you answer?" Kate whispered. "Someone might need you."

Someone's head was going to roll. "Not yet." He did not want to let her go. The knock was more insistent this time, very close to pounding.

Marc shouted, "What do you want!"

A long moment of silence passed before the offending party said, "I am sorry to disturb you, Your Elusiveness, but I must speak with you."

Nicholas.

What in the hell was he doing here?

Obviously bent on losing his job, Marc thought. Unless there was some dire emergency. That brought Marc to his senses and sent him away from Kate to gather his robe from the end of the four-poster bed. He discarded the condom, shrugged on the robe and stalked to the door, tempted to throw it open from the force of his fury over the interference. Realizing Kate was still in his bed, naked, he opened the door only wide enough to confront his attendant.

"This better be good," Marc said, not bothering to hide his irritation.

"My apologies for the intrusion, Your Virileness,"

Marc gritted his teeth and spoke through them. "Just spit it out, Nicholas."

"The queen mother has asked me to summon you. It seems that our youngest guest will not go to sleep without Dr. Milner's assistance. The household is at its wit's end. I would have called, but you left your phone behind."

Marc regretted leaving behind information on where he and Kate would be. "For God's sake, Cecile is an infant. Getting her to sleep is not that difficult. Tell my mother to have Beatrice practice more persistence."

"It's okay, Marc."

Marc turned to find Kate clutching the sheet to her neck. "Cecile's still trying to adjust," she said. "I don't mind seeing about her."

Marc minded, and he was bloody well having a difficult time adjusting to the thought that his night with Kate had come to an abrupt halt. "We will be returning within the hour. In the meantime, tell my mother she owes Dr. Milner a huge debt, and myself as well."

Nicholas nodded. "I will pass on that message, and again my apologies for the interruption."

Nicholas walked away, muttering under his breath. Marc couldn't really blame the man. After all, he hadn't come here to retrieve them of his own volition.

Making his way back to the bed, Marc snapped on the floor lamp and sat on the edge of the mattress. Kate stared up at him, regret etched in her expression. Marc could certainly relate.

He brushed her hair away from her forehead and planted a kiss where the faint bruise now resided. "Will she ever sleep through the night?"

"Yes, she will, as soon as she learns to go back to sleep on her own. She won't do that unless you stop your little midnight visits."

Hell, he'd been caught. "How would you know about that?"

She raised his hand to her lips and kissed his palm. "Because I've been sleeping the past few nights in the room next to the nursery. I don't return to the guesthouse until a couple of hours before dawn when Beatrice relieves me."

"I thought I was doing the right thing."

She held his hand against her warm cheek. "I think you're doing a wonderful job, although you might want to reconsider so she will learn to get herself back to sleep."

"I admit it. I've grown soft. I cannot stand to see her cry." He kissed her gently. "I cannot stand to see any woman cry, especially if I am the reason for her tears."

Kate smiled. "I promise you, a few minutes ago, I wasn't crying."

He returned her smile. "I know. You were moaning."

Her eyes widened. "Was I?"

"Yes, you were, and quite sufficiently. So was I."

"Do you think Nicholas heard us?"

"If not the moans, then he probably heard the headboard hitting the wall."

"We did that?"

"Yes, we did."

Kate covered her face with her hands. "I won't be able to face him now."

Marc took advantage of Kate's release of the sheet and lowered it, revealing her bare breasts. He played his thumb back and forth over one nipple. "I had hoped to make more noise throughout the night."

Kate dropped her hands from her face and sighed. "Me, too. I still haven't seen the royal birthmark."

Grinning, Marc stood, turned his back on Kate and lowered the robe to immediately below his waist.

"Wow. It looks like an inverted ice cream cone."

First, he felt Kate's fingertips outlining the birthmark above his right buttock, then the play of her warm lips against his flesh. That was all it took to convince Marc that he could not take Kate anywhere at the moment except back to bed.

When he turned and dropped the robe to the floor, Kate's lips parted in surprise. "I thought we were leaving, Marc."

"Not yet." He climbed back in beside Kate and hovered over her. "Cecile is relatively cheerful this time of night. My mother and Beatrice can entertain her while I finish entertaining you."

"Marc, she's going to know what took us so long."

"And your point?"

"I don't want to her to think—"

"That we are engaging in very hot and very hard…" He pressed against her, letting her know it would not be long before he recovered. "Lovemaking?"

"Well, since you put it that way."

He winked. "I am going to put it another way. Kate, I do not care what my mother thinks we are doing. I only care about doing it, and I promise you that's exactly what I intend to do."

With that, he slid down Kate's body, leaving wet kisses in his path, determined to show Kate that he was a man of his word.

Nine

Together Kate and Marc put Cecile back to sleep, just like a real family. But Kate acknowledged that the concept was only an illusion, even after their evening together. And she had to decide how much more she could take before she lost herself to him completely, although she was probably already too late.

Standing outside the nursery, Marc pulled her into his arms and murmured, "Come to my bed with me."

Kate would like nothing better, but every time he kissed her, made love to her, he stole another chunk of her heart. "I think I should just go back to the guesthouse. Otherwise, we'll never get any sleep."

Marc dropped his arms from around her and shoved his hands into his pockets. "I suppose you're right. We wouldn't want the staff to start making assumptions. That would only serve to make matters worse."

Kate was hoping Marc might put up a little more of a fight. But once again, his reputation and rumors prevented them from having their relationship out in the open. "First, I need to tell you what Beatrice told me today."

"You spoke with her? Why did you wait until now to tell me?"

"I think it's because you've kept my mouth occupied most of the night."

Marc released a gruff sigh. "If you continue to make those comments, then I'll say to hell with the staff and carry you to my bed."

"Promises, promises."

He looked mock-serious. "Kate, I'm warning you."

And she'd learned to heed those warnings that afternoon. "Okay, okay. Back to Beatrice."

Kate wasn't sure how to proceed except to be blunt and hope Marc took the news well. "Basically, she said that she heard your brother did have a lover aside from the countess. She saw them together at the guesthouse one night while she was walking in the gardens. But she couldn't give me a name or any description."

Marc didn't look pleased, but at least he didn't look angry. "That's not much to go on, but it's a start."

"Yeah, I guess it is, although I'm not very optimistic we'll find out much more any time soon."

"We have to keep trying. I have to know for certain if Cecile is Philippe's child, then decide how much information I'm willing to release. Regardless, at some point in time, we will have to reveal Cecile is not your child, or mine."

Kate sighed. "You know, I'm really too tired to even think about it now. I just wish I could go to bed and wake up to find this whole rumor mess is nothing more than a nightmare."

Marc's expression turned all too serious. "This is beginning to take its toll on you, isn't it?"

"I'll survive."

"I'm certain you will, but you have to realize that it could get much worse before it ends."

"How so?"

"You could be shunned at the clinic. Patients could refuse to see you if they begin to believe the rumors."

"If it happens, I'll just ignore it."

"It will not be that easy to ignore if it does happen, and you might have to make some choices in terms of your career."

Had she not been a knowledgeable doctor, Kate would have sworn her heart just stopped. "What are you saying?"

"I'm saying that you might consider returning to the States, at least until this is all cleared up."

"Is that what you want me to do?"

"This isn't about what I want. It's about protecting you from the brutality that I've experienced my entire life. It's not an easy thing to deal with."

Until that point, Kate had been prepared to deal with it. Now, she wasn't so sure. Marc was telling her that he believed it would be best for her to go home. Maybe he was right. Maybe she should walk out of his life. Maybe that's exactly what he intended to do, provide her with an easy out.

"I'll seriously consider what you're saying," she said, trying to keep a tight hold on her anger and hurt, "and I think you could be right. If I'm not around, then that would at least end the rumors of our clandestine affair that just happens to really be taking place."

"Kate, I want you to be—"

"I know, Marc. You want me to be careful. You want me to be safe. And I want…" You to love me. "I want to go to bed, alone, so I can finally get a good night's sleep."

She turned to leave before the annoying tears paid her another visit.

"I'll be by to see you in the morning, Kate."

Kate stopped in the hall and without turning around said, "I'd prefer to be by myself tomorrow."

She hurried away, yet still hoped that maybe Marc would

call her back and tell her he didn't want her to leave, that he wanted her to stay for good.

It didn't happen.

But what could she expect? Marc DeLoria was a good-time guy who had enough to worry about besides Kate Milner. And obviously she'd misunderstood when he'd said "My love" when they'd made love earlier. Maybe he'd meant nothing by it. Maybe he'd said that to many more women.

But Kate wasn't competing with a woman; she was competing with a kingdom. And she would do well to remember that from now on, even if she would never forget the time they'd spent together—or him.

On Sunday, Marc granted Kate's wish and left her alone. Even when she went to the palace to help tend to Cecile and then dined with Mary, she didn't see him. Again, he had totally withdrawn from life—her life. But then, she had told him she'd wanted to be by herself. In reality, she'd hoped he would have ignored her request. Instead, he'd totally ignored her, period.

By Monday morning, Kate regretted that she hadn't sought him out and insisted they talk one more time, and she regretted that she hadn't just laid it on the line and told him she was in love with him. At least then she would have lessened some of the burden. But she felt the full weight of the decisions she would have to make when she entered the clinic, a place where she had found satisfaction in doing what she did best—treating people who truly appreciated her efforts.

Kate had opted to come in early to complete the paperwork she'd left last Friday. She wouldn't want to leave any unfinished business in case she did decide to return home. And that included unfinished business with Marc. But that would have to come later, if she could ever get him alone again.

As she passed through the corridor, the sound of heated voices coming from Renault's office halted her progress. She stopped to listen, realizing that the devious doctor had obviously ignored Marc's dismissal. She also recognized a woman's voice, at first believing it to be Isabella, the lustful nurse. She was very much Renault's type. But when the woman spoke again, Kate was shocked to realize it was Caroline, her linguistic aide and clinic champion.

Although it went against her grain to eavesdrop, Kate remained outside the door to listen, shock holding her in place when she heard Caroline say, "I have done what you've asked of me. I delivered the baby to the palace with the note. I will not do any more, Jonathan."

"The king is forcing me to leave my job. I will not stop until I ruin him."

"Well, you'll have to ruin him all by yourself."

"Then it is over between us," Renault hissed.

"This will be no hardship for me, I assure you," Caroline said.

Kate wasn't surprised that Renault had set his sights on the blond-haired, brown-eyed beauty, but she was surprised that Caroline had succumbed to his suspect charms. Still, she wanted to cheer, both from Caroline's insult and the knowledge she had gained about Cecile's mysterious arrival at the palace. Then she wanted to shriek when the door flew open and Renault stormed out. He shoved her arm on his way down the hall, sending her a look of disdain over one shoulder as he tore through the doors leading to the waiting room.

"Good riddance," Kate muttered as Caroline joined her in the hallway.

The nurse placed a shaky hand to her throat as if she feared someone might strangle her. "Dr. Milner, I didn't know you had come in."

"Well, I'm here, and we need to talk." She gestured toward the office Caroline had just left. "In here."

When they both entered, Kate shut the door and faced Caroline, who looked as though she might faint. "I overheard your conversation with Dr. Renault."

"All of it?"

"Enough to know that you're the one who left little Cecile at the palace gates. Are you her mother?"

Caroline shook her head and her eyes filled with tears. "No, but I did raise her from the time she was born."

"Then you know the identity of her mother."

She looked away. "Yes. She was my best friend."

Was? "Where is she now?"

Caroline sniffed. "She died after giving birth to Cecile."

Kate experienced a twinge of sympathy. "Why haven't you come forward with this information?"

"I promised I wouldn't say anything."

"Who did you promise?"

"Jonathan."

Kate's sympathy went the way of the wind. "That creep? He has no right to ask that of you. Why would you get involved with him?"

Caroline withdrew a tissue from her pocket and blew her nose. "He threatened me, told me that he would have me fired from my job if I didn't do as he asked. He can be very convincing."

Not as far as Kate was concerned. "Why did you tell him in the first place?"

"Because we were lovers. Because I thought I could trust him when I decided I needed to come forward. He was the one who came up with the plan to leave Cecile at the palace with the anonymous note indicating she was a DeLoria. In order to protect me, or so he said, since it took me so long to make the decision. It turns out that Jonathan saw this as a way to exact revenge after King Marcel threatened to fire him because of staff complaints. He's very envious of Marcel DeLoria. He despises him."

That much Kate already knew. "Now let me get this

straight. He convinced you to give the baby away and leave a note that claimed she's a DeLoria?"

Caroline raised her red-rimmed eyes to Kate. "She is a DeLoria, Dr. Milner."

"Then one of the DeLoria sons is her father?"

"Yes."

Drawing in a breath, Kate prepared to ask the question she would rather avoid, but she had to know. "Which son?"

"King Philippe."

Kate wanted to collapse from relief. "Your friend and Philippe were lovers?"

"They were more than that, Dr. Milner. They were married. No one knew because King Philippe believed the country could not accept Lisette. She was a commoner. She worked at the tailor's in St. Simone. That's how they met. They loved each other very much, but they had to keep it hidden from the world."

Kate took a moment to let the information sink in before she said, "But Philippe was engaged to a countess."

"Yes, and that was a front. Countess Trudeau knew all along about the marriage and agreed to pose as his fiancée, at least until King Philippe decided how to break the news to his family that he planned to abdicate the throne to his brother. He wanted to be with Lisette and raise their child together, whether anyone accepted her or not. That was the reason for the countess's and the king's two-year engagement, and the reason why the countess married so soon after King Philippe's death."

Kate sighed. "He was willing to give it all up for the woman he loved."

"Yes, but before he could, it was too late. He never had the opportunity to tell anyone." A tear escaped and rolled down Caroline's cheek. "He never saw his beautiful baby girl."

The tragedy was beginning to unfold, piece by piece, and

it was all Kate could do not to cry a few of her own tears. "Were you there with Lisette when she gave birth?"

"Yes. I tried to save her, I swear it. But when I realized I needed help, I called the king. He had just returned from Paris and he was on his way to take Lisette to the hospital when he lost control of the car."

"And Lisette—"

"Died only hours after Cecile was born. She made me promise to help Philippe take care of little Cecile and to tell him that she would always love him. I never had the chance, but I did take care of the baby and loved her the best way I knew how, and I do love her still. But I've always believed she belongs to her rightful family. I just didn't know what to do, since no one knew about Lisette and Philippe."

Even though her evasiveness had threatened Marc's standing with his people, Kate very much understood the woman's dilemma. "Caroline, I'm so sorry you got caught up in this mess, but you did take care of Cecile very well. She's happy and healthy. The family owes you a great deal for that."

Caroline's tears came full force now. "I will tell King Marcel the details if you wish me to. And I am prepared to suffer the consequences of my deception."

Kate recognized that the nurse's only real mistake had been her involvement with the devil doctor, Renault. "I'm sure the royal family will understand that you were put in a very precarious position and will choose to be lenient. They may not be so kind to Jonathan Renault."

Anger turned Caroline's eyes a deeper brown. "He deserves the harshest punishment. He is responsible for the rumors and the attempts at discrediting the king. And you."

"Well, at least we can clear everything up now with King Marcel."

Caroline stuffed the weathered tissue back into her pocket.

"I will gather my things and leave today. The clinic has the number where I can be reached."

"You can't quit, Caroline."

"But I assumed—"

"That you would lose your job? Not if I can prevent it. You're a wonderful nurse. The clinic needs you. I do, too." Kate smiled. "How else am I going to be able to tell the difference between a sore throat and a sore back?"

Caroline hugged Kate for a few moments, then drew back with a joyful expression. "My sincerest gratitude, Dr. Milner. The clinic most definitely needs you, too. The patients are much more fond of you than they ever were of Jonathan. Many of them have refused to see him since your arrival."

That concept gave Kate pause. The patients did need her, and if she left now, she would be leaving them in a lurch. She would definitely need to stay, at least until a suitable replacement was found, or if Marc tried to change her mind about going home.

Marc.

She had to call him immediately and tell him the puzzle was finally solved. Now if she could just put the pieces of her heart back together if he didn't ask her to stay.

Marc hadn't waited long enough for them to bring round the car before he'd climbed inside the Corvette and taken the hairpin mountain curves at excessive speeds, leaving behind the armored car full of guards as well as his mother, who waited back at the palace for word. He'd reached the hospital in record time, forced into action by Kate's phone call stating she had solved the mystery of Cecile's parentage. Now he sprinted down the hospital corridor toward Kate's office and burst inside, startling Kate, who sat at her desk, looking very unnerved.

"Tell me now," he demanded. "Is Cecile Philippe's child?"

Kate rose, rounded the desk and perched on the edge. "Yes, she is your brother's child."

Hearing the confirmation sent shock spiraling through Marc. "And the mother?"

"She was a commoner, a tailor's assistant."

"Where is she?"

Kate's gaze faltered. "She's dead, Marc. She died following Cecile's birth, the same night Philippe died trying to reach her to bring her back here."

Marc streaked a hand over his forehead, now covered in beads of sweat, both from his harried departure and the unfathomable information. "Then he did have a lover other than the countess."

"No, Marc, she wasn't his lover. She was his wife. And he was about to abdicate the throne to you so that they could be together."

And Marc had thought he couldn't suffer more shock. "No one knew?"

"Only Caroline, the nurse I've been working with. She was Cecile's mother's friend and she raised the baby until she returned her to the palace. Jonathan Renault was also involved, with Caroline and with the worst of the schemes."

"He was behind this after all?"

"Yes, and there's more."

Kate recounted what she'd learned earlier about Philippe and the woman named Lisette, the nurse and her connection with Renault, and Renault's plans to destroy Marc. When she was finished, she said, "Now that everything is cleared up, I'm asking that you not be too hard on Caroline. She's a good employee and she didn't ask for any of this. She's been a victim of Renault's deceit and had it not been for her, who knows what would have become of Cecile?"

Caroline remaining as an employee of the clinic was the least of Marc's concerns. "I will see to it she keeps her job. But

I have no recourse other than to have Renault arrested for treason."

"He's on his way to Paris," Kate said. "I spoke with his landlord, who informed me he'd gotten in his car about an hour ago and taken off. Or at least I think that's what he said. His English wasn't too good, and we know my French isn't too great."

"You talked to him by phone?"

"In person."

"You went to Renault's house to confront him? That was dangerous, Kate."

She smiled. "Believe me, I wasn't worried. I planned to tell him you were on your way. If that didn't work, a swift kick would have."

Marc was too uptight to smile, too wound up to find any humor in the situation. "That was unwise, Kate, a huge risk."

She shrugged. "Well, I said I wanted some adventure, and this has been quite an adventure."

Marc didn't like the way she'd said that, as if the adventure was over. "At least now you can go back to your duties here without worrying about the press or Renault."

She studied her hands clasped tightly in her lap. "Marc, I've decided to stay here only until you find someone to replace me. You were probably right about me returning to the States. Maybe that would be best for everyone, especially you."

Marc fought an unfamiliar panic. "You have no reason to leave now, Kate. Everyone will know that you are not Cecile's mother." He sounded almost desperate, probably because he was.

She glanced up at him. "If you decide to reveal the truth, and I'm not sure you would want to do that if you consider what it might mean to Philippe's reputation."

Marc wondered if the truth would damage Philippe's reputation if everyone knew the whole story, that his love for a woman had driven him to deceive his people. But would his mother be receptive to telling all? He wasn't certain he would be willing to take the chance if it meant destroying his brother's memory. As much as he'd despised trying to live up to Philippe's example, he wanted his brother to be remembered for the great man he had been—a man who had been willing to give up his title for the sake of love.

That concept was as unfamiliar to Marc as driving the speed limit on rural roads. Or it had been before he'd met Kate.

He didn't want her to leave, yet he could not hold her against her will. "If you want to return to the States, that's your decision. But I would like for you to stay."

"Why, Marc?"

"You're very much needed here at the hospital."

"Is that the only reason?"

"Cecile needs you, too." *Just say it, dammit.* "And I—"

The loud knock at the door cut off Marc's declaration and provoked a foul curse bursting forth from his mouth before he could stop it. He threw open the door, again finding Nicholas there. The man had seriously bad timing.

"Beg pardon, Your…Majesty, but your mother insists you return to the palace immediately. It seems the media are calling for a statement from you in regard to charges leveled by a Dr. Renault, who says you've threatened to kill him, which is why he has fled the country."

"That bastard," Marc snapped. He turned to Kate, recognizing that now was not the time to make any confessions. "Kate, I have to—"

She flipped her hand toward the door. "Go on. I have a few patients to see anyway."

"I'll speak with you as soon as I have the time."

"Guess I'll see you in about a month, then." She smiled, but not before he saw the disappointment in her eyes.

"We'll talk about this later. I promise." If only he could promise her more.

Marc left her then, hating that he had caused her more pain. Hating himself because he had been such a coward. He'd had the prime opportunity to tell her that he needed her and that he cared for her more than he could express, but he'd blown it—with some help from his attendant.

Once more, duty had intruded on his private life, and that caused Marc to consider several things. Would she be willing to give up much of her privacy to be by his side? Would he be selfish to ask that of her?

Unlike Philippe, he had no one to replace him should he decide to give up the crown for love. But he didn't know if he could live with the decision to give up Kate.

Ten

"So that's it, Mother. The whole story of how Cecile came to be."

In the library, Marc sat on the settee across from Mary, awaiting her reaction and finding it odd that she seemed so calm. He, on the other hand, felt as if someone were banging a drum in his head and lighting a torch to his gut.

"I suppose I didn't know Philippe as well as I thought," she said. "And I'm sad that he didn't believe he could come to me. I would have understood if he'd fallen in love."

"You might have, Mother. But the country as whole might not have accepted his choice."

Mary toyed with the bracelet at her wrist, turning it round and round. "The country is more accepting than most people realize. They accepted me when your father brought me here."

"Perhaps that's because you have more charm that most women. And you aren't exactly a commoner."

"They recognized that I loved your father greatly, and two people in love are a wonder to behold."

"How is that possible when you knew each other so briefly?"

"I knew it the moment I laid eyes on him, and he felt the same. It's not so very difficult to understand once you have been in that position."

Marc actually did understand. But he didn't have time to consider love at the moment—his love for Kate—even though he needed to think about it, and soon. Before Kate left him. "I have to decide how to handle this whole media fiasco. The people are demanding answers from me."

Mary sighed. "Those answers call for serious deliberation, especially Renault's claim that you threatened to kill him. Did you threaten him?"

"It was a veiled threat, and it did not involve killing him, although that thought did cross my mind."

"I'm very surprised, Marcel. You've always been very diplomatic."

"He called Kate a whore."

"Then you should definitely do him bodily harm."

He couldn't suppress his smile, but only allowed it for a moment. "I will deal with him without resorting to violence, Mother. Renault and his ramblings are not my greatest concern. Deciding what to reveal about Cecile's parentage is."

Mary sighed. "I am proud to claim Cecile as my grandchild, but I hate that Philippe's birthright put such pressure on him, enough to cost him his life because he felt he had to deny his true love. And now I see it happening to you. At times, I wish you weren't subjected to living your life for your people."

No one wished that more than Marc at this moment. "I have no choice."

"You should have choices, Marcel, especially when it

comes to whomever you choose to love. That is a given as far as I am concerned."

Marc understood she was referring to Kate, and he wasn't ready to discuss that with her yet. "What do you think we should do about Cecile?"

"That is your decision, my son."

"I want to know what you wish me to do."

"I want you to raise Cecile as your own."

He could not consider anything else. He loved the baby as if she were his own child, and he would continue to protect her at every turn. "I had planned to raise her, regardless of the fact that she's Philippe's daughter."

"Therein lies your answer. And I wish for you the love you deserve with Kate."

He knew it would eventually come to this. "Mother, I—"

"Marc, you have never feared much in your lifetime. You were always the one climbing the tallest tree, scaling the wall surrounding the castle." She smiled. "Chasing the most unattainable women. Do not be afraid to love."

"I'm not afraid of it. I'm just not bloody good at it."

Mary's demeanor went stern in a matter of seconds, as it often had when Marc had climbed those trees and scaled those walls. "You will never know unless you try, Marcel. Kate deserves that much from you. Unless you've been trifling with her feelings. If that is the case, I will not be pleased."

Marc thought for a moment and realized he had been guilty of many things where Kate was concerned, the least of which had been his inability to express his feelings. "In some ways maybe I haven't been fair to her, but not intentionally. I've believed all along that I could not give her what she needs. A life of her own, not a life where everyone is scrutinizing her every move."

"Have you given her that choice?"

Marc looked away. "No."

"Do you love her, Marcel?"

God, he did. "Yes, Mother, I do love her." It hadn't pained him to admit it. The ceiling did not fall down around his head, and the earth below his feet did not open up and swallow him.

"And what did she say when you told her?" Mary asked.

He braced for the fallout. "I haven't told her yet."

The fallout came swift and sure. "Oh, good grief, Marcel. What are you waiting for? A royal edict?"

He'd been waiting for the right time, the right place, the right words. "It's not as if I've had nothing better to do, Mother." A very weak excuse.

"You have certainly found the time to bed her, my son."

Touché. "I do not care to discuss this with you."

Mary flipped her white lace handkerchief in his direction. "Oh, posh. I am not brainless, Marcel. I know why you took her to the cabin, and what went on there, if not before. And I assure you that Kate takes your intimacy very seriously, and I hope you do as well this time."

This time. The anger came back to Marc once more. Would he ever live down his playboy reputation? "I'm not the same man I was before, Mother. I've changed, whether you care to believe it not."

Mary joined him on the settee and rested a delicate hand on his arm. "But have you changed enough to love only one woman? Enough to be a good father and a man whom your own father would be proud of?"

He'd never loved another woman as he loved Kate. He'd never really loved any woman aside from her. "I don't know, Mother. Why don't you tell me?"

"I truly believe you have changed, *mon fiston.*"

"If that were the case, then you would stop referring to me as your little boy."

She leaned and kissed his cheek. "You will always be my

little boy, but you are a man now, and I am very, very proud of you."

Marc had waited what seemed like a lifetime to hear those words. "Thank you, Mother. I appreciate your faith in me." A faith he had seen in Kate as well. He reveled in the fact that the two women he loved the most believed in him...or at least Kate had at one time.

Mary patted his arm. "And I would be even more proud if you would do something else for me."

Now why did that not surprise him? "What would that be, Mother?"

"Make Kate your wife."

Marry Kate? Was he ready for that? "We've had too little time together to make such a monumental decision."

"You've spent enough time together to fall in love. If it happened to your father, it most likely has happened to you. After all, you are your father's son. Had I not settled him down, he probably would have been globe-trotting well into his golden years."

But Marc had no idea if Kate loved him. After all, time and again she'd said she only wanted adventure. And a few hours ago, she'd said she planned to leave him. "Kate is considering returning home to the States."

Mary looked totally taken aback. "Why did you not tell me this sooner?"

"I didn't want to upset you further. I know how much you admire her."

"And what do you plan to do to prevent this from happening?"

Marc rested his elbows on his knees and rubbed both hands down his face. "I honestly don't know. I have too much to think about now with Renault's threats and the rumors. I'm torn between duty to my country and my commitment to Kate."

"You will simply have to consider both. Life is very short, Marcel."

And Marc was very short on time. Feeling drained, he leaned back against the sofa. "What if Kate decides to leave regardless of what I tell her?"

"Then you will have to convince her to stay."

She made it sound as if that involved no more than saying, Kate, I love you, marry me, and we'll live happily ever after. "How do you propose I do that?"

She released a mirthless laugh. "Marcel, you've spent your life wooing women. You are a highly intelligent man. I have no doubt you will find a way."

"I hope your belief in me is warranted." He hoped Kate's belief in him still existed.

"I have all the confidence in the world in you. And I assume you've decided to take my advice?"

He smiled reluctantly. "I will follow your advice and try to win Kate's heart."

"You have her heart, Marcel. Now all you have to do is come up with a plan to win her hand."

A sudden bout of determination sent Marc abruptly to his feet. "I will get on that immediately. And we'll hope that Kate hasn't left for Paris to catch the next plane out of Europe."

"I doubt she has, dear. If I know her, she's probably coming up with some way to convince you that love isn't really a four-letter word."

"And I hope I am not making a mistake by asking her to take on this life and my problems."

She stood and touched his face. "You're asking her to be by your side. Throughout history, every successful male leader has had a remarkable woman by his side. And of those women who have chosen to stand behind their mates, you can rest assured they've given their husbands a few swift kicks in the arse for good measure."

Marc grinned. "I've always wondered why my father looked as though it sometimes pained him to sit on the throne."

He held out his hand and drew her into an embrace, thankful to have rediscovered his mother's love—a love that had always existed. He'd simply been reluctant to accept it.

"Love well, my son," she whispered. "There is no greater power on this earth."

Marc kissed her cheek, realizing that what she'd said about love was patently true, and his love for Kate propelled him out the door and to his office, with Nicholas following behind him.

Once in the study, he told Nicholas, "Find Brigante and tell him to meet me here immediately."

"Are you calling a press conference, sir?"

"I am certainly not planning a ball, Nicholas."

"And when will this take place?"

"This afternoon, if all goes well. And I'll need your assistance."

Nicholas bowed. "As always, I am at your service, Your Majesty."

"Your Majesty? Are you getting soft on me, Nicholas?"

"Why, of course not. I will address you as I see fit, depending on what you are planning to do."

"Meaning?"

"If your plans include marriage to Dr. Milner, then I will address you as you so deserve to be addressed, Your Wiseness. And if they do not, then I will have to address you as Your Foolishness."

Marc scowled. "Were you listening in on my conversation with my mother?"

"I am appalled that you would think such a thing. I am only relying on my observations."

"Good."

"However, I do agree with your mother on the point of having a good woman by your side, and I must say that Dr. Milner is the crème de la crème of women. You could not do better."

"Thank you, Nicholas, for your counsel. And if you are quite finished with your commentary on what you did not overhear, I will tell you what I expect from you in the next few hours."

In the next few hours, Marc's life was about to take a turn. And if it spiraled out of control, he would welcome Kate as his anchor. He wanted her in his life, in his bed. As his wife, his life partner.

He wanted her more than he wanted the crown.

And damn anyone who told him he could not have her.

Kate would give anything if Nicholas hadn't interrupted. Marc had been about to say something. He wanted her to stay because… He liked the way she looked standing by a stove? He liked having her around for a little slap and tickle when the spirit moved him? If she went back home, would he even miss her?

She considered what she would be giving up if she did decide to leave. She loved her job. She loved Cecile as if she were her own child and Mary almost as much as she loved her own mother. And she definitely loved Marc.

Of course, the big question was—did Marc love her? If not now, could he ever love her? She could darn sure try to convince him that he could. And she would, even if he was the most stubborn, headstrong, sexy, to-die-for man she had ever known. She'd never backed down to challenge before, so why start now?

If Kate could have one wish, at the moment she would wish she were two people. One available to take care of her responsibilities, the other available to go after Marc.

Fifteen patients down, one more to go, then a long night of decision-making ahead of her. A lot of hours to choose between responsibility to her life's work and responsibility to her own life. If Marc ended their relationship completely, she wasn't as sure as she had been before that she could stand facing him on a regular basis, knowing what might have been. But she also couldn't stand the thought of leaving little Cecile or Mary. Or Marc.

Kate stopped in the break room long enough to indulge in a stale croissant and a cup of cold coffee, all she'd had to eat that day. Her appetite had gone out the door with Marc and hadn't returned because Marc hadn't returned. He also hadn't bothered to call.

Considering what he now faced, Kate couldn't blame him for putting her on the back burner. She didn't like it, but she didn't blame him. Hopefully, they would find a few minutes to talk, at which time she'd have plenty to say to him.

"Dr. Milner, I have orders to escort you to the town square."

Kate glanced from the beginner's French book she'd carried with her into the lounge to Bernard Nicholas, who stood at the door looking decidedly concerned.

And she was definitely confused. "Is there a medical emergency?"

"No, there is no emergency."

"But I still have one patient to see."

"That has been covered by Dr. Martine. This is of the utmost importance."

She stood, clutching the coffee cup tightly. "Can you give me a hint?"

"I have been instructed to say no more." He gestured toward the hall. "Now if you'll please follow me."

Kate started to issue a protest, but thought what the heck. Just another adventure in a long line of many. And maybe even the last one for a while.

After exiting the hospital's main entrance, they were immediately surrounded by armed guards, one in front, one in back and one on either side of Kate and Mr. Nicholas. And thankfully no press, unlike the last time Kate had dared to leave through the front door.

Instead of taking the car, they walked the four blocks in silence until they reached a mass of people and media members gathered round the statue of a white marble angel, her face turned to the sky, centered in the cobblestoned square. Mr. Nicholas motioned to Kate to follow him into an area cordoned off with bright yellow tape and protected by several members of local law enforcement. It wasn't until they had worked their way a few more feet that Kate glimpsed the makeshift platform. And standing behind the podium was the king.

Kate felt that old familiar longing when she looked at him. His neatly combed hair revealed his incredible face. His impeccably tailored navy suit enhanced his broad shoulders. His absent smile and confident stance made him seem every bit the monarch—until he looked to his left and their gazes met. Then she saw a fleeting glimpse of some mysterious emotion in his eyes before he turned his attention to the crowd.

He spoke in French and Kate could make out a few words, but not enough to understand what this was all about. She turned to Nicholas and asked, "What's he saying?"

"He's talking about the hospital and his plans for improvements." He waited a few moments then raised an eyebrow. "Now he's saying he's going to give away his car for auction with all proceeds going to hospital expansion."

"The Corvette?"

"It appears that way."

Kate couldn't believe he would actually give up his revered vehicle. "What's he saying now?"

"He's explaining the difficulties he's had with Dr. Renault and he's denying the threats. He does say that he dismissed the physician and he's giving his reasons for that decision. It's not very flattering."

Probably more restraint than Kate would have exercised when it came to Jonathan Renault. "Good. I hope they believe him."

At that moment, an attractive young woman walked to the podium and stood by Marc's side. As irrational as it seemed, Kate wondered if this might be some girlfriend he hadn't bothered to tell her about. Or maybe it was darling Elsa. But no, the woman wasn't a blonde, and she wasn't buxom. But she was looking at Marc as if he'd hung the sun hovering above them.

Oh, God. Was he about to announce his engagement? Had he chosen this woman next to him to be his wife? That thought halted Kate's breathing altogether.

She couldn't stand it any longer when Marc sent the woman a smile. "Who is that?" she asked Nicholas.

"That is Gabriella Collarde. The king is about to speak English and she will translate his words into French."

"Thank heavens. Maybe now I can understand him." Maybe now she could relax knowing this wasn't some paramour he'd been hiding in the palace broom closet.

"I would like to move on to the topic of the mysterious 'palace' baby," Marc began. "Her name is Cecile, and it has been rumored she is a DeLoria. I am here to confirm that she is."

Several people gasped, then a chorus of whispers ensued until Marc raised his hand to silence them. "All I will say at this time is she was conceived in love and she will be raised with love as my child."

He paused to seek out Kate and gave her his smile. "I would also like to publicly acknowledge another very special woman in my life—someone I've known for quite some time, yet it wasn't until recently that I've had the privilege of knowing her very well."

Kate locked firmly into his gaze. Her pulse fluttered and her heart pounded like a kettledrum from anticipation of what might come next.

"And if she would do me the honor of coming to my side, I have something I would like to ask her."

Stunned and absent of coherent thought, Kate turned to Nicholas. "Is he talking about me?"

Nicholas smiled. "He is certainly not talking about me, Doctor, unless he's suffered a severe loss of testosterone, which I greatly doubt. So I assume he does mean you."

Kate wasn't sure she could move; it felt as though someone had plastered her feet to the pavement. She definitely couldn't speak because a lump the size of a basketball had formed in her throat. And as far as her vision went, that proved to be a challenge, too, since her eyes were foggy with tears.

Had it not been for Mr. Nicholas's assistance, Kate would have stumbled blindly to the podium. But once they reached the platform, Marc reached for her, taking her hand and her heart as he helped her up the steps and pulled her close to his side.

When he turned her to face him and pushed the microphone away, it was as if everything around them disappeared—the masses, the mountains and even the clear skies above. Kate saw nothing aside from his cobalt blue eyes, his beautiful smile, his endearing dimples. She heard nothing aside from him saying, "I love you, Kate, and I want you to be my wife."

Kate opened her mouth, closed it, and opened it again, but the words wouldn't form around her threatening tears.

Marc looked concerned. "Do you love me, Kate?"

She sighed. "Yes. I always have. I always will. But Marc, I'm not royalty. I'm just…well…me."

He palmed her cheek in his large, warm hand. "And it's you that I want. You that I've chosen. The rest doesn't matter."

"It could matter to your people."

"I suppose we'll have to find out then." He pulled the microphone back into position and said, "I have asked Dr. Milner to marry me. Now, what do you think her answer should be?"

In many different languages, in many different voices, the word Yes! reverberated around them, growing into a chant that vibrated the platform.

He looked at Kate, his valiant heart in his eyes. "I believe you have their answer, and now I need yours."

When Kate didn't respond, he leaned to her ear and said, "One simple word, Kate. One big adventure. Together. Always."

How could she refuse such an ovation—or the man she loved with every solitary beat of her heart. "Yes."

Marc turned to the onlookers. *"Oui."* He laughed. "She said yes."

More cheers rose from the crowd as Marc drew Kate into his arms and kissed her without hesitation. A moving, tender kiss that Kate felt to the depths of her soul. After they parted, Marc smiled, Kate cried and Mary joined them, shedding a few tears of her own.

All three embraced for a moment and then left the podium together, Marc and Kate's arms around each other's waists. As the guards led them away, Kate caught sight of one cameraman with a white bandage spread across his nose. He moved a considerable distance back when they passed by him. Then someone called from the crowd, "Dr. Milner, what is your relation to the baby named Cecile?"

The crowd went deathly silent and Marc muttered, "You don't have to answer that," as he tried to move her forward.

"Yes, I do." Kate paused and turned toward the man making the query. "She's mine." Or she would be.

"Good show, Doctor Milner," Nicholas said from behind them.

Marc gave her a squeeze. "Very good show, *mon amour.*"

As Marc, Mary and Kate stood by the Rolls awaiting the return to the palace, Mary touched Kate's face with reverence. "I have always trusted my instincts, dear Kate, and I see they have not failed me now."

Kate hugged her again. "And I guess I have to learn to trust mine, too."

Mary smiled at them both. "You two go ahead with Nicholas. I have another car waiting."

"We'll see you at home," Marc said, finally feeling truly at home.

As he turned to Kate and studied her beautiful green eyes, he realized home had been there all the time, waiting for him to fill it with a remarkable woman with whom he could share his life, the good and the bad. The woman who had long ago rescued a prince from a frog before he had become a king. The woman who was worthy of bearing the title queen. His queen.

The woman who had taught him how to love.

Epilogue

Today, Katherine Milner DeLoria had become a queen.

Three months ago, she'd been common Kate, the doctor, but on this fair September day, she'd been set right in the middle of her very own fairy tale.

In a white horse-drawn carriage, bedecked with assorted flowers gathered from the last blooms in the palace gardens, she rode through the cobblestoned streets lined with villagers and the ever-present press, including television cameras capturing the event.

Maybe it hadn't been the royal wedding of the century, but to Kate, it had been everything she'd ever dreamed of—a white-lace wedding gown that had been worn by generations of Doriana's queens, a traditional ceremony held in the stunning, stone cathedral that had witnessed many a regal wedding. And most important, a gorgeous groom who could steal any woman's heart with just a look.

The atmosphere seemed surreal, dreamlike, but Kate's *hus-*

band—would she ever get used to that?—was so very real. Marc sat beside her with his left hand, sporting a wedding band, entwined with hers, the other lifted to wave at the on-lookers who cheered as they passed. He wore a black suit, a gray striped ascot and a smile designed to please the crowd—until he turned it on her. It melted into a smile full of prom-ise, of love, and Kate's heart melted, too, knowing it was only for her. Knowing he was hers for the rest of their lives, as he'd promised without hesitation during their vows. He hadn't seemed the least bit nervous during the ceremony—until he'd almost dropped the platinum-and-diamond ring he'd bought her in Paris two weeks before. But she could forgive him that momentary show of nerves. She could forgive almost any-thing, as long as she had his love.

When the coach stopped to allow the guards to clear the streets of some persistent reporters trying to best each other for the perfect photo, Marc leaned over and whispered, "You know something, with all that fabric you're wearing, I could slip my hand underneath your skirt and no one would know."

"I would definitely know," Kate said, imagining it in great detail.

"True, you would. Are you wearing those demonic panty hose?"

She grinned and shook her head. "White stockings held up by only a band of lace at the thighs."

He blew into her ear, exposed due to her upswept hair. "What else is under there?"

She shivered. "If you keep that up, King Marcel, I'm going to let you find out even if we are being watched on worldwide television."

"Damn the camera crews, but I suppose that might not be deemed proper, although very tempting. But just another mile or so, then we're off to Greece on a private jet, where we can do whatever we please, anywhere we please. The first order of business when we're airborne will be to get you out of that dress and those stockings and have some champagne, naked."

"Sounds like a very good plan, Your Studliness."

"Have I told you what I plan to do with that champagne?" he said as he again waved to the crowd, looking as if they were discussing the weather, not hot and heavy lovemaking.

Kate waved as Marc did, even though she really wanted to kiss her husband. Badly. "Do tell."

"I'm going to pour it all over your incredible body, and lick it off slowly."

She turned her face to his and brushed a kiss across his lips, the crowd cheering its approval. "And I'm going to do the same thing to you."

Marc groaned. "Could this procession go any slower? I'm going to die from wanting you before we begin our honeymoon."

Kate smiled. "If I remember correctly, we started the honeymoon last night when you showed up in my bedchamber even after your mother told you to leave me alone so I could get a decent night's sleep."

He raised a dark eyebrow. "Bedchamber? Spoken like a true queen. And I didn't hear you complaining last night. I did hear you moaning."

"Stop it or you are going to make my makeup melt."

He turned his attention from the crowd to her, surveying her face. "That wouldn't matter. With or without makeup, you're still the most beautiful queen Doriana has ever known, with my mother running a close second."

Kate sighed and squeezed his hand. "I'm going to need time to get used to being labeled a queen."

"The first gainfully employed queen in the history of Doriana, I might add."

Thanks to Mary, Kate thought. Her precious mother-in-law had insisted Kate continue her work at the clinic, even if

Mary had to go before the council and argue the point. Hopefully that wouldn't happen. The unrest involving the last scandal had finally died down after everyone had learned of the impending marriage between the playboy king and the common doctor. No one knew about Philippe and his wife yet, but Mary had promised she would write it all down and reveal the news after more time had passed. In the meantime, Marc and Kate would raise Cecile as their own child, eventually telling her about the way she had come to be. A story of love worthy of being passed down through the ages.

Marc leaned forward and groaned again, his attention now focused on an alley to their right. Kate followed his visual path and noted the reason for his obvious distress. A handsome young man sat on the hood of a black convertible, several young women fawning all over him.

"That's your Corvette, isn't it?" she asked.

Marc frowned. "Yes, and they're going to ruin the paint."

Kate fought a sudden bite of apprehension. "Are you going to miss the attention from all those women, now that you're a married man?"

He wrapped his arm around her shoulder and pulled her close to his side. "I'm only going to miss the car." He kissed her cheek. "I have the only woman I want."

"I still can't believe you gave up your car. Couldn't you have kept it and just given some money to the building fund?"

"Actually, I gave the car away to fulfill the terms of a wager."

"A wager?"

"Yes, with two friends from Harvard. We wagered that none of us would be married within ten years. If we did marry, we would have to give up our most prized possession. Although I did not adhere to the terms of the wager, I did last nine years."

"Any regrets?"

He touched her face with tenderness. "Only if I would have given you up. That would have been my greatest loss. I could live without the car, but not without you."

For the second time today, Kate was on the verge of tears. She willed them away and welcomed back the joy. "So have your friends married yet?"

"No. Mitchell Warner is living in Texas as a rancher."

Kate's eyes widened. "*The* Mitch Warner, from the Warner political dynasty? The senator's reclusive son?"

"Yes, that would be the one. Dharr Halim is a sheikh and his wife has been predetermined. But as of yet, he has not married."

"Are they here?"

"No, but Dharr sent best wishes and an intricate vase made by an artisan in his country, Azzril. Mitch sent a note that said, 'I knew you couldn't hold out,' along with a model of the Corvette. We're to meet again at a reunion in the spring." He discreetly moved their joined hands from Kate's lap to his thigh and slid it upward. "I'm certain they will understand why I could not resist you."

Kate understood only one thing at the moment—the way Marc was looking at her now, with unmistakable hunger in his eyes, made her want to tap the driver on the shoulder and tell him to hurry the heck up.

Kate glanced back at the carriage behind them that carried the queen mother, Cecile and her own mother and father. "I think my parents are getting along well with Mary. She's giving them advice on their tour across Europe."

"Mother enjoys that sort of thing."

"Honestly, I can't believe they're actually going to take a real trip. And when they return home, they're going to travel even more. When I lived with them, they wouldn't go anywhere or do anything. My mother wouldn't even get on a plane. I had to provide their entertainment."

"I can understand why they enjoy your company," Marc said. "I certainly do."

"Well, it's nice to have someone need you. To a point." Kate's parents had long ago crossed that point, but it seemed they had learned to live without her constant companionship, which was a very good thing.

He turned his serious eyes to her. "But I need you, Kate."

"That's different, Marc." With him, she had learned that having someone needing her didn't have to be stifling. "We need each other. And you do have a life beyond only me. We both have lives."

"We will continue to have a life together. That much I promise you."

"I know. But I also understand you have responsibilities." She batted her eyelashes in her best southern belle imitation. "Being as how you're a little old king and all."

Marc grinned. "There's that Tennessee accent I do love. I thought you'd lost it after learning French. I'm glad you haven't."

Kate rested her head on his shoulder and held his hand tightly when the carriage again lurched forward. "I could stand losing the accent, as long as I don't lose you."

Marc tipped her face up to meet his gaze. "You will never lose me, Kate."

She looked at him with all the love in her heart. "And I think it's wonderful that you've given up something you've greatly treasured for the sake of your people."

"You and Cecile are my greatest treasure. The three of us make a good team. And when she is older, we will have more children to add to our family."

Kate realized it was a good time for a few revelations, now that they were moving again, preventing him from jumping out of the coach. "Marc, there's something I have to tell you. Actually, two things."

He frowned. "Why so serious?"

"Because I don't know how you're going to feel about this."

"Kate, nothing you could say would disappoint me."

"It might surprise you, though."

"My life is full of surprises. You are a prime example of that. A very welcome surprise, in your case."

"Okay. Here goes." She drew in a deep breath. "Bernard and Beatrice are married."

"What?"

"I know. It's shocking."

Marc scowled. "When did this happen?"

"A month ago, in a quiet ceremony."

"Is everyone bent on keeping their marriage a secret in this family?"

Kate squeezed his arm. "Ours has been very public."

"True." Marc ran a hand along his jaw then looked at her again. "So I'm assuming that's all the shocking news you wish to tell me."

Kate chewed her bottom lip. "Actually, no."

"What else?" Marc asked, his tone wary.

"I'm pregnant."

His expression filled with awe as he laid his palm on her abdomen. "Are you certain?"

She rested her hand atop his. "Yes. I took the test two days ago. I wanted to wait until the right time to tell you. I figured this was as good a time as any since I have you captive in a coach, in case you decided to run."

"I promise you I'm not going anywhere." He proved it by taking her completely into his arms and kissing her deeply, thoroughly, eliciting a few whistles and catcalls from the crowd. When they parted, he told her, "You have blessed me twice today, Kate. I hope it's another girl, a sister for Cecile. I admit I favor girls. Much less trouble than boys. Ask my mother."

Kate was buoyed by his optimism, his love. "If we have a boy, I want him to be just like you."

Marc brought her hand to his lips. "I want him to be better than me, Kate. I want him to have your spirit, your strength."

"Marc, how can you say that? You're the strongest man I've ever known."

"You give me strength, Kate, through your love."

"And you do the same for me."

Kate recalled what Mary had said to her in the garden not long after she'd arrived in this beautiful country—to find a place in the world with this beautiful man.

I wish for you that kind of rare and precious love, my dear Kate.

Mary's wish had been granted, and so had Kate's. The consummate playboy had been replaced by the consummate king. The ultimate friend, an accomplished lover, the best father a child could know—loved her with all he had to give.

Truly a man for all seasons, and Kate's husband for all time.

* * * * *

UNMASKING THE
MAVERICK PRINCE

KRISTI GOLD

To the Ditzy Chix, the greatest group of authors on earth, for their wonderful camaraderie. And to the Chix-a-Dees, a fantastic group of romance readers whose commitment to the genre never ceases to amaze me.

Thanks to you all for your continued support.

Prologue

Tomorrow morning, Mitchell Edward Warner III planned to get the hell out of Harvard and return to the Oklahoma cattle ranch where he'd spent every summer since his birth. The place where he'd been taught to ride a horse and rope a steer without breaking too many bones. Where at fifteen, he'd fumbled his way through sex with a country girl down by the creek, high on adrenaline and teenage lust, as well as the prospect of getting caught. By the summer of his eighteenth year, he'd gotten pretty damn good at all three.

But he'd never been any good at being what his father wanted him to be—the heir apparent of a dynasty spanning four generations of high-powered politicians. He'd made the decision to shun his legacy, first by rejecting the preferred Texas alma mater in favor of an Ivy League school, and then going further against tradition by choosing business over law. He refused to enter the world of partisan politics and social-climbing suck-ups where both his father and betrayal reigned supreme.

The hoots and hollers filtering in from outside made Mitch long for a freedom that still wasn't quite within his reach. Instead, he was hidden away with two friends, Marc DeLoria and Dharr Halim, in their shared apartment. An unlikely trio to most observers, but they had one very important thing in common—unwelcome attention from the press because of family ties. Tonight was no different from the rest. Sons of kings and senators had a hard time remaining invisible.

While the post-graduation party raged outside, Mitch claimed his favorite spot on the floor with his back to the wall, appropriate since at times he felt that way in a very real sense. He tossed aside the ranching magazine he'd pretended to be reading and picked up the champagne bottle to refill his glass, wishing it were a beer. "We've already toasted our success. Now I suggest we toast a long bachelorhood." He topped off Dharr's and Marc's drinks, replaced the bottle in the bucket and then held up his glass.

Dharr raised his flute. "I would most definitely toast to that."

Marc hesitated, champagne in hand, and after a few moments said, "I prefer to propose a wager."

Dharr and Mitch glanced at each other before turning their attention back to Marc. "What kind of wager, DeLoria?" Mitch asked.

"Well, since we've all agreed that we're not ready for marriage in the immediate future, if ever, I suggest we hold ourselves to those terms by wagering we'll all be unmarried on our tenth reunion."

"And if we are not?" Dharr asked.

"We'll be forced to give away our most prized possession."

Oh, hell. Mitch could only think of one thing, something he valued more than any material object he had ever owned, and he'd owned plenty. "Give away my gelding? That would be tough."

Dharr looked even less enthusiastic when he glanced at the

painting hanging above Mitch's head. "I suppose that would be my Modigliani, and I must admit that giving away the nude would cause me great suffering."

"That's the point, gentlemen," Marc said. "The wager would mean nothing if the possessions were meaningless."

Mitch found it kind of strange that Marc hadn't mentioned anything he would be willing to give away. "Okay, DeLoria. What's it going to be for you?"

"The Corvette."

Damn, that vehicle was legendary, and Mitch had a hard time believing Marc would actually part with it. "You'd give up the love mobile?"

"Of course not. I won't lose."

"Nor will I," Dharr said. "Ten years will be adequate before I am forced to adhere to an arranged marriage in order to produce an heir."

"No problem for me," Mitch said, and it wasn't. "I'm going to avoid marriage at all costs."

Again Dharr held up his glass. "Then we are all agreed?"

Mitch touched his flute to Dharr's. "Agreed."

Marc did the same. "Let the wager begin."

Mitch smiled, the first sincere one in days. Team players to the end.

Without a doubt, Mitch would beat them all. Marc was too damn fond of women not to get caught in someone's trap. Dharr would probably buckle under his father's pressure and marry the woman chosen for him. Which left Mitch to do what he did best—stand on his own.

He figured the press would eventually get tired of stalking him if he didn't give them anything to talk about. He would blend into the real world in a single-stoplight town where people didn't look at him like he were some kind of a god. He'd get rid of every suit he'd ever owned, spend his days in jeans and chaps and his nights in the local bar, with women who didn't expect anything but a few turns on the dance floor and an occasional good time after closing.

And if he was lucky, he'd finally be left alone to live his life as he pleased, however he pleased, and finally walk into a place without being noticed.

<u>One</u>

Nine years later.

When he strode through the doors with all the self-assurance of a living legend, Victoria Barnett almost dropped her plastic cup of cheap chardonnay into her lap.

The pair of Wranglers washed out in places too difficult to ignore, the denim shirt pushed up at the sleeves revealing tanned forearms covered by a veneer of dark hair and the black Resistol tipped low on his brow gave the appearance that he was any hard-working, testosterone-laden cowboy searching for a way to spend a Friday night—probably between the sheets.

But he wasn't just any cowboy. He was Quail Run's favored son, the next best thing to American royalty, and Tori's possible ticket to a pay raise and promotion.

The journalist in her reacted with excitement at the prospect of obtaining the story of the decade. The woman in her reacted with heat to his diamond-blue eyes assessing the crowd with guarded interest as he worked his way to the jam-packed bar.

A few men acknowledged his presence with a casual, "Hey, Mitch," as if his appearance in this dusty down-home dive was a common occurrence. More than a few women eyed him as if he were the answer to their wildest dreams.

Tori couldn't imagine why a man of his caliber would frequent a place like Sadler's Bar and Grill, or choose to reside in this unforgiving southern Oklahoma town. Had it not been for her best friend's upcoming wedding, Tori would never have returned to Quail Run, where she'd grown up in hand-me-downs and a hard-luck shack. Poor little Tori, whose mama hadn't bothered to marry her dad—not that he'd bothered to ask.

But for the first time in two days, she was glad she had come back. And if luck prevailed, Mitch Warner would give her exactly what she needed.

"You really should give it a whirl, Tori."

Tori turned to her right and gave her attention to Stella Moore, the reason for her presence in the local bar—a final girlfriend get-together before Stella married Bobby Lehman tomorrow night. "Give what a whirl?"

Stella nodded toward the small stage at the front of the dance floor where some bearded, beer-bellied deejay wearing a T-shirt that read Bite Me was setting up for karaoke. "You should sing. You know you want to."

"Just do it, Tori," Janie Young said with an added nudge in Tori's left side. "Plainie Janie" as she'd been known in school. But with her waist-length blond hair, perfectly made-up green eyes and lithe five-foot, eleven-inch frame, Tori concluded that Janie couldn't lay claim to being plain now. On the contrary, her chosen career involved gracing the runways from New York to Paris as a renowned model known simply as Jada.

"One of you can sing," Tori said. "I'd rather sit here and finish my wine." Even if it was really bad wine.

"Come on, Tori," Stella cajoled. "You had the best voice in the high school choir. Show it off."

A hot blush crawled up Tori's throat and settled on her cheeks. "That's not saying all that much, considering there were only ten of us in the choir."

Janie frowned. "Don't put yourself down. You know you're talented. Besides, it'll be good practice before you sing at the wedding tomorrow night."

Tori grabbed a lock of hair and twirled it round and round her finger, a nervous habit she'd begun at the age of three, when she'd finally acquired some hair, according to her mom. Back when her mom still remembered all the little milestones in her daughter's life, before she'd forgotten her only child's name. Back when her mom was still around.

Pushing away the sadness, Tori said, "It's been a long time since I've sung in public." A long time since she'd had anything to sing about.

Brianne McIntyre returned to the table from the restroom, her red curls bouncing in time with her exuberant stride, completing the "Fearsome Foursome," as they'd labeled themselves during their youth. Another of the prodigal daughters who rarely returned home, Brianne resided in Houston where she was currently attending her third college and studying nursing, still undecided on what she wanted to be when she grew up.

Something sinister was stirring, Tori decided, when her friends displayed some fairly devious smiles. "What are you three up to now?"

Stella rested a hand on her belly, slightly swollen from the pregnancy that had been the reason for the hurry-up wedding. "Nothing at all, Tori. We're just here to have some fun."

Stella's assertions did nothing to silence the suspicion running at full steam in Tori's head.

Janie leaned forward and grinned. "Don't look now, girls, but Mitch Warner's sitting at a table on the other side of the dance floor."

Tori didn't dare look again. Not unless she wanted to be totally obvious in her admiration. "I know. I saw him come in."

Janie, however, opted to be obvious and fairly drooled after turning back to the group. "Oh my gosh, what I wouldn't do to that man if I had the chance. He's hotter than an Oklahoma sidewalk in August."

So was Tori, thanks to Mitch Warner, even it was October, not August, and forty degrees outside. "He's okay."

"Okay?" Stella's hazel eyes went almost as wide as the round table where they were seated. "He's drop-dead gorgeous. And last week, Bobby told me he and Mary Alice Marshall finally broke up. She's going to marry Brady the banker."

Brianne wrinkled her freckled nose. "I still can't believe he was dating her. Everyone knows she's slept with every cowboy under thirty in this town."

All three of them, Tori thought wryly.

Stella shook her head, sending her dark curls into a dance as she sent Brianne a warning look that wasn't lost on Tori. "No one knows that for sure, Brianne. People here are too judgmental for their own good."

Tori considered that to be a colossal understatement. The town's residents had said the same thing about her own mother many times, which was probably the reason for Stella's scolding. Or maybe Stella's unplanned pregnancy had sent the rumor mill back into full swing.

"The way I understand it, she and Mitch did the deed the first time one summer over fifteen years ago," Janie said in a conspiratorial whisper. "They've been on and off, literally, since he came back here to live."

Tori had heard about Mitch's and Mary Alice's extracurricular activities when she'd still been living in Quail Run, but she'd been too young to care. Five years her senior, Mitch Warner had been the elusive, enigmatic rich boy who'd only come to town during the summer. And she'd only caught a glimpse of him a time or two when she'd been riding her bike and seen the limousine drive past on the way to his maternal grandfather's ranch. During those times, she'd found the car much more fascinating than him.

Besides, boys like Mitch Warner hadn't been interested in Tori

Barnett, who'd lived on the wrong side of the social dividing line. Even though she could have spent her days ostracized from the mainstream and hanging her head in shame, she hadn't. Instead, she'd graduated valedictorian, worked her way through college and now struggled to establish herself at the Dallas women's magazine, where she currently served as a staff reporter.

An interview with a revered United States senator's reclusive son could propel her career to unknown heights, and provide much-needed money. She might even be able to pay off the bills she'd incurred when her mother had been in the hospital. If Mitch Warner cooperated.

"Yoo-hoo, are you in there, Victoria?"

Tori snapped to and stared blankly at Janie. "I was just thinking."

Brianne presented a wily grin. "About Mitch Warner?"

As a matter of fact. Tori finger-combed her bangs, surprised they weren't cemented to her forehead because of the perspiration gathering there. "Just thinking about work."

Stella blew a raspberry between her full lips. "Stop thinking about work, and try to enjoy yourself. I am, even if I can't have anything fun to drink."

Reminded of her own drink, Tori took a quick swallow of the less-than-palatable wine. "Okay, I promise I'll have some fun. But I'm not going to sing."

"Our first singer tonight is Tori Barnett, one of Quail Run's own, so let's give her a big Sadler welcome back!"

Tori sent her friends a bitter look and didn't bother to budge, even when the deejay called her name again.

"Get up there, Victoria May," Janie insisted, followed by several patrons chanting, "To-ri! To-ri!"

Making a total fool of herself in front of her friends was the very last thing Tori wanted at the moment. And more important, making a fool of herself in front of Mitch Warner wouldn't help her cause. But she hadn't forgotten how to sing, so she might as well meet the challenge head-on.

After all, what was the worst thing that could happen?

Tori confronted the worst thing when she stepped up on the stage, took her place behind the microphone and realized her brain had gone back to the table.

She knew the Patsy Cline song by heart, but this would be a nightmare, not a sweet dream, if she couldn't choke out the words now lodged in her throat, because Mitch Warner—kicked back in the chair, a beer wrapped in his large hands and the full extent of his blue, blue eyes and jet-black hair revealed because he'd removed his hat—had chosen that very moment to smile at her.

Tori felt naked under his perusal, totally exposed and definitely warm. As the song's intro began a second time, she had only one thought. If she couldn't sing in front of him, she'd never have the nerve to ask him for an interview.

That alone drove her to close her eyes and open her mouth to perform in public for the first time in years. She might have momentarily forgotten the lyrics, but she would never forget that Harvard cowboy's perfect smile.

Mitch Warner had never seen an angel dressed in black leather.

That's exactly how she sounded, this woman named Tori—like an angel. But she looked like a passport to sin. It wasn't her voice that made him imagine her beneath him, naked, her long legs wrapped around his waist, her silky brown hair brushing over his chest as they took a slow trip to heaven. And he'd probably go straight to hell in a handbasket if he decided to act on that fantasy. But as his gaze tracked the snug leather pants that showcased her curves and her breasts that rose beneath the form-fitting red turtleneck sweater with each breath she took, Mitch engaged in a battle below his belt buckle that he wasn't sure he could win.

When he'd entered the bar, he'd planned to stay only long enough to meet his foreman and rescue him from an all-day drinking binge in honor of the end of his bachelorhood. He didn't care for crowds or socializing except when necessary. Trust wasn't something that came easily for him. He never knew when some member of the press might be lurking in the shadows, waiting to catch him doing something that might be deemed newsworthy. For that reason, he was reluctant to talk to strangers.

But tonight…. Well, tonight he might make an exception with this stranger named Tori. Bobby could find another ride home since Mitch planned to meet the woman responsible for his current predicament. Whatever happened after that was anyone's guess.

He gave his full attention to Tori, who was now singing the final chorus. It was all Mitch could do to keep his boots firmly planted on the floor when she smiled, tossed a long lock of hair over her shoulder and then left the stage. He hadn't done this in a long time, but he remembered enough to know that appearing too eager would most likely turn her off.

He waited for two more singers to finish—if you could call drunken geezers, who couldn't carry a tune in a front-end loader, singers. A slow ballad now played on the jukebox, providing the opportunity to have Tori polish his belt buckle. Damn, he didn't need to think about that. Otherwise he'd have to remain seated indefinitely.

After finishing the last of his beer, Mitch replaced his hat, stood and worked his way across the dance floor crowded with mostly married couples, since the town still held true to a strict moral code. And those who ignored the code maintained rooms by the hour at the Quail Run Court.

He arrived at the table to find his foreman's fiancée, Stella, sitting with two other pretty ladies whom Mitch didn't know, nor did he want to know them. His interest was tuned solely into the singing angel who kept her gaze centered on the empty plastic cup clutched in her hand.

"Hey, Mitch," Stella said. "I thought you might be with Bobby out at the Greers' ranch, drinking yourself into a stupor."

"No time for that." Mitch kept his eyes trained on Tori who had yet to look at him. "We're getting ready to move the cattle into the south pasture before the first real norther hits."

The redhead bent her elbows and braced her jaw on her palms. "Isn't it kind of early for that, since it's only October?"

"Nope," Mitch said, and left it at that. He didn't have the desire to explain the workings of a cattle ranch or the weather to this particular woman. He only had the desire to get this brown-haired angel into his arms to see if her body felt as good as it looked. "Care to dance, Tori?"

Her gaze zipped to his and she looked as if he'd asked her to strip naked. "Are you talking to me?"

"Unless there's someone else named Tori at the table."

She stared at the hand he offered like he'd grown claws. "It's been a long time since I've danced."

"It's been a long time since you've sung, too," Stella said. "I doubt you've forgotten that, either. And even if you have, I'm sure Mitch would be glad to show you how, wouldn't you Mitch?"

"I can do that." He'd be glad to show her a lot of moves, none that he'd dare undertake in public. First things first. Right now, he had to get her away from the table and onto the dance floor.

She finally stood, but didn't take his hand. She did follow him to the middle of the floor, where Mitch faced her and took her palm to rest in his palm and then circled his other arm around her shoulders. She linked two fingers of her free hand on to his belt loop, like she was afraid to really touch him. Hopefully she would relax after a while, once she realized Mitch was only interested in dancing. For now.

Despite the fact they weren't that close, Mitch might as well have been covered from head to toe by a goose down blanket, not denim, considering he was quickly warming up. She could dance better than most and he imagined her skills were far-reaching. But that was all he could do—imagine—since she continued to maintain a safe distance.

She also refused to look at him until he said, "I'm Mitch."

"I know who you are."

Damn. He'd hoped she didn't know, but he shouldn't be all that surprised. His notoriety had followed him to Oklahoma, even if the media attention had waned over the past few years. But that was subject to change at any given moment, especially if the rumors about his father's retirement were true. Then it would start all over again, the speculation about whether Mitch would step in and take up the political reins. That would be a hot day in Antarctica. The only reins Mitch cared about were attached to a horse's bridle.

He decided to focus on something more pleasant, namely the woman with the big brown eyes who was sort of in his arms. He figured if he drew her into a conversation then maybe he could work his way in to drawing her closer. "How long have you lived in Quail Run?"

"I don't live here."

That disappointed the hell out of Mitch. "But the karaoke guy said—"

"I'm one of Quail Run's own, I know." And she didn't sound too pleased by that fact. "I grew up here, but I've been gone for almost ten years. I moved to Norman to go to college after I graduated from high school."

About the same time Mitch had come back from Harvard. "So what brings you to town?"

She lowered her eyes again. "Stella's wedding. I'm her maid of honor."

At least they had something in common. "Oh, yeah? I'm Bobby's man of honor."

The comment earned him her full attention and the full effect of a smile that threatened to knock the sawdust floor from beneath his boots. "Not the best man?" she asked.

"Not in Stella's opinion."

Her smile disappeared. "You and Stella dated?"

"Hell, no!" He hadn't meant to say that with such force, but that's all he needed, a rumor he'd bedded his friend's fiancée. That would be enough to send the rag reporters running back to Quail Run. "Stella's only a friend. She wanted Bobby to ask her brother to stand up for him. He picked me instead."

"I can't really blame Bobby. If I had to choose between

you and Clint Moore, I'd have to say you would be my choice."

"You have something against Clint?"

She frowned. "I have something against guys who can't control their hands in movie theaters."

Mitch wondered if that rule applied to guys on dance floors. At least he'd been forewarned. "So you dated Clint Moore?"

"I dodged Clint Moore. I'm basing my opinion on hearsay, and that's probably not fair at all. I'm sure Clint's really a nice guy beneath that playboy exterior."

"Are you dating anyone now?" *Good, Mitch. Nothing like being subtle.*

She shrugged. "I don't have time to date."

That pleased Mitch. Nothing stood in his way of seeing her again, at least while she was still in town, if she was willing. "What takes up your time?"

"Mainly work."

"What do you do for a living? Sing?"

"No."

"Then what?"

She looked away and sighed. "I really don't want to talk about my work right now. I'm trying to forget about it. Besides, I'd only bore you."

He doubted anything involving her mouth would bore him. "What do you want to talk about?"

She gave him another energetic smile, which also gave Mitch a rush that went straight to his head. "Tell me about you," she said.

Mitch wasn't sure he wanted to go there. "What about me?"

"I want to know what it's like to live on a working ranch."

At least she hadn't asked what it was like to be a revered politician's son. Mitch would have two words to describe that—pure hell.

They talked for only a minute until the karaoke resumed with a few more wannabes trying their hand at singing in voices that could rouse dead driftwood. Frustrated, Mitch showed

Tori to a table in the corner near the dance floor and away from the crowd to continue the conversation.

The noise in the bar seemed to fade away as they turned the discussion to their favorite pastimes. He learned that Tori loved riding horses, and he told her about his prize gelding, Ray. She asked about his grandfather but never asked about his father, and he appreciated that more than she knew. He liked the way her laughter sounded when he told a joke, liked the way she twisted a strand of her hair when she described her disdain for Dallas traffic and big-city hassles. And it suddenly struck him that he'd told her more about himself in an hour than he'd told anyone in a lifetime. At least those aspects of his life he was willing to reveal.

After a while, Mitch moved to the seat next to her to hear her better, or so he'd told her, when in fact, the bar had quieted down after the karaoke had ended. In reality, he wanted to be close to her. He wasn't having a damn bit of trouble hearing her, but he was having one helluva time not touching her.

When a slow-dance tune filtered through the overhead speakers from the jukebox, Tori sighed and sent him another smile. "Gosh, I love this song."

He loved the way her dark eyes sparkled with pleasure. He imagined they would probably do the same when it came to a different kind of pleasure. And man, he'd like to find out. "Do you want to dance again?"

"Sure."

This time, Tori didn't hesitate coming to her feet or taking his hand to pull him up—not that he was resisting.

Mitch normally preferred something a little livelier than a love song, but he didn't mind at all when Tori didn't bother with his belt loop and instead, brought her arm around his back and laid her head against his chest.

He doubted she was much more than five foot five, and since he was six foot three, her head fit perfectly beneath his chin. Her hair smelled like flowers despite the fact the bar was hazy with smoke. Her body pressed against his brought back the desire in a rush of heat.

He slid his hand down her back to the dip of her spine but didn't dare go any farther, considering her comment about guys with roving hands. He didn't want to be put in the same class with Clint Moore. Besides, he wasn't a teenager anymore, and he didn't have to resort to blatant seduction to gain a woman's attention. He'd learned a long time ago not only how to satisfy a woman, but also how to read the signs. So far, Tori's body language told him she was comfortable only with dancing.

But that only lasted for the next two songs. By the third ballad, the first of a series of tunes involving torrid affairs in tangled sheets, things started to heat up between them. Mitch felt it in the way Tori's body dissolved into his, knew it when he moved his hand to her hip and she didn't protest.

They soon abandoned traditional country-dance form and wrapped their arms completely around each other. Their bodies touched in all the right places—her full breasts to his chest, thighs to thighs, pelvis to pelvis. Their hands roved over each other's backs where dampness had formed from the heat of the bar, the heat of their close proximity, the heat of the fire building between them.

Mitch let her go long enough to shed his denim shirt and hat, leaving him wearing only a plain white tee. Tori followed suit, removing the black leather jacket to reveal the sleeveless red sweater that formed to her breasts perfectly.

They left what clothes they could discard in public piled on the table, while Mitch imagined removing the rest of their clothes and taking her to his bed, beneath the patchwork quilt where he could end this torture. Where he could touch her with his hands, taste her with his mouth, satisfy the unbearable pressure building in his groin. But he had no right to ask that of her, even if he wanted her so badly he could carry her out of here at the first sign that she wanted it, too.

They came back together, moved together but remained mostly in one spot, in the corner away from the rest of the dancers, only occasionally drifting into another couple's path, disregarding the muttered cautions and the occasional near-collision.

Mitch buried his face in her neck, tested the shell of her ear with the tip of his tongue. She responded with a soft, pleasurable sound that drove Mitch wild. He nudged her bottom toward him with his palms, until not an inch separated their lower bodies and only one thing could bring them closer. If Tori, with the sweet sexy smile, the voice like an angel and the body that could turn Mitch into a devil, hadn't known how this unconventional foreplay was affecting Mitch down south, she did now. No way could she ignore his aroused state. No way could he ignore it, either, though he realized it was best if he tried.

God, he wanted to kiss her, but he wasn't sure whether to take the chance. If he made the move too soon, she might hightail it out of there, and he couldn't stand it if she did. First of all, he'd lose his dignity, considering he was hard as a horseshoe and was relying on Tori to hide that fact. Secondly, he didn't want this time to end without eventually knowing how her sexy mouth would feel against his, engaged in something besides small talk, even if that's all he would know tonight.

Maybe someone would play a fast song, something to help him regain control of his libido. He was surprised someone hadn't, but when he glanced at the jukebox and found Stella and her friends feeding in quarters and giving him a thumbs-up, he realized they'd been the reason behind the barrage of sex songs.

Then Tori tilted her face up, her warm lips settling against his neck, and Mitch gave up the fight. He danced her toward the dark, recessed area near the far end of the room, lit only by a flickering beer sign and far away from what was left of the late-night crowd.

Once they stepped off the floor, he guided her to the corner and backed her up against the wall. He braced one hand over her head and the other on her waist, angling his lower body away from her, at least for the time being. Her eyes, dark as a desert at midnight, looked hazy as he brushed a kiss over her forehead.

"Mitch, this is crazy," she said in a breathless whisper.

He trailed kisses along her jaw. "I know. Real crazy."

She turned her head slightly, giving him access to her neck. "We probably shouldn't do this."

He pressed fully against her once more, letting her know his body didn't agree. "Yeah. We probably shouldn't."

"Mitch," she murmured when he worked his mouth up her throat.

He lifted his head and palmed her face with one hand, running his thumb along her soft lower lip. "Yeah?"

She closed her eyes. "It's hot in here."

It was now or never. He chose now. "Do you want to go someplace else?"

"I want you to kiss me."

She didn't have to tell him twice. He lowered his lips to hers, only a breath away from finally having what he wanted from her now—what he'd wanted all damn night since the moment he'd laid eyes on her—until, "Get the hell away from my woman!" drew him away from her to look around the corner.

Bobby Lehman stood by the table where Stella was seated, his fists raised and aimed at the hulking deejay named Carl, a man who was twice the ranch foreman's size with a temper second only to a raging bull defending his herd.

Mitch could stay here and do what he wanted to do—kiss Tori senseless.

Or he could rescue the groom from getting a beating the night before his wedding.

Damn Bobby Lehman for ruining his night.

Two

Twenty minutes later, Tori found herself crammed into the front seat of Mitch's fifteen-year-old faded black truck. She was closest to the passenger door while Bobby Lehman, the big burr in her butt, occupied the place where Tori preferred to be—next to Mitch. But when Bobby had threatened to throw himself out of the truck after they'd pulled away from the bar, Tori had agreed to switch places and block the exit, saving Bobby from the clutches of concrete even if he had insisted, loudly, that he had to go after Stella. However, at the moment, Tori would gladly open the door and shove him out, doing them all a favor.

She'd never really understood what Stella saw in Bobby Lehman, a stocky-built, non-descript sort of guy with a brown flattop haircut that accentuated his receding hairline, hazel eyes and an overblown opinion of his attributes. Tori liked him less now that he was whining, "Oh, God, Stella's not going to marry me," blowing his whiskey breath on the side of her face since she refused to look at him. And she'd liked him even less when Mitch had gotten between Carl and Bobby to stop the brawl and Bobby had inadvertently slugged Mitch in the mouth. If she added the fact that Bobby had stopped Mitch from kissing her in the bar because of his hot head, she would literally despise the pavement he'd crawled upon on his way to the truck.

Now that Mitch had a small split on the left corner of his bottom lip, Tori doubted he'd kiss her tonight. Maybe that wasn't a bad thing. If she wanted him to grant her an interview, she needed to start acting like a professional, not some smitten woman willing to hop into bed with a pedigreed cowboy just because he looked great in jeans, danced like a pro and made her melt with his smile. Besides, she hadn't really wanted to hop into bed with him. She'd wanted to hurl herself into bed with him without a second thought.

"I gotta see my woman," Bobby slurred when they arrived in front of Stella's tiny white frame farmhouse, situated between the edge of town and the verge of nowhere. Tori's accommodations until Sunday.

"That's not a good idea, Bob," Mitch said, bracing an arm across Bobby's chest to hold him back. "You better let her calm down first."

"I'll talk to her," Tori said as she grasped the handle. After she opened the door and slid out of the truck, she smiled at Mitch over Bobby, who was now leaning to one side. "Thanks, Mitch. I guess I'll see you tomorrow night at the wedding."

"If she marries me," Bobby whined again.

Mitch sent Tori a regretful look. "Yeah. Maybe we can finish our *dance*."

His grin, lopsided due to his swollen lip, did things to Tori that she felt all the way to the soles of her feet. "That's a deal."

Just as she reached the gate, Tori heard, "Dammit, Bobby. Get back here!"

Bobby rushed past her, pushing her against the fence as he tore into the house. Stunned, Tori turned to find Mitch rounding the hood, verbalizing the curses she had silently uttered at the drunken groom-to-be.

"He's determined to talk to her," Mitch said when he reached Tori's side.

"I think we both should go in there and referee."

"I think you're probably right."

Tori entered the house with Mitch behind her, finding wobbly Bobby facing off with stern Stella.

"Carl was only congratulating me, you jackass!" Stella shouted, her face stained with tears.

"He had his hand on your back…Stel…" Burp. "…la."

Mitch approached Bobby and grabbed his arm. "Come on, Bob. You need to sleep it off."

Bobby wrenched his arm away and stumbled back against the wall. "I ain't goin' nowhere till she talks to me."

Stella folded her arms beneath her full breasts. "I'm not talking to you right now, Bobby Joe Lehman. I'm not sure I'm even going to marry you."

Without warning, Bobby pushed off the wall and snatched the keys out of Mitch's grasp. "Stella and me are going for a drive."

"No way, Bob," Mitch said. "You're drunk, so give them back."

But before Mitch could snatch them away, Stella grabbed the keys from Bobby, dropped them down her maternity blouse and grinned.

Bobby growled and then went in search of Mitch's keys, running his hands up Stella's blouse like a security guard doing a strip search. Stella squealed and said, "You brute!" but didn't put up one ounce of a fight.

And just like that, Bobby and Stella were kissing and groping like a couple of horny kids, as if all were forgotten, especially that Tori and Mitch were standing there, playing witness to their foreplay.

Tori turned her back on the disgusting scene and told them, "Get a room."

And they did, running hand in hand into the bedroom adjacent to the living room, slamming the door behind them. Tori stared at the closed door, mouth agape and totally shocked into silence.

"Which one of us is going to get my keys?"

Tori turned to Mitch and shook her head. "Not me. Not on your life. You should have put them in your pocket."

"That's the last thing I wanted, Bobby rifling through my pocket." Mitch ran a hand over the back of his neck. "What do you propose I use to get home?"

"Stella's car?"

"You have any idea where she keeps her keys?"

Tori visually searched the room. "In her purse, which is probably in the bedroom with her and Bobby. So I guess you can either call a cab, walk or wait." She really hoped he'd choose the last option.

"No cabs in Quail Run, and no way am I going to walk twenty miles in forty-degree weather." He sauntered over to the floral sofa and set his long, lean body down on the cushions, easy as you please. "I'll wait."

Suddenly very warm, and very thrilled, Tori slipped out of the black leather jacket and hung it on the hook by the opening leading to the kitchen before facing Mitch again. "You know, it could take a while."

"Probably not. Bobby's pretty drunk. I'm not sure he can even get it…" He rubbed his shadowed jaw. "Get anything done."

Tori had no doubt Mitch could get it done, and quite sufficiently, drunk or not. But he wasn't drunk, and neither was Tori, except she felt rather woozy seeing Mitch leaning back on the sofa, his raven hair shining in the light since he'd left his hat in the truck, his long legs stretched out in front of him, his large hands clasped over his board-flat belly, right above the big gleaming silver-and-gold belt buckle, and below that, the big….

Tori forced her gaze back to his eyes. "Bobby's been here the past two nights. From what I've heard, he's rather…determined." So was Tori, determined not to faint over the sheer maleness of Mitch Warner.

"Don't mind me," he said. "You can go on to bed."

Don't mind me? How could she possibly ignore him? "You're sitting on my bed, Mitch."

His grin arrived slowly, bearing down on Tori with the force of an eighteen-wheeler hell-bent for the border. "Oh, yeah? I thought Stella had a spare room."

"She does, but it's full of boxes and furniture ready for the move to the ranch where Bobby works."

"Bobby works for me."

Another shocking revelation. "She didn't tell me that."

"Well, he does." Mitch patted the seat beside him. "Come here. We can talk while Stella and Bob take care of business."

Tori thought it might be better if she suggested they sit at the dinette, not on her makeshift bed, in case she found it difficult to behave. But she was so drawn in by Mitch's diamond-blue gaze that she moved toward the sofa as if he were pulling her forward with an invisible lasso.

She dropped down beside him, keeping a decent berth between them, in case she did forget herself and tackled his fine cowboy bod.

They remained silent for a few moments while Tori worked up the nerve to tell him what she did for a living and then ask him for an official interview. But before she could open her mouth, the trouble commenced, beginning with an "Oh, baby," then an "Oh, Bobby, oh, Bobby, ohhhh...." The thumping against the wall behind the sofa sent both Mitch and Tori off the couch simultaneously.

"Get your jacket and let's get out of here," Mitch said.

Tori complied and met Mitch at the front entrance. "Where are we going?"

"Anywhere but here," he said as he opened the door.

They walked to the truck but when Tori headed for the passenger side, Mitch said, "I locked it."

She faced him again. "No one locks their vehicles in Quail Run."

"I do. I never know when some reporter is going to get it in their head to rummage though my glove box, looking for family secrets."

Tori swallowed hard. Maybe now wasn't a good time to tell him she was a reporter. She'd wait and do it tomorrow night, after the wedding, since she assumed it was still on. The honeymoon obviously was.

On the brink of freezing to the sidewalk, Tori pulled her jacket tighter around her. "Okay, so now what do you suggest we do? Go for a walk?" She nodded toward the closest neighbor's house, which happened to be one pasture over. "We could beg the Wilsons for mercy."

Mitch strode to the back of the truck and pulled the tailgate down. "We can get back here for the time being. I have some hay and a couple of heavy blankets. That'll keep us warm until Stella cries uncle. Or, 'Oh, Bobby!'"

Tori had no doubt that being under a blanket with Mitch Warner would keep her very warm and could get her into serious trouble. But that didn't stop her from saying, "Okay. Guess it's the best we can do for now."

Mitch stepped up into the pickup's bed and held out his hand to help Tori up. Turning his back on her, he crouched down and pulled a wire cutter from the built-in metal toolbox backed up to the cab, snapping the string of wire binding the hay bale while Tori stood on the tailgate and watched.

After scattering some hay and laying a blanket over it, he sat and again patted the spot beside him. "Soft as a feather bed."

As dangerous as one, too, Tori thought. But her teeth were about to chatter right out of her head if she didn't get some heat.

She slipped down beside Mitch where he covered them both with a red-and-black plaid blanket that smelled faintly of hay and oats, their heads propped against the partial bale of hay padding the toolbox. They stared straight ahead, the silence broken only by the occasional gust of wind whistling around them and rustling the leaves in the nearby maple tree. The lone guard light and a sliver of the moon high in the sky provided the only real illumination in the clear, dark night.

"I really can't believe that just happened," Tori said, the heat of her blush offering some relief from the biting cold.

"Me neither. Didn't know old Bobby had it in him."

"Obviously he does since Stella's pregnant."

Tori could feel his gaze lingering over her, caressing her as did his deep, seductive voice when he said, "I wonder if they broke the bed."

"If they haven't by now, it's a pretty sturdy bed."

"So you've had to put up with that every night?"

"Yep, every night. And every time Stella started with the Oh, Bobby, I rolled my eyes and said, 'Oh, brother.'" She turned her head and found he'd turned to his side to face her. "It's absolutely ridiculous, isn't it?"

He smiled, giving the moon and stars some hefty competition. "Which part? The moaning or the fact that they're that passionate about each other?"

Tori rolled to her side, bringing their faces so close she could feel the whisper of his breath against her forehead. "I don't know. Maybe I'm just jealous. My boyfriend never said, Oh, Tori! during…you know."

He frowned. "I thought you didn't have a boyfriend."

"Ex-boyfriend," she corrected. "We broke up a few months ago."

"What went wrong?"

Everything. "He stayed in Oklahoma City when I moved to Dallas. We tried the long-distance relationship for a while, but it didn't last."

"Did you try phone sex?" he asked in an amused tone.

"A guy who considers reading a stock market report as foreplay isn't inclined to having phone sex."

"Yeah, well he must've been a real idiot."

"Honestly, Mike was a nice guy. Just not all that romantic." And not all that easy to love.

"Does that interest you, having someone talking to you during sex?"

Tori shivered at the way Mitch had said the word "sex" as

if he literally knew all the ins and outs. She trembled from the way he studied her with those heavenly blue eyes that made her want to sing a tribute. "I can't really say what I prefer since I haven't had that much experience. I've only had the one boyfriend."

When Mitch pulled the blanket up under their chins, Tori remembered he didn't have on a jacket. "You must be freezing since you're only wearing a shirt."

"Two shirts, and I'm pretty hot-natured."

He was simply hot, Tori decided, and shivered again.

"But you're cold, so let me give you some of my heat," he said in a low, slow-burn voice. He wrapped his arms around her and pulled her closer, doing exactly as he'd promised—giving her his *heat*. And Tori absorbed that heat in some places that were more than adequately covered.

Noting his lip was beginning to swell more, she carefully touched the corner of his mouth above the cut. "You should really make Bobby pay dearly for this."

He surveyed her face for a long moment before his gaze came to rest on her mouth. "Yeah. Bobby owes me for a lot of things, especially for his damn interruption back in the bar."

"No kidding," she said, surprised at how winded she sounded. Even more surprised when Mitch kissed her forehead, her cheek, then rested his oh-so-warm lips against hers.

Tori pulled back. "If we do this, your mouth is going to hurt."

"Not if you kiss it and make it better."

Oh, jeez. Oh, gosh. Oh, my, Tori's final thought when Mitch parted her lips with his tongue, slipping it inside her agreeable mouth.

He tilted his head to avoid touching the slight cut to her lips, but he had no trouble at all kissing her completely, moving his tongue against hers, softly, painstakingly though he didn't appear to be in any pain. Tori was. She ached like the devil from wanting him, knowing that only he could make her particular ache all better.

As the kiss went on and on, deeper and deeper, hotter and hotter, Tori reasoned that the tension that had been building between them in the bar, the sounds of Stella's and Bobby's lovemaking, the sex talk, had added kindling to the campfire. The combination was proving hazardous, threatening to drive them to a possible point of no return. Unless she stopped Mitch, and soon.

But Tori didn't stop him. She didn't want to stop him. Not when he kept kissing her until she thought she'd go up in a blaze of glory. Not when he tugged her sweater up and slipped his hand underneath to cup her breast through black lace. Not when he worked the front closure of her bra, opening it with ease.

She gasped when he contacted her bare flesh.

"I'm sorry my hands are so cold," he murmured in her ear, but kept his callused fingertips working her already rigid nipple.

"Your hands are wonderful," she said, prompting him to kiss her again, this time more deeply, more ardently, more suggestively as he moved his tongue back and forth, imitating the act foremost on her mind.

The next thing Tori knew, she was on her back on the blanket-covered hay and Mitch was partially on top of her, still kneading her breasts with finesse, first one, then the other. She didn't care that they were in a truck bed, not a real bed. She didn't care that it was cold as a well digger's shovel. She didn't care about anything when Mitch lifted her shirt completely, burrowed his way beneath the blanket, and replaced his hand with his lips.

His mouth was definitely hot and so was his tongue that flicked across her nipple before he suckled her with an unyielding tug that made her want to cry, Oh, Mitch!

Tori totally abandoned any arguments against this as she slid her fingers through his silky black hair. She'd never felt so carefree in her life, so totally consumed by a man with a mouth that should be registered as a weapon since it was shooting holes in her common sense.

She was keenly aware of Mitch's erection pressing against

her thigh, the movement of his hips grinding against her, telling her exactly what he needed without saying a word.

Mitch lifted his mouth from her breasts, came up from beneath the blanket and kissed her again, still off-centered but still as effective.

He broke the kiss and whispered, "I want you, Tori, so tell me to stop."

Stop! her mind called out as he worked the button on her pants. Stop! sounded again as he tracked her zipper down. Stop! filtered into her hazy brain as he pushed the leather pants and her panties down her hips to her thighs.

Don't stop! was the voice she chose to heed when he sifted his fingertips through the covering of curls, finding the source of all that need she desperately needed him to satisfy. And he did, with small circular motions, coming nearer and nearer until he hit the mark, causing her hips to rise abruptly from the jolt.

Mitch muttered, "Easy, babe," before kissing her again, not once halting his slow, deliberate ministrations.

"Easy" would describe Tori at the moment and what Mitch probably considered her to be, but again she didn't have the will or wherewithal to stop this, stop him.

She moaned against his mouth when he fondled her with the pad of his thumb and slipped a finger inside her, then another. Such a sweet invasion, such a skilled man, her final grasp on reality before the climax completely took over all reasoning with a pulsating rhythm and sharp, succinct spasms.

But it simply wasn't enough, and wouldn't be until she had all of Mitch. She pulled his denim shirt and T-shirt from his waistband as he had hers, reached up beneath both and glided her palm down the flat plane of his abdomen, over the slight spattering of hair at his navel that thinned when it reached his waistband. It took two hands to loosen the buckle, and two seconds for Mitch to halt the kiss and suck in a deep breath when she released the snap and lowered his fly. He pulled her against his chest and tucked her head beneath his chin. But that didn't prevent her from going forward, going all the way.

He exhaled slowly when she opened his jeans and tugged at his briefs, freeing him. She worked her palms beneath his shirts once more, over the taut terrain of his broad chest, pausing to touch his nipples, then back down, back up again, heating her palms from the friction, sufficiently warming them up so she could do some exploring of her own.

But she didn't have that opportunity since Mitch rose up on his knees, threw back the blanket, pulled her pants and underwear down to her ankles, pushed his jeans and briefs down to his thighs and then pushed inside her before she could draw her next breath.

"Oh, man," Mitch said.

"Oh, wow," she murmured, now totally, completely addicted to the feel of his weight, his tempered thrusts stoking the fire, burning away the last of the cold with his body. Big body…every bit of it.

She ran her palms over his muscled back then down to his buttocks to feel the power as he moved, a little faster and harder each time.

Amazing, Tori thought as he slid his hands beneath her bottom and pulled her fast against him. Incredible was another thought when he whispered sexy words in her ear—words that would send a proper Southern mother for the soap. His breath came in sharp gasps at her ear, hers came in soft puffs as he stroked her with his body and his hand again, and again. Thrust again and again and again…

The second orgasm hit Tori like a tidal wave, knocking her back into oblivion. Mitch's body went rigid in her arms and he stopped moving altogether.

Everything seemed to stop then as Tori shuddered from the impact and Mitch released a long hiss between his teeth, then collapsed against her.

After a time, the stars came back into view, the world started turning again, the cold nipped at her nose and rode out on a fog from her parted lips. But Tori knew that although everything seemed to be back to normal, except for her heartbeat, she would never, ever be the same again. Never.

* * *

This wasn't the first time Mitch Warner had made love to a woman in the bed of a truck, but that had been years ago when no other options had been available. It *was* the first time he'd totally lost control to the point he'd felt like he'd had an out-of-body experience. And the first time that he'd been so tuned into a lover that he'd failed to use a condom.

He thought he should probably move off of Tori, offer some lame excuse for his carelessness, but he didn't have the strength. The cold night air bit at the back of his bare thighs and if he didn't at least cover himself, the tails of his shirt might freeze to his butt. If he didn't roll away from Tori, *they* might freeze this way only to be discovered by the sheriff tomorrow morning, still tangled together, not such an unappealing prospect. But if he didn't get Tori back in the house, he would be tempted to go at it again, not a great idea considering he'd already screwed up once in the protection department, and he hated to think what the consequences might be. Stella and Bob would be the first ones to tell them that unprotected sex leads to unplanned pregnancy.

"I guess this is probably a good time to tell you I've never done this before," Tori said against his shoulder.

Stunned, Mitch raised his head and stared down at her beautiful face. No way would he have not known she was a virgin. Mary Alice had been one all those years ago, but then so had he. He sure as hell wasn't a novice now. He would have known. "I thought you said that you and your boyfriend—"

"I meant I've never had sex with someone I've just met. Ever."

Mitch couldn't lay claim to that, but for the past decade, he'd settled for convenience and comfort with Mary Alice instead of hot, unrestrained sex with a virtual stranger—hot unprotected sex—until tonight. Until Tori.

Finally, he rolled away from her onto his back, reached down and pulled the blanket back into place, not only to keep her warm but also to keep the temptation to make love to her again corralled.

After they pulled their clothes back into place, redid and re-snapped, they resumed their original positions staring at the sky, not touching, not speaking, until Mitch couldn't stand it any longer. He had to know exactly how dire their situation might be.

"Tori, are you on the Pill?"

"Kind of late to be asking me that, Mitch."

No kidding. "I know."

"The answer is no."

Oh, hell. "Then—"

"But I have taken a birth control shot, so we should be okay. At least where pregnancy is concerned. I know I'm safe in the disease department. I've only been with one man."

"So am I. I've only been with one woman for the past nine years."

"Mary Alice."

He glanced at her but she continued to study the stars. "How did you know about that?"

"This is a small town, Mitch. People talk. That's why you have to promise me you won't say anything about this."

The concern in her voice led to his reassurance. "I'm not going to tell anyone, Tori. You can trust me."

"Good. I wouldn't want anyone to think that I'm...."

When her voice trailed off, Mitch turned to his side again and pulled her over to face him. "Wouldn't want anyone to think that you're what?"

"You know. Someone who would do this kind of thing." She released a humorless laugh. "That's really stupid considering I did do this, and we are consenting adults, and it's really no one's business—"

Mitch stopped her words with a kiss then bracketed her face in his palms. "I don't think any less of you, Tori. It's just one of those things that happens when two people are attracted to each other."

She laid a dramatic hand on her chest and grinned, though Mitch still saw the worry in her dark eyes. "Does this mean you still like me?"

Mitch laughed, something he didn't do that often, especially not in the presence of a woman. "Yeah, Tori, I like you." And he did, a lot.

"Okay, that's great. But if you really like me, then you'll find a way to get your keys before we both turn into human icicles."

Mitch started to protest, to ask her to put her incredible body back against his so they could have a little more time together, something that was damn out of character for him. He normally wasn't the let's-hold-each-other-after-sex kind of guy, but then this wasn't exactly a normal situation. And Tori wasn't just any woman. But he also realized that they both needed some sleep so they wouldn't pass out during the wedding tomorrow night.

Tomorrow night. Maybe they could have a repeat performance, out of the elements and in a real bed. His bed. And he wouldn't be so careless the next time.

That alone spurred Mitch from beneath the covers and onto his feet to hold out his hand and help Tori up. Once they were standing, he took the opportunity to pull her against his chest one more time, feel her against him one more time, kiss her one more time before letting her go.

After they left the truck, they walked the path in silence and stopped at the front door, where they found the pilfered keys taped to the screen.

Mitch yanked them down and tossed them up, snatching them in midair. "At least I didn't have to go frisk Stella to find these. That would have really sent Bobby over the edge."

Tori's smile was soft and self-conscious. "I'm sure Bobby's out like a light. At least I hope so."

They stared at each other for a solid few seconds before Mitch leaned over and this time kissed her cheek, fearing if he did more he'd be tempted to ask her if he could join her on the sofa.

"I had a good time tonight, Tori." A serious understatement. He'd had a great time. The best time he'd had in a long, long time.

"So did I." She rubbed her hands down her arms. "But I think it's probably wise if we don't have quite as good a time tomorrow night."

So much for his plans. "You're probably right." And she probably was, but Mitch couldn't help hoping that maybe he might have more of what he'd experienced with her tonight, just one last time before she left. But he wouldn't ask that of her, not now. Not when he could see the guilt calling out from her dark eyes.

"Tell Bobby I'll be by to get him in the morning since it's bad luck to see the bride on the day of the wedding."

"Okay, but it's too late for that. He's going to see her unless I blindfold him."

"Probably not a bad idea at that. He's going to have one hell of a headache and the sun isn't going to help."

"Serves him right." Tori sent him another smile as she opened the screen. "Guess I'll see you at the altar."

Mitch experienced a sharp stab of fear. "At the altar?"

She frowned. "Stella and Bobby's wedding?"

Damn. He was acting like a total fool. "Yeah. The wedding. Stella and Bob's wedding at Stella's parents' house. Tomorrow night."

When she opened the door, he said, "One more thing."

She faced him again, her long, slender fingers curled around the handle. "What?"

"I just want you to know that I'm not normally this careless."

"Me neither. Guess we were just feeling a little frisky."

When she smiled again, he wanted to kiss her again. Real bad. "'Night Tori."

"Good night, Mitch."

He watched her slip inside the house and close the door, then watched the door some more, hoping she might come back out. Hoping she might invite him in. Like that was going to happen. He'd totally screwed up everything by doing something he should never have done. Something he hoped wouldn't affect both his and Tori's future. But he had to trust that what she'd said was true—she couldn't get pregnant.

Shoving his hands into his pockets, Mitch walked back to the truck and slid inside, calling himself ten kinds of a fool for losing control, vowing to forget this ever happened. But when he started the engine and turned on the heat full blast, he could smell Tori's floral scent flowing through the truck—a scent that was all over his clothes, all over his body.

The taste of her was still fresh in his mind, on his tongue, jump-starting his desire back to life when he recalled in great detail how it had felt to be inside her. How he had totally, completely lost himself in the moment. And just as important, how it had felt to talk to a woman who'd actually listened to what he'd said, a woman who'd treated him like a man, not like a means to maintain her status among Quail Run's limited elite— like Mary Alice Marshall, who'd recently turned her affections to Brady Stevens, the banker. More like to his checkbook.

Mitch really didn't care. The relationship had been going nowhere for years, and they'd both realized that for a while now. In fact, he'd been relieved when Mary Alice had called it off. He was really glad she had, especially tonight. Otherwise, he might still be settling for convenience, missing out on making love with an angel. An experience he wouldn't soon forget.

Regardless, he would try to avoid repeating the reckless behavior tomorrow night, even if he couldn't avoid Tori. He would be a gentleman and keep his hands to himself, if that was what she wanted.

But he wasn't going to like it. Not one damn bit.

Tori leaned against the closed door with eyes shut tight. Even though it was warm inside the house, she felt chilled to the marrow.

"Where have you been, Victoria May?"

Her eyes snapped open to find Stella seated on the frayed tan chair wearing a tattered robe, her hair in curlers and her eyes blurry with sleep. "Why are you still awake?"

"Bobby's snoring like a freight train."

Tori pushed away from the door. "What? No, 'Give it to me Stella?'"

Stella blushed like a vine-ripe tomato. "You heard that?"

"I heard plenty. So did Mitch. That's why we left." Tori re-hung her coat back on the rack and started toward the small hall that led to the bathroom. "I'm going to take a shower." And try to wash away the remnants of the mistake she'd just made.

Stella stood and blocked the path. "You didn't answer my question. Where did you and Mitch go?"

"We sat in the back of his truck."

"What did you do back there?"

"Uh, we talked."

"Only talked?"

Tori didn't dare tell Stella anything different and not because she didn't trust her. She just didn't want to have to explain her imprudent behavior. "Yeah. We talked. General conversation. You and Bobby ought to try it."

Stella grinned and yanked a piece of straw from Tori's hair, holding it up as if she'd found the prize egg at Easter. "Looks to me like someone had a roll in the hay."

Tori strode to the sofa, perched on the edge and covered her face in her hands to hide the guilt. "We did it," she blurted out, then peeked between her fingers to see Stella's reaction.

Stella hovered over her with eyes as wide as world globes. "You mean you 'did it' as in made love with Mitch Warner?"

Tori dropped her hands to her lap and fell back against the sofa. "We had sex, Stella. You can't make love with someone you barely know."

Stella took a seat beside her. "Was it great?"

Tori could feel the flames rise to her face. "Oh, yeah. Better than great."

Stella slapped Tori hard on the thigh. "It's about time you took a few chances."

Unfortunately, Tori had taken a huge chance that she wished she could take back. "We didn't use anything for protection."

Tori didn't think Stella's eyes could get any wider, but they did. "Oh, no. Don't you know what can happen when you do that?"

Oh, yes, Tori knew exactly what could happen because it had happened to her mother and to Stella. She'd been certain that she was above such carelessness. A fine time to have a common sense lapse.

"Do you think you might be pregnant?" Stella asked.

"I'm hoping I'm not. I took a shot a while ago."

"Define 'a while.'"

"About five months ago."

"Isn't that a little long for it to still be of use, Tori?"

"Yes, although sometimes it takes women up to a year to get pregnant. I just didn't have any reason to get another one after Mike and I broke up." Until tonight.

"If you are pregnant, what are you going to do?"

Have a baby, Tori decided. Her mother had done it without a husband; she could do it, too. But hopefully it wouldn't have to come to that.

Tori came to her feet and headed toward the bathroom. "I'm not going to worry about it now. I'd just be borrowing trouble."

And if she let things get out of hand with Mitch again, she'd be borrowing a national debt's worth of trouble. She still wanted the interview, but she doubted she would have the nerve to ask. She wasn't sure she could even face him again.

But she had to face him tomorrow night at the wedding. Beyond that, she would just take it one step at a time—and hope that she didn't find herself repeating her mother's history and stepping into his arms because she just couldn't resist him.

She had to resist him. She also had to consider that she still had an opportunity she couldn't pass up. But if she didn't get him to agree to giving her a story, she would be leaving on Sunday. Leaving him and this intolerant town behind. And hopefully she wouldn't be leaving with a little reminder of the night she'd found sheer heaven in a maverick cowboy's strong arms.

Three

The following evening, Tori stood in her best friend's bedroom where she'd spent many a day during her youth, giggling over boys and even crying over them a time or two. The house had been her haven, her home away from home. The place where she'd felt welcome, never judged or pitied. She had known unconditional love and acceptance from Stella's parents, who now waited downstairs to witness the marriage of their only daughter. Tori would never know the pleasure of having her mom in attendance should she decide to wed, and that made her sad on a night that should be filled with joy.

The soft sounds of taped music signaled the ceremony was about to take place in the Moores' living room among select family and friends. Mitch was downstairs, too, and that created havoc on Tori's heartbeat, more than the prospect of singing in front of a whole slew of people. She'd hidden out that morning when he'd come to retrieve Bobby, and he'd nixed the brief rehearsal right before noon due to ranch obligations, sending his apologies and assurances to Stella that he knew what to do.

Tori couldn't argue that one bit. Last night, he'd known exactly what he was doing.

At least she wouldn't have to talk to him during the service. Of course, she couldn't very well avoid him at the reception without looking obvious. Exactly what did one say to someone following one reckless night? She didn't have a clue, nor could she afford to think about that now.

Smoothing a hand over the long-sleeve, tea-length red velvet dress, Tori hoped she hadn't left a spot from her perspiring palms. Stella sat at the dressing table while Janie and Brianne applied the finishing touches on her makeup. All of them had been uncharacteristically quiet in light of the event—the first of the "Fearsome Foursome" was about to embark on matrimony and parenthood.

Tori wondered if in a few short years they would all be soccer moms. Not her, she decided. She wanted to make a solid go of her career before she even considered settling into a normal routine. She also wanted a two-parent home, something she hadn't had. She could not in good conscience subject her child to that kind of existence, even though she'd done okay. She wanted more than okay. She wanted it all—the career, the home, the husband and the kids. All in good time, unless....

Her interlude with Mitch Warner once again weaseled its way into her mind. Carelessness, plain and simple, and hopefully without repercussions.

The bouquet of red roses and stephanotis began to shake in Tori's hand when she recalled their lovemaking. How was she going to face him if she couldn't maintain a good grip on a bunch of posies?

"Okay, we're ready," Brianne proclaimed, drawing Tori's attention.

Stella was standing now, the fingertip-length veil somewhat concealing her face but the plain lace sheath couldn't conceal her pregnancy. However, the dress was tasteful—and white— something that would have been unheard of a decade ago, especially in this hypercritical town. Maybe things had changed. Or maybe Stella just didn't care what everyone else thought.

"You look beautiful, Stella," Tori said sincerely, her voice shaky as she fought back sentimental tears. "Bobby is going to be so proud of you."

Stella frowned, although her eyes misted. "Bobby's lucky I'm still marrying him."

"And he's very lucky to have you," Brianne said as she swiped a hand over the moisture on her own cheeks.

Janie walked to the door and opened it wide. "Okay, let's go before we all start blubbering and ruin our makeup. Single file. I'm first, then Brianne, then Tori. Stella, you're bringing up the rear."

Brianne blew out a frustrated breath. "We know, Janie. We've already been through the routine."

Janie shot an acrimonious look over one shoulder. "I just want to make sure we have it straight."

Tori couldn't hide her smile over Janie's assertiveness and need to organize. Some things never changed, at least inwardly. She patted Stella's arm and said, "Break a leg, kiddo," before moving in front of her.

"Not a nice thing to say to a pregnant bride who's expected to walk down a flight of stairs in heels," Stella muttered from behind her.

The sound of the *Wedding March* filtered in from the parlor below. Janie sent them all a "thumbs-up" then began her descent. As earlier rehearsed, Tori waited until Brianne had taken three steps then started down the stairs behind her.

The makeshift aisle was flanked by four rows of white chairs on either side, all filled to capacity. Some guests lined the walls and although the living room was larger than most, the masses made the room seem to close in on Tori. Anticipation and adrenaline sent her pulse on a sprint as she continued her descent.

When she reached the red runner covering the carpet, Tori scanned the front of the room, namely the groomsmen. With his sandy stylish hair and charmer's smile, Clint Moore looked handsome as always, even if he was a playboy extraordinaire. Bobby's older brother, Johnny, bald as a bowling ball and grin-

ning like a madman, stood at Clint's right. And on his left, nearest the groom, one man literally stood above the crowd.

Dressed in a standard black tuxedo, Mitch Warner had
morphed into the senator's son, his boots the only indication
that he preferred prime cattle to a political caucus. His eyes
were as blue as his blood, his hair as black as the dark before
the dawn, a perfect masculine package that could be marketed
as Every Woman's Fantasy.

In that moment, Tori felt about as "country bumpkin" and
nondescript as she'd ever felt in her life. Mitch was luminous
and charismatic, especially his smile that he now aimed on her.
A smile that could wilt her bouquet.

Tori's steps faltered for an instant. If she didn't watch it,
she'd take a misstep, end up posterior over pride in the aisle
and be forced to sing "Send in the Clowns" instead of "The
Wedding Song." Of course, if Bobby had had his way, she'd
be belting out "I've Got Friends in Low Places." Lucky for her,
and the esteemed guests, Stella's good taste had won out.

After she took her position before the red brick fireplace
where the pastor, Janie and Brianne now stood, Tori turned to
watch Stella gliding down the aisle on her father's arm, glow-
ing like a summer firefly. Tori hoped that she would be so
happy when her time finally came, *if* her time finally came.

Stella reached the front of the aisle, accepted a kiss from her
dad, then joined hands with Bobby. The intro of the song began
and for a minute, Tori thought she might miss her cue when
her traitorous gaze landed on Mitch. But instinct took over and
she sang the lyrics without fail, focusing on a framed family
portrait across the room to avoid looking at the guests, particularly the best man.

When she'd ended the song, the minister began the simple
ceremony. Stella's voice trembled as she repeated her vows, yet
she said them without hesitation. Bobby sounded a little shaken
up, but he didn't waver with the "I dos" either. Tori didn't dare
venture another glance in Mitch's direction when Bobby engaged Stella in a rather lengthy kiss. But she couldn't avoid him

when the service ended and he joined her for the trek back down the aisle behind the happy couple.

Gosh, he smelled great, Tori thought as she rested her hand in the bend of his arm. He murmured something but she couldn't quite hear him due to the resounding applause. As it turned out, Mitch's words would remain a mystery, since the wedding party was quickly ushered into separate limousines brought all the way from Oklahoma City for the reception—the bridesmaids in one car, the groomsmen in the other. Bobby and Stella climbed into Bobby's truck, now sporting a lengthy string of beer cans, inflated condoms tied to the antennae and She Got Him Today, He'll Get Her Tonight emblazoned in white letters across the closed tailgate.

"Classy," Tori muttered as they traveled the mile to Sadler's that had been reserved for the private reception. "I've never understood why men get such a kick out of writing dirty sayings on the wedding vehicle."

Janie sighed. "I've never understood why Stella chose Bobby, but she's stuck with him now."

"She's in love," Brianne said. "And we're all just jealous."

Tori remained silent even though she secretly acknowledged that in some ways Brianne was right. Human nature dictated a need to be loved. She was no different.

After they arrived, Tori trailed her friends into the club, her heart doing a jig when she considered Mitch was probably already inside. Her assumptions were confirmed when she glimpsed him standing near the beer keg talking to a leggy blonde with a neat upsweep and a neck as slender as a swan's. Her strapless dress revealed abundant breasts that looked as if they might launch from the bodice if she raised her arms even a tad. Her lips were unnaturally full and her diamond-encrusted hand kept landing on Mitch's arm. It wasn't until she glanced her way that Tori recognized the woman—Mary Alice Marshall.

Stung by an utterly ridiculous prick of jealousy, Tori wandered away from the disconcerting sight to stand in line with

the guests waiting to congratulate the bride and groom, while
Clint kept Janie and Brianne entertained near the bar with Lord
only knew what kind of stories. But she couldn't keep her eyes
off the harlot and Mitch still involved in a conversation. And
by the way, wasn't Miss Mary Alice engaged? Tori wondered
exactly where the fiancé might be. Maybe he hadn't been invited. She seriously doubted that. She did not doubt that Mary
A. still had designs on Mitch, apparent by the way the woman
kept moving closer to him, touching him with a familiarity
shared by longtime lovers. Lovers who were still lovers.

Tori experienced a sense of satisfaction when Mitch began
tugging at his bow tie and glancing around the room. After he
frowned and pointed toward Stella and Bobby, Mary Alice left
his side with a flip of her wrist and swayed away, tossing a suggestive look and steamy smile over one shoulder.

In order not to look too interested in Mitch's whereabouts,
Tori studied the groom's cake as she waited for the crowd surrounding the honored couple to dissipate. Leave it to Bobby to
request a plastic pickup truck and toy horses as decoration. But
then, Mitch might prefer something similar at his wedding.
Boy, wouldn't he make a terrific-looking groom? And she
wouldn't mind being his bride.

Heavens, where did that thought come from? She needed to
quit thinking about him on those terms. After all, they'd spent
only one night together in the bed of a truck. Pure and simple
lust, spontaneous sex. That's all it had been, and she didn't plan
on an encore. She had to start considering how she would ask
him for the interview, now that she gathered he was still speaking to her. But how long would that hold true once he learned
she was a member of the hated media?

She'd give it her best shot at explaining why she hadn't told
him sooner, ask for the story and, if not successful, return home
tomorrow and forget everything that had happened between
them…in a year or two.

The tap on her shoulder startled her, stealing her breath
when she considered that maybe Mitch was standing behind

her. Even though her heart was running at sprinter speed, she retained enough composure to turn slowly instead of spinning around like a frenzied top. Disappointment, then surprise, overtook her when she realized Mary Alice Marshall, not Mitch, had taken her place in the dwindling receiving line.

"Do I know you?" she asked, her tone just a little too sweet for Tori's taste.

"I graduated from Quail Run High three years after you."

Mary Alice tapped a perfect pink nail against her chin. "Oh, that's right. You're that really smart poor girl."

And you were that stuck-up, cheerleader hussy. "True, I was valedictorian."

"How nice. Why are you back?"

Sheesh. Wasn't that obvious? Tori decided Miss Mary Alice probably didn't make it into the top seventy-five percent of her class of twenty-five. "I'm Stella's maid of honor."

The light came on in Mary Alice's expression. Dim, but still on. "Oh, of course." She made a sweeping gesture toward Tori's gown. "That's the reason for the, um, dress. You know, velvet would not have been my choice."

Tori graciously chose to ignore the dig at Stella's taste. "I didn't see you at the wedding."

"That's because Brady and I didn't go to the wedding. We had a prior commitment."

Probably engaged in riveting conversation about the new hardware store the bank had financed, Tori decided. "Ah, yes. Brady, your fiancé."

Mary Alice wrinkled her nose. "How did you know about him?"

She pointed at the comet-sized diamond on Mary Alice's left hand. "Well, that's a dead giveaway. And people are fairly free with the latest gossip."

"True. The news of mine and Brady's engagement has been the talk of the town."

A prime example of a definite lack of excitement in Dullsville. "So when's the big day, Mary Alice?"

"Oh, not until next summer. Brady's building us a new house. Four-thousand square feet on Hunter's Hill." She nodded toward two men conversing in the corner. "That's my sweetie over there, talking to Daddy. He's absolutely wonderful. He will do anything I ask of him."

Anything that involved money, no doubt, because Tori couldn't imagine, or didn't want to imagine, Mary Alice having randy sex with Brady Stevens.

Tori smiled and raked her brain to try and think of something complimentary to say about the town's banker. That was a tough one considering he was at least two inches shorter than Mary Alice, suffered from the beginnings of male pattern baldness and wore the most ill-fitting green suit Tori had ever seen. She found it hard to believe that Mary Alice Marshall had traded in Mitch for a milquetoast. Or maybe Mitch had traded her in. She couldn't imagine what Mitch had seen in her. Actually, she could imagine. It probably involved her bra size, not her brain.

Enough with the nastiness, Victoria.

She gave Mary Alice a benevolent smile. "I'm sure he's great." And rich.

"He is. He's going to make a fine husband." Mary Alice presented an artificial grin. If she were any more transparent, she'd be invisible. "How long will you be staying? Maybe we could do lunch."

Oh, yeah. Down at the local barbecue joint gnawing on messy ribs with the local debutante. What a nice way to spend a day. "That depends. I could be leaving tomorrow or hanging around for a week or so."

"And what will determine that?"

Tori didn't dare go there, although it was tempting to tell Miss Mary Alice she might be spending her days with the former boyfriend. "If Stella and Bobby need my help settling in, I'll be here a little longer."

"Then you'd be staying out at the Independence Ranch?"

Tori simply couldn't resist getting a rise out of the woman.

"I haven't talked to Mitch about it yet, but I'm sure I'd be more than welcome there."

The smile dropped from Mary Alice's overly painted lips. "You've met Mitch?"

"We met last night at Sadler's. He's been very accommodating." If Mary Alice knew exactly how accommodating, she'd probably fall over in her fake designer heels. "He's a very nice man."

"Yes, he is, if you like that cowboy sort. Frankly, I prefer someone more refined."

As Tori suspected, Mitch had dumped the deb. "Like Brady?"

"Yes, and that reminds me. I should join him now. I'm sure he's wondering where I am."

Tori glanced to her right to find Brady chatting with a roving waitress, not looking at all concerned. She hid her smile when she turned her attention to Mary Alice. "Aren't you going to congratulate the bride and groom?"

"Actually, no. I don't know Stella all that well and I've never cared much for Bobby. I just think it's so sad they had to get married."

Tori saw red, and it wasn't the beer sign in the corner. "Bobby and Stella love each other very much."

Mary Alice flipped her ring-bedecked hand in a dismissive gesture. "I'm sure they do. They're perfect for each other. Down home without a pot to pee in. I hear they can't even afford a real honeymoon."

Tori had the sudden urge to kick off her heels, hike up her dress and take Mary Alice down to the ground for a good hair-pulling cat fight. She'd never done that before, but then she'd never done what she'd done last night, either. Neither would qualify as classy, so she chose to verbally sink in her claws. "Stella and Bobby chose not to go on their honeymoon right away because Mitch needs him on the ranch for now. And speaking of Mitch, I think I'll go find him and ask him if he has room for me. You have a nice night with Brady."

Mary Alice's eyes narrowed into a menacing glare. "Oh, I'm sure Mitch has room for you out in the bunkhouse. He's always kind to the common folk."

With that, she pivoted and headed away, leaving Tori clamoring for some scathing comeback. But wasting energy on the likes of Mary Alice Marshall was futile. She had learned that at a very early age.

Finally, Bobby and Stella were alone, holding each other in a death grip and acting as if no one else existed. Tori hated to interrupt, but she wanted to congratulate them one more time before she grabbed some champagne to bolster her courage before she sought out the senator's son.

When she approached, Stella held out her hand and they hugged each other for a long time. Tori pulled away first and said, "Guess you're an old married woman now."

Stella held up her left hand that now sported a plain white gold band. "Yep, and one of these days, I expect to serve as your maid of honor, as long as you don't make me sing."

Bobby sent Tori a comical grin. "That would clear a room real fast."

Stella smacked him on the arm. "We've been married less than hour, and already you're in trouble." She turned back to Tori. "Speaking of singing, you did a beautiful job."

"She looked damn beautiful doing it, too."

Tori went into freeze mode at the sound of the voice behind her. A deep, provocative voice that generated enough heat to thaw her quickly.

She faced Mitch and murmured, "Thank you."

"So here we are again," he said when Stella and Bobby turned their attentions back to each other.

Obviously, the feline Tori had momentarily become in Mary Alice's presence had its claws in her tongue. Or maybe it was Mitch's smile, his face, his hair, his tuxedo or any myriad aspect of the man that kept her momentarily mute.

"You look nice tonight," she finally managed. "Very debonair. And your lip is barely swollen."

"And you look great in that dress. I told you that when we were walking down the aisle."

Mystery solved. "I guess I didn't hear you. But thanks again."

"I'm also wondering what you have on underneath it."

Tori had definitely heard that, loud and clear. But that was the last thing she heard, because the hired band picked that moment to begin a lively number, making normal conversation impossible, which became evident when Mitch said something else that Tori couldn't begin to understand. "What?" she practically shouted.

He leaned closer to her ear, his warm breath trailing over her jaw. "We need to talk. Alone."

Exactly what Tori had been thinking all night. "Okay. I have something I need to ask you, too. After Stella and Bobby cut the cake. "

Mitch nodded toward the dance floor now containing the bride and groom melded together, cheek to cheek. "That could be a while. I suggest we talk in the meantime."

Tori looked around. "Where?"

"Outside. In the truck."

"Are you sure that's a good idea?"

He gave her a knock-me-out grin. "Inside the truck this time."

This time. A vision of another bout of lovemaking in the cab of Mitch's truck attacked her.

No! No! No!

She could not go there again, even if she dearly wanted to take that trip. This encounter would be about business, and she hoped that after she made her proposal, he wouldn't boot her out of the truck onto her behind. "Okay. But I need to be back soon."

"No problem."

Mitch gestured toward the door and on the way out, picked up two champagne glasses, stuck one in each pocket, and then grabbed an open bottle of bubbly from the startled bartender.

Tori followed Mitch out the door, thinking his charisma mixed with cheap champagne could prove to be a fatal combination. She would only have a small glass, just enough to give her a little bravado.

Once they were settled in the truck—Mitch behind the wheel and Tori crouched in the corner of the cab—he turned on the ignition.

"Are we going somewhere?" she asked.

"No. I just want to turn on the heat before you freeze to death."

Although the temperature was somewhat milder tonight, Tori still shivered when a draft of air from the blower hit her full force.

"It should warm up in a minute," Mitch said as he poured the champagne.

Tori was already heating up from his presence alone. Just watching his hands in action turned her on. Ignoring him would be a lost cause.

After he was finished, he situated the bottle between his thighs, drawing Tori's gaze to the male terrain much more obscure in dress slacks than in jeans. But she remembered how those thighs had felt against hers, the tickle of masculine hair, the tensile muscles, the absolute power.

"Tori, do you want some of this?"

Oh, yeah.

Mortified, Tori tore her gaze from his lap and focused on his chin. Darn him, he didn't even try to hide the fact that he knew what she'd been thinking. That knowledge was etched all over his gorgeous face, sparkling in his eyes, present in his smile that sent the mercury rising in her body despite the chilly interior.

She took the glass he offered and a quick drink of champagne. The bubbles tickled her tongue, but not as strongly as Mitch Warner tickled her feminine fancy.

He held up his glass and said, "To the happy couple. Thank God they actually went through with it."

Tori tipped her glass to his. "Amen."

They sipped in silence until Mitch grimaced and said, "You know, I've hated this stuff since my first glass at sixteen. I've only had it once more in the past ten years."

"Another celebration?"

"The day I graduated from Harvard."

A reminder of exactly who he was and why Tori needed to tell him who she was. First, she would concentrate on congenial conversation. "I would have taken you for a beer drinker."

"I am. But the Warner household didn't serve something as lowly as beer, unless it was a high-dollar import."

The venom in his tone took Tori aback. Obviously he did have somewhat of a temper. She gulped another quick drink, keeping her distance in order to thwart the temptation to smooth the tightness from his clean-shaven jaw.

"I guess I should say I'm sorry about last night," he said after a bout of silence. "But I'm not sorry it happened."

Neither was Tori. "I really can't believe we did it in the bed of a truck."

"All things considered, it was still great."

"Was it?"

His gaze zipped to hers. "You didn't think so?"

She chewed her bottom lip. "I guess on a scale from one to ten, I'd give it an eight." In reality, she'd give it a twenty.

He set his champagne on the dash, tipped his head back against the seat and streaked both hands through his hair. "Only an eight?"

"Well, considering it was rather frigid—"

"I don't think anyone qualified as frigid."

"You know what I mean. We didn't really get undressed, understandably so."

"I thought we did pretty well improvising."

"You could say that."

He lifted his head and aimed his intense blue eyes on her. "I could also say that I didn't notice the cold at all because, lady, you were pretty damned hot last night."

Oh, Lordy. Hot behavior was not normally her forte. But then, Mitch Warner was pretty darned hot himself. She'd spent her life learning to compose words to fit the situation, describe the mood, in this case, the man. "Powerful," came to mind. A sensual, magnetic field. A lean, mean love machine. Not enough adjectives of praise existed to do him justice.

Tori stared at her glass instead of him. "If you say so."

He reached over and tipped her chin up with his thumb, forcing her to look at him again. "I definitely say so." He ran one fingertip over her jaw then down her neck. "And I want to apologize again for being so careless."

"We really don't have to go there, Mitch."

His toxic blue eyes melted her from the inside out. "I want to go there again, Tori. With you. All night."

Before Tori had a chance to prepare, he leaned over and slid his tongue across the seam of her lips. "Champagne tastes pretty damn good on you."

"Mitch, I don't think—"

"Don't think, Tori." He took her glass and placed it next to his on the dash, then shoved the open bottle between his seat and the door. "Thinking is overrated."

Tori was overheated, on the brink of incineration when he took her into his arms and kissed her deeply. The tart taste of wine lingered on his tongue, his slow, steady thrusts displaying his need that matched her own. In spite of her previous goal, she couldn't garner the strength to stop him. Couldn't even consider anything but the softness of his tempting lips, the scent of his tantalizing cologne, the glide of his talented hand over her hip as he pulled her closer.

Breaking the kiss, he murmured, "This velvet feels great."

So did his mouth on her neck, hot and damp as he graced it with soft kisses, working his way to her ear. "I want to take this dress off of you. Then I want to rub it all over your body. And mine."

Tori wanted that too. Boy, did she want that.

And she just might get it, she decided, when he reached for

the back zipper and slid it down. "You mean take it off here? Now?" Her voice sounded unnaturally tinny and shrill.

"Not completely," he whispered. "Only a little. I just want to touch you a little. Then I want to take you to my bed where we can do this right. I want to see you naked." His voice sounded smooth, but his breathing sounded shallow. So was Tori's, what little breath she had left.

Tori lost all her will, all her logic, when he slipped the dress off her right shoulder, exposing the top of her bra. She clung to his head, threading her fingers through his thick, dark hair while he brushed kisses across the rise of her breast, using his tongue to make tempting incursions beneath the red lace. Slowly he inched the fabric down until he revealed her nipple for the wicked workings of his lips. The steady pull of his mouth hurtled heat straight to her thighs where his hand now worked the dress upward. In a matter of minutes, she would completely forget why she'd agreed to this rendezvous if she didn't put an end to this now.

Framing his jaws in her palms, she pulled his head up and gave him a beseeching look. "Mitch, we have to stop before we can't."

He straightened and sighed. "I know."

After redoing her dress, he scooted over to his side of the truck and tipped his forehead against the steering wheel. "You're going to be hard-pressed to believe this, but I don't normally come on that strong. It's you. You make me crazy."

Tori couldn't recall when a man had ever said that to her, but she couldn't let flattery or his sensuality rule her head. And she wondered how crazy he would be once she told him the truth.

He lifted his head and glanced her way again. "Now, what did you want to ask me? Let's make it quick so we can get out of here, get on with the festivities, then get on with some more pleasurable activities."

Damn his confidence. She hadn't even said she was willing to go to bed with him again, even though, if things were different, she certainly would.

The man was sufficiently sucking her mind as dry as an Oklahoma gulch in late summer. For that reason, she focused on the two barely touched glasses of champagne sitting side by side on the dash. "Actually, I have a request. But first, I need to tell you something."

"You have a boyfriend."

"No, that's not it."

"Husband?"

"I'm serious, Mitch."

"I can tell. So if you don't have another lover, what is it?"

"I need something from you." And that sounded totally questionable to Tori. She could only imagine how it had sounded to him.

She knew exactly how it had sounded when he said, "I've already told you I'm ready to give you whatever you need, all night long, this time in a real bed."

Oh, how tempting it would be to tell him to take her away and make good on that promise. But she couldn't. "I'm not referring to sex."

His sigh sounded highly frustrated. "Okay, Tori, you're confusing the hell out of me here. Just spit it out."

She drew in a long breath and released it slowly. "I'm a journalist, and I want your story."

Four

This was the closest Mitch had ever come to being sucker punched by a woman. He sat silent for a few moments to let the revelation sink in. Shock gave way to anger and the bitter taste of betrayal overrode the sweet taste of Tori still lingering on his lips.

He risked a look to find her studying her joined hands. "Why the hell didn't you tell me this last night?"

She lifted one shoulder in a shrug, the same shoulder he'd kissed only moments before. "I was going to say something when we were at Stella's, but when you made the comment about the press rifling in your glove box, I just lost my nerve. Later, I, uh, had other things on mind."

She'd had her hands all over his body. He didn't need to remember how great last night had been, or how much he had hoped for a repeat performance tonight. He needed to hang on to his anger. For all intents and purposes, she was the enemy.

"I'm not your enemy, Mitch," she said as if she'd read his mind.

"I've never found one friend among the media."

"Not every journalist buys into sensationalism. Some of us are responsible."

He shot her a hard look. "I have a difficult time believing that, especially since you didn't bother to let me in on your little secret."

She touched his arm then drew back, like she'd forgotten herself. "If you'll just listen for a minute, I'll explain why I think it will be to your advantage to let me do an interview."

Under normal circumstances, Mitch would admire her persistence. But nothing about their relationship so far had been even remotely normal. Not their initial meeting. Not their sexual beginning. Not his undeniable attraction to her that still lived on even after what he now knew. "There's nothing advantageous about spilling your guts. I value my privacy. I've worked damn hard to escape the attention. No need to stir it up again."

"It's going to get stirred up since your father's probably about to announce his retirement."

"I don't give a damn about politics."

"Then you might consider stating your position now rather than let the speculation start to fly. Define your aspirations before someone does it for you. I'm willing to help you."

He ran a hand over his face and stared straight ahead. Some of what she'd said made sense, but he wasn't into logic right now. "You have no idea what it's like to have every detail of your life exposed so everyone can take a jab."

"Actually, I do."

The hint of pain in her voice brought Mitch's attention back to her. "How so?"

"It doesn't matter."

It did to him, even though it probably shouldn't. "Hey, if you expect me to open up to you, it's only fair you do the same."

"This isn't about me. This is about an opportunity you shouldn't pass up."

"I don't want my life plastered all over some newspaper."

"It's not a newspaper. I work for a Dallas women's magazine. We feature stories about successful men in Texas."

"I don't live in Texas, in case you haven't noticed." He couldn't control his sarcasm, yet it didn't seem to dissuade Tori.

"But you're from a prominent Texas political dynasty, so that counts. I'm proposing a story that focuses on your life as a rancher, not as a politician's son. If you don't intend to follow in your father's footsteps, then this is the perfect venue to let that be known."

"And what's in it for you?"

"Well, honestly, it would mean more visibility for me. Possibly a promotion."

The anger came back with the realization he'd been set up by a woman who'd incited his total loss of control and moved him more than any woman he had known. "You had this planned the minute you stepped into town, didn't you? Pretty damned convenient to have Stella and Bob's wedding as a front."

She looked on the verge of getting mad, and he wanted her that way. He wanted her as mad as he was at the moment. Mad over the deception. Mad because this wasn't the way tonight was supposed to end. "For your information," she said, "it didn't occur to me to ask for the interview until you stepped into the bar last night."

Irrational anger overwhelmed his usual common sense. "So was that what our little interlude was all about, sex for a story?"

First, she looked as if she'd been slugged, then her brown eyes flashed fury. "I'm not even going to justify that with an answer." She grabbed the door handle. "Forget about it. I'm sorry I asked. I'm sorry about everything."

Damn, he wasn't being at all fair. She didn't deserve this much animosity. And in reality, he didn't want her to leave. "Wait."

She hesitated, the door partially ajar. "Why? So you can rake me over the coals some more because of my chosen profession?"

"No. So I can apologize."

"Apology accepted."

"Good. Now close the door."

"Why?"

"Because I need more details about what you're proposing."

She looked hopeful and sweeter than she had a right to be. "Then you'll actually consider it?"

"I'm willing to listen."

After closing the door, she settled back into the corner of the seat. "First, I'd follow you around for a week, focusing on Mitch Warner, the rancher, and his life. It's also an opportune time to reveal a lighter side of your personality. For example, what you do in your spare time. Your favorite activities. What you admire most in a woman."

"Honesty."

Again, she looked as if she'd been slapped. Why the hell couldn't he control his mouth where she was concerned? "I guess I deserve that," she said. "But I promise I'll be honest with you from now on. In fact, I'd be willing to let you see the final draft. You can approve or disapprove any of the content before it's put to bed."

Speaking of bed.... Even though he didn't like that she'd hidden the truth about her questionable occupation, Mitch was still commanded by their chemistry, and he didn't see any end to it anytime soon. Especially if she spent a solid week in his world. "What about us?"

"What about us?"

"This thing between us."

She sighed. "Our relationship would have to be strictly professional from this point forward."

"And this is supposed to sell me on the idea?"

She hinted at a smile. "Whatever's existed between us on a personal level until now will have to be ignored."

He'd bet his back forty acres she couldn't ignore it any more than he could, and he intended to put her to the test. Scooting across the seat, he cupped her chin, running his thumb over her lower lip. "You really think that's possible?"

"Sure." She didn't sound at all convinced.

He trailed his fingertip down her throat and outlined the scoop neck of her dress, following the path where his mouth had been only a few minutes before. "Just like that, you're going to turn it off?"

"Yes."

When he palmed her breast, this time through the fabric, she released a ragged breath. "Are you sure about that?" he asked.

"Positive."

"Your nipple's hard."

"It's cold."

"You're lying again."

She pulled his hand away and rested it in his lap. "I'm a lot stronger than you think. If you'll let me do this story, I'll prove it to you."

For the second time, Mitch collapsed against the seat and stared at the truck's faded headliner. "I'll have to think about."

"Fine. My plane leaves from Oklahoma City at noon. That means I'll need to leave Stella's tomorrow by 9 a.m. If you're not there, then I'll take that as a no and head back to Dallas. We'll forget any of this ever happened."

Regardless of whether he decided to do the interview, he would never forget what had happened between them last night. What had almost happened again tonight. He would never forget her. "Okay. Agreed."

She nodded toward the bar. "We need to go back inside. I'm sure they're wondering where we are."

"Suit yourself."

She frowned. "Aren't you coming in?"

"No. I'm going to say here for a while. I need to calm down."

She pinched the bridge of her nose as if she had one helluva headache. "I'm sorry I made you so angry. I never intended to do that."

"Anger isn't my problem at the moment."

She sent a pointed look at his lap, which didn't help matters at all. Even with the loose fit of the slacks, his problem was more than evident.

"Oh," she muttered then glanced away.

"Oh, yeah."

"I'm sorry about that, too."

Mitch was only sorry he couldn't do anything about it, at least not with her tonight. But maybe later. If he agreed to her request.

He had a lot to consider tonight, not only her current proposal but also the fact that he was hard as hell just thinking about what they could be doing in his bed. He'd just have to decide if having her around for a week would be worth it.

Who was he trying to fool? Damn straight it would be worth it.

When he didn't speak, she opened the truck and slid out. "I really hope I see you in the morning."

He really hoped that if he did decide to do it, he wouldn't be making a major mistake.

Tori's hope began to fade when she glanced at her watch. Half past nine, and no Mitch. She'd already mopped the kitchen floor twice in order to ready Stella's rental house for the next tenants. In fact, the family could probably eat off the vinyl tiles. And worse, she was ruining her good black slacks and favorite white crepe de chine blouse. She should have changed into something more casual but she'd wanted to save her one pair of jeans for later, in case Mitch decided to take her up on her offer. That obviously was not going to happen. Stalling for time wasn't going to make Mitch Warner magically materialize.

Last night, she'd seen him only briefly back at the bar after their tense encounter in his truck. He'd stayed long enough to toast the couple and then headed away with only a quick goodbye. He hadn't witnessed the cake-cutting, the garter toss or Tori miraculously catching the bouquet. Of course, if she hadn't made the grab, the cascading flowers would have hit her dead in the face. No doubt, the whole thing had been rigged by the bride.

And most likely, those final few moments in Mitch's presence would be her last, at least for a while. She didn't plan to return to Quail Run until after the birth of Stella's baby. She could manage that visit in a day and never even have to run into him, if she was unlucky.

Resting her palms on the top of the mop handle, Tori muttered, "Stubborn man. Stubborn, sexy man." Not only would she have to return to work without the story of the decade, she would also have to face her boss with the news that she hadn't been successful. She should've asked Mitch first before she'd called Renee yesterday morning about the possibilities. Oh, well. The plan had been a good one, even if it hadn't come to fruition.

"Time to go, Cinderella. Looks like Prince Charming isn't going to show. If we don't hurry, you'll miss your plane."

Tori looked up to see Stella standing in the hall, holding Tori's battered black duffel against her chest. She propped the mop by the back door and frowned. "You don't need to be lifting anything, Stella."

"You sound just like Bobby." She held out the bag. "Here."

Tori took the duffel and headed toward the door. She turned and scanned the house one more time, proud that she'd accomplished so much with so little sleep. The sounds of Bobby's and Stella's official consummation the night before hadn't plagued her as much as thoughts of Mitch. She doubted those would dissipate any time in the near future, even after she was back to business as usual.

Tori opened the screen and stepped out into the sunshine— then nearly fell off the porch. Leaning against his truck, Mitch Warner looked as gorgeous in the daylight as he did deep in the night. Funny, she hadn't even considered that she'd never seen him during the day. And she sure as heck hadn't considered he would actually show up considering the time. She would forgive him his tardiness. Forgive him just about anything. How could she not pardon a man in faded denim and blue flannel that matched his eyes, his arms folded over his broad chest and his long legs crossed at the ankles stretched out before him? How could she ever forget the picture he now presented? Picture. Darn, her camera was in the front seat of the car. Otherwise she might take a shot or two as a souvenir. Probably not a great idea since he wasn't exactly smiling.

When he didn't bother to move or speak, Tori strolled to Stella's car and slid her bag into the open trunk on the off chance that his sudden appearance involved a friendly visit, not a business proposition. If he had decided to nix her offer, she would be gracious. She didn't feel the need to hold anything against him—except maybe her body.

Cut it out, Tori.

If he did happen to agree to her proposal, from now on she couldn't afford to entertain any lascivious thoughts about Mitch Warner. Or at least she couldn't be obvious about it.

After Tori straightened her shoulders and closed the trunk, she turned to face Mitch. "Good morning, Mr. Warner."

He pushed off the truck and approached her slowly. "Sorry I'm late. I'm running behind this morning."

Tori's heart was running at full speed. "That's okay. Cleanup took longer than we thought." After waiting for confirmation, Tori glanced over her shoulder to find Stella had disappeared back into the house, evident by the slamming of the screen door. Some friend.

When she brought her attention back to Mitch, she noticed he'd moved closer. She also noticed that his eyes looked tired. Translucent blue, but tired. He also had a day's worth of dark beard blanketing his jaw and surrounding his lips. That would mean some heavy-duty whisker burn if she kissed him. However, she was not going to do that again, even if the temptation was stronger than the morning sun.

Tori shifted her weight and tried to relax her frame, a futile attempt at a nonchalant façade. "So what brings you here this morning?"

"You know why I'm here."

She was still too afraid to hope. "Breakfast? I have a whole-grain bar in my overnight bag."

"Are you determined to change my mind about this whole thing?"

"That depends on which way it would change. Are we going to do it?"

He grinned then, revealing dazzling white teeth accentuating his dazzling smile. "Sure. Stella's car or my truck?"

"I meant the interview."

"Too bad."

"So?"

"What do you think?"

She thought she would die on the spot from the suspense. "I don't know what to think."

He rubbed a hand over the back of his neck. "Yeah, I'll do it."

Tori kept her feet firmly fixed to keep from flinging herself into his arms. "Great. You won't regret it."

"I'm going to hold you to that."

She'd settle for him holding her. "Okay. We're agreed."

"First, I have a few ground rules I expect you to follow."

She suspected as much. "Okay."

"I don't want to answer a lot of really personal questions."

She certainly didn't intend to reveal that their first up close and personal encounter happened in the back of a truck. "Fine. I'll avoid the boxers or briefs query." She already knew the answer to that one anyway—briefs.

"And I don't want to talk about my father."

That could put a severe kink in her plans. "Mitch, we're going to have to talk about him in terms of your insistence you're not going to assume his role in politics."

"You can mention that briefly, but I don't want to talk about why we haven't spoken more than three times in fourteen years."

"Only three times?" Tori couldn't suppress the shock in her tone.

"Yeah, and that's all I'm going to say about that."

The media had speculated that father and son didn't get

along, but Tori had no idea the rift in their relationship was this acute. She made a mental note to handle that situation with fine-crystal care. "Anything else?"

He leaned forward and positioned one hand on the truck near her hip, the other in his back pocket. "Yeah. We reconsider the hands-off clause."

With him so close, Tori considered taking him up on the offer. That wasn't at all advisable. "It's necessary that we maintain a professional relationship while I'm interviewing you. Otherwise, I might lose my objectivity."

"You might gain a little more insight on my likes and dislikes, at least between the sheets."

"I don't plan to go between your sheets."

"You'd like my sheets."

"Behave yourself or *I'm* going to reconsider."

With a push of his palm, he took away his body, but not the heat that had worked its way beneath Tori's skin, as he had from the first time she'd seen him saunter into the bar like a cowboy king. "If I have to behave, I will."

She didn't believe that for a minute. "Good. Now if you'll give me an hour or so, I'll settle into the motel and then I'll have Stella give me a ride to the ranch."

"That's not going to work."

"Okay, less than an hour. I just want to change into some jeans."

His gaze raked down her, slowly, and back up again. "You look fine to me, but I meant you staying at the Quail Creek Inn. That won't work. It's a seedy place."

"Unfortunately, it's all that's available."

"You could stay in the main house." He hooked his thumbs in his pockets. "It's big enough."

Not big enough to avoid him, Tori decided. "I don't think that's a great idea."

Tori hadn't noticed Stella's reappearance until she said, "You could stay with me and Bobby."

Tori regarded her friend standing by the car's fender. "I

couldn't do that, Stella. You and Bobby are practically on your honeymoon."

Stella engaged in a little eye-rolling. "Bobby and I have been on our honeymoon for months, and if I recall, you were in the house last night."

Yes, attempting to sleep to the sounds of Stella and Bobby doing the horizontal cha-cha. "Do you have a spare room?"

"Three bedrooms but only one bath," Mitch said. "It's the original house."

"We'll manage fine," Stella said. "In fact, I'd love to have you for a little longer, Victoria. Since I've quit work, I could use the company."

Mitch sent a less-than-friendly look at Stella. "My place would be much more comfortable."

Not for Tori. Mitch Warner was the definition of temptation. Even if he slept in a galvanized steel chastity belt instead of pajamas, she could probably pick the lock with her teeth to get to him in a fit of adrenaline brought about by uncontrolled desire. She didn't trust him to keep his distance. More important, she didn't trust herself around him, especially at night.

"So what's it going to be, Tori?" he asked. "My place or Stella's?"

"Yeah, Tori," Stella said. "Which one?"

Tori felt as if she'd been thrust into an accommodation war. However, she did see certain advantages to being on Mitch's property. Rental cars were non-existent in town and she'd have to rely on Stella to cart her back and forth to the ranch every day if she stayed in the motel. That would definitely get old very quickly.

"I'll stay with Stella and Bobby."

"Then it's settled," Stella said and opened the driver's door. "Let's go. I want to be there when Bobby comes in for lunch. You can help me do a little unpacking."

Great. Tori wouldn't be a bit surprised if she was left holding a box while Bobby and Stella grabbed a nooner, just liked they'd grabbed a dawner while she'd been slaving over the floors.

When Tori rounded the car, Mitch followed her to the door. But before she could open it, he stopped her progress with a palm on the window. "If you get tired of listening to the Stella and Bobby show, come on up to my house and stay with me. I won't bother you. Much."

An hour later, she emerged from Stella's faded green sedan wearing second-skin jeans and a tight-fitting sweater—a brown-eyed angel with a she-devil body that could drive a man to his knees in worship. Mitch just might have to do that in the next few days.

Maybe Tori wasn't open to taking up where they'd left off, but that wouldn't stop Mitch from trying. Of course, she would have to be willing, otherwise it might seem that he was trading sex for a story, and he wasn't that low. But he wasn't above trying a little subtle persuasion to change her mind.

Standing on the old home place porch, Stella passed by him and said, "I'll be inside. When she gets off the phone, come on in and make yourself at home."

He turned his attention to Tori who was now conversing on a cell phone. When she laughed and tossed her hair back from one shoulder, Mitch couldn't quell the sudden jealousy. Maybe she did have a boyfriend back in Dallas. After all, she'd lied to him about her job. Okay, she hadn't exactly lied, but she had withheld the truth, at least until last night.

But if he looked at it logically, she could've led him on a merry chase, gathering information under the pretense of an extended visit, only to hightail it out of Quail Run to write a story and he wouldn't have been the wiser until it came out in print. Instead, she'd opted to be up front and honest about her plans, and he had to respect that. He wasn't quite ready to trust her, though. Not until he knew for certain she wasn't bent on making a buck on a bunch of falsehoods.

After Tori finished her conversation and opened the trunk, Mitch approached and took the suitcase from her. "Calling for backup?" he asked.

Even her frown was damn pretty in the daylight. "Calling my boss. I had to let her know I'd be staying for a week."

"She didn't have a problem with that?"

"Not when she considers what I have to gain."

Tori had no idea what she could gain if she would only say yes to him. And sure as the sun set she would say it before she left.

He set the case on the porch. "I'll leave this here for now. I want you to come up and meet my granddad."

"I've met him. I used to live here, remember?"

"Then I'm sure he'd like to see you again."

"Is that the only reason you want me in your house?"

He grinned when he noticed her blush. "What other reason would I have?"

She folded her arms beneath her breasts. "I could think of a few. I guess I'm having a little trouble trusting you."

"Guess that makes two of us."

"Good point."

He held out his hand to her, which she failed to take. He could live with that reluctance, for now. "Come on up. I'll only occupy you for a few minutes." Or longer, if she was willing.

"Okay. For a while."

At least she walked fairly close to him as they traveled up the path while he explained they owned almost three thousand acres, land that had been in his mother's family for over five generations, purchased when Oklahoma was still a territory. The conversation was so dry that by the time Mitch reached the front porch, he realized he'd missed his calling as a history professor.

"Nice house," Tori commented when he pushed open the pine door. "And very large."

"I had the Austin stone shipped from Texas, but basically it's pretty simple."

When they entered the great room, Tori looked around, her eyes wide as she honed in on the massive rock fireplace. "This is simple? The ceilings are what, twenty feet?"

"Twenty-four, and that makes the room look bigger."

She ran her hand over the brushed suede sofa. "This feels really nice."

"Kind of like the velvet last night, huh?" Mitch just couldn't help himself when he thought about her running her hand over him in the same way. He imagined taking her to that sofa and getting inside her again. He hadn't initiated that couch yet, but he just might real soon.

Or maybe not, he decided when he noticed the acid look Tori sent him over one shoulder. She turned and faced him with a strained smile. "Where's your grandfather?"

Truth be known, Mitch had no clue where Buck had gone. His '56 Chevy truck was nowhere in sight. "Guess he stepped out for a minute. I'm sure he'll be back soon. Not many places for a seventy-six-year-old widower to go in town."

Her eyes narrowed with suspicion. "Did you know he had left before you brought me up here?"

"I didn't notice his truck was gone until we got on the porch."

She sent him a skeptical look. "Are you sure?"

Man, this mutual mistrust thing wasn't going to bode well for the interview, or Mitch's plans to make love to her again. "Look, let's just get this out on the table right now. I won't question your motives, if you won't question mine."

He offered his hand again and this time she actually accepted it for a shake. "Deal."

But in that moment, neither one of them made a move to part. Mitch couldn't resist running his thumb along the smooth skin on her palm, couldn't resist hanging on a little bit longer. Obviously Tori could. She tugged away and slipped both hands into the back pockets of her jeans. He'd give a month's wages to be her hands about now.

"Anything else you want to show me?" she asked.

His grin made an appearance in spite of his effort to stop it. "You know, you might want to quit asking those kinds of questions. That would make it a lot easier for me to behave."

Her sultry smile nearly knocked the wind out of him. "My questions are innocent. I can't help it if your thoughts aren't."

"Your questions contain a lot of double entendre."

"Entendre? Now there's a word you rarely hear coming out of a cowboy's mouth."

If she only knew what other words were running around in his brain, she'd be out the door in a matter of seconds. "I know a few more. Want to hear them?"

"Would that be ranch lingo or the articulation of a Harvard grad?"

"Just simple words for a simple man." He saw more than mild curiosity in her eyes. He also saw his chance and moved a little closer. "Take sexy, for instance. That would describe you in that sweater."

A trace of self-consciousness flickered in her brown eyes. "It's blue, basic, just like me."

"How about beautiful? There's nothing basic about your beauty, Tori. It's real. Appealing. Do you want more words?"

"Why not? You're obviously on a roll."

Another kind of roll came to mind. He reached out and snagged her belt loop to pull her against him. "Tempting. That's another I don't toss around that often, but that also describes you."

"Mitch—"

He stopped her protests with a fingertip against her lips. "Dangerous. You're dangerous, Tori, in the worst kind of way, because you don't realize your power. You're deadly to a man's control."

She pulled his hand from her mouth and held it against his chest. "I could say the same thing about you and your power over women."

"That's where you're wrong. I'm not that strong, at least not around you. And you know something? I don't even begin to understand it." With his left palm, he reached down and nudged her hip until not even a scrap of air separated them. "No woman has ever done this to me so easily."

Her breath caught and her pupils flared. "Mitch, we said we wouldn't."

He ran his hand over her bottom before traveling up to the small of her back. "You said it, not me."

She wet her lips, a subtle sign of encouragement in Mitch's opinion. "What do you really want from me, Mitch Warner?"

"I want to kiss you, but only if you say yes."

He saw the hesitation in her eyes, the questions, immediately before he saw her give in and heard her whisper, "Yes."

He bent his head and brushed a kiss over one cheek, then the other, savoring the moment before he reached his ultimate goal....

"Why, looky what my grandson brung me for my birthday."

Mitch dropped his hands and hissed out an angry breath.

He'd be damned if Buck Littleton didn't have timing as bad as Bobby Lehman.

Five

Mitch's grandfather had good timing, or at least Tori assumed the pencil-thin man with the shaggy silver hair, handlebar moustache and battered straw hat was his grandfather. A long time had passed since she'd seen him and even back then, she hadn't seen him too often. He had definitely aged, but then so had they all.

Mitch stepped to her side and said, "Buck, this is Tori Barnett. She used to live in Quail Run."

Buck snatched his hat from his head and nodded. "Your mama was Cindy Barnett, Calvin Barnett's daughter, right?"

Tori managed a smile in light of her discomfort. "That's right. My granddad used to run the gas station." She wondered if Mitch had caught the fact that she had the same name as her maternal grandfather, a sure indication that her mother had never married her father.

Buck rubbed his stubbled chin. "Your mama used to do some sewing now and then for my Sally." He winked at Mitch. "Your grandma was like a race car driver on a sewing machine. She couldn't get the seams straight."

Tori was propelled back into her past by an old man's recollections. A past that had included hand-to-mouth and hard times. But her only parent had done the best that she could under the circumstances. "My mother was a very good seamstress. The best in the county."

"Last I heard, you were off to college," Buck said. "Are you back for good?"

"No. I live and work in Dallas now."

"And your mama?" he asked. "How is she faring these days?"

"She had a stroke and passed away a little over a year ago."

Buck crimped his hat in his fists. "I'm mighty sorry to hear that. She was a real good woman, as I recall."

"Yes, she was."

Mitch cleared his throat as if uncomfortable over the course of the conversation. "Tori's here to do a story on me for a magazine, Buck."

Buck's mouth opened, then snapped shut. "Well, I'll be damned. I don't know how you convinced him to do that, Tori, but it's not for me to question."

"Good." Mitch turned to Tori. "Come with me and we can get started."

Tori didn't dare ask what he wanted to start, or possibly finish. She would just follow Mitch, remind him of the rules and then silently scold herself for being proverbial putty in his presence. If she didn't grow a solid backbone soon, she'd be on her back in record time.

"Well, it was nice talking to you again, Mr. Littleton. Maybe we can have a conversation about yours and Mitch's relationship. Readers would love to know about your influence on his life."

Buck chuckled. "That's easy. I taught him how to drink beer and rope a calf and romance a woman. And if he gets out of hand, you let me know. I'll put him in his place."

Mitch took her by the elbow. "Let's go, Tori, before he starts telling more wild tales."

"Oh, and happy birthday, Buck," she tossed over one shoulder as Mitch guided her toward the adjacent hallway.

"His birthday is four months away," Mitch said as the sound of Buck's laughter followed them all the way down the corridor.

Tori counted the number of rooms, three to be exact, on the way to an unknown destination. Two were sparsely furnished, one was a bath, and all were oversized. At the end of the hall, they entered a comfortable room containing a small fireplace, battered plaid furniture, a cluttered desk complete with a computer and rows of bookshelves.

"I hang out here in the evenings," Mitch said as he closed the door behind them. "Most everything in here I've had for a lot of years."

Although she had a bad case of the nerves from being alone with him, Tori felt as if she'd discovered a treasure trove. A person could tell a lot about a man by what he kept in his private domain.

When he remained at the door, staring at her expectantly, she turned toward the shelves, grasping for something to focus on other than him. If not, she ran the risk of repeating what had almost happened before Buck's interruption. Right now, she had to concentrate on the business at hand—his interview.

"Very interesting assortment of books," she said as she perused the collection.

"I have eclectic taste."

Eclectic. Another glimpse of the Ivy League boy. Man, she corrected. Very much a man. "I can see that."

She tracked a visual path from the top shelf that held numerous Louis L'Amour books to the one below where she found several business digests. But the volume of poetry caught her immediate attention.

Tori looked back to find Mitch had taken a seat on the sofa, his tanned arm thrown casually over the back, one leg crossed over the other as if he planned to stay a while. She held up the book. "Is this a leftover from college?"

"Is there some reason why I wouldn't like a little poetry?"

Keeping her back to him, she flipped through the pages. "It

just doesn't fit your persona. I'm betting you've kept it to impress the girls."

"You're wrong."

She turned and leaned back against the shelves, the book clutched to her chest. "Prove it. Name one poem—"

"'Twice or thrice I have loved thee, before I knew thy face or name. So in a voice, so in a shapeless flame. Angels affect us oft, and worshipped be.' John Donne. From *Air and Angels*."

Tori couldn't find her voice, couldn't find the strength to look away from his intense gaze. For the first time in a long time, she'd been stricken speechless.

He smiled, but only halfway. "Proof enough?"

"You could say that." She turned and replaced the book before facing him again. "You are certainly full of surprises, Mr. Warner. I'm very impressed."

"Haven't you heard someone recite poetry before?"

Not a to-die-for enigmatic man with a voice so strong, so resolute, so masculine that the verse had sounded like an invitation to seduction.

"My mother was a sucker for *The Itsy Bitsy Spider*. Does that count?"

He unfolded from the sofa and approached her slowly. "This was one of my mother's favorites."

Tori did well not to gasp when he brushed her arm as he reached around her. She took the weathered book he offered, *The Little Engine That Could*, opening it to the first page, yellowed from time yet holding a message that would probably never fade.

My dear baby boy. Happy first birthday! Never let anyone tell you that you can't.—Love, Mama.

"She read that to me every night until I turned eight and decided I was too grown up to hear it again," he said, a trace of sadness in his tone. "She was a large part of my success."

A mix of emotions ran through Tori. She was flattered he had shown her something so special, and somewhat confused as to why he had. Touched by the fact that he'd kept the book all these years, and saddened by the reminder of her own mother. "My mom contributed to my success, too. She was always there when I needed her."

"I still miss mine and it's been almost fifteen years since her death."

Tori recognized that was his reason for sharing, to let her know that he could relate to her loss, her pain. A connection. Common ground. What a totally thoughtful thing to do. If not careful, she was going to take a plunge and land totally in love with this man.

"What about your father?" he asked quietly.

Tori shifted her weight from one foot to the other. "He's not in my life. Good riddance, as far as I'm concerned."

"I'm sorry."

"I'm not. My mother handled both roles very well." Tori handed him the book and sent him a shaky smile. "Life goes on, and so should this interview."

He slid the book back into place. "So when do we start the process?"

"Actually, we already have."

He frowned. "Aren't you going to take some notes?"

She tapped one finger against her temple. "Right now, I'm relying on this. Later, I will use a recorder when we get into detailed specifics and quotes."

"About the ranching business?"

"Yes, and that's next. But it's nice to know a little more about the man beneath the façade now that I've seen your choice in books."

He kept his gaze trained on her eyes. "You really think you know me by my taste in literature?"

"I know that you like westerns and probably fantasized about being a cowboy from a very early age. I know that beneath the tough guy exterior you have a poet's soul and a great love for your mother. I learned all of that in about ten minutes, tops."

"There's a lot you don't know about me, Tori." His tone sounded serious and edgy.

"I'm sure there is. And when I leave here, I still won't know everything about you. But I will know enough to do a fantastic story." She would also know the incredible high of making love with him, if only one wonderful time.

He propped one hand against the shelf above her head and leaned toward her. His expression went from solemn to seductive. "What about you, Tori? When are you going to tell me a little more about what you like?"

Considering the grainy quality of his voice, Tori decided he might as well have added "in bed" to the end of the query. His blue eyes had enough power to light an entire metropolis, enough to make Tori forget once more why she was there.

Ducking under his arm, she played nosy reporter and assessed the mess on his desk. "Let's talk about your business now."

"You're being evasive."

She turned and used the desk for support. "I'm being a journalist. Journalists interview subjects, and you are the subject, not me."

He moved in front of her, this time keeping a comfortable distance, but not far enough away to alleviate Tori's discomfort. "One of these days, I'm going to make you talk more about yourself."

"Are you going to tie me up and threaten to brand me?"

He rubbed his chin, looking thoughtful. "Hadn't thought about tying you up, but that might be interesting."

"Cut it out, Mitch, or I'll go get your grandfather to put you in your place."

"Speaking of places, I have one special place I need to show you."

"That wouldn't be down the hall, would it?"

His grin made another showboat appearance. "If you want to see *that* particular place, I'll be glad to show you any time. You just say the word."

Oh, but she wanted to say it. She wanted to find his bed and stay there with him the rest of the day and well into the night. "Thanks for the offer, but I don't think so. Now exactly where are we going?"

"Somewhere that involves both business and sex."

* * *

"We call this the Happy Place. It's where we collect semen from the bulls."

Mitch expected Tori to be somewhat shocked, as Mary Alice had been when he'd shown her the sterile room situated in the main barn. He figured the reporter might as well become accustomed to every aspect of his business, even the less than pleasant ones. But she didn't seem at all bothered by this particular setting.

Instead, she turned to him and asked, "Do you practice artificial insemination on your own herd or do you ship frozen semen? My guess is that you do both."

Mitch was more than a little bowled over by her query. "How do you know about livestock AI?"

She shrugged. "I worked part-time for a horse breeder during college. He taught me how to collect from his stallion. I can't say that it thrilled me exactly, but I learned a lot, the most important lesson being to hang on to the lead rope when you've got a stud who's hot after a teasing mare."

If Mitch had less presence of mind, his mouth would've hit the ground. "He got away?"

"Almost, but I caught him before he mounted the mare instead of the dummy. That would have been a disaster, since she was a Welsh pony and he was a seventeen-hand thoroughbred. He might have hurt her."

Even though Mitch was used to the breeding terminology, even though he'd seen both horses and bulls collected for the process of artificial insemination, it seemed kind of odd coming out of Tori's mouth, a woman with a face as innocent as they come. And considering his recent questionable state of mind, he didn't need to hear her say words like "mount" and "hot" and "teasing" either.

He swiped a hand over the back of his neck. "Guess I don't need to go into great detail about what happens then."

"No, you don't."

"Okay, then come with me back here."

He showed her to his business office, the oak paneled walls containing only his framed diploma, his desk clear of any signs of chaos, the way that he liked his life. He suspected Tori was somewhat surprised by his organization considering the demolition mess in the den.

"This is quite different from your home office," she said, confirming his suspicions.

"That's my private study I showed you earlier," he said. "Buck's in there a lot and he's not real neat. He likes to use that computer to play games and wander into a chat room now and then."

"It's nice that the Internet provides a place for senior citizens to go."

"Yeah, but he doesn't go there. He likes to hang out with the 30-something crowd. He says the old fogies are boring."

She laughed, a soft musical sound that brought back Mitch's reminiscence of the first time he'd heard her laugh. The first time he'd heard her sing. The first time—and the last time— they had made love.

Once more, his body reminded him that it only took a thought or two to propel him back into lust mode. But he was quickly realizing that with Tori Barnett, the lust was secondary to the fact that he really liked her, probably a lot more than he should. After all, she would only be here for a few more days and then they'd both go back to pursuing their careers instead of mutual pleasure. Unfortunately, she hadn't agreed to exploring that pleasure thing again—yet.

Tori slid her fingertips back and forth over the edge of the desk, causing Mitch to look away for the sake of his sanity. "You obviously have a good program going on here," she said.

That wasn't all he had going on. "Yeah. We raise a few Red Angus, the last of Buck's herd. We have two top-grade bulls and about fifty heifers for breeding."

"That's all?"

"Yeah."

"And you make a living on that?"

He bypassed her and slipped behind his desk to retrieve a business card. "Here," he said as he slid it forward.

Tori studied the card for a few minutes before raising her eyes to his. "This says L and W Consulting. What kind of consulting?"

"Cattle consulting. I've developed several methods that ensure quality stock. I employ a few men and women who go out in the field to present workshops to various ranchers all over the country. We teach them how to get the most out of their breeding programs. We also distribute instructional software and videos that I helped develop with Rand Wilson."

"Rand?"

"He's one of my ranch hands, but he's also a computer wiz."

"I assume you do this to supplement the ranch income."

"It isn't a sideline; it's a very lucrative business. I've made enough money to retire at least twice and live in Maui. I needed to put my business degree to good use. Of course, there are a few young ranchers who need a hand in getting started. I usually provide my services for free to them."

"You're an enigma," Tori said. "A true renaissance cowboy."

"I'm driven. I always have been."

And she was driving him crazy every time she looked at him, not to mention every time she nibbled on her bottom lip. What the hell was wrong with him? Could he not spend more than fifteen minutes in her presence without wanting to crawl all over her? Hell, a thirty-three-year-old man shouldn't be this wildly out of control over a woman he barely knew, even if at times he felt as if he'd known her a lot longer than three days. That was nuts.

She strolled to the small window facing the back paddock. "Well, I see a horse out there. I suppose that means you still work cattle the old-fashioned way."

Mitch walked up behind her, keeping his hands fisted so he wouldn't touch her. He needed to take this slowly from now on, otherwise she might keep running away. He didn't want her to run away. He didn't want her going anywhere in the near future except maybe into his arms again.

"That's my gelding, Ray. Buck gave him to me for my seventeenth birthday. He's on up in years, but he still has a few miles left. One of these days, I'm going to have to retire him."

"He looks like he's in great shape."

So was she, Mitch decided as he took a visual tour down her back and over her butt. She had a great body, and he had a building pressure below his belt buckle in response.

Mitch hadn't realized how close he had moved to her until Tori turned and practically ran into his chest. Deciding to give her a little space and a reason to trust him, he took a step back.

She crossed her arms over her breasts as if trying shield herself from him. "Okay, you have a successful business and a wonderful house that's probably at least four bedrooms."

"And four baths."

"You must be planning to have a large family with lots of kids."

"That has never been in my plans."

"Why?"

This was a subject he didn't really care to broach, but he needed to be honest with her now. "Because I've never put much stock in marriage."

"Your parents were happily married for quite a while, as I recall."

"Before my father…" *Whoa, Mitch.* He was getting a little carried away with his open book bit.

Her gaze didn't waver. "Before your father did what?"

Betrayed his entire family by not sticking around when he was needed most. "I don't want to talk about that."

She sighed. "I'm sorry. I didn't mean to intrude since that subject is apparently very painful for you."

Damn. She could see right through him. No one had been able to do that before, especially not a woman. But Tori was an extraordinary woman and too intuitive for Mitch's own good. "I'm over it."

"But you can't forget it, can you?"

"Tori," he said in a warning voice.

"I know. I know. Nothing too personal." She grabbed a lock of her hair and began twisting it into a spiral. "So what shall we see next?"

If Mitch had his way, he'd show her his bedroom and release all his frustration, his latent anger, in one long, hard session of lovemaking. "You need to go back to Stella's to settle in and I need to do some work."

"Can I watch for a while?"

"No. If you're in here, I won't be able to concentrate."

"I'll try to be really quiet."

And he'd be trying to silence her with his mouth. "You don't have to say anything to distract me, Tori. You only have to stand there, looking pretty."

"I'll definitely make a note of your penchant for flattery."

She had no clue about her beauty, and Mitch found that very engaging. "I don't throw out compliments that often, so accept it graciously and go visit with Stella for a while. I'll see you later."

She stuck out her lip in a pretend pout. "Okay. I guess I need to get my camera loaded anyway."

"Camera?"

"Yes, I brought it for the wedding, then promptly left it at Stella's house without taking a single picture. I have plenty of film left and that's where you'll come in."

Hell, he didn't like the sound of that. "You plan to take pictures of me?"

"Sure. A few candid shots of you and the ranch. And if you're concerned, I've taken tons of photography classes. I'm fairly good at it."

"I have no doubt about that." He had no doubt she was good at everything she endeavored.

"Normally I'd have a staff photographer come and do it, but I assumed you wouldn't want anyone else involved in this. That means you're stuck with me."

Funny, Mitch didn't feel at all stuck with her. He did feel incredibly hot at the moment, and on the verge of compromising his dignity. For a man who'd always prided himself on self-control, he was bordering on the edge of losing it big time. He collapsed into his chair and laced his hands behind his head before she caught him having a weak moment. "Get out of here, Tori, before…"

"Before what?"

Before he changed his mind, locked the door, and tried one more time to seduce her out of her sneakers, and everything else. "Before it's dinnertime and I don't get a thing accomplished today."

"Oh, but you've accomplished a lot."

"What would that be?"

"You just spent the last twenty minutes without trying to kiss me. Now that wasn't so hard, was it?"

He leaned forward and locked into her gaze. "You have no idea how hard it's been." Or how hard it was going to be as long as he wanted her this badly, and that could be for a long while.

Dinner with Stella and Bobby had been pleasant enough. The evening entertainment was not.

Tori covered her face with her hands following the first moan, then crushed the pillow over her head when the succession of name calling began.

Admittedly, tonight the love sounds bothered her on a different level. She didn't want to be reminded that if she would just say the word, she could be in Mitch's bed enjoying a little love fest of her own. In fact, she was beginning to wonder why she'd continued to fight Mitch, fight her overriding attraction to him. Sure, she should try to remain objective while gathering information. But no one would have to know what they did in the dead of night.

In reality, her resistance to intimacy with Mitch had more to do with her fear of falling for him. He wasn't really commitment material, something he had made quite clear today. Granted, he had spent nine years with one woman, but he hadn't asked that woman to marry him. No, siree, Bobby…who happened to be groaning loud enough to call the cattle home.

That did it.

Tori vaulted out of the feather bed and her feet hit the cold hardwood floor, reminding her that the weather was not conducive to taking a walk. However, she would rather face the elements than endure one more thwack of the headboard hitting the wall in a torrid tempo.

Not bothering to turn on the lamp, she snatched her robe from the bedpost and slid her feet into the ridiculous furry brown gorilla slippers Stella had given her as a gift for serving as maid of honor. The other two bridesmaids had received frogs and pigs, so she supposed she got the better end of the deal.

The floor creaked beneath her feet as she felt her way along the wall. She finally reached the small living room illuminated by a lamp in the corner—a good thing considering the area was littered with unpacked boxes. Grabbing her leather jacket from the coat tree, she yanked open the door and stepped onto the porch. The moderate breeze flowed over her and until that moment, she hadn't realized how hot she'd been. She could attribute that to the down comforter, or her own desire for Mitch that she'd warred with all day long…and most of the night.

"I figured you'd be out soon."

With her heart lodged firmly in her throat, Tori spun toward the sound of the deep voice to find a dark figure silhouetted against the limited light. She laid one shaky hand against her throat. "God, Mitch, you scared the hell out of me!"

"Sorry. I didn't mean to do that."

She walked to the glider where he now sat and hovered above him. "What are you doing here?"

"Couldn't sleep."

"And you walked all the way here to alleviate your insomnia?"

"I decided you'd probably need some company eventually."

"You were certainly taking a huge chance that I would come outside."

"Not really. I know Stella and Bobby's habits well enough

to know they'd eventually drive you out of the house. If you hadn't come out when you did, I probably would've left in an hour or two."

"An hour or two?"

His gaze raked over her in a slow excursion. "If you'd agreed to stay with me, then you wouldn't be traipsing around in the cold in your nightgown."

He was nothing if not tenacious. "Okay, I'm here, you proved your point, so you can go back to bed now."

"Not until you come back to my house with me."

"I really don't think that's necessary. They can't keep going at it all night."

"Wanna bet?"

No, she didn't, because she wasn't at all sure when Stella's and Bobby's antics might end, possibly not before dawn. "I would have my own room?"

She could see a flash of white teeth before he said, "Do you think I'm going to make you bunk with Buck?"

"That never entered my mind."

"But you thought I might offer my own room."

"That thought did cross my mind." Several times, in great detail.

"You can stay in the bedroom on the opposite side of the house from mine."

"I'm still not sure that's wise."

He released an impatient sigh. "Would you rather spend a week listening to the Stella and Bob parade on a nightly basis?"

No, she wouldn't. But she wasn't sure she could trust Mitch not to pursue the lovemaking issue. And worse, she didn't really have a lot of confidence in herself not to eventually concede.

The glider whined as he pushed out of it to stand before her. "Tori, I do solemnly swear I am not going to pull any funny stuff while you're in my house. Not if you don't want it."

She did want it, and that was the problem. Yet she didn't think she could stomach more nighttime sex noise that didn't involve her. And Mitch. "Okay. Let me just grab a few things and I'll spend the night tonight."

He inclined his head. "Only tonight?"

"That depends."

"On what?"

"On whether you behave yourself."

"The door has a lock. Then you can be assured I won't bother you while you're sleeping."

Predictably, he hadn't said he would adhere to that when she wasn't sleeping. "Fine. I'll be right back."

As she pulled open the screen, Mitch said from behind her, "Nice slippers."

She turned and stuck out a gorilla-covered foot. "Yeah, I like to monkey around now and then."

He gave her a crooked smile. "Oh, yeah?"

Releasing a groan, she turned away from all that charisma and hoped she had enough strength to keep turning away for the remainder of the week.

Mitch felt a little guilty over being grateful that Bobby had a penchant for hamming it up in the bedroom. But Tori really would be more comfortable in his house. She'd also be nearby in case she changed her mind.

"This is it," he told her as he pushed open the door. "Nothing fancy, but it does have its own bathroom."

Tori walked into the room still wearing her leather jacket over her nightclothes. When the light hit the pale blue gown, he could see the outline of her bare legs all the way to her thighs beneath the sheer fabric. Best not to look there if he intended to go back to his own room and get some sleep.

She set her duffel down on the red plaid spread and faced him. "It looks comfortable enough."

"The bed was from my room in the old house but it has a new mattress." Mitch was having a hard time not looking at her breasts.

When Tori clutched the jacket closed, he realized he'd been

caught. "You know, the old house is nice enough," she said. "Why did you build a new one?"

The memories had been too much for Mitch to bear—memories of the time he'd spent with his mother during the summers when his dad had been too busy for them both. Memories of the last days of her life. Too many ghosts, and facts that Tori didn't need to know, even though he had the strongest urge to tell her.

Instead, he said, "I wanted something that was solely my contribution to the ranch, a symbol of my putting down roots here. Buck was resistant at first, but I finally talked him into living here and letting Bob use the old place instead of staying with the other hands in the bunkhouse out back. He did insist we bring in some of the furniture so he'd feel more at home."

Tori pointed at a picture hanging on the opposite wall. "Did he insist on that, too?"

Mitch moved closer to her to see what had caught her attention. Damn. He'd forgotten all about that stupid photo of him on a pony wearing a red felt cowboy hat, complete with a jockey string cinched beneath his chin and matching red chaps. "Yeah, that was definitely his idea."

"Nice outfit," she said, grinning. "I think it's adorable."

He could say the same about her with those damned ape house shoes hugging her feet. He gestured toward the closet. "You can hang your stuff in there."

She glanced at the bag on the bed. "I didn't bring that much stuff. Since I wasn't planning on staying, I'll have to borrow some clothes from Stella."

Right now, he'd like to help her shed her clothes. "Tomorrow, you can bring whatever else you need."

She propped both hands on her hips. "Now what makes you so sure I'm going to stay here for the remainder of my visit?"

"Because you want to get some sleep."

"True, I do." She stretched her arms and yawned, causing the jacket to gape, revealing the outline of her breasts and the shading of her nipples.

If he didn't get out soon, there was no telling what he might do. "If there's nothing else you need, I'll go to my room now. Buck's two doors down, but he shouldn't bother you."

"Actually, I do need something from you." She perched on the end of the bed and patted the mattress. "Come here."

Before he could sit, she pointed a finger at him. "I only want to talk, so get rid of that look on your face."

He scowled. "What look?"

"The one you always give me when you have certain things on your mind."

Good going, Mitch. He might as well have I Want You, Tori tattooed on his forehead. "Fine. I won't look at you." He didn't dare sit by her, either, not if he wanted to control himself. "I'll just stand here and you talk."

"All right. I have an idea I want to run past you."

If it didn't involve them assuming a prone position, he wasn't sure he wanted to hear it. "Okay. Shoot."

"I've been thinking about us, our relationship, and I've decided we need to start over."

"Start over?"

"Yes. As friends. Maybe then we won't be so inclined to skip ahead to the next step."

"We've already gone way beyond the next step, Tori. We can't go back." Nor did he want to. He wouldn't take back one moment of their first night together.

"It's all a mindset, Mitch. Besides, we do have a few things in common, a good basis for a friendship."

Mitch could think of one in particular—they were damn good together in bed. Or at least in the bed of a truck, since they hadn't actually made it into a real bed. "What things?"

"We've both lost our mothers."

"True." Their shared loss had made him feel even closer to her. "What else?"

"We like to dance."

"Friends don't dance, at least not as close as we do. You're going to have to do better than that."

She sat silent for a moment, then snapped her fingers and pointed. "I've got it. We both know about the breeding process."

Mitch couldn't help smiling over Tori's obvious chagrin. "Yeah, we do."

"You know what I mean. Anyway, I think if we build on that friendship, then when I leave here, we'll both be the better for it."

In other words, she was saying she wanted nothing more than friendship. That should have been okay with Mitch, but for some reason, it wasn't. "I've never really had a woman friend before."

"You and Mary Alice weren't friends?"

He could've gone all night without Tori mentioning her. "Maybe years ago, when we were younger. But basically, we didn't talk all that much."

"I see."

Mitch was surprised by her sober tone. "Mary Alice and I are over. We should've been over a long time ago."

She leaned back on her bent elbows, thrusting her breasts forward and adding to Mitch's increasing discomfort. "Why did you finally break it off after nine years?"

He wasn't sure he needed to go there, either, but it would be better if Tori knew up front his opinion on the subject wasn't bound to change. "She wanted to get married and as I've told you, marriage isn't something I plan to undertake."

"Did you love her?" Mitch could tell she regretted asking when she looked away and said, "Never mind. That's none of my business."

No, it wasn't, but he wanted her to know the reality of his relationship with Mary Alice. Taking a huge risk, he sat on the edge of the mattress, keeping his hands clasped together between his parted knees. "She didn't want me exactly. She wanted my money and my name. She's always been that way. When I didn't bend to her will, she went looking for someone who would, namely Brady Stevens."

"Now he's quite a catch."

"Yeah. He always kind of reminded me of an anemic perch."

Tori's laughter started out as a chuckle then grew into a full-fledged guffaw. Mitch tried to refrain from joining her, but he couldn't.

"Cut it out in there!" came the very irritable voice of Buck.

Tori slapped her hand over her mouth until she recovered. "I'm so sorry. I forgot about your grandfather."

"Don't worry about him. In fact, I'm not sure he's really awake. He's been known to talk in his sleep."

"Does he walk in his sleep?"

"No. And if you're worried, neither do I."

"I'm not worried." She glanced at the bedside clock. "Speaking of sleep, it's past one. We both need to go to bed."

"I'm all for that."

"Alone."

Double damn.

Mitch rose from the bed then faced her. "I'll think about the friends thing." When he wasn't thinking about making love to her.

"It's not going to be that difficult, I promise. In fact, I'll prove it."

Taking Mitch by surprise, she came off the bed and wrapped her arms around him. "See? We're hugging and that's all it has to be."

He kept his frame as stiff as a split-rail fence post and his arms loosely around her. Right now it would take him a split second to back her up and lay her down on the bed so he could try a little urging.

She stood on tiptoe and kissed his cheek. "Good night, Mitch. Sweet dreams."

The sweetest dream was in his arms, but he wouldn't make a move now. If she wanted to be friendly, he could do that. At least tonight. He swept her bangs away and kissed her forehead. "'Night, Tori."

Again, neither of them moved away, same as it had been earlier that day. And the real shocker came when Tori, who'd insisted on friendship only a few moments earlier, grabbed his neck and brought his lips to hers.

As far as kisses went, this one had little to do with simple friendship. Simple need, yes. It was hot. It was deep. It was killing Mitch not to take it further.

Tori pushed away first and Mitch held up his palms. "That was not my fault."

She slid both hands through her hair. "I know. It was mine. It won't happen again."

Mitch headed for the door but before he walked out, he turned to her and said, "You just keep telling yourself that, Tori. Maybe then you'll start to believe it."

Six

She could not believe she'd been such a fool.

That was the first thought that entered Tori's mind when the sun streaming into the window hit her face. She'd been a complete and absolute idiot last night. What had possessed her to kiss Mitch after she'd been so adamant about establishing a friendship with him? Well, that was obvious. Mitch had possessed her since the night she'd met him. The little devil.

Rolling to her side, she checked the clock, then bolted upright. Almost noon. Why hadn't Mitch woken her? Probably because he was determined to avoid her after her behavior last night. She sure as heck couldn't blame him. But on the other hand, she wasn't going to let him. She still had a job to do.

After a quick shower, she completed her morning routine and then slipped on a plain gray sweatshirt and a pair of Stella's low-riding, pre-pregnancy jeans. They were a little loose, but they would have to do since Tori hadn't brought enough casual clothes to last through the week.

After slipping on a pair of sneakers, she hurried into the living room to find it deserted. The kitchen showed no signs of life with the exception of a couple of coffee cups and a discarded copy of the weekly *Quail Run Herald* on the dinette table. Although she was sorely tempted to peruse the news and find out if anything had been added to the usual gossip, she didn't have time. Her next stop would be the barn in hopes that she could catch a few minutes with Mitch.

Tori left the house and walked the path at a fast clip, admittedly driven by anticipation and excitement over seeing him again. When she caught sight of several men gathered in the arena adjacent to the barn, she pulled up short. She walked to the pen and propped one foot on the bottom rung, shading her eyes against the sun to survey the activity. Two cowboys on horses turned profile conversed with the other onlookers standing near the roping chute. One of those cowboys happened to be Mitch Warner.

His long leg, the one she could see, dangled at the horse's side, bypassing the stirrup. He had one large hand draped casually on the saddle horn, the other resting on his thigh encased in faded jeans. He wore a black felt hat, a pair of brown roughout boots and a confidence that couldn't be ignored, even at this distance. Tori cursed the fact she still hadn't retrieved her camera because this picture was definitely worth a thousand words.

Old West magnificence. Raw machismo. Undeniable magnetism.

Mitch Warner was all those things and more.

Tori tried to overlook the sudden rush of heat, the heady bout of chills, the desire for him that never seemed to let go. In her head, she knew it would be best to return to Stella's and wait until later to catch up with him. In her heart, she knew she couldn't leave. Not yet. Not until she had a longer look, before someone noticed her presence.

Too late, she realized when Buck sauntered around the pen and headed toward her with a bowlegged gait.

"Hey, missy," he said as he stood next to her, one ragtag boot propped on the rung not far from her foot.

"Hey, Buck." She nodded toward the gang who so far had failed to heed her appearance. "Are they about to brand a calf?"

"Nope. They've been playin' all morning. Breakaway roping just for the fun of it."

"I'm not sure I understand the 'breakaway' part."

"They rope the calf, then let go of the rope. Then a man goes into the pen, takes the rope off the calf and they do it all over again. Best time wins."

"What do they win?"

"Braggin' rights. That's about it. Most of those boys don't have all that much. Mitch employs as many as he can full-time. Sometimes he gives the others part-time work when he has something extra he needs done. Next week, they'll help him move the rest of the herd in closer to the barns before winter sets in. Easier to feed them that way."

Tori surveyed the motley crew, men of all shapes, sizes and ages. Then she noticed the twenty-something man on the horse next to Mitch, a ruggedly handsome man with massive shoulders, longish golden hair and a winning smile. But her attention was soon drawn to what he was missing—his right arm below his elbow. "Does he work here?" she asked Buck, pointing to the cowboy.

Buck chuckled. "Yeah. We call him Bandit, for one-armed bandit."

Tori frowned. "That seems kind of cruel."

"Nah. He's the one that started it. It kind of describes his way with the ladies. He's been known to steal their…. Well, never mind about that."

Tori laughed. "He sounds like an interesting guy."

"He's a good guy. Back when Gus came to visit during the summer, he'd follow Gus around like a pup looking for a teat. After Rand—that's his real name—lost his arm when he was sixteen, Gus kind of adopted him, taught him how to rope with one hand and his teeth. It's the strangest sight you'll ever see."

Rand, the software developer Mitch had mentioned yesterday. "He's the computer expert?"

"Yeah, but he wanted to be a horse vet. Even went to school and came close to finishing before he quit. He said it wasn't for him, but we figure it was too much for him to handle, with his missing arm and all."

Tori suspected there was quite a story there, but she had to concentrate on the one that presently needed her attention. "Why do you call Mitch 'Gus'?"

"At first I called him 'Grumpy Gus' cause he was so grumpy as a boy. Damn serious from the day he was born. 'Course, I could make him laugh by showing him my teeth." Buck thrust a partial containing his top two teeth out with his tongue, then shoved them back in the same way.

"Ouch," was all Tori could think to say.

"Don't hurt a'tall. Now when that horse kicked me in the mouth, it hurt somethin' fierce."

She wrinkled her nose. "I can imagine."

She could also imagine why Mitch was so fond of this man. Buck was salt of the earth, as good as gold, and those kind of men were hard to come by in this day and time. Obviously his grandson had picked up some of those same traits, considering he was inclined to hire the down-and-out from town. That must have been what Mary Alice had meant when she'd said Mitch was kind to the common folk. To look at him now, he appeared just as common. To know him as she was beginning to know him, he was anything but common—in appearance, in personality, in his ability to mesmerize, as he was doing right then when he rode around the pen, looping the rope with both hands and guiding the horse with the sheer strength of his legs.

She was vaguely aware that Buck had said something, but in her daze, she hadn't heard a thing. Tearing her gaze away from Mitch, she said, "Huh?"

"I said he's a good man."

"I'm sure he is." She knew he was.

"All he needs is a good woman."

Tori continued to watch Mitch in an effort not to appear too interested as he chased after a calf someone released from the chute. "I'm sure he'll find one eventually."

"I'm beginning to wonder. He wasted nine years on the wrong woman."

Only then did she turn to Buck. "You weren't disappointed when it didn't work out between him and Mary Alice?"

"Nah. She's too prissy. Gus needs someone who understands him. Not too many gals around here to choose from."

She gave her attention back to Mitch. "I'm sure that's true. It's a small town."

Tori sensed Buck staring at her in the moments of passing silence before he said, "How long do you plan to stay?"

"Until Sunday."

"I couldn't talk you into staying longer?"

She glanced at him briefly. "I have a job and an apartment waiting for me back in Dallas."

"You got a boyfriend?"

She dropped her foot from the rung and leaned one shoulder against the rail to face him. "Now, Buck, you know you're much too young for me."

In his grin, she saw a glimpse of his grandson. "Yeah, but you ain't too old for Gus. He could use a woman like you, someone to keep him grounded."

"You don't even know me."

"I know you well enough, Tori. You're like him. You're smart and you hung in there when people weren't so nice to you."

"Why do you think people weren't nice to me?"

"I know about your mama and how she never got married. I heard a few people talk, but I was never one to pass judgment on anyone. You don't know a person's situation till you've walked in their shoes."

She lowered her eyes and studied the dried grass beneath her feet. "It wasn't bad all the time. I have a few very good memories. But I've since moved on. I don't intend to live here permanently again."

"This town ain't so terrible, as long as you have someone to lean on when the going gets tough."

The crowd scattered and headed away in all directions, while Mitch dismounted and started toward the barn. Tori saw that as an excuse to avoid any further matchmaking attempts by Buck, as well as her chance to finally talk to Mitch. She patted Buck's shoulder and smiled. "Got to get some work done now. I guess I'll see you later."

"You can go with me to the fair if that grandson of mine won't take you."

"Fair?"

"The Harvest Festival. You remember that. Happens the same time every October and ends with the rodeo this weekend."

Once more, Tori was thrust back into her past. She'd been conceived following that rodeo almost twenty-eight years ago, the only thing she knew about how she had come to be, and her father—a roving rodeo bum. "I remember, but I hadn't thought about going."

"You need to go. Best barbecue and beer in the state. Not that I touch the stuff."

Tori grinned. "You expect me to believe that?"

"Nope, but you do need to believe one thing." He pointed at the barn and closed one eye as if preparing to take a shot. "That boy in there has it bad for you."

Tori couldn't think of any response, so she gave him only a friendly goodbye as she walked away to seek out Mitch.

Mitch had it bad for *her*? Not hardly. Maybe her body, but that was it. On the other hand, she was starting to have it bad for him, and that might not be so good.

But it could be so good, if she continued to weaken in his presence. And if the devastating cowboy kept pressing the issue, she had no doubt her resolve would eventually wane.

After rinsing Ray off, Mitch stepped out of the wash rack to find Tori leaning back against the opposing stall. She had her hair pulled into a ponytail high atop her head and the sweat-shirt she wore looked like a jogger's reject. The jeans were too big, and if she wasn't the cutest thing he'd ever seen, he'd eat his roping saddle for lunch.

She lifted her hand in a flat-palm wave. "Hi. Got a few minutes to spare?"

He'd give her a few minutes. Hell, he'd give her hours if she would just give it up and acknowledge they wanted each other. He could see it in her dark eyes, feel it in his bones. The heat between them was so fierce that it could fry the shavings in the stalls.

"Sure. I'll just leave Ray tied up until he dries. We can go into my office."

Tori followed behind him, keeping her distance even after they were tucked away behind a closed door. She hadn't noticed that he'd locked it, but if she had, he would offer the explanation that anyone was bound to come in, and he didn't want to interrupt the interview. That sounded logical, even if it was a stretch in the truth department.

He'd stayed up most of the night, literally up, hard and aching for her. That ache had yet to subside, nor would it until he made love to her again, this time with slow precision, until he'd convinced her that answering their mutual need was only natural.

While Tori stood with her arms folded tightly over her middle, Mitch claimed a seat on the edge of his desk.

"Did you sleep well?" he asked, thinking that was the most innocuous thing he could say at the moment.

"Obviously. You should've gotten me up earlier."

He'd wanted to rouse in ways that she could only imagine but had resisted with the little scrap of will he had left. "I figured you needed your rest. Besides, this is the only time I've had a break since dawn."

She nodded at the computer. "What are you doing there?"

"Tracking the herd and adding in a couple of new calves into the program. They all have numbers."

"They should have names."

"If you can come up with twenty-three, then have at it."

"That could be a challenge, I guess."

The challenge right now came when she wet her lips. Mitch had to grip the edge of the desk to keep from grabbing her and kissing her into mindlessness. "Anything else you want to know about the business?"

Her gaze shifted to the diploma hanging on the wall to her right. "I'm sure I'll think of something, but first, I want to apologize for my behavior last night."

He was tired of both hearing and voicing those words. Tired of fighting their attraction. "When's it going to stop, Tori?"

She centered her gaze on him. "It won't happen again."

"I meant our apologies for wanting each other. Maybe it's time we just quit saying we're sorry and accept the fact that this thing is stronger than both of us."

"It's not, Mitch. We're adult enough to control ourselves."

"This has nothing to do with how old we are. It has everything to do with how hot we are for each other."

"You certainly are making some fairly big assumptions."

"Assumptions or truths?"

"Assumptions."

Mitch pushed away from the desk and moved closer to her. "You're not even a little bit hot and bothered right now, knowing we're alone? Knowing we could do anything we please and not a soul would know about it?"

"No." She turned away from him and walked to the window, but not before he saw the uncertainty in her expression, the desire in her eyes.

He came up behind her and this time, he didn't bother to keep his hands off of her. He couldn't.

Circling his arms around her waist, he pulled her against him. She didn't resist, but she also didn't relax. "I don't believe you, Tori. I think right now, you're about to go up in flames. So am I."

"I'm about to go up to Stella's and get my camera."

He worked her sweatshirt up and rested his palm on her bare abdomen. "I wouldn't mind taking a few pictures as long as we do it without our clothes."

Her breath hissed out when he began to trace the waistband on the loose-fitting jeans with a fingertip. "Not a good idea. They could fall into the wrong hands."

Mitch slid his palm right beneath the jeans until he contacted the band on her panties. "I'd make sure they stayed in my hands."

"Mitch, we can't." Tori tipped her head back against his shoulder, belying her protest.

He inched his palm lower, beneath the lace. "You don't have to do anything, Tori, except enjoy it."

The gasp that slipped out of her mouth was soft, needy, and so was her flesh as he searched for the place that would ensure her pleasure.

"You're hot, Tori," he told her as he caressed her with his fingertips, his strokes deliberate in their intent. He wanted her weak and wanting. He wanted to hear her moan, feel her come apart.

When the rap sounded at the door, Tori yanked his hand from beneath her jeans and wrenched away.

"Hey, Mitch, are you in there?"

Mitch walked to the desk, braced both palms on the edge and lowered his head. "Yeah, Bob. I'm here." He sounded winded, something that wouldn't be lost on his foreman.

"Is Tori with you?"

"Yes," she answered in a raspy voice. "We were just talking."

Bobby chuckled. "Okay. Stella wanted me to tell you she's made some lunch, so when you and Mitch are done *talking*, come on up."

"She'll be there in a minute, Bob," Mitch answered for her.

"If it's only going to take you a minute, Mitch, then maybe you should grab something to eat so you'll have more stamina."

One more word and Mitch was going to rearrange his foreman's face. "Get out of here, Bob."

"I'm leaving, boss. Take your time, Tori." Bobby's retreating footsteps could barely be heard over his laughter.

"Mitch, I'm—"

"Don't say it, Tori. Don't you dare say you're sorry."

"I was going to say I'm totally losing my mind."

He shoved back from the desk and faced her. "Join the club."

She linked her hands behind her neck, causing the sweat-shirt to ride up where Mitch caught a glimpse of her navel. He did not need to see anything that even resembled bare flesh.

Dropping her arms to her side, she blew out a slow breath. "Okay. Maybe this thing is stronger than both of us."

"What clued you in? Was it before or after I almost made you—"

"Before."

"What are we going to do about it?" he asked even though he knew exactly what he wanted to do—carry her up to the house and into his bed.

"Well, right now, I'm going to get some lunch, then I'm going to write down a few notes."

He allowed a disparaging smile to surface. "Until we fin-ish what we started a minute ago, your notes are going to be incomplete."

She came as close to a scowl as Mitch had witnessed so far. "Notes as in your business skills."

He took two steps toward her. "That's not going to be as interesting."

She smiled and took two steps back. "I've got a great idea. Mitch Warner's ten favorite ways to please a woman."

He advanced one more step. "Only ten?"

This time, she didn't move. "You know, I don't think you really want to go there in the article. You'd never have a mo-ment's peace for all the women lining up the drive to find out if you live up to the hype."

One more step and he'd be in her face, and back into trou-ble. "Do I live up to the hype?"

She hesitated and pretended to think a moment. "I'm not sure yet. As you've said, my notes are still incomplete."

Five more minutes of this kind of talk and he was going to

back her up against the wall, to hell with the bed. "Maybe we should do some more research tonight."

"Your granddad invited me to the festival."

Mitch had totally forgotten about the event that he'd attended for the past ten years without fail. "I'll go with you."

"You will?"

"Yeah. You probably need some protection from all the cowboys. Once they get a good look at you, you'll be fighting them off in record numbers."

"Yeah. Sure."

"I'm serious, Tori. It's not too often that a woman as good-looking as you comes into town." And he'd be damned if he'd let any of them touch her.

"And who is going to protect me from you?"

Man, he'd really done it now if she was that wary of him. "You don't have to worry about that. I'll be on my best behavior."

She walked up to him, adjusted his collar and then patted him on his chest. "We could consider this a friendly date."

"A date?"

"Does Mitch Warner not date?"

The last real date he'd been on had been a wreck—dinner with Mary Alice and her daddy. Clyde Marshall had spent the entire evening blowing cigar smoke in Mitch's face while he'd tried to sell Mitch on the benefits of becoming a member of the family. "I might shock a few people in town if I stroll in with you on my arm."

Her expression sobered. "No one has to know it's actually a date, Mitch, if that's what's worrying you."

"I didn't say I cared what anyone thought."

"You might, considering you'll be with me."

He didn't understand this one damn bit. "You're not making any sense, Tori."

She sighed. "When I was younger, people assumed that since my mother had me out of wedlock, I would automatically follow in her footsteps. I heard the speculation many times before I got out of this godforsaken town. For that reason, I didn't date. I didn't give anyone any reason to believe that I was anything but a good girl who didn't dare step out of line."

Now it was beginning to make sense. On one level, she was the self-assured career woman. On a deeper plane, she was still that vulnerable teenager trying to prove her worthiness to walk among society. "Then you're saying I might not want to be seen with you because people might assume that you, a grown woman, might be sleeping with me?"

"Something like that."

"Tori, you don't have anything to prove to me or anyone else. Whatever happens between us is our business, and no one else's. It doesn't make you a bad person." When she lowered her head, he lifted her chin. "I would be honored to escort you through the streets of town. To hell with what anyone thinks."

Her smile illuminated the room, and something in Mitch lit up, too. It felt good to bring out that smile with such a simple gesture. Unlike Mary Alice, it took so little to please Tori, only one more reason why he enjoyed her company. One more reason to show her more pleasure than she'd ever known.

"Great," she said. "I'll get to work, you get to work then we'll go to the fair. What time?"

"Seven. I'll pick you up."

Her smile withered. "Are you sure you want to do this? I could always go with Stella and Bobby or Buck."

He brushed a kiss across her cheek. "I wouldn't do it if I didn't want to. I don't do anything I don't want to do." Except he didn't want to feel what he was feeling for Tori, but it seemed he had little choice in the matter.

"Okay. I'll see you at seven," she said, followed by a quick kiss on his cheek.

When she turned and headed for the door, he said, "One more thing, Tori."

She faced him with her hand curled around the knob. "What?"

"You and I both know that what's going on between us isn't going to change anytime soon."

"And your point?"

"Would it be so wrong to just enjoy each other while you're here?"

"Why don't we wait and see how it goes tonight?"

He knew exactly how it was going to go. He'd be pretending that everything between them was casual, but deep down he would be wanting her with every breath he drew. "All right. I can live with that." If it didn't kill him.

"Fine. I'll see you later."

When Tori closed the door, Mitch dropped down into the chair behind his desk and rested his face in his hands. He couldn't help but wonder if his behavior, his uncontrolled desire for her, had her believing that he saw her as an easy target because of her history. Very far from the truth.

Tori Barnett was smart and sexy. A class act. A woman that any man with half a brain would like to know better. He had revealed more about himself to her than he'd ever revealed to any woman. She'd begun to melt his emotional walls and although he found that troublesome, he couldn't ignore the anticipation every time she walked into a room—and that had little to do with sex, as reluctant as he was to admit it.

Yet he had offered her no more than a date to the local shindig and a few sessions of lovemaking while she was in town. But then she hadn't asked anything else of him. Still, he intended to put on the brakes. Tonight, he would treat her like the one-in-a-million woman she was. He wouldn't expect more than her company and, in turn, prove that he did respect her enough to ignore his own needs. Anything that happened between them from this point forward would be up to her.

He would be the gentleman his mother had taught him to be. In the meantime, he would remind himself that in a matter of days, she would leave him to return to her own life. He would also try to ignore that bite of regret struggling to the surface every time he thought about her departure.

He still had six days in her presence and even if they never made love again, Mitch would always be glad for this time with Tori Barnett—an honest-to-goodness good girl.

"Bobby tells me you were doing Mitch in his office."

Tori stopped mid-bite and swallowed quickly in order to deliver a retort to her former best friend. "I was not *doing* Mitch anywhere."

Stella pushed her plate back and smiled. "And why weren't you, Tori?"

"Oh, good grief." Snatching her own plate from the table, Tori walked to the kitchen counter, shoved the uneaten half of her turkey sandwich into the trash, then set the dish in the sink. "Give me one good reason why I should be sleeping with Mitch Warner."

"Because you want to."

Exactly, Tori thought, staring into the suds as if they could foretell the future. "What I might want to do and what I should do are two different things."

"Tori, don't you think it's time to stop being the good girl?"

How weird that Stella should bring that up considering Tori's recent conversation with Mitch. For a second, she wondered if they'd been plotting the demise of her resistance together. "If you recall, I was not a *good girl* four nights ago."

Stella came up beside Tori and rested an elbow on her shoulder. "Knowing you, you've been beating yourself up inside ever since."

Tori shrugged off Stella's arm and began washing the dishes with a vengeance. "I haven't exactly been beating myself up, although I probably should."

"Why? What happened between you and Mitch was nature having a field day. You should be glad you've had the opportunity, and you should be trying to grab a few more."

She ran the dishrag round and round in a glass until it squeaked. "To what end, Stella? I'll be leaving here in a few days and then it's over."

"So?"

A stretch of silence passed before Stella said, "Oh, gosh. You're falling in love with him!"

"I'm not. I can't."

"Sometimes you don't have a choice. I certainly didn't want to fall in love with Bobby, but I'm glad I did." She patted her belly. "Now I have a baby on the way and a man who loves me more than his horse."

Tori chuckled. "That's nice to know, but that's exactly the reason why I can't fall for Mitch. He doesn't love me more than his horse, and he never will."

"He could. Stranger things have happened."

After rinsing off one plate, Tori leaned a hip against the counter and faced Stella. "Not with Mitch. He gives the term 'confirmed bachelor' a whole new meaning. His determination to avoid commitment is etched in cement."

"Then my advice is to make a few memories to take back to Dallas with you. If you're going to fall in love with him, you'll do that without going to bed with him again. You can't make it any worse by having a little fun while you're falling."

Stella was probably right. If she was going to lose her heart to Mitch, she would do that without ever kissing him again.

Until this point in her life, she'd been a model citizen. She didn't even have a citation on her driving record. She'd been a devoted daughter. She'd waited until she'd been in a long-term relationship before she'd made love for the first time. She'd walked the straight and narrow for so long she was surprised she didn't step heel to toe. Enough was enough.

Saint Victoria vowed to say goodbye to the good girl, at least for tonight.

Seven

The fair had packed the streets to capacity, both with vendors and townsfolk from across three counties. As it had been from the time Tori was young, all the citizens looked forward to the event as a nice diversion from the everyday grind. Back in her youth, she'd always attended the festivities with her friends. Not once had she ever been on the arm of a boy, taking in the games on the midway provided by the same Oklahoma City carnival company for fifty years. Not once had she sat in Horner's pasture on a blanket with a date to watch the fireworks light up the sky after sundown. Not once had she kissed on a Ferris wheel.

Those were nothing more than unrealized teenage dreams. Tonight she enjoyed the company of a dream man dressed in a starched pale blue shirt that enhanced his eyes, just-right jeans that highlighted his attributes and a tan felt hat that crowned him the consummate cowboy. And his cologne— well, that should just be labeled lethal.

Yes, tonight Tori walked the sidewalk amidst the chaos of

the crowd, the gorgeous Mitch Warner by her side—when he wasn't shaking hands with all the passersby. His political roots were showing, whether he cared to admit it or not. She wouldn't be a bit surprised if he started kissing babies. That was okay, as long as he saved a few for her later on.

Right then she stood on the sidewalk in front of the hardware store, waiting while Mitch visited with Lanham Farley, the town's mayor who happened to be older than Red River dirt. However, he was still upright and able to take nourishment, evident by the fact he was gnawing on a smoked turkey leg with his dentures.

Tori engaged in people watching to pass the time. She had to admit the excitement in the air was palpable. Strident screams came from the vicinity of the belly-flopping rides scattered around on the vacant lot at the end of the street. That lot used to house the livestock auction barns before people took their business to bigger cities and better markets. She was amazed that Quail Run hadn't completely died out as so many small towns had. In many ways, she was glad it hadn't, even if she never planned to live here again. As she'd told Buck earlier that day, not every memory was a bad one. And she hoped tonight that with Mitch, she might make a few more good ones. If he ever escaped the esteemed mayor.

"Well, my, my, you did stick around."

Tori glanced to her right to see Mary Alice Marshall, her jeans painted on her narrow hips and her lips painted fire-engine red. Her perfectly curled long blond hair trailed from beneath a white cowboy hat as she clutched an armful of stuffed animals that Tori would like to tell her to stuff in a place where the sun don't shine. "Hello, Mary Alice. Looks like you made a haul."

Mary Alice squeezed the animals to her ample chest. "Actually, Brady won these for me. Aren't they cute? I plan to give them to the children's home in Bennett."

"That's nice."

"And it's nice of you to support the festival, considering your limited means. But you shouldn't just stand here." She pulled a strip of red tickets from the pocket of her jeans. "Take these and go have some fun."

Tori intended to, starting now. "Actually, I'm waiting for Mitch, so I won't be needing any freebies."

"Mitch?" Mary Alice's voice cracked like an adolescent boy's.

"Yes." She nodded toward the cowboy-in-question. "He's talking to Mayor Farley. I'm sure he'll be finished in a moment."

Mary Alice inclined her head and gave Tori a hard stare. "Are you and Mitch an item, or is he just being charitable?"

Tori gritted her teeth to halt the litany of insults threatening to spew forth. "Actually, he's—"

"Ready to go."

Mitch's surprise appearance couldn't have been better timed. The arm he draped over Tori's shoulder couldn't have been more welcome. "Let's go, Tori." He touched the brim of his hat and said, "'Night, Mary Alice," but didn't wait for a response.

Tori sent Mary Alice a smug smile over one shoulder as they walked away. "Have a good time with Brady."

After they'd traveled a block, Mitch asked, "What did she say to you?" concern in his voice and his eyes.

"Nothing much. She just wanted to make sure I remembered my place and wished me a good time, until she found out I'm having it with you."

"She's just blowing steam."

"She still has a thing for you."

"She's jealous of you, but it's not only because you're with me."

A perfect blonde with big breasts and more money than God was jealous of her? "That's a stretch, Mitch."

"That's the truth. Believe me, I've known her a long time, and I can see envy written all over her face. She covets your independence because she wanted to leave here, just like you, but she was too afraid of her father to make a move."

"That's really a shame."

"That's the past and I want to forget about it and her."

When Mitch dropped his arm from around her, Tori couldn't ignore the disappointment. But then he took her hand and said, "Let's go play some games on the midway. I usually win."

And Mitch did at the basketball toss on the first try.

The carnie pointed to the myriad stuffed animals clipped to a string above their heads. "Which one do you want, little lady?"

Tori studied them for a few moments but before she could make her choice, Mitch said, "She'll take the monkey."

"One monkey it is," the carnie said as he handed Tori the miniature ape with a yellow plastic banana glued to his hand.

Tori gave Mitch a bewildered look as he took her by the arm and guided her past the fortune teller booth. "I was about to pick the white tiger."

"I thought the monkey complemented your house shoes."

Holding the ape up, she said, "You're right. And he needs a name."

"He reminds me of the mayor, so you should call him Lanham."

Tori laughed. "You're right. Lanham it is. Lanny for short."

Once more, Mitch draped an arm around her shoulder. "What now?"

"I want some cotton candy."

"I can do that."

She waited near the stand while Mitch waited in line. Several people passed by her and stared, but she couldn't say that she recognized any of them. And she doubted anyone recognized her, considering how long it had been since she'd been in town. Still, she suspected that their covert glances had to do with her "date" tonight. Before she returned home, no doubt she would be the notorious nobody who'd wrangled the local icon out of an evening.

A few minutes later, Mitch returned with the fluffy cloud of pink sugar on a stick and offered it to her. "Here. It was either this or some weird shade of green."

"This is great."

Tori's first bite of the candy brought back memories of a simpler time. So did the smells of frying funnel cakes and popcorn. Yet everything seemed much more special with Mitch at her side. For the first time, she walked the midway with a man, but not just any man. A special man who so completely tugged at her heartstrings every time he smiled.

"How about we try out a ride?" He snagged a hunk of the cotton candy and popped it into his mouth.

"I don't go for anything too daring," Tori replied. "But I do like the Ferris wheel."

He grinned. "I can't interest you in that kamikaze roller coaster?"

"Not if you value your boots."

"I do, so the Ferris wheel it is."

Again Tori hung back as Mitch purchased tickets from the booth. While waiting their turn to board, they maintained a comfortable silence, Mitch standing behind her with his palms braced on her waist. She resisted the urge to toss the monkey and candy aside to turn into his arms. Definitely not a good idea at the moment. But when they were alone on the ride, she had a good mind to fulfill one of her fantasies, if he proved to be agreeable.

After the wheel executed two go-rounds, their turn finally came. Tori climbed into the red car first and Mitch followed, Lanny positioned between them like a hairy, inanimate child. They pulled the safety bar over their laps and as they ascended backward, Tori's tummy took a pleasant dip. It dipped again when they sat suspended at the top while more riders loaded, providing her with the perfect opportunity to make her request.

Mitch rested his arm along the back of the seat, their thighs touching. That alone made her breathless. She sounded breathless when she said, "Mitch, can I ask you a question?"

He frowned. "I thought maybe we'd forget about the interview tonight."

"This isn't for the article. This is something that I want to know. Off the record."

"Okay."

"Have you ever kissed anyone on a Ferris wheel?"

He took off his hat, ran a hand through his hair, then settled it back on his head. "As best I can recall, I tried that once when I was about thirteen. I got slapped."

Tori twirled the white cone round and round. "I wouldn't slap you."

"You really want me to do that in front of the entire town?"

She kept her eyes focused on the lights spread out before them. "Not if it's going to ruin your rep—"

He stopped her words with a kiss as soft and as sweet as the cotton candy. Even when the ride started moving again, he didn't stop. Tori was barely mindful of the wheel's rotation or the moderate breeze blowing her bangs back from her face. Her awareness centered only on Mitch and the absolute thrill of his mouth moving against hers. He took her hand into his and rubbed her wrist with his thumb in a motion as gentle as the glide of his tongue against hers, as easy as the swaying car.

All too soon, the ride stopped and so did his kiss.

He leaned back against the seat, taking his hand from hers to adjust his hat that had tipped back from his forehead. "That probably melted your candy."

Tori looked down at the said candy to find it gone. "I think it flew away."

Mitch leaned over the side of the car and looked down at the ground below. "Oh, hell. Hope it didn't end up in some matriarch's beehive hairdo."

Tori released a laugh that seemed to float away on the wind along with the last of her heart. "That should make it in the *Quail Run Herald* if our little adolescent display doesn't first."

He patted the monkey's head. "At least you hung on to Lanny."

If only it would be so easy to hang on to Mitch, yet that was as elusive as the whereabouts of the candy. "I guess the earth didn't move just because you kissed me in public."

He regarded her with luminescent blue eyes that gave the

midway lights some serious competition. "I wouldn't necessarily say that."

The wheel jerked forward and soon stopped on the platform, bringing an end to the ride, bringing about Tori's disappointment over the end of a few very memorable moments.

As soon as the attendant lifted the bar, Mitch climbed out and offered his hand for her to take. And he didn't let her go even after they started down the wooden walkway, where they were met with random applause and hoots and hollers from several of the onlookers. Someone shouted, "Way to go, Gus!", prompting Tori to spin around to find Buck standing nearby, a handsome-looking older woman by his side. She sent a quick glance at Mitch to find he didn't look at all pleased at being caught by his grandfather.

Heat rose to Tori's face when she considered the number of people who had played witness to their behavior—particularly the blond bombshell standing near the exit, two furry friends dangling from her hands and two lying on the ground at her feet as she glared at Tori.

As juvenile as it seemed, Tori experienced a strong sense of satisfaction that Mary Alice Marshall had seen poor valedictorian Victoria Barnett in a lip-lock with Mitch Warner. Very petty, but pretty amusing at that.

Again they took to the busy streets, strolling along at a leisurely pace, hand in hand, Lanny clutched tightly in Tori's arm. The magical evening and Mitch's equally magical kiss had taken its toll on Tori. With every whiff of his cologne, every casual touch, she realized how she wanted this evening to end. But not yet. Not until they spent a little more time together. She didn't want to seem too enthusiastic, even if she was.

The masses began to move past them, mothers and fathers and kids, along with assorted couples, young and old, all heading toward Horton's pasture. "The fireworks are about to start in a few minutes," Tori said. "Are you interested in watching?"

Mitch stopped in the middle of the hordes and looked around. "I have a better idea."

Before Tori could inquire about that idea, Mitch turned and tugged her in the opposite direction, against the flow of the crowd. He stopped at the place set up for hayrides provided by a couple of local farmers with tractors and flatbeds. Leaving her behind once more, he spoke briefly with one of the men, handed him what looked to be a few bills, then returned.

He took Tori's arm and said, "Let's go."

A few people had gathered to await their turn, but the farmer waved them away. "This is a private hire, folks. The next ride will be here in about ten minutes."

A collective groan rang out from the bystanders, yet Mitch didn't give them a second glance as he helped Tori onto the trailer covered in hay. They positioned themselves with their backs to the bails lining the perimeter, Lanny between them once more.

The tractor headed out with a spew of fumes and a grating groan, bumping Tori closer to Mitch's side and practically crushing the poor stuffed animal. Some smart kid with a big mouth yelled out, "Give her a hickey," triggering a boom of laughter from those left behind.

"No hickeys," Tori said as she settled closer to him.

He pulled Lanny from between them, tossed him over his shoulder, then wrapped both his arms around her. "Damn. You're going to ruin all my fun tonight."

"You just ruined all of Lanny's fun. Now he's going to get cold."

"Lanny can get his own woman."

"He could borrow a friend from Mary Alice."

Mitch nuzzled his face in her hair. "I don't want to hear her name again, okay?"

"Fine by me. I'd rather concentrate on us having fun."

"That sounds real promising, ma'am." His voice was a rough whisper in her ear. "Here we are again, in the hay under the sky."

Tori trembled but it had nothing to do with the night air because it wasn't that cold. "We didn't have a chaperone the last time we were in this situation."

"And we did have a blanket, which we don't have now."

"I guess that means we should both be on our best behavior."

Mitch scooted down, taking Tori with him and slipped his hand beneath her jacket, bringing it to rest on her rib cage immediately below her breast. "Not necessarily. It's dark out and unless he has night vision, he couldn't see us anyway."

"Mitch Warner, you are a very wicked boy."

He rimmed the shell of her ear with his tongue. "And I can give you a mean hickey."

Tori giggled as he nibbled on her neck. "Don't you dare!"

"Can I at least give you a kiss?"

"Please do."

And he did, only this one wasn't quite as tempered as their Ferris wheel folly. This one was hotter, more insistent, intense. They sank lower and deeper into the hay until they were practically lying down. Their respiration sounded harsh and ragged when they managed to stop for a breath.

Mitch tracked a path with his thumb along the side of her breast, then moved his hand in slow increments until he found and fondled her nipple through the sweater. The snap of fireworks in the distance couldn't compete with the pounding in her ears. The lights flashing in the sky above them had nothing on those sparking behind her eyes when Mitch slid his leg between her legs, rubbing against her in a suggestive rhythm.

When Mitch broke the kiss to slide his tongue down her neck, a needy sound escaped Tori's parted lips. "How much longer is this ride going to go on?" she murmured.

Mitch lifted his head. "Not long enough. He turned around about five minutes ago."

"I didn't notice."

She definitely noticed when Mitch curled his palm on the inside of her thigh where their legs met. "I can't be just your friend, Tori, when I want to make love to you so bad, I physically hurt."

Tori, the former good girl, guided his hand between her

legs, letting him know exactly what she needed and where. "I want to be your friend, Mitch. But I also want to be your lover, at least tonight."

"And tomorrow night and the next, until you have to leave," he said as he plied her with heavenly strokes through the denim of her jeans. "But we can't do this here and do it right."

Tori was on the verge of going over the edge again until Mitch pulled his hand away and shifted them into a sitting position. "Luckily, we're almost there."

"Yes, I was. For the second time today."

He kissed her soundly one more time. "I'll damn sure finish this, baby, if you're sure that's what you really want."

"It is."

"Then let's get off this ride and go home."

Mitch rode all the way home with his hand on Tori's thigh while Bob, who'd had a few too many beers, talked incessantly in the back of the company's extended-cab truck and Stella kept telling him to stuff a sock in it or he wouldn't get any when they got home. Bobby responded by telling Stella they didn't have to wait until they got home, then the smacking kisses and giggles commenced.

By the time they pulled up the drive and deposited the uninhibited couple at their house, Mitch was so on edge he thought his skin might crawl off his body. And worse, the ape stared at him from his seat on the dash, looking as if he might open his monkey mouth and chastise Mitch for his inability to control himself enough to keep his erection reined in until he got Tori alone.

He waited until he saw Bob and Stella close the front door before he turned all that edginess on Tori with a down and dirty kiss, brief but to the point. Then he sped up the drive to his own home, spewing dirt as he braked harder than he'd intended. He yanked open his door, intending to help Tori out but she met him at the hood of the truck. They kissed hot and heavy again before he took her hand and led her inside the foyer, where he claimed her mouth one more time.

He couldn't remember the last time he'd kissed a woman so much in one night. He also couldn't recall when he'd enjoyed kissing a woman this much. Probably never. But kissing wasn't all that was on his mind at the moment, the reason why he tore himself away from Tori's tempting mouth, clasped her hand and led her down the hall faster than he should.

"What about Buck?" Tori asked when they entered his bedroom, her voice little more than a breathless whisper.

Mitch closed the door and tripped the lock. "I really don't give a damn where he is, as long as he isn't in here with us." Although from the looks of things at the fair tonight, his grandfather might be getting lucky, too.

When he turned to Tori, she brushed away her windblown hair, her face flushed. "We left Lanny in the truck," she said.

He approached her slowly. "And that's where he's going to stay. I don't want anything between us." He took two more steps until he stood immediately before her. "No stuffed animals. No clothes. And no apologies for what we're about to do."

"Definitely no apologies, if you continue to live up to the hype."

"I guess you'll know soon enough."

Time seemed to suspend in that moment, the tension so thick Mitch could cut it with his pocketknife. Tori put an end to the hesitation by tugging his shirt from his waistband, tearing at the snaps and peeling it off his shoulders.

Clasping the hem of her black sweater, he lifted it over her head and tossed it aside. Her hair was even more mussed now and she looked sexy as hell standing there in a scrap of a black lace bra that barely concealed her breasts. Mitch didn't attempt to remove that because she beat him to the punch. And what a punch he received when she shrugged it off, revealing tawny nipples drawn tight. He'd never had the pleasure to inspect them in the light until now, but that inspection was short lived when Tori dove for his buckle and popped it and the button on his fly open.

Determined to slow down and savor the moment, Mitch

gathered her up into his arms and laid her on the bed. He sat on the edge of the mattress and worked her jeans down her legs, tossing them aside to join her clothes on the floor, leaving her clad in only a scrap of black satin. Although his own jeans were as tight as a vise, he chose to remain dressed for the time being and simply study her for a few moments, with his eyes and hands.

"You're so damn beautiful." When he brushed his knuckles over her abdomen below her navel, she began to tremble, from her belly to her legs.

Concerned, Mitch glanced up to see that her eyes were tightly closed. He leaned over, his arms on either side of her. "Tori, are you okay with this?"

She opened her eyes and sent him a slight smile. "I'm very okay with it."

"You're shaking."

"I can't help it. I'm excited."

"Are you sure? Because we can stop if you—"

"Mitch, if you stop now, I'll never forgive you."

He traced her lips with the tip of his tongue. "I couldn't have you holding a grudge, now could I?"

"Precisely. Now take off your clothes and let's get on with it."

"Not yet," he said. "Not until I get a good look at you."

He bracketed her pelvis between his hands and rubbed downward with his thumbs, performing an impromptu massage as he lowered her panties. When he had them resting at the tops of her thighs, he lifted her bottom and pulled them completely away.

For a man who needed to be inside her more than he needed air, the pace had been agonizingly slow, but well worth the time it had taken. He didn't intend to pick up speed, not until he had her exactly where he wanted her to be.

"Open your legs for me, babe," he told her, using his palms to encourage her. "And don't close your eyes."

Her uneven breathing told him she was wound tight, and so

was Mitch, to the point of possible combustion. But that possibility didn't stop him from taking his time as he slid his fingers through the soft cloud of curls, remaining there to play for a few moments before seeking her slick, warm flesh. She was so primed for his touch that he knew it would take no time at all for her to climax. For that reason, he tempered his strokes, alternating between watching her face and watching the movement of his hand as he explored her, both inside and out.

Her respiration increased and her body tightened around his fingers as the first signs of orgasm overtook her. He wanted to replace his hand with his mouth, but she was already too far gone. Instead, he kissed her until every last ripple of the release subsided. Now he could join her in that state of oblivion.

He pushed away from her and stood at the side of the bed, fumbling for his zipper in harried anticipation.

"Mitch." He looked up to see Tori seated on the edge of the mattress where he had been. "Come here," she said, her voice much calmer now, as if she had regained her control where Mitch had done anything but.

He walked to her and watched as she lowered his fly, then did the same with his jeans and briefs. After he shrugged out of them completely, she held out her arms and, with only a look, invited him inside. But before he could join her, he still had something else to consider. Something he'd vowed not to forget again.

Pulling open the nightstand drawer, he withdrew a gold foil packet and held it up. "Should I use this?"

She failed to look at him as she tossed back the quilt and slid beneath the sheet. "I think that's a good idea, just to be on the safe side."

Her tone, her hesitant gaze, sent a sliver of apprehension up Mitch's spine. Maybe the other night she hadn't been honest with him. Maybe they had taken a huge risk. Yet as he studied her lying there in his bed, her skin flushed and her eyes wide, his desperate need for her outweighed any concerns over what might have been. He only wanted what could be. What would be.

After rolling on the condom, he snapped off the lamp and tossed back the sheet to take his place beside Tori. The three-quarter moon filtering in from the open curtains cast her face in muted light, her eyes as dark as the night.

Holding her face in his palms, he took another moment to just look at her. "I've wanted you non-stop since we were together in the truck. You've had me on a slow burn for four days. Every time I think about you, I get hard."

"Hard is good."

"Not when you're riding a horse. When I saw you standing outside the arena today, talking to Buck, it was all I could do not to tell the boys to go away, toss you over my shoulder and take you to this bed."

"And I might have let you."

"Oh, yeah?"

"Yes, even though my original goal was strictly friendship."

His only goal at the moment was to please her. To make her feel so good she wouldn't consider being anywhere else but his bed for the time they had left. "Tell me what you want, Tori. I'll do anything you want me to do."

With her hands on his hips, she encouraged him to move over her. "I want you inside of me. I want it deep. I want it hard."

Nearing the point of madness, Mitch reached between them and guided himself inside her, pausing before he was completely immersed in her heat. "How deep?" he asked, inching in a little more.

"I want to feel all of you."

He moved a little more. "How's this?"

"Is that the best you can do?" Her voice was low and throaty, enticing as hell, driving Mitch to the brink.

With one hard thrust, he seated himself completely and nearly came undone in the process. "Better?" That one-word question took a lot of effort and so did his determination to hold on a little longer.

She slid her fingers through his hair and moved her hips beneath him. "The best."

He wanted to be the best she'd ever had.

With all the strength he could muster, he reached over and grabbed the other pillow then pulled her up to prop it on top of the pillow already positioned beneath her shoulders. Then he lifted her bottom in his palms and drove into her.

Even if he'd wanted to slow it down, he couldn't. Not with her welcoming this wild, unrestrained rhythm resulting from all the desire they'd held for each other from the moment they'd met. Not when she kissed him, her tongue meeting his in time with their thrusts and her nails raking down his back. Not when he felt the first contractions of her climax pulling him even deeper still.

His heart pounded against his chest as the pressure built and built, then exploded, fast and furious. He rode the waves with Tori in his arms, his face buried in the softness of her neck, his body jolted from the intensity of the climax.

In the aftermath, they were now covered in sweat, surrounded by the heady scent of sex and finally calmed by the long-awaited satisfaction. Or at least Tori seemed calm. Now Mitch was the one who was shaking.

Tori lifted his head in her hands and stared at him. "Are *you* okay?"

"If I were any better, I'd be dead." He rolled to his side, taking her with him. "I don't want you to leave."

The words jumped out before he'd even had time to register exactly what he was saying.

"I wouldn't want Buck to know I'm in your bed," she said, obviously misunderstanding his meaning. He thought it best not to enlighten her, at least not until he analyzed why he hated the thought of her returning home. Right now, he had to keep her beside him all night.

He kissed her softly and rubbed her shoulder. "Buck might not be in until morning. And even if he's here right now, he doesn't know where you are. Stay with me tonight. All night."

She settled her cheek against his chest. "Okay. I'll stay tonight."

That promise seemed inadequate to Mitch because he

wanted more than tonight with her. He recognized some sort of transformation was occurring inside him. He damn sure didn't know what to do about that, or why Tori Barnett was making him feel things he'd never felt, never wanted to feel.

But he did know that as long as he had this lady in his arms, he was going to enjoy it. Tomorrow, he'd think about the rest.

Two hours later, Tori sat in the small chair positioned in front of the picture window in Mitch's bedroom, hugging her legs to her chest as she stared into the night. She wore his discarded shirt, the only thing she could locate in the darkened room. The fabric held the trace scent of his cologne, and so did her body.

The moon looked hazy, but then that might have to do with her unexpected tears. She could chalk up the irrational emotions to hormones. Or she could go ahead and admit that her current state resulted from the realization that she was falling in love with Mitch Warner.

She had never intended to do such an inadvisable thing, but her mind had been a giant jumble since the first time she'd danced with him. So had her heart.

She recalled when he had graced the pages of tabloids and teen magazines, an enigmatic young man who'd captured nationwide attention with his looks alone. He'd been born into wealth and a political legacy, a favorite pick to fashion the nation's future—smart, handsome and eligible.

At that particular time, Tori's interest in Mitch had been limited to the news coverage, due to her first thoughts of becoming a journalist, not desire for him or his kind—a typical, spoiled rich kid who'd had the world handed to him while she'd had to struggle for everything she'd obtained. She also remembered viewing one photo immediately after he'd been accepted to Harvard and another when he'd been caught on film escorting a beautiful co-ed to a college formal. But she'd never really seen him smile. She'd believed him to be arrogant, that he'd thought himself above showing any true emotion.

Now she recognized that she'd seen sadness in those magnetic blue eyes, not snobbery or self-absorption. And if all those women who'd fantasized about him really knew the man beneath the façade, as Tori now did, they would have worshipped him even more.

Still, she and Mitch hailed from different societal positions. They had very different aspirations. She longed for a successful career and recognition for her efforts. He yearned for obscurity and a normal life.

And she was beginning to feel guilty that in some ways she had been using him to attain that success and security. But she had to rationalize that she could assist him in maintaining his privacy by stressing that he wanted to be left alone. They both would win in the end.

Except Tori would suffer a loss in exchange for that success when she left him behind.

For that reason, she needed to start viewing this liaison exactly as it was—nothing more than a brief affair between two consenting adults. She needed to shore up her emotions, beginning now.

Standing, she turned and took one last look at Mitch. He slept on his side facing the window, the sheet draped carelessly over his hips, exposing only the tops of his thighs and the flat plane of his belly, his arms tucked beneath the pillow, his eyes closed against the limited light of the moon and Tori's scrutiny.

She wanted desperately to climb back beneath the covers and mold herself to his strong back. She wanted to wake him one more time and fuel the fire between them with a few touches. Instead, she bypassed the bed and headed out the door, leaving her discarded clothes, and Mitch, behind.

Tori needed time to think and assess. She needed to sleep. She couldn't do either with him so close.

Tomorrow, she would continue the interview process. If more intimacy occurred between them, she would strive to keep her feelings out of it. She would take what he had to offer, engage in a little self-discovery and enjoy their remaining time together without inhibition.

A solid plan. A good plan. Now she just had to stick to it.

Eight

Mitch had hated waking at dawn to find Tori gone. He'd had every intention of making love to her again before they started their day. At breakfast, he'd planned to confront her over the disappearing act but she hadn't shown up. When he'd gone to her room to seek her out, he'd found her bed made and the place totally deserted. As irrational as it seemed, he'd worried she'd taken the first plane back to Dallas after last night. It wasn't until Bob had told him Tori was up at the old house with Stella that he'd allowed himself to relax—as much as a man with an illogical need for a woman could relax.

After he accomplished something constructive, Mitch planned to let her know that he wanted her in his bed until she left on Sunday, no argument. If she appeared reluctant, he'd just have to find a way to convince her, and he could think of a lot of ways.

That brought about a smile as he sat at his desk, checking the status of pending software shipments. He wasn't having a whole lot of luck concentrating on his business when the business of making love to Tori was still so fresh on his mind. His concentration went completely by the wayside when the knock came at the door followed by, "Mitch, can I come in?"

"Door's open," he replied as he braced himself for the impact of seeing Tori again, as if he could prepare. Just hearing her voice had him on edge.

Tori entered the room dressed in a navy blazer and a skirt that hit just above her knees, revealing her legs and a pair of matching moderate high heels. Her straight brown hair flowed over her shoulders, stopping where the collar formed a V above her breasts. The suit was business conservative, tasteful, but to Mitch, she might as well have been wearing nothing at all, considering the impact on his libido.

Mitch leaned back in his chair. "Where have you been?"

She hooked a thumb over her shoulder. "Actually, I've been talking to some of the hands. I wanted to ask them a few questions."

"And you did it dressed like that?" His tone sounded gruff and jealous. He'd be damned if he wasn't.

Tori smoothed a hand down the skirt. "They didn't seem to mind."

"I'm sure they didn't mind at all. In fact, you probably made their day, showing up in that outfit."

"I meant they didn't seem to notice."

Mitch tented his fingers beneath his chin. "I never pegged you as being that naïve, Tori. They're men. They noticed. Especially Rand. He might seem like the quiet type, but you have to be careful around him."

As if bent on ignoring him, she slid the black bag off her shoulder and set it down on the sofa then pulled out a yellow notepad. "I have some interesting comments here. The overall opinion is you're fair and generous. One man said that he, and I quote, 'considers you a good friend, second only to his bluetick hound.' The only real criticism came when Rand said you're not always pleasant if you haven't had your coffee. Have you had your coffee today, Mitch?"

"Are you saying I'm not pleasant enough for you?"

"You are a little testy." She went back to the notes. "However, I am happy to report that the general consensus is that you're a generous employer and a good man."

When she swept her hair away from her shoulder and smiled, Mitch had the strongest urge to show her exactly how good he could be. "I still don't understand why it was necessary to get all dressed up to talk to the help."

"I'm dressed up because I plan to go into town with Stella. She wants to shop for some fabric for the nursery curtains. While I'm there, I'll interview a few people to give the story some local color. In order to do that, I need to appear professional."

Did she have to look so sexy doing it? "Fine. I'm sure they won't tell you all that much."

"I'll take my chances, but first...." Rifling in the bag, she exchanged the pad for a camera and waved it at him. "Picture time. I want to show you in your element. The cowboy working at the computer." She lifted the camera and said, "Smile."

Mitch didn't feel like smiling. The only thing he wanted to do right now was make her smile, utilizing his hands and mouth. To appease her, he sent her a halfway grin. She seemed satisfied and snapped the camera, nearly blinding Mitch with the flash.

"Great," she said. "One more."

She didn't wait for a smile or for Mitch's vision to return before she took two more shots.

"Enough," Mitch said. "I can't see a thing." That wouldn't do at all since he didn't want to miss a minute of seeing her, especially in that suit.

"Sorry," she said. "That's enough for now."

Not by a long shot, Mitch decided. He moved from behind his desk and held out his hand. "Give it here. I want to take a couple of pictures of you."

"Me?"

"Yeah. I want a souvenir."

She laid a dramatic hand above her breasts. "Well, if I must. Where do you want me?"

He grinned. "Honestly?"

She frowned. "For the picture, Mitch."

Stepping aside, he gestured toward his desk. "Sit there."

"You want me on the desk?"

Oh, yeah. That was a fine idea. "We could do it on the sofa, but I think the desk adds a unique perspective."

"If you say so." Finally she complied, hoisting herself up with her palms, her legs dangling and her hands folded primly in her lap.

Mitch didn't want prim and proper. "Cross your legs and pull the hem of your skirt up a little. Show me some leg."

She complied and leaned back on her palms, then topped off the pose with a coy look. "How's this?"

Pretty damn good, but he wanted to see a little more skin. If he had to settle for a picture as a replacement after she left, he wanted a good one. "Unbutton the top button on your jacket."

"Mitch—"

"Just do it, Tori. You might actually enjoy it." He sure was, and he'd only just begun.

Tori got the button undone after a couple of attempts. Mitch suspected she was nervous, but he also wondered if maybe she was a little turned on by it all. He planned to find that out, real soon. Stepping back, he snapped a picture then narrowed his eyes. "Open your jacket up a little."

"If I do that, you'll be able to see my bra."

"I know."

She drew in a shaky breath and released it slowly. "Why, Mitch Warner, I didn't know you were serious about taking naughty pictures."

"Sexy pictures, Tori. Just a little suggestive."

"Oh, so you want suggestive, do you?" she said, challenge in her tone and her dark eyes.

She released every last one of the jacket buttons and opened it completely, exposing her navy satin bra and shocking the hell out of Mitch in the process. She shook her head, mussing her hair so that it now looked as untamed as Mitch felt. And when she inched her skirt up to the tops of her thighs, he reclaimed enough coherency to back up and lock the door.

"Is this suggestive enough?" she asked when he stepped forward.

"Oh, yeah. That looks real good."

When he continued to stand there, greatly enjoying the sight, Tori asked, "Are you going to take the picture?"

He didn't want another picture. He wanted her. Now.

After tossing the camera into the bag, he strode to his desk and moved in front of her. Her skin was flushed, either from self-consciousness or excitement. He hoped it was the latter. Hoped that she was experiencing the steady burn she'd incited in him.

Mitch pulled her up from the desk and into his arms, wrapping her legs around his waist as he carried her to the sofa and deposited her there. He leaned over to kiss her, deep, hard, unrelenting, before he worked the jacket off her slender shoulders and pulled her arms from the sleeves. He trailed his lips down her neck, pausing to slide his tongue along the edging of her bra. When he heard her gasp, he raised his head and found her staring at him with anticipation.

"This morning, I didn't like finding you gone from my bed," he told her as he played with her nipples through the bra.

"I thought it might be better if I slept in my own bed, in case Buck should become suspicious."

"I don't care what Buck thinks. I just want to make you feel as good as you made me felt last night. Let me do that, Tori."

"What if someone wants you?"

"I want you, and that's all that matters."

Her sigh echoed in the room. "Mitch, you're making it hard for me to be a good girl."

"Tori, you're just making me hard."

Mitch crouched before her and propped both her legs on his

shoulder. He removed her shoes, one at a time, before reaching beneath her skirt to tug her panties up her legs slowly, then lifted her heels to completely pull them away.

Tori stared at Mitch, mute, the rasp of her respiration the only sound disturbing the quiet. The power of his gaze, the soft strokes he breezed up and down her thighs with his callused palms, the anticipation, robbed her of any desire to protest anything he might attempt.

For a fleeting moment, she questioned his goal when he lifted her bottom and pushed her skirt up until it bunched below her waist. All doubt dissolved, and so did she, when he dropped to his knees, nudged her legs apart with his shoulders and lowered his head.

Tori wasn't exactly a novice when it came to sex, definitely not a schoolgirl virgin. She had knowledge of the ways a man and woman could express themselves during lovemaking, but mostly through girl talk, not through practice.

The gentle sweep of Mitch's tongue, the unyielding tug of his lips, the caress of his fingertips went beyond her realm of experience. Beyond anything she had ever known before with a man, even her former lover.

The tempting taboo of it all sent her into an abyss where nothing existed except pure feeling. Her head listed to one side as Mitch continued to assail her, using his mouth as a lovely weapon to daze and weaken her, leaving her helpless to do anything but stare in wonderment.

When the climax claimed her, she tried to prolong it with every last bit of her strength. But she didn't have the will to stop it any more than she had the will to stop Mitch from keeping her captive with his mouth.

As Tori drifted back to reality and her heartbeat began to slow, she tipped her head back and closed her eyes, only mildly aware of the rasp of a zipper and the rattle of paper. She recognized then that Mitch was not quite done with her yet, and she wasn't quite sure she could handle more of his sensual torture.

But she was darn sure going try, she thought when he said, "Come here, Tori," in a low, controlled voice

She opened her eyes to see his jeans pushed to his knees, his shirttail doing little to conceal his erection. Like a boneless puppet, she didn't resist when he clasped her waist and directed her onto his lap to straddle his thighs. While she watched, he released the buttons on his shirt, allowing it to fall open.

Keeping his eyes locked on hers, Mitch lifted her up and guided her to his erection. Now it was Tori's turn to level her own brand of torture on him. She moved her hips in a slow, teasing rhythm, taking him inside her in small increments. She watched his face as she quickened the tempo, his jaw clenched tight. The power she experienced was a little hedonistic, and well-deserved considering the power he'd held over her. She bent to kiss him, nipping at his lips as she moved in a wilder cadence. A groan escaped his lips and she leaned back, knowing that in a matter of moments, he would be exactly where she had been minutes before, where she was going again because of Mitch's touch.

This release hit her as hard as the first, sending shock waves through her body as she took Mitch completely inside. A long breath hissed out of his mouth and she felt the steady pulse of his climax.

Tori collapsed against his bare chest, her palms curled over his solid shoulders as if she needed to hang on for dear life, her cheek resting over his strong heart. For such a reckless ride into oblivion, she felt incredibly content.

After a time, Mitch pressed a kiss to her temple and said, "I could get used to this."

So could she, and that was dangerous. "Guess there's something to be said for having outrageous sex in an office."

"It's not just the lovemaking, Tori. I could get used to having you around for more than a few days."

She raised her head and met his solemn gaze. "Unfortunately, I have to go back to work."

He brushed her hair away from her shoulders. "I know, but I want to see you again after that."

A tiny glimmer of hope radiated from Tori's heart. "That might be difficult since I live in Dallas and you live here."

"Maybe we could work something out."

"I'm open to suggestions."

He brushed a kiss across her lips. "Here's a good suggestion. I want you in my bed until you leave. We'll discuss the rest later."

That sounded more like a demand than a suggestion, but she didn't have the strength or desire to refuse. "Okay, but what about Buck?"

He grinned. "Three's a crowd."

She playfully slapped at his arm. "You know what I mean. I wouldn't want him to think badly of me."

"Don't worry about Buck. He always minds his own business."

"I know it's none of my business, but you're heading for trouble."

Seated at the dinette in the kitchen, Mitch looked up from his beer and glared at his grandfather. "What are you talking about?"

Buck turned a chair around, straddled it and rested his arms on the back. "You're stringing that girl along, and I don't like it one damn bit."

Mitch scratched at the label with a thumbnail. "In case you haven't noticed, we're both adults and well above the legal age."

"I know that. I also know that she's got feelings for you and I don't want to see them trampled."

"I don't intend to do that."

"What you intend to do and what you will do are two different things."

Mitch continued to stare at the brown bottle, dotted with condensation that was no match for the beads of sweat on his forehead. "What makes you think I'm going to hurt her?"

"Have you asked her to marry you?"

That garnered Mitch's full attention. "No."

"Why not?"

Mitch felt as if he were being reprimanded for staying out past curfew, only this was a much more serious offense, apparent by Buck's tone. "One, we barely know each other. Two, I have no plans to marry anyone and you know that."

Buck tipped his straw hat back from his brow. "Maybe you need to reconsider what you're doing by keeping her in your bed. Tori's a nice girl and she deserves a man who isn't gun-shy when it comes to matrimony."

"You're getting way ahead of the game, Buck. She's got a career that's important to her. As far as I know, she's not interested in anything too serious, either."

"Are you sure?"

Tori didn't strike him as being the kind who wanted a husband and babies, but he'd been wrong about women before. "Tell you what. If you'll stop grilling me about the women in my life, then I won't ask where you've been the past few nights."

"I've been with Eula Jenkins if you hafta know."

"You've been bedding the town's most proper widow?" Mitch shook his head. "Talk about trouble."

Buck snorted. "We're both a little long in the tooth for you to be passing judgment."

Mitch couldn't resist turning the tables on Buck. "Tell me something. Are you going to marry her?"

"Stranger things have happened. And you'll be the last to know if I propose."

Mitch barked out a laugh. "That'll be the day, you getting married again."

"It's a lot more possible than you going to the altar." Buck rubbed a gnarled hand across his stubbled chin. "Just a little more advice, Gus. One of these days you're going to have to let go of your anger over your daddy remarrying or it's going to eat you up inside and ruin your chance at being happy."

Mitch didn't think he would ever get over the betrayal, and he resented his grandfather for shoving it back in his face. "Don't you have something to do?"

Buck climbed from the chair with more agility than many twenty-year-olds. "Yeah. I gotta go get on the Internet. My chat buddies are expectin' me."

"Have a good time."

"I will. And you have a care because if you break that little girl's heart, you're going to hear it from me."

As Buck strode away, Mitch took a swig of his beer and set it down hard on the table. Maybe his grandfather was making some sense. Maybe he should just let it be over after Tori left.

But deep down, he couldn't stomach the thought of letting her walk away without ever seeing her again. He'd just have to take that out and think about it later. Right now, he needed to get some work done.

At least Tori had accomplished something besides having a little afternoon delight with Mitch Warner. She'd talked to several of the town's more prosperous citizens, including the owner of the feed store, who'd been highly complimentary about Mitch's community involvement, and Betty Galloway, the city secretary, who'd been forthright about Mitch's commitment to the local school through his elected position on the board. Obviously he wasn't so averse to politics after all, something Tori found somewhat amusing.

Mentally and physically exhausted, Tori now sat in the corner booth of Moore's Drug and Soda Fountain—the business that had been in Stella's family for sixty years—waiting for her best friend to finish up at the grocer's so they could head back to the ranch. Her thoughts continuously kept drifting back to the interlude in Mitch's office, and his declaration that he wanted to see her again after she returned home. Maybe they could try it for a while. And maybe their relationship might progress into something solid. A girl could always play at optimism.

Tori sipped at her cherry cola and almost choked when she heard the familiar feminine voice coming from the counter to her right. Her gaze zipped to the leggy blonde chatting away about the new house with Gracie, the waitress who'd worked at the fountain since Moses was in knickers.

She wanted to slink down in the booth to avoid another confrontation with Mary Alice but instead remained upright, pretending to look out the window at the limited traffic on Main Street.

"Is this seat taken?"

Tori cursed Stella's tardiness as she stared up at Mary Alice. "I'm expecting someone."

"Mitch?"

It would be too easy for Tori to lie but she opted for the truth. "Actually, Stella. She should be along any time now."

Mary Alice slid into the booth across from Tori and rested her cheeks in her palms. "I'll leave when she gets here, but first, I just wanted to say that you're the talk of the town."

Tori internally cringed. "How so?"

"It's my understanding your doing some sort of story on Mitch. Is it true?"

Relief relaxed Tori's stiff shoulders. "Yes, I am."

"Is this for a newspaper?"

"It's for a magazine."

Mary Alice sat back and folded her arms across her middle. "Oh. One of those grocery store rags?"

Tori quelled the urge to wipe the smug look off the bimbo's face. "It's a monthly magazine and very reputable. We do features on prominent Texas businesswomen. Every now and then, we cover successful men, the reason why I'm interviewing Mitch."

"Tell me something. Is making out with those men part of the interview process?"

Stay calm, Victoria. "That was just a friendly kiss. Spontaneous. It didn't mean anything." A whopper of a lie. It had meant everything.

"I take it this job of yours pays well?"

"It's a great job."

"I guess you live in one of those posh downtown apartments."

"It's a nice apartment." A small one bedroom apartment that happened to be in a Dallas suburb, the only thing she could afford until she paid off the medical bills, a fact Mary Alice did not need to know.

Tori was surprised that Mary Alice actually looked interested, and wistful, when she continued her queries. "Is there a lot going on in Dallas? I mean, do you go to museums and that sort of thing?"

"Sure. When I have time. Dallas has great opportunities in terms of culture. Haven't you ever been there?"

Mary Alice frowned. "Once, a long time ago. I considered moving to Houston to go to college right after high school."

"Why didn't you?"

"Well, because Daddy…" Her gaze faltered. "Because I decided to go to the community college in Halbert County. I studied business so I could help Daddy out at the mill."

Tori wasn't buying any of her bull. "You could have done that in Houston."

She presented a fake smile. "I like living in Quail Run, close to my family."

As unlikely as it seemed, Tori actually felt sorry for her. "It's never too late, Mary Alice. There's a whole wide world out there. You shouldn't settle."

Mary Alice looked totally incensed. "I'm not settling. I'm going to marry Brady and have a nice life."

"I'm sure you will," Tori said, unconvinced that Mary Alice believed her own shtick. "But if you're having second thoughts, it's best to stop now before you find yourself stuck in a marriage you don't really want."

Mary Alice slid from the booth, this time more quickly than she'd entered, her expression stony with anger. "Thanks for the advice, Tori. Now let me give you some about Mitch."

"I don't need any advice about Mitch."

Ignoring Tori's protest, Mary Alice set a palm on the table and leaned into it. "Has he taken you down to the creek yet? That's his favorite place to make love."

"I assure you we have not been to the creek."

"But you have been in his bed."

Tori wondered if she had guilt scribbled all over her face. "What makes you think something intimate's going on between us?"

"Because Mitch Warner is a hypnotist, especially when it comes to sex. He's good at everything he does, and he's great at giving a woman what she needs, although I'm betting you already know that."

This time Tori looked away. "Mitch is only a friend."

"I hope that's true, otherwise you'll spend nine years of your life trying to convince him to settle down. He won't do it, Tori. He's not the marrying kind so you can get that out of your head."

"I don't have that in my head."

"Good, because he's a lost cause when it comes to commitment. I found that out the hard way."

The sadness in Mary Alice's voice drew Tori's gaze to her melancholy expression. "You're still in love with him, aren't you?"

"Sure. He's very easy to love. But I guess you know that. And if you don't now, you will."

With that, Mary Alice walked away, leaving Tori alone with food for thought and shattered hope. She knew all too well that the advice Mitch's former lover had bestowed on her was good counsel.

It would be best to think of Mitch as only her friend and nothing more. She would physically accept what he offered for the rest of the week, then she would walk away while her heart was still relatively undamaged. Before she agreed to be his good-time good girl with no future in the offing.

For the first time in ten years, Mitch had failed to attend the annual rodeo. Instead, he'd opted to spend the night with Tori—the night before she returned to Dallas, leaving him behind.

As far as he was concerned, the week had passed too fast,

although he couldn't complain about the time they'd spent together, especially when they'd made love. And they'd made love a whole lot, at night and in the morning in his bed. During the day, in his office or behind the hay in the barn. She'd been willing to experiment, to try new positions, and they'd mastered quite a few. The only thing she'd refused was his offer to make love at his favorite fishing spot down by the creek.

Right now she sat on the sofa in the den across from him, wearing only his shirt at his request, her feet propped in his lap so he could give them a rubdown. He planned to give her a rubdown all over her body as soon as she quit asking all the damn questions.

She flipped through her notes, then tucked the pen behind her ear and set the pad down beside her. "Okay, I have about everything I need here except for one thing. I need some sort of quote about your father."

Mitch paused with his hand on her instep. "I told you I don't want to talk about him beyond the fact that I don't want to inherit his kingdom."

"Can't you think of anything nice to say about him?"

"I respect his abilities as a national leader."

"That's a start."

"That's the end of it, Tori. I'm not budging on this issue."

She slid her feet off his lap and scooted forward on the sofa, studying him with intense dark eyes. "Do you want to say anything about your mother?"

If he listed all her good points, that would take an entire page, maybe two. "She was a great lady and much more than my father deserved."

Tori slid the pencil from behind her ear and tapped it on the pad before gripping it in both hands. "A few nights ago, I went into the den while you were sleeping to do some more research on the computer. From everything I've read, it seems your parents were very much in love."

Although Mitch had never understood it, his mother had adored his father right to the end. "Don't believe everything you read."

"I don't, but I've seen pictures of them together. Stories that talked about how they were inseparable before she became ill. Are you telling me that wasn't the case?"

Mitch forked a hand through his hair. "When she was sick, he didn't have time for her. In fact, he wasn't even there when…" He let the declaration fade away because he didn't want to get into that with Tori. Resurrecting those old memories, the bitterness, wouldn't bode well for their last night together. And it could be their last night if he didn't convince her to see him in the future, a subject she hadn't wanted to broach to this point.

She leaned forward and touched his knee. "Are you telling me your father wasn't there when your mother died?"

"I don't want to talk about it."

"I think you need to talk about it. Maybe you'll feel better."

He attempted a forced smile. "The only thing that would make me feel better is if you take off that shirt and come sit in my lap."

"No you don't," she said. "No sexy talk. Not until you answer my question."

Fueled by his sudden anger, Mitch bolted from the chair and began to pace. "Okay, Tori, if you really want the truth, I'll tell you. But it's ugly."

"I can handle it."

He braced one arm on a bookshelf, determined not to look at her, otherwise he might not get this out. "My mother wanted to die at home, and she considered the ranch home, not the Bellaire mansion my father bought to impress all his cronies. So I made the arrangements for her to travel here by ambulance, against my father's wishes. He was royally pissed at me for doing it."

"And he wasn't at her side for that reason?"

"He was here the morning she died, but he had to get back to D.C. to do the nation's business."

"He left knowing she was going to die?"

Mitch hated to admit the truth, but he felt it only fair to do so. "We didn't know it was going to be that day exactly, but we knew she was close. He should've stayed anyway."

"Were you with her when she died?"

"Yeah." This was the most difficult part—the memories of his mother going to sleep and never waking up while he watched. "She slipped into a coma that afternoon while I was reading to her from this." He pulled out the book of poetry. "She revered John Donne. She taught me to appreciate poetry."

Sadness turned her dark eyes even darker. "I did something similar the day my mother died."

"You read to her?"

"I sang to her."

Mitch wasn't at all surprised, and he could imagine how much that had meant to her mother. "What did you sing?"

"The same song I sang the night we met. She loved Patsy Cline. I think that particular song had to do with her feelings for my father, although we never discussed that. It seemed to hurt her to talk about him."

"Where is your father now?"

"I don't know. In fact, I don't even know his name because I never asked, and my mom never offered. She did give me an envelope on my sixteenth birthday that contained his identity. I've never opened it."

Mitch had erroneously assumed that she didn't see her dad by choice. He'd never begun to consider she hadn't met him. "Why haven't you tried to find out more about him?"

"Maybe I just want to keep hanging on to the resentment. I guess we're alike in that respect, resenting our fathers because of what they have or haven't done. But at least you had a father to lean on after your mom was gone."

"Buck, yeah. My dad, no." Mitch shoved the book back into place and faced Tori. "Then the bastard had the nerve to remarry six months later."

Tori's confusion was apparent in her expression. "I thought he remarried a year later."

"That's what he wanted everyone to believe, and he had the

means to cover it up. That whole wedding the following year was only a show for the media. He betrayed my mother's memory and he came out of it without suffering a scratch on his well-regarded record."

"Do you think he was seeing your stepmother before your mother's death?"

"He denied it to me. But I've never believed it."

Tori rose from the sofa and laid a hand on his shoulder. "Sometimes things happen between people that are beyond control, especially when it comes to grief. Maybe he's telling the truth."

Mitch shook off her hand and turned his back to her again. He expected her to listen, to understand, not to side with his father. "It's not important anymore. That was a long time ago. I don't care to rehash it, so let's drop it."

"I understand. You're not willing to forgive your father. But at least you have one, even if he isn't perfect. That's more than I've ever had."

Remorse for his insensitivity turned Mitch toward Tori again, only to find she was at the door. "Where are you going?"

"To bed."

"I'll be there in a while."

She finally faced him. "To *my* bed, Mitch. I think you need some time alone tonight. And I'm sorry if I've made you dredge up some painful memories. I was only trying to help."

She had helped him in many ways, if only by listening, that much Mitch acknowledged. But his pride prevented him from protesting, even though he wanted to be with her this last night more than he'd wanted anything in a long, long time. "Fine. If that's what you want."

"I'll see you in the morning," she said, then left without a glance in his direction.

And more than likely, tomorrow morning might very well be the last time he would see her. He couldn't blame her for walking away from his bitterness. He understood why she wouldn't want to be involved with a man who'd made it his goal to steer clear of committing to anything aside from his business. A man who had been so caught up in his own anger that he hadn't even stopped to consider that she'd never known her own father.

Spending the night without her in his arms would be his punishment, and he should just accept it like a man. But he'd be damned if he would.

Nine

Lying on her side facing the window, Tori felt the bend of the mattress behind her and smelled the trace scent of summer-fresh soap. She sensed his heat a second before he settled against her back and his arms came around her.

"I'm sorry, babe," he whispered. "I don't know what else to say."

As far as Tori was concerned, he didn't have to say anything else. Although she believed it unwise to accept his apology so easily, she felt powerless to do anything else. An even trade for spending a last night with him.

Turning into his arms, she buried her face against his bare shoulder. Although he had removed all of his clothes, he simply held her for a long while, as if reluctant to make another move. Or perhaps this was what he needed from her at the moment, someone to absorb the pain and anger that still haunted him like a restless spirit.

Tori did want more from him. She wanted to remember being so closely joined with him that she didn't know where she began and he ended. To remember what it was like to be totally lost in love with a man, something she'd never understood until now.

She breezed her hand down his back, over the curve of his hip and then back up his side before reaching between them to touch him. He was already aroused, even before the first steady stroke of her fingertips. When she continued to explore, a slight groan slipped from his lips before he gave her a meaningful kiss propelled by pent-up emotion and the ever-present passion. He clasped her wrist and brought her hand to his lips for a kiss, then sent his hands over, touching places both innocent and intimate. Rolling her onto her back, he kissed his way down her body, breathing soft sensuous words against her skin, stopping to finesse her breasts then working his warm, wonderful mouth lower, bringing her to the sweetest release she had known in his arms.

He moved over her without a sound, entered her with a sigh, made love to her carefully as if she were precious. Then the passion prevailed, setting them on a frantic course. When they were spent in each others' arms, their skin damp from the heat of the lovemaking, their ragged breathing echoing in the silent room, only then did Tori realize what they'd forgotten. Again.

Although the timing wasn't conducive to pregnancy, she felt she should be honest with him about the chance they'd taken, both tonight and the first night they had been together. Yet when he whispered, "I can't get enough of you," in her ear, she couldn't quite find the strength to tell him. Not yet. But she had to tell him before night's end.

He rolled onto his back and settled her against his chest, stroking her hair and kissing her forehead as he always did in the aftermath, a habit of his she had come to appreciate and cherish. Only one more of the many reasons she loved him, and she did love him, wise or not.

Mitch's rough sigh signaled the end of the comfortable silence. "I've never told anyone about the moments before my mother's death. Not even Buck. He left the room because he couldn't handle it."

Tori found it odd that Mitch hadn't blamed Buck for his absence where he had blamed his dad. She also suspected that he was concerned she might use that information in the article. "I promise it will stay between you and me."

"And if you ever decide to find your father, I have a few connections who could probably help."

"I really appreciate that, Mitch." And she did. "But I'll only consider doing that when I decide to have children. I would want to have a medical history, if that's possible. I doubt I would pursue any kind of relationship with him, and that's assuming he would even want that."

"You plan to have kids?" His incredulous tone cut Tori to the quick.

"In the future." Quite possibly in the near future, if she'd become pregnant that first night they were together. It was now or never. "Speaking of children, there's something I need to tell you."

He tensed against her side. "You already have a kid?"

"No. The birth control shot I told you about, well, it's been a while since I had it. It might not be effective. I don't think there's a huge chance I could be pregnant, but nothing's fail safe."

She closed her eyes tightly and waited for the fallout. Waited for him to bolt from the bed and run like the wind. Instead, he said, "Condoms aren't one hundred percent fail-safe, either. We'll just hope there won't be any consequences. And if there are, we'll deal with it if and when the time comes."

Tori didn't dare ask how he intended to deal with it. She only knew that if she happened to be pregnant, she would love and care for the baby as well as her mother had loved and cared for her. She would tell her child about its father. But would she tell Mitch and face his rejection, the same as her mother?

He lifted her chin and kissed her lips softly, thrusting all the concerns from her mind. "Are you sleepy?"

"Not really."

"Neither am I. Any ideas how we might pass the time?"

He was drawing her in again with only the idle touch of his fingertips stroking her shoulder. "We could go grab a bite to eat in the kitchen," she said, even though she couldn't imagine choking down a bite of anything.

"I'm not hungry."

"Go for a midnight ride in the truck?"

His finger drifted down between her breasts. "Why don't we just go for another midnight ride?"

"But Mitch, it's only been about twenty minutes."

He pulled her over until they were face to face, body to body once more. He pressed against her, making it quite clear that twenty minutes had been more than sufficient. "You're insatiable," she told him.

He palmed her breast. "Downright rapacious."

"Rapacious? How about voracious?"

He slid his hand down her belly and taunted her some more. "Horny."

Tori laughed but not for long. She was too caught up in his caresses to laugh. Too overwhelmed by the fact that he could make her want him so desperately. Too aware that tomorrow would come too soon.

But tonight was theirs—all theirs—and she planned to enjoy it to the fullest.

After last night, Mitch knew every inch of Tori's body, every sweet curve, crevice and furrow. He knew every sound she made when he pleased her, every soft sigh and steady moan. He knew the feel of her hands on him, all over him, and thinking about that now brought his need for her back to life, even if he hadn't slept in over twenty-four hours.

He valued her as a lover, would miss her in those hours before dawn, but he would long for her friendship just as much. That's why he couldn't let her leave until she agreed to see him again.

Determination drove him out the front door that he let slam behind him, startling Tori, who was now standing at the passenger side of Stella's car. He slid his hands deep into his pockets before he did something stupid, like carry her back to his bed to engage her in a little sensual torment until she agreed. But that wasn't the answer right now. She needed to know that this wasn't only about sex. Not by a long shot. How he was going to express that, he had no idea. He'd just have to wing it and wish for the best.

"Need any help?" he asked, realizing he was a little late in making the offer since her bags were already positioned in the trunk. His fault, since he'd stayed way too long in the shower, hoping she might change her mind about joining him after she'd refused the offer. He'd begun to sense the distance she was putting between them long before she'd left his room to pack.

She smiled but it faded fast. "I've got it all. Thanks."

He'd never noticed the flecks of gold in her brown eyes until now, or how the highlights in her brown hair took on the appearance of fire in the sunlight. So much he hadn't noticed and he wanted more opportunities to correct that. "Are you sure you don't want me to take you to the airport?"

"You're needed more here. Buck told me you're all about to saddle up and move the herd."

"I could take a couple of extra hours." Man, he sounded almost desperate. Maybe he was. "The boys won't be back from church until lunchtime."

"That's okay," she said. "Stella needs to pick up some things in the city that she can't get here."

He clenched his jaw tight against protests he wanted to issue over her stubbornness. "Fine. But before you go, we need to talk about when we're going to see each other again."

She leaned back against the car and toed a rock with her sneaker. "I really don't think that's going to be possible."

Damn her resistance. "Sure it is. I either come there or you come here a couple of weekends a month. If money is a problem, I'll buy you a plane ticket."

Her gaze shot to his. "It's not the money, Mitch. But there is a problem."

"What?"

"I've been in a long-distance relationship before. It doesn't work."

"We could try it. It might work for us."

"Yes, it probably would work for you, but not for me."

"I don't understand what you're saying, Tori."

She released a slow breath. "I don't want to be your weekend girl, Mitch. I don't want to end up like Mary Alice, spending the next nine years of my life in a relationship that's never going to go anywhere."

How could he explain that she was nothing like Mary Alice? How could he tell her that she'd meant more to him than any woman he'd been involved with in his thirty-three years? "What do you want from me, Tori?"

"Nothing, Mitch. I don't want anything from you. But I might if we stay involved and I know that scares the hell out of you."

Mitch couldn't deny that. He also couldn't deny he didn't want to lose her completely. "If you mean marriage, you know how I feel about that."

"Oh, yes. You've made that clear as glass."

Turning away, she opened the door but Mitch closed it with his palm before she could climb inside. "Tori, I'm asking you to think about it. You don't have to answer me now."

She faced him again and framed his jaw in her palm. "Yes, I do have to answer you now. And the answer is no. I'm already halfway in love with you, and I don't want to go all the way alone. I don't want my life to be full of goodbyes. So let's just leave it at this." She stood on tiptoe and kissed him as gently as her touch. "I'll send you a copy of the article when I'm through with the final draft."

Still reeling over her declaration, he didn't know what to say. Could he really offer her more than his time in bits and pieces? Could he even consider committing to her? Right now, he wasn't at all sure, so he offered her the only thing he could until he sorted everything out. "You don't have to send the article, Tori. I trust you."

She looked as if he'd given her his entire ranch. "I won't let you down."

She already had, but it wasn't her fault. It was his.

"I have something for you," she said, then pulled a brown clasp envelope out of her back pocket. "Here. But don't open it now."

Mitch took it in his hand and turned it over. "What is it?"

"The picture you took of me in the office."

Damn. "When did you get it developed? *Where* did you get it developed?"

"Stella let me in the drugstore yesterday morning before they opened. I used their equipment."

Man, that was the worst move Tori could've made. "What did you do with the negative, because I don't have to tell you what could happen—"

She patted his arm. "I destroyed it, so don't look so worried."

Something else was also weighing heavily on his mind and he needed to get it out in the open. "You will tell me if you're pregnant, right?"

"We've got to go, Tori," Stella called from the driver's side.

Tori consulted her watch. "She's right. I've got to go. Bye, Mitch. It's been great." Without another word, she slid into the car and closed the door.

It's been great? How many times had he said that to a woman before he sent her away to resume his solitary existence? He was getting a bitter taste of his own medicine, and it burned like acid all the way to his gut.

Angry at Tori over her casual dismissal, at himself for not being the kind of man she needed, Mitch spun around and headed for the house, determined not to watch her drive out of his life. But as if he'd lost command over his will, he turned and leaned a shoulder against the rock support on the front porch. Stella pulled the sedan out of the circular drive and headed away, then stopped abruptly.

When the passenger door opened, Mitch believed Tori had changed her mind. Believed she was coming back to tell him that she didn't want it to be over. At the very least, coming back for one more kiss. Hell, he didn't care why, just as long as she did come back.

All his hope dulled when she exited the car with camera in hand and snapped a picture of him, favoring him with a sweet smile as his final keepsake.

Mitch remained in the same position until the car disappeared from view, the ache that he'd had since that morning growing more intense with each passing moment. But this time it was centered in his chest, right around the neighborhood of his heart.

"Are you going to tell him if you're preggers?"

Avoiding Stella's scrutiny, Tori continued to stare out the side window at the passing scenery on the interstate, what there was to see aside from billboards and the occasional fast-food joint. "I hope I have nothing to tell."

Stella turned down the radio, a good thing since the love song was greatly aiding in Tori's temptation to cry. "He has a right to know."

"And I have a right to live my life as I choose, so butt out."

"My, my, you're testy. I bet you are pregnant."

Tori sent Stella a look as sour as her stomach. "I could be premenstrual. Have you considered that?"

"I guess that could be it, but I don't think it's likely."

"You sound like you want me to be pregnant."

Stella took one hand from the wheel and patted her belly. "Misery loves company."

Miserable was exactly how Tori felt at the moment, and she didn't welcome any advice from her friend or anyone else, for that matter. "Look, if I did happen to be pregnant, I don't see any reason to involve a man who doesn't want kids or marriage or anything that even remotely resembles commitment. It wouldn't be fair to subject my child to that."

"Mitch isn't like your father, Tori. I know he'd want to do the right thing. And if you dig down deep past all that pain you're in now, you'd know it, too."

Tori shifted to one side as far the seatbelt would allow. "What is the right thing, Stella? Marrying only for the sake of a baby?"

She saw a flash of hurt cross her friend's face. "Bobby and I married because we love each other. The baby only sped things up a little."

How could she have been so careless with her words and Stella's feelings? "I didn't mean you and Bobby. I know you love each other. But Mitch doesn't love me."

"Did you ask him?"

"I shouldn't have to ask. I did tell him before I left that I was falling in love with him."

Stella's eyes went wide as the wheel. "What did he say to that?"

"Not a thing, and there's my answer."

"Maybe he's scared, Tori. Bobby nearly swallowed his tongue before he got out the 'love' word the first time."

Tori was terrified. "Love's a scary business, especially where Mitch is concerned. I'm not even sure he's capable of it."

"Oh, he is. It's just going to take the right woman, and I honestly believe that could be you."

If Tori could really believe that, then she would have agreed to see him again. She would have returned to Quail Run on weekends, showed him the sights of Dallas and made love to him as often as she could. But he'd given her no hope of that ever happening. He'd given her no promises. And hopefully, he hadn't given her a child, even though, under different circumstances, that would be the greatest gift of all.

"Speed up a little, Stella," she said. "I'm going to miss my plane."

"You're going to miss Mitch Warner, Tori. You won't be able to escape him, even when you get home."

"I have too much work to do on the article to think about him."

Even before Stella snickered, Tori realized how ridiculous that sounded. "Considering the story's about him, that's going to be tough, Victoria."

Regardless of what had transpired between them, Tori vowed to do the best work she had ever done. She was professional enough to paint a favorable picture of the man, even if he'd considered her only a convenience. Even if he happened to be the man she loved and could never have. He was still a good man. And no one knew that better than Victoria Barnett.

He lives in obscurity in Oklahoma with his grandfather who calls him Gus. The town folk consider him the consummate community leader. To see him on the street, he appears to be a classic contemporary cowboy. But in reality, he's a Harvard-educated rancher whose roots run deep in a political dynasty…

And he was going to be a father.

That morning, Tori had taken three tests to confirm what she already knew—she was pregnant. As her mother had done before her, she'd traded common sense for charisma in the arms of a commitment-phobic cowboy. Another sad case of repeating history.

She had no idea how to tell him. Or even if she should tell him, although he did indicate he wanted to know so they could "deal" with it. But what then?

Tori didn't have time to ponder the hows and whys when her boss breezed in, holding the last draft of the article, number five at Tori's last count.

"I think this is almost it," Renee declared, her smile accentuating her apple cheeks. "It's got everything. Great quotes. Local color. Love the pictures. But…"

Tori hated it when people ended a sentence with "but." "What is it now?"

"You're missing a very important aspect, namely a comment from Edward Senior."

"This is about Mitch Warner, not the senator."

"It just won't ring true unless we interview his father."

She could just imagine what Mitch would have to say about that. "I promised I wouldn't involve his father—"

"You don't make promises you can't keep, Tori."

Renee had that look about her, the one that said she wasn't about to budge short of a sudden Texas tornado, signaling certain defeat for Tori. "And how am I supposed to get this interview when the article goes to press in a few hours?"

Renee tossed the draft on the desk in front of Tori. "I've taken care of that. Senator Warner has agreed to give you fifteen minutes."

Tori felt the internal panic button depressing. "When?"

"Now. He's on his way up. Be nice to him."

With that, Renee swiveled on her heels and strode out of the office before Tori could manage another argument.

A few minutes later, Senator Edward Warner arrived in the open door, an impeccably polished statesman and a glimpse of the future Mitchell Warner. Tori had seen him in numerous photographs and on TV, yet the images had not done him justice.

His black hair was painted silver at the temples and his eyes, though not as light as Mitch's, were sky blue. He was slighter in build and probably two inches shorter than his son, yet his air of confidence and palpable control made Tori's office seem to shrink.

Rising slowly from her seat, Tori regained enough composure to extend her hand. "Senator Warner, I'm Victoria Barnett. Thank you for coming on such short notice."

He stepped forward and took her hand for a brief shake. "Very nice to meet you, Ms. Barnett. I do have a plane to catch back to D.C. in two hours, so I don't have much time."

Tori gestured to the chair opposite hers. "Then please, have a seat and I'll explain why you've been asked here today."

He sat and sent her a practiced politician's smile. "It's my understanding you would like some sort of statement from me concerning a feature on my son."

"Yes, that is what my editor is requesting."

"This wasn't your idea?"

"Actually, no. Mitch doesn't…" She studied the paper-weight on her desk, hating how ill-prepared she was for this meeting. "I'm afraid your son—"

"Doesn't care to have my opinion."

She finally looked up and found his expression somber. "That's correct."

"Then I assume you know that our relationship has not been on the best of terms."

"That's been common knowledge for some time. But Mitch did mention it to me a time or two."

"That surprises me, considering my son is a very private man. He also has a strong contempt for the media, and right-fully so. Until the past few years, he's spent his life in the spot-light. He was forced to grieve for his mother on national television. My position has left us all open for scorn."

The disdain in his tone disturbed Tori. "Senator Warner, you are under no obligation to say anything at all."

He smoothed a neatly manicured hand down the lapels of his navy silk suit. "If I thought that I could say something to mend my relationship with my son, I'd do it. I'm afraid it's too late for that."

"It's never too late. I only know that whether he admits it or not, he needs you in his life." Two minutes in his presence, and she'd already revealed too much.

"You sound as if you have a personal investment in Mitch's well-being."

How was she going to dig herself out of this one? Honesty was the best course. "I spent quite a bit of time with him dur-ing the interview process. I consider him a friend." And so much more. "He's a good man who happens to be in a lot of pain. I don't like to see anyone suffer."

"And you're suggesting that by adding my thoughts to this story, I'll alleviate some of his resentment toward me?"

"It's worth a try."

"I admire your optimism, Ms. Barnett, even if I don't embrace it." He crossed one leg over the other and adjusted his red tie. "If I speak to you off the record, can I trust that you won't repeat what I'm about to tell you?"

Tori pushed the recorder to one side and folded her hands in front of her. "Of course. But again, I don't want you to feel you have to say anything more."

"Normally, I wouldn't. But I've spoken with Mitch's grandfather and he seems to think you have more than a passing interest in Mitch. He also speaks very highly of you."

Tori nearly choked. "You've talked to Buck?"

"Yes. He's been much more understanding and forgiving than Mitch."

"What exactly did he say?"

"He claims that you're the woman who could bring my son around. I might have passed that off as the ramblings of a hopeful grandfather, but after listening to you for the past few moments, I believe he could be right."

Lord, her feelings for Mitch must be flashing like a neon sign across her face. "As I've said, we're only friends. I think Buck would like it to be more, but that's not very likely."

He looked more than a little skeptical. " Mitch could use a friend. Someone who understands why his wounds run so deep."

Tori already recognized the depths of Mitch's wounds. She also realized every story had two sides. She'd heard Mitch's version; she might as well hear his father's since he was willing to provide it. "Okay, then. If you think it will help, I'm willing to listen."

He shifted in the chair, the first sign of a chink in his composure. "I'm assuming Mitch told you he has never forgiven me for marrying only months after his mother's death."

"Yes. He sees it as a betrayal of her memory."

"It's difficult to explain why things happen the way they do," he continued. "Caroline was there to see me through a very tough time in my life. Not only had I lost my wife, I'd lost my son as well."

"And grief drew you both together." Not so different from Tori's and Mitch's connection brought about by their shared sorrow over the loss of their mothers.

"I suppose in some ways I couldn't face the prospect of living my life alone. Maybe that's a sign of weakness, and maybe that held true in the beginning. But Caroline and I have had a good life that's developed into a solid, loving relationship. Unfortunately, it hasn't included Mitch, by his choice."

"Maybe now that you're relinquishing your senate seat, it might be easier to repair your relationship. If you do intend to retire."

"I do, and my reasons have to do with something that is not yet public knowledge." He gave her a meaningful look. "Again, I'm taking a chance by trusting you, but because you obviously care about my son, I believe this is something you should know. Another reason why Mitch and I might never heal the breach in our relationship."

Tori could not imagine what he was about to say, or if she really wanted to hear it. But if it directly involved Mitch, she needed to know. "Go ahead."

"I'm leaving the senate because my wife's pregnant."

Great. Mitch was about to have a sibling and a child. Fine fodder for the scandal machine. "Congratulations. When's the baby due?"

"My daughter should be here in five months."

"A girl? That's wonderful."

He flashed a father's smile full of pride, but it quickly faded. "Caroline is in her early forties, so it's a high-risk pregnancy. But so far everything is going well. I pray that continues."

Tori witnessed sincere concern in his eyes, maybe even a hint of fear. Understandable. He'd already lost one wife; he was worried he might lose another. "I'm sure everything will be fine. And maybe this blessing will be the first step in repairing your relationship with Mitch."

"I'm not sure if or when I should tell him."

Ironic that Tori was in the same boat. "He probably should hear it from you instead of someone else." Advice she should follow, something that was becoming all too clear. "When the press gets wind of this, it will be all over the country."

"I know. I'll have to decide how to handle that soon."

"In the meantime, if you could find something favorable to say about Mitch for this article, that could help open the lines of communication."

When another long span of silence commenced, Tori feared he might not agree. Then he pointed to the recorder near her hand. "Turn that on."

Tori fumbled for the switch, earning a genuine smile from the senator. "Okay, I'm all set."

He settled back in the chair, as if a weight had been lifted from his shoulders. "Mitch is a fine man and I respect his decision not to carry on the tradition of politics in the family. I'm very proud of what he's accomplished, and I know his mother would be as well." He hesitated for a long moment and in his eyes Tori saw the depth of his pain and remorse. "I love him as much as any man could love his son."

He rose from the chair and said, "You may quote that."

Tori swallowed around the fullness in her throat, struggling to keep the threatening tears at bay as she stood. "Wouldn't you rather tell him that in person?"

He released a resigned sigh. "I gave up on convincing Mitch that I've always had his best interest at heart, even if I've made more than my share of mistakes."

"Maybe he'll be ready to listen after the article comes out."

"That would be great. And a miracle. But if he isn't willing to communicate with me, you can tell him for me. All of it. And take care of him."

With that, he was out the door, and Tori was left alone, stunned by his assumption that Mitch would ever consider letting her take care of him. Shocked that he had so easily read and accurately interpreted her feelings for his son, with a little help from Buck and her own inability to hide her emotions.

At least she had a quote she could use to appease Renee. A sincere, heartfelt quote from a father who was suffering as much as his son. But would Mitch welcome his father's words, or would he take exception to Tori including them? She had no choice. This involved her standing with her editor, her job. Possibly better pay and a promotion, something she would need if she were forced to raise her baby alone as well as pay off her debts. Yet deep down, Tori remained hopeful that this would be a catalyst for opening a dialogue between Mitch and his father. An opportunity for both men to heal. Then again, maybe she was being overly optimistic.

The other two decisions she now faced weighed even heavier on her mind—if and when to tell Mitch about the baby, and whether to open the faded envelope resting atop her desk. Right now, she would deal with the latter.

Drawing a cleansing breath, Tori slit the envelope's seal with one shaky fingertip and unfolded the single page. A faded photo dropped onto the desk—a snapshot of her youthful mother and a smiling cowboy. Presumably, Tori's father.

She gripped the letter in one hand while covering her mouth with the other, her vision blurred from tears as she read the information she'd avoided most of her life.

His name was Rick Ballard. He'd had medium brown hair, dark brown eyes and a pirate's smile, a sweet-talker of the first order. He'd hailed from Wyoming and spent his life on the road as a bull rider. One weekend in October, he'd come to Quail Run to participate in the local rodeo and had sufficiently swept Tori's then seventeen-year-old mother off her feet and into his arms. Eventually into his motel bed on their last night together—the night Tori had been conceived.

The final two revelations sent a sob climbing up Tori's throat that slipped out on the heels of her unexpected sorrow.

He had died two months before Tori's third birthday in a

tragic rodeo accident while doing what he loved to do. Before that fateful day, he had never known that Victoria May Barnett existed, because he'd never known about the pregnancy. And her mother had lied to her daughter all those years by claiming it had been careless disregard that had kept him away from his child.

Tori cleared away her shock to read the four simple words closing the letter, a plea for forgiveness.

"I'm so sorry, honey."

Caught in a stranglehold of emotions, Tori swiped furiously at the tears now streaming down her cheeks. She experienced regret over the loss of her father and anger over her mother's deception. And confused. Why hadn't she been forthcoming with the truth? Maybe Cynthia Barnett had been so ashamed that she'd needed to blame her lover. Maybe she'd inherently known that the man she loved was not interested in commitment and she couldn't change that.

Since the letter offered no explanation for her mother's motives, Tori would never know the whys. But she did know two things.

She would forgive her mother and let go of any bitterness. Otherwise, she would end up like a man she knew. And she had to tell that man about their baby. She would not let her own child suffer the same fate of never knowing its father, regardless of what Mitch chose to do with the information.

For the remaining five workdays, Tori would prepare for the article's release the following Monday. That left the weekend open to do what she had to do. Come Saturday night, she would return home to face her past…and her future.

Ten

I love him as much as any man could love his son....

For the third time in the past half-hour, Mitch read the words in total disbelief. He'd received the advance copy that morning by courier and he realized Tori had probably sent it. Yet she hadn't enclosed a note or an explanation. In fact, he hadn't heard a thing from her since she'd left.

"Smart girl, that Tori," Buck said from the desk chair in the den while he surfed the Internet. "She made you look like a saint in that story."

Mitch had no argument about the content of the article...until he'd come upon the quote from his father near the end. He tossed the pages aside and leaned his head back on the tattered sofa. "She didn't have to go to *him* for his opinion."

Buck swiveled the chair away from the monitor and glared. "Didn't you read what your daddy said? He's proud of you, thinks you're a good man and—"

"I read it, Buck."

"But you ain't paying attention."

He knew his grandfather well enough to know he wouldn't let it go until he'd had his say. Well, Mitch intended to have his say, too. "Why shouldn't I believe this isn't just another ploy to win over his constituency?"

"Because he never needed you for that before. And he's about to take his bow. He's not running again."

"He hasn't confirmed that yet. I'll believe it when I see it."

"Believe it. He told me it's so."

Mitch straightened, every muscle in his body taut with both shock and fury. "When did you speak with him?"

Buck shrugged. "Last Sunday, like I've done almost every Sunday for the past fifteen years. He calls me to check on you since you won't give him the time of day."

Obviously everyone he cared about was bent on subterfuge. "Why the hell didn't you tell me this before?"

"Probably because of the way you're reacting right now."

"And you didn't think I had a right to know or any say-so in the matter?"

"No. I can say whatever I please to whoever I please. I didn't live almost eighty years to have a wet-behind-the-ears grandson telling me otherwise."

Overcome by blinding anger, Mitch swept the article off the couch with his forearm. "And I don't appreciate you going behind my back."

Buck bolted from the chair and stood over Mitch, the fires of hell in his rheumy eyes. "You listen here, young man. You might not respect your daddy, but you will respect me. You've been mule stubborn for much too long. If I can forgive him, then you can, too. She was my daughter, for God's sake."

"And she was *my* mother! Tell me one good reason why I should forgive him for not bothering to be at her deathbed, then marrying another woman before his first wife was barely cold in her grave?"

Buck yanked the magazine from the floor and jabbed a finger at the page. "The reason's right here, plain as the nose on your face. He loves you."

Mitch didn't need this. He didn't want to deal with it. For two solid weeks, he'd done nothing but think about Tori, the loss eating at his insides like rust. Now she'd betrayed him by talking with his father when she'd known all along how he felt about that. "Good for good old Dad. Might have been nice if he'd said it to me in person instead of in print for the world to see."

Now Buck tossed the magazine onto the couch. "Good God, Gus. Don't you remember him telling you every time he left you here in the summer? He said it until you got too big for your britches and quit listening."

"And he quit listening to me a long time ago. He didn't listen when I asked him—begged him—to stay when Mom was sick. He ran off to serve his country, as always. We weren't important enough for him to stick around for any length of time."

"You were important to him, Gus. And it was tough on him, leaving you behind to deal with your mama's sickness. But he tried to get back that night. He didn't know she was going to pass before he made it here. None of us knew."

Mitch felt incredibly tired at the moment. Too tired to re-hash old recriminations. "We've been through this before."

Buck snatched his decrepit straw hat from his head and crushed it in his hands. "And we'll keep going through it until you get it through your hard head. Your daddy has never stopped loving you, even when you turned your back on him, just like you turned your back on Tori."

Where the hell had that come from? "This has nothing to do with her."

"It has everything to do with her. You're making the same mistakes. Just like you won't admit you love your daddy, you won't admit that you love her either."

Mitch's gut burned and he closed his eyes against the pounding in his temples, the truth of that statement digging at his heart. "You're crazy, old man."

"I might be crazy, but you're a coward."

Mitch's eyes snapped open. "What did you say?"

"You heard me. You're a coward. A yellow, lily-livered coward."

"I'm not afraid of her."

"You're afraid of your feelings for her, dammit," he hissed. "Admit it to me. You love that girl, otherwise you wouldn't be moping around here, biting anyone's head off if they come within fifty feet of you. You're so sick in love you can't even think straight. Hell, if it hadn't been for Rand, you would've shipped sperm instead of software to that college in Idaho."

He would spend years trying to live down that mistake and no telling how many more. "Let it go, Buck."

"Not until you say it."

This time Mitch vaulted from his seat. "I said let it go."

"I'm going to stand here until you say it, or I die in my tracks, whichever comes first. You know I will."

"Okay, I love her!" Mitch blurted. "Are you happy now?"

Buck's grin looked victorious. "Nope. Not until you tell her."

Mitch paced the room, restless with the admission and the knowledge that he'd blown it with Tori. "I haven't heard a word from her in two weeks. The day she left, I told her I wanted to see her again, but she refused."

"Maybe that's because you didn't offer her more than a quick tumble every now and then. That don't set too well with the womenfolk."

Mitch stopped at the shelf and faced Buck again. "What am I supposed to offer her?"

"Marriage."

"You are crazy. We've only known each other a short time." Yet Mitch felt as if he'd known her for years. She certainly knew him better than any woman ever had. She knew him better than any living soul.

"That don't matter, Gus. Why, I met your grandmother on a blind date one weekend and we got married the next, before I shipped off to the army. Your mama went down to college in

Austin, met your daddy her second year, then married him two months later. You came along about ten months after that."

"That's you and my parents, not me. I prefer to wait a little longer before I decide something that will affect the rest of my life."

"You've waited too long as it is. It's time to grow up, Gus. Be a man. Commit to something other than this place cause it won't keep you warm in the winter. Have a few babies, too. I'd like some great-grandkids hanging around before I get too old to take them fishing by the creek."

Mitch held up his hands, palms forward. "Whoa! You're getting way ahead of yourself. I haven't said I'm going to propose, not to mention Tori's not even speaking to me."

"She will, as long as you say the right thing," Buck said with certainty. "By the way, me and Eula are going to get married in the next week or two, so I'll move in with her. That'll give you and Tori this place all to yourself."

A banner day for bizarre news, Mitch decided. "You're serious?"

"Yep. Eula's a good moral woman and I got to buy the package before I get the goods."

"You're marrying her so you can have sex?"

Buck chuckled. "I'm marrying her because I love the woman. Sex at my age is just topping on the cake."

Despite Mitch's determination not to, he laughed. "Congratulations, Gramps. I hope like hell you know what you're doing."

"I do." Buck pointed a bony finger at him. "And if you call me Gramps again, I'll take you down a notch or two. I also expect to be saying congratulations to you real soon. Maybe we can have a double wedding."

Buck's senility had obviously set in. "No thanks. If I decide to get married, I want my own service. And that's a big if." Mitch couldn't believe the words had left his mouth with such ease. He couldn't believe he was actually considering something as insane as proposing to Tori. Now he was getting ahead of himself. First, he had to find her and then convince her to talk to him. That could prove to be an enormous challenge. One he was ready to undertake. Now.

He started to leave the room before Buck called to him, "Where are you going in such a hurry?"

Mitch stopped at the open door and faced his grandfather. "I'm going to go pack a bag so I can head to Dallas."

"She won't be there, Mitch."

Mitch turned to find Bob standing in the hall, baseball cap in hand. "How do you know?"

"She called Stella yesterday and said she was coming here tonight. We're supposed to meet her at Sadler's around 8 p.m. because she's driving in."

"Did she say why she was coming back?"

"You know women, boss. Stella only told me what she thought I needed to know. But I have a sneakin' suspicion she wanted me to pass the information on to you so you'll show up."

"I might just do that." No might about it. He'd be there and nothing would stop him, not even the case of cold feet threatening to work its way beneath his boots.

In a little over eight hours, Mitch would grab some courage and lay it on the line. In eight hours, he'd finally see Tori again, this time in person instead of in his dreams. Eight hours seemed like a helluva long time to wait.

He guessed if he'd waited half his life to find a woman like her, he could wait a few more hours.

"He's not coming."

Stella patted Tori's hand from across the same table they'd occupied the first night she'd met Mitch, only tonight, Janie and Brianne had been replaced by the now-absent Bobby. "Sure he's coming, sweetie," Stella said. "It's only been an hour."

An hour that had seemed like a millennium to Tori. "Now tell me again what Bobby said to him?"

Stella rolled her eyes. "He told him to meet us here at eight, and Mitch said he would be glad to."

"Are you sure that's all Bobby told him? He didn't say anything about me being here?"

"As far as I know, that's all he said. But you know how men are. They don't go into great detail unless it involves sex or sports. If you want, you can ask Bobby as soon as he gets back from the restroom."

As if Bobby would really tell Tori if he'd slipped up and mentioned her appearance. She rested her cheek on her palm and glanced around the crowded bar. If Mitch happened to come in, she would have a hard time seeing him immediately among the local masses. And if he had wandered in earlier and seen her, he might have left before he'd been discovered. That just made her plain depressed.

"I've got an idea on how you can pass the time, Tori," Stella said.

Cry? That's exactly what Tori wanted to do at the moment. Her roller-coaster emotions were threatening to leave the track for the umpteenth time in a week. "Maybe count Carl's chest hairs spilling out from his T-shirt?"

Stella yanked the spiral lock of hair Tori had been twisting like an old-time washing machine wringer. "You should sing. You know you want to."

Oh, sure. Like she really had something to sing about. "No, thanks. And might I remind you, it's Saturday night. Karaoke's on Friday."

"Carl would probably make an exception. You were really popular the last time you performed. Besides, it would help you to relax."

Tori let go a mirthless laugh. "Singing in front of a jam-packed room is not my idea of relaxing, especially in my nervous state."

At that moment, Bobby returned to the table, saving Tori from having to further argue the no-singing point with her best friend. For once, she was glad to see Stella's other half.

He hitched up his pants, yanked back his chair and dropped into it. "I don't think he's coming, girls."

Tori was no longer glad to see Bobby Lehman, even if she did agree with him. "I just said the same thing a minute ago."

"You want Bobby to go call him, Tori?" Stella asked.

Frustrated, Tori slapped one palm on the table, rattling Bobby's beer bottle and startling the couple. "I feel like I've been thrust back into high school study hall when everyone passes notes. I should've just gone out to the ranch and taken my chances instead of coming here."

"Why didn't you?" Stella asked.

Good question. "I guess I thought this was a more neutral place, in case he decided to slug me for sticking his dad's quote in the story."

Stella looked mortified. "Mitch would never hit a woman, Tori."

"I know that. I meant in case he wants to give me a large piece of his mind." He already owned a large piece of her heart.

Bobby streaked a hand over his square jaw. "Yeah. He wasn't too thrilled about that."

Panic gripped Tori. "You talked to him about it?"

"I kind of overheard him talking to Buck. He'll get over it eventually."

Eventually. Maybe by the time their child turned twenty-one, if she ever had the opportunity to tell him about the baby. "I wouldn't bet on it. He tends to hold grudges." One of the few faults Tori had discovered, but a major one, especially if he turned his resentment on her.

So far nothing was going as planned for Tori tonight. And it only got worse when Carl tapped the microphone and said, "Listen up, people. By special request, you're about to enjoy an encore performance by Tori Barnett doing a little Patsy Cline number! Get up here, little lady, and sing!"

Tori now understood the whole grudge thing. "Stella, if you weren't in such a delicate state, I'd ask you into the parking lot."

She had the gall to laugh. "Oh I'm so sure, Tori, since you're so tough."

Tori didn't felt tough at all. In fact, she felt fragile and frightened, void of confidence in her singing or anything else, for that matter.

The chanting commenced, rumbling through the crowd until Tori was forced to stand and answer their pleas. On her way to the stage, she gave Stella a look that said this was not over.

While Carl put on the music, Tori adjusted the microphone and cleared her throat. If she'd known what Stella had been up to, she would have requested another song. But it was too late to even consider that as the intro began to play.

Tori admitted the song was very appropriate. After she told Mitch about the baby—if she had the chance to tell Mitch—she might only have her sweet dreams of him, forced to start her life anew without his support or the prospect of his love. At least she would have a special reminder in her child, hopefully the best part of them both.

When her cue came, Tori belted out the lyrics as if she had all the strength the world. Sang as if her life depended on the act. And cried despite her efforts to avoid that very thing.

She closed her eyes, willing her voice to remain steady as the tears rolled down her cheeks and onto the red sweater she'd worn the first night she'd met her stubborn cowboy. She didn't bother to brush them away, didn't care who might notice.

This might have been her mother's favorite song, but right now Tori sang to Mitch Warner—wherever he might be.

Standing back at the corner of the crowded bar, Mitch watched Tori give another heartfelt performance. She wore the same clothes and sang the same song from that first night he'd laid eyes on her. But this time, the feelings she stirred deep within him had nothing to do with lust and everything to do with his love for her. He wasn't accustomed to having his control sabotaged by emotions, yet he had no will left to fight it. He was totally unarmed and ready to surrender. From now on, she would call all the shots.

Several patrons greeted him, but he didn't respond beyond

an occasional nod. He moved closer to the stage to get a better look, concerned when he thought he saw moisture dampening her flushed cheeks. Yet her voice remained clear, almost reverent, and now that he knew this had been her mother's favorite, he assumed that was the reason for the tears. But she hadn't cried before, and that led him to believe it could be more than bittersweet memories causing her turmoil.

Seeing her standing there in the spotlight, her sorrow bared for everyone to see, he wanted to go to her and hold her, protect her, yet he had no call to interrupt at the moment. He wasn't even sure she would welcome the intrusion. But when her voice faltered and she stopped before the song's end, he elbowed his way through the muttering crowd, practically shoving several people aside, strode to the stage and caught her hand in his.

She opened her eyes and stared at him, as if she didn't quite believe he was real. When she didn't move, he clasped her waist, pulled her from the platform and into his arms.

They held each other as the music continued, danced as they had that first night together, clung to each other, this time driven by a closeness they'd established during their time together, not chemistry. Mitch recognized their relationship went far beyond desire. Far beyond anything he'd ever expected.

When the original version of the song began to play, several couples drifted onto the dance floor. Mitch didn't care if the whole town decided to three-step. He couldn't imagine letting Tori go, not yet. Not until he felt her continued tears bleeding through his shirt, where her cheek rested against his chest.

He sought her ear and whispered, "Let's get out of here."

She nodded and he took her hand, guiding her toward the exit through the gawking crush of people. On the way out, they passed by Bob, who gave Mitch a salute, and Stella, who grabbed Tori's hand, winked, then let her go.

By the time they reached the door, Mitch was determined to get as far away from this place as possible. He steered Tori toward his truck, opened the door for her and helped her up into the cab, amazed when she didn't ask where he was taking her. He climbed in behind the wheel and shot out of the parking lot, sending a gravel hailstorm in his wake as he sped down the highway toward home.

He tugged Tori close against his side and let silence prevail for the time being. When he arrived at his destination, then they could talk.

After pulling up the drive that led to the old house, he diverted to his right and traveled down the makeshift road leading to the creek. A full moon had risen over the open field, guiding him to the spot that had served as his refuge on more than one occasion, including the day his mother had died. If he needed to come to terms with his feelings for Tori, and reveal them to her, this was the logical place to do it.

After putting the gearshift into Park, he slid out of the truck, rounded the hood and opened Tori's door. Again she didn't refuse his offered hand or his direction, as if she totally relied on his guidance.

He led her to the back of the truck, yanked down the rusty tailgate then seated her there. He stood before her, both her slender hands wrapped securely in his. The moonlight cast Tori's face in gold, a face that Mitch wanted to see every day for the rest of his life. He'd never wanted anything so damn bad. Not his degree. Not his business. Not even his freedom.

But first, he needed to find out what had her so sad, and he hoped like hell it didn't have anything to do with him.

Tori focused on their joined hands, still silent. At least her tears had dried, but that did nothing to alleviate Mitch's concern.

"What's going on, Tori?"

She blew out a shaky breath but failed to look at him. "It's been a tough two weeks."

"I know. I've missed you." More than he'd missed anyone since his mother's death.

"I've missed you, too" she said, keeping her head lowered.

"Tori, look at me." When she complied, he continued. "When I found out you'd be there tonight—"

"Bobby told you?" Both her tone and expression reflected her surprise.

"Yeah. Didn't you know that?"

"No. I asked him not to and he said he wouldn't. I was afraid if you knew I'd be there, you wouldn't come because of the quote from your father in the article."

"I'm not going to lie to you, Tori. I was pretty mad at first since I didn't understand why you did it."

She raised her eyes to his. "I did it for you."

He brushed a strand of hair from her cheek. "I know. And I appreciate that more than you know."

She looked genuinely pleased, and as pretty as Mitch had ever seen her look. "I think you should try to work it out with him," she said. "It's important, especially since I've recently found out my father never knew about me. And I'll never know him because he's gone. He died when I was three."

He felt her pain as keenly as if it was his own. "You read the letter."

"Yes. That's why I think it's important you reestablish a relationship with your own father. He's all you have."

"I realize that now," he said. "But before I deal with that, I have a few things I need to say to you."

Her gaze drifted for a moment and then came back to rest on his eyes. "I need to say some things to you, too. You can go first."

Mitch had every intention of going first, before he lost his courage. "You're going to have to bear with me because I don't have a whole lot of experience with this kind of thing."

"You're a smart guy, Mitch. And articulate. I'm sure you can handle it."

"Just a few simple words from a simple man, Tori. That's all."

"I'm listening."

He tightened his hold on her hands to anchor himself. "Since I left college, I've carefully calculated my life, planned everything down to the last detail. But I've recently realized some things throw all those plans off course."

"I know what you mean. Sometimes things just happen."

"Yeah. I sure as hell didn't plan on you. I didn't plan to stay up at night for two weeks, dealing with this pain I didn't understand. I sure didn't plan to pick up the phone at least a hundred times to call you before I decided that wasn't a good idea."

Now she looked hurt. "Why wasn't it a good idea?"

"First, you told me you didn't want to see me anymore. Second, I didn't know what I wanted from you until today."

"What do you want from me, Mitch?"

"To be with you, and not only tonight." He tipped his forehead against hers. "I can't stand the thought of you walking away and never coming back. I don't think I can take that a second time."

She released a small sob and bit her lip, he assumed to halt another round of tears. He planned to kiss those away eventually—if she let him after he said what he needed to say.

He was down to the wire. The moment of truth had arrived—a moment he'd never thought to confront. "I love you, Tori. God knows I didn't want to, but I do."

Tears threatened at the corners of her eyes but she blinked them back. "Are you sure?"

"It's real, Tori, and I don't want to let it go. I don't want to let you go."

"But there's so much we have to deal with. You're here, I'm in Dallas."

"Marry me and we'll live wherever you want to live." There it was, and not so difficult after all. Not when it was so right.

When she tugged her hands from his grasp, she might has well have knifed him in the gut. "What did you say?"

"Marry me, Tori. Be my wife. I would be honored to be your husband."

"Do you realize how crazy that sounds, Mitch? What are people going to say since we've known each other for such a short time?"

"I don't give a damn what anyone has to say about it, except for you."

She spun a lock of hair around her finger. "First, let me say what I have to say to you. Then we'll see if your offer still stands."

Fear momentarily immobilized Mitch. Fear that he'd screwed everything up by his unwillingness to acknowledge his feelings until now. "I don't think you could say anything that would change my mind. Unless you don't love me."

She dropped her hands to her lap. "Oh, I love you all right."

"But only halfway?"

"All the way. That's not the problem."

Relief reared its head. But frustration and impatience attacked him all at once. "Then what the hell is it?"

"I'm pregnant."

Mitch waited for the urge to run. Waited for the cold sweat, the burning in his gut. It didn't come at all. In fact, what he experienced at the moment felt a lot like pride and joy. "When did you find out?"

"Earlier this week. Actually, the day I met with your dad. That's why I'm here tonight, to tell you."

The same old mistrust came home before he could stop it. "Did you tell him?"

She frowned. "Of course not. I wouldn't tell anyone without telling you first. Even Stella doesn't know. She thinks I'm here just to see you again."

Mitch rubbed his chin and grinned. "I'll be damned."

"I'll be damned? Is that all you can say?"

"You know something, babe. I think subconsciously I wanted to get you pregnant. I could've pulled a condom out of my pocket that night in the truck."

"You had a condom with you?"

"Yep, but I also had a woman in my arms that made me lose my mind because I wanted her so badly." He touched his lips to hers. "I still want her."

Tori swiped at her eyes. "I'm so glad you do. I figured you'd be back at the house by now, locking yourself in."

Overcome with a sense of happiness he'd never before experienced, Mitch lifted her off the truck and set her on her feet, pulling her close. "Buck told me he wanted a great-grandchild before he was too old to enjoy one. Looks like he's going to get his wish. Now am I going to get mine?"

He saw pure love shining in her eyes, all for him. "Yes. I'll marry you. Gladly."

"Thank God." He kissed her again, this time more deeply to drive home his feelings for her. "I love you, baby. And I don't want to wait to get married."

"Just when do you propose we do this?"

"Next week wouldn't be soon enough. But I guess we have to make a few arrangements and decisions about where we're going to live."

"I really don't see why we can't live here."

That totally caught Mitch off guard. "What about your job?"

"It seems that news of your story has already created a lot of buzz, even though it's not out until Monday. I've already started getting some offers. I can work freelance, as long as you understand it might mean quite a bit of traveling at times."

"That's fine, as long as I can go with you most of the time. Because babe, from this point on, I don't want to be without you." And he didn't, not even for a minute.

She brushed a soft kiss over his lips. "And I don't want to be without you, either. Besides, it's been good to be back here. I didn't realize how much I've missed the small-town life, even though we will be the latest topic of gossip."

He saw right through her attempts at false humor. "Tori, I'll make sure no one in this town will ever do or say anything to hurt you again."

"You know something? I'm not really worried. When I think about it, there were very few people who didn't accept me and my mom. People like Mary Alice."

Hopefully that would be the last time he had to hear that name, at least coming from Tori's sweet mouth. "You won't have to worry about her. She broke off her engagement to Brady and she's moving to Chicago. Something about going to culinary school, although I can't imagine Mary Alice doing anything that involved getting her hands dirty."

"I'm glad she's decided not to settle for a mediocre marriage." She gave him a smile and a squeeze. "I'm not."

"I want to make you happy, Tori. The whole thing kind of scares me since my example has fallen short."

Her expression went serious. "Mitch, your father explained a lot to me about the reasons why he married Caroline and why he's now retiring. You need to let him explain it to you, too. And you need to really listen with your heart."

"I'll call him tomorrow. I can tell him about the wedding. But I'm not making any promises on how it will go."

"At least it's a beginning."

He lowered his hand to her abdomen, the place that sheltered the child he'd never believed he would have. A child he already loved. "Here's to new beginnings."

Pulling his hand up, she kissed his palm. "And good memories." She sent a quick glance over her shoulder and grinned. "Want to make a few more?"

Mitch returned her smile. "Yeah, but I'm thinking we should go back up to the house and use a real bed. You need to be comfortable."

Ignoring him, Tori hoisted herself into the truck bed and slipped off her jacket. "I'm thinking we should take advantage of the fact that I'm still mobile enough to do it in unusual places. In a few months, that might not be true."

Without hesitation, Mitch hopped up into the bed and covered it in hay, a repeat of that first monumental night together.

"You know what I'd really like," she said as they settled onto the hay.

Mitch cupped her breast beneath the sweater. "Yeah, baby, I think I do."

"Aside from that."

Her mild scolding didn't stop Mitch from lowering his hand to the zipper on those coronary-inducing leather pants. "Yeah, I know all about that, too."

"Mitch, I have to say this now." She pulled his hand up and held it against her heart. "I want a big wedding. The works. Just like Stella's. As long as I don't have to sing."

"I really like hearing you sing. How about at the reception?"

"I can do that." She gave him a mock-suspicious look. "You're not going to make me sing all the time for my supper, or for sex, are you?"

He slid her zipper down. "No, but I will make you want to sing during sex."

She worked his belt buckle open. "We'll see about that. And I'll make a deal with you. If I promise to sing at our reception, then you have to promise to recite some poetry."

He halted the downward progress of her jeans. "In front of people?"

She gave him a coy look followed by a wink. "If you'll at least think about it, I promise you'll be rewarded for your efforts."

"That's a deal." And he sealed that deal with another kiss, another slow, mind-blowing session of lovemaking under the stars with the woman he would soon make his wife.

As he held her in his arms, Mitchell honestly believed he could accomplish anything. Except maybe poetry reading in public.

What the hell. He would consider it for Tori. Anything for Tori.

Epilogue

*"**T**wice or thrice I have loved thee, before I knew thy face or name. So in a voice, so in a shapeless flame. Angels affect us oft, and worshipped be…"*

Three days ago, Mitch Warner had surprised the entire congregation by reciting that verse following his wedding vows. Yet no one had been as shocked—or as touched—as Victoria Barnett-Warner.

The ceremony had been held on a perfect November day in the small country church Tori had attended during her youth every Sunday with her mother. Tori wore Mitch's mother's wedding gown, a gift from Mitch, since her own mother sadly never had the opportunity to wear one. The "Fearsome Foursome" had been reunited when Stella, Janie and Brianne served as attendants, escorted by Bobby and Rand, with Mitch's father assuming the role of best man, at his son's surprising request. Proof positive that the healing process had finally begun.

Both Mitch's and Tori's mothers had been honored with white roses and their framed portraits set out on the pews on each side of the aisle. And Buck, dressed in his Sunday best, sans straw hat, had gladly given the bride away.

They'd chosen Sadler's for the reception—which was quickly becoming a tradition in town, according to Carl who had served as musical host, despite Bobby's protests. But Bobby hadn't complained about the medley of honky-tonk songs Tori had sung at Stella's request.

All in all, it had been a grand party, but it paled in comparison to the honeymoon Tori and Mitch now enjoyed.

For the past two days, she'd been sequestered with her new husband in a massive cabin situated in a small country called Doriana, compliments of Marcel DeLoria, one of Mitch's Harvard friends, who just happened to be the king. Yet they hadn't been very hospitable guests, not bothering to leave their accommodations since their arrival. Mitch had assured Tori that as a newlywed himself, Marc understood completely.

Wrapped in a downy-soft red blanket, Tori stood at the window of their comfortable room, wood smoke rising from the rock hearth positioned in the sitting area opposite the ornate king-size bed. She studied in awe the fat snowflakes drifting over the forest surrounding the cabin, the Pyrenees providing a picturesque backdrop rivaling any panorama Tori had witnessed in her limited travels. But her favorite scenery dozed in the bed behind her, naked as the day he was born and as majestic as any mountain. At one time she might have been known as poor little Tori, but now she was truly rich, steeped in a wealth of love provided by a man who adored her and the baby growing inside her. Thanks to him, she had far too many blessings to count.

She also had a very masculine arm snaking around her middle to pull her back against a muscled chest that she'd come to know very well.

"What are you doing up?" Mitch asked in a husky voice.

She wriggled her bottom against him. "I should be asking you that question."

His soft laugh made her shiver. His hand on her breast made it worse. "If you haven't learned by now what that means, then I guess you need a few more lessons."

She turned into his arms and smiled. "If I wasn't pregnant already, I would have been before the end of this trip."

With a flick of his finger, he dropped the blanket from around her, leaving her naked again. She frowned and said, "It's cold in here, Mitch. The fire's dying down."

He slid his hand down her belly and cupped her between her thighs. "I don't think so."

What an insatiable man. Not that Tori was inclined to complain. "Can we at least get back under the covers?"

Sweeping her into his arms, he laid her back on the four-poster bed and hovered over her, giving her his heat. "Seriously, we probably ought to cool off a little bit. I don't want to hurt you."

"You haven't and you won't. But we could try just holding each other for a minute?"

"No problem." He rolled to his back and took her with him, positioning her close to his side in the crook of his arm. "This is one of my favorite parts of married life. Can't imagine how I lived without it so long."

Tori couldn't imagine how she'd lived without him. "You know, we should really think about getting dressed."

Mitch groaned, loudly. "Why? I've kind of enjoyed being naked all day. And all night. Eating naked. Watching television naked."

Tori rolled her eyes. "We haven't watched any television, Mitch. In fact, I haven't even seen a television."

He grinned. "I'll concede that."

"Right now we need to get ready for the party Marc and Kate are throwing for us. Marc's sending the Hummer up the mountain in less than an hour to escort us back. I don't think that would make a good impression, showing up buck naked, not to mention it's freezing outside. And speaking of Buck, why didn't you tell me he married Eula?"

"For the same reason you didn't tell me about my stepmother's pregnancy. He wanted to tell you himself."

"I'm glad your dad told you at the wedding. I'm also glad you've called a truce."

Mitch's rough sigh echoed in the room. "We still have a lot of work to do. A lot of baggage to overcome."

Tori rose onto one elbow and studied Mitch's stoic expression. "He's worried about the risk Caroline's pregnancy poses. He needs your support."

"I'll do the best I can, as long as you're there with me."

"I promise." She traced the outline of his full lips surrounded by a shadow of dark whiskers. An ever-present surge of desire, of need, flowed through her in a stream of warmth. "Caroline asked us to come over for dinner the weekend after we return home."

"I don't even want to think about going back yet."

"I know, but I have several loose ends to tie up."

"And I have to say goodbye to Ray."

Tori gasped. "Oh my gosh! Is he sick? Do you have to—"

He gave her a reassuring kiss on the cheek. "Nothing like that. I'm donating him to a therapeutic riding program for kids with disabilities. The ranch is about fifty miles away. I can visit him any time."

"I thought you said he still has a few good years left."

"Actually, I promised to give him away if I lost a bet."

Another shocking revelation. "What kind of bet?"

"Marc and me and Dharr Halim—you haven't met him yet—wagered we wouldn't marry before our ten-year reunion. Marc blew it and so did I. Dharr's still a hold-out but since he's a sheikh and destined to rule his country, he's bound to have to marry sooner or later. Hopefully before next May."

"And since you lost, you had to give up your horse?"

"Yeah. The thing that meant the most to me. Ray qualified, until I met you."

Tori's eyes clouded with tears, but this time from pure joy. "You know, I didn't realize the extent of your love until now."

He breezed his fingertips along her cheek and studied her with a world of love in his eyes. "How could you even doubt it, Tori?"

"I don't. But you love me more than your horse, and that says so much."

Mitch laughed and hugged her hard. "I guess that does mean a lot, coming from a cowboy."

"A Harvard cowboy," she said, then planted a kiss on his chest. "A very sexy Harvard cowboy."

As Tori worked hot kisses down his torso, Mitch sucked in a hard breath. "Listen, lady, if you keep going, we're not going anywhere for a while."

She lifted her head from his belly and smiled. "I know."

"You're the one who told me our ride will be coming shortly." And if she didn't quit, the vehicle wouldn't be the only thing.

"I guess you're right." She slithered up his body and planted a warm, wet kiss on his mouth. "But I'm suddenly in a very needy state, so we'll be fashionably late. Now show me exactly how much you love me."

He framed her face in his palms. "First, I'll tell you. I love you more than my horse. I love you for giving me our baby. I love you more than anything, even my life. Today. Tomorrow. From here on out, as long as you're willing to put up with me. Now that's not exactly poetry, but it's the truth."

"You're wrong, Mitch. It sounded exactly like poetry to me. And now I'm going to show you just how much I love you."

Mitch reveled in Tori's lack of inhibition as she made sweet love to him once more. Sure, she was more than a little wicked when it came to pleasing him, but Mitch didn't mind in the least. Every angel was entitled to fall from grace now and then, especially *his* angel.

In the past few weeks, Mitchell Edward Warner III had learned how to love, how to forgive and how to accept life's little surprises. Now he intended to prove himself a devoted husband, a better son and a loving father to his own child. By the end of next year, he planned to be pretty damn good at all three.

* * * * *

DARING THE DYNAMIC SHEIKH

KRISTI GOLD

To Marilyn P, my favourite "Red Hat" lady,
talented writer and good friend.

Prologue

During his university career, Sheikh Dharr ibn Halim had learned the finer points of economics, yet he had mastered the art of seduction. He knew how to take a lover beyond the limit, how to use the cover of night to reveal a woman's secret passions and the light of day to heighten the pleasure. Yet over the past year, he'd learned all too well the devastation of love, a bitter lesson he would take with him the rest of his life.

Dharr was only mildly aware of the activities commencing outside the apartment he'd shared with two roommates during his Harvard career. He was in no mood to celebrate his accomplishments, for with his degree came the end to his time in America and the beginning of his responsibility to his country. Tomorrow he would be leaving everything behind, including his friends, Prince Marcel DeLoria, second born son of a European king and Mitchell Warner, a United States senator's son who knew all too well the burden of notoriety. Their time together had been a welcome distraction from the media's attention, a means for escape and an opportunity for revelations.

Dharr did not plan to make any disclosures during this farewell gathering. He chose to withhold the secret housed deep in his soul, never to be revealed to anyone. It was that secret that kept his thoughts occupied tonight as it had over endless nights in the recent past—he had fallen in love with a woman who had not loved him in return.

Seated in his favorite chair, Dharr turned his attention to his friends. As always, Mitch had positioned himself on the floor of their shared apartment as if he had an aversion to furniture. Marc had claimed his usual place on the sofa.

After a time, Mitch picked up the champagne bottle from the coffee table to refill each of their glasses. "We've already toasted our success," he said. "Now I propose we toast a lengthy bachelorhood."

Dharr leaned forward and raised his glass in agreement. "I would most definitely toast to that."

With champagne in hand, Marc paused a moment before offering, "I prefer to propose a wager."

Dharr and Mitch exchanged suspicious glances. "What kind of wager, DeLoria?" Mitch asked.

"Well, since we've all agreed that we're not suited for marriage in the immediate future, if ever, I suggest we hold ourselves to those terms by wagering that we'll all be unmarried on our tenth reunion."

Dharr knew he had a battle on his hands in showing his father the logic—and necessity—of waiting ten years to wed. He would endeavor to hold off at least that long, if he decided to marry at all. "And if we are not?"

"We will be forced to give away our most prized possession."

Mitch grimaced. "Give away my gelding? That would be tough."

Dharr could consider only one thing, the painting hanging above Mitch's head on the wall. That valuable piece was definitely his most cherished possession—now that the other had left him. "I suppose that would be my Modigliani original, and I must admit that giving away the nude would cause me great suffering."

"That is the point, gentlemen," Marc said. "The wager would mean nothing if the possessions were meaningless."

"Okay, DeLoria," Marc asked. "What's it going to be for you?"

"The Corvette."

"You'd give up the love mobile?" Mitch's tone resounded with the astonishment Dharr experienced over the offer. Marc coveted the blessed car as much as he coveted women.

"Of course not," Marc said. "I won't lose."

"Nor will I," Dharr said. "Ten years will be adequate before I am forced to produce an heir." And hopefully enough time to heal his wounds so that if he had to enter into a marriage, he would do so with honor, even if without love.

"No problem for me," Mitch said. "I'm going to avoid marriage at all costs."

Again Dharr held up his glass. "Then we are all agreed?"

Mitch touched his flute to Dharr's. "Agreed."

Marc did the same. "Let the wager begin."

Though Dharr would greatly miss the company of his friends, destiny dictated he accept his legacy and live up to his responsibilities. If the circumstances demanded he adhere to the marriage arrangement set out years before, at least he would have some satisfaction knowing that the young woman chosen for him had been born into his culture. She would understand his duty, his position, and what it would entail to be queen when the time came for Dharr to take over rule of his country, Azzril.

Should that prove to be the case, and if he could not have the woman he loved, then he would settle for Raina Kahlil, simply because she was the same as him.

One

Ten years later

She was nothing like he remembered.

Shading his eyes against the April afternoon sun, Dharr Halim realized the extent of Raina Kahlil's transformation from girl to woman as he covertly watched her from the deck of her California beachfront cottage. Several years had passed since those days when she'd possessed gangling limbs and unkempt braids. Today she was quite different, at least from a physical standpoint.

As she waded along the surf's edge, Raina moved with a grace as fluid as the ocean waves, her legs still long and lithe only with much more substance. Her gold-brown hair flowed over her shoulders like a cloak, trailing down her back where it touched the hollow of her spine below her waist. But it did not provide enough cover to completely conceal her golden flesh exposed by a two-piece swimsuit that left little to the imagination.

As far as Dharr could discern, she had yet to detect his presence, her gaze focused on a seashell she was examining as she headed toward him. Her distraction allowed more time to assess the unanticipated conversion.

She wore three silver loops in the lobe of each ear and a turquoise beaded necklace the color of her swimsuit. Her limited attire revealed the rise of her full breasts and her bare torso where Dharr's gaze tracked a path down her abdomen to her navel that sported a half-moon silver ring. Below that, the curve of her hips and thighs heightened his awareness of the drastic changes in her. And his awareness that as a man, he could appreciate those changes.

But the last time Dharr Halim had encountered his intended bride, she'd been in her early teens and engaged in hand-to-hand combat with a young boy who had dared to challenge her. Dharr wondered if she would attempt the same tactics when she discovered that he'd come to escort her back to Azzril.

Considering the way she carried herself—with unmistakable poise and confidence—Dharr suspected that her hellion attitude had undergone little alteration. When she sent him a look that might wither another man, he realized his assumption had been true. He had prepared himself for her reluctance, bolstered by information that should convince her to return home, despite the fact she had chosen to ignore his recent correspondence. He had not exactly prepared for the way his body reacted when he considered her fiery attitude might translate well beneath the cover of satin sheets, in the light of day or the dark of night. And that would be a fantasy he should resist. He had recently decided that he had no intention of upholding the marriage contract, cemented by the knowledge that she had rejected their culture. Out of respect for her and her father, he would maintain his distance even though he recognized he might be sorely tempted to do otherwise.

Without halting her progress, Raina strode up the stairs leading to the deck, assessing him much the same as he had her, yet she did not look happy over his unexpected presence. Somewhat surprised, yes, but definitely not pleased.

Stopping before him, she tossed the shell over one shoulder and braced both hands on her hips. "Well, as I live and breathe, if it's not the dashing Dharr Halim. Are you here to torment me like you used to?"

Her voice had lost all semblance of an Arabian accent, replaced by a distinct American tone, with a touch of sarcasm Dharr chose to ignore. He could not quite ignore her proximity or her body. "It is good to see you again, Raina."

"Answer my question. Why are you here?"

"Do I need a reason to visit?"

"As a matter of fact, yes, you do. It's been what? Fifteen years since we last met?"

"Twelve, to be exact. I was attending Harvard at that time and came home the summer before you left Azzril with your mother. Your father brought you to the palace for a visit. You were fighting with the cook's son."

"And you intervened, as usual." She hinted at a smile that quickly disappeared. "That was a long time ago, so don't you think I'm entitled to be a bit suspicious over your sudden appearance?"

"I promise my intentions are honorable." Even if his thoughts at the moment were not. A man would have to be struck blind— or a eunuch—not to have a reaction to her attire, the soft lines of her form that would feel quite exquisite against his hands.

She chafed her palms down her arms. "Let's continue this inside. It's kind of chilly out here."

She did not have to inform him of that fact, Dharr thought wryly when his gaze rested on her breasts. On the other hand, he was extremely warm.

Stepping to one side, he made a sweeping gesture toward the cottage. "After you."

"Good thing you didn't say 'ladies first.' I wouldn't have let you in."

As he'd suspected, she had not changed in regard to her independent spirit, but at least she had said it with a smile. "I would not presume to make such an error, Raina."

"Good." She glanced toward the drive where he'd parked the plain white sedan. "No limousine? No armed guards?"

"It's a rental car. Guards are not necessary at the moment." He smiled. "Unless you intend to throw me out."

"That depends on why you're here."

With that she passed by him, bringing with her the smell of sea and sun and a pleasing citrus scent. Once inside, she indicated a high-back stool at a bar that divided the small kitchen from the living area. "Have a seat. It's not much, but it's home."

Modest came to mind as he surveyed the area containing only a few pieces of furniture, followed by the awareness of light when she flipped two switches, completely illuminating the room and revealing a host of colors. Many different colors in varying hues, as if an artist's pallet had exploded, sending paint throughout the room. It suited her, Dharr decided, for she had always been a rather colorful character.

Dharr pulled back the stool and seated himself, expecting Raina to take the chair next to him. Instead she said, "I'm going to change and while I'm at it, you can tell me why you've come."

She swayed toward a bath diagonal to the counter and within his view, yet she left the door open, offering no protection or privacy from prying eyes—his eyes, in this instance. He could see the front of her torso in the vanity mirror she faced due to the open door. Although he thought it might be best to avert his eyes, he couldn't seem to force his gaze away from her body, admittedly intrigued that she would be so uninhibited.

When she reached for the ties around her neck, hidden beneath her hair, Dharr asked, "Do you not have a bedroom?" His voice held a noticeable edge, reflecting the sexual jolt he'd suffered when considering he might see more of her than he should.

The suit now unsecured, she anchored the top with one arm across her breasts. "You're looking at it."

Yes, he was, and he liked what he saw when she lowered the top—teardrop breasts tipped with russet nipples that would fit perfectly in his hands and mouth. The house, however, did not interest him. He scooted the stool beneath the counter to hide his reaction to her.

"Now tell me to what do I owe this visit?" she said as she slipped the bottoms down. Dharr could only make out faint details of her well-shaped buttocks due to the vanity concealing the reflection from her waist up and her hair, which covered most of her back. Yet it was enough to leave him nearly bankrupt of all thought.

He cleared his throat. "Had you read my letters, then you would know why I have come."

"What letters?" She slipped a silky coral shirt over her head and Dharr watched the fabric slide down, imagining his own hand doing the same over her hair, or her bare back. Only he would keep going, lower and lower…

"Dharr, what letters?" she asked as she pulled her hair from beneath the shirt and tugged on a pair of underwear made of sheer lace. Black lace, and barely enough fabric to be considered an article of clothing.

He shifted on the stool once more. "I've recently sent two letters. Did you not receive them?"

Finally she worked a pair of loose-fitting slacks up her hips, turned and came back into the room. "I didn't get any letters. Did you send them here?"

"I had my assistant send them. Perhaps they went to the wrong address."

She pulled her hair up and secured it with a black band high atop her head. "I've just recently moved from my mother's house. Maybe she has them."

"Perhaps she does."

She leaned over the counter and scrutinized him with golden eyes as clear as a fine gemstone. "I could call her and ask, but since you're here, why don't you just tell me in your own words what they said?"

The news that Dharr had to deliver would not be pleasant, therefore he would work his way into it. He rose from the stool and walked past her into the small living area, stopping to view a canvas resting on an easel near the large paned window facing the driveway. The painting was of a young girl turned profile, standing in the midst of a desert, looking out over mountainous terrain. The child appeared small and lost among the expanse of sand.

He glanced at Raina now leaning back against the counter. "Did you do this?"

"Yes, I did. It's a memory I had of Azzril when I was a little girl. I remember feeling very insignificant in all that open space."

"It's very good," he said, then strolled back to the counter and reclaimed his place across from her. "Do you support yourself with your art?"

She crossed her arms and propped them on the counter. "No. I teach at a small private college. I have a master's in art history. And you still haven't answered my question. What did your letters say, and what are you doing here?"

"I am here at the request of your father."

Her eyes narrowed, flashing anger. "This better not have anything to do with that archaic marriage arrangement."

"I assure you it does not. As far as I am concerned, that no longer exists."

She rolled her eyes to the ceiling. "Try telling that to my father. I'm sure he'll have something to say about it."

"You will have to take that up with him when you see him in the next few days."

She straightened. "Papa's coming here?"

"No. Your father wishes you to come to Azzril immediately. He sent me to escort you back."

She sighed. "Dharr, I'm an adult, not a child. I don't just up and leave when my father says so, I don't care what he wishes."

"What if it is your father's final wish?"

"I don't understand." Raina sounded unsure and looked almost as forlorn as the child in the painting.

Dharr had hated saying something that he did not exactly believe to be the truth, but Idris Kahlil had insisted Dharr present a dire situation to convince Raina to come to Azzril. Yes, the former sultan did have a potentially serious illness, yet suggesting he was pounding on death's door was somewhat an exaggeration.

"Your father quite possibly has a heart condition, Raina. He has been restricted to bed rest at this time."

Her face was shrouded in disbelief. "He was just here to see me two months ago."

The revelation took Dharr aback. As far as he'd known, the sultan had not been in contact with his daughter beyond phone calls. "He has been here?"

"Yes. Every year, sometimes twice a year, since I left Azzril. The last time I saw him, he looked fine."

"He's not a young man, Raina."

"But he's so strong. I can't believe…"

Dharr thought he detected tears before she lowered her eyes. He felt compelled to provide comfort and took her hand into his, somewhat surprised when she failed to pull away. Her long, delicate fingers seemed fragile in the well of his palm and he experienced a surge of protectiveness toward her, as he had many years before. "You are his only child, Raina. His only family. He needs you to be with him during his recovery."

She raised her gaze to his, optimism replacing the distress on her beautiful face. "Then he's going to recover?"

Undoubtedly he would, Dharr thought. The sultan was not a man to let illness restrain him for long. "The physicians are not certain about the extent of his condition at this time, but he's in no imminent danger. They are being cautious and watching him closely. He has been resting comfortably since his departure from the hospital."

She pulled her hands from his grasp, leaving Dharr feeling strangely bereft. "He's not in the hospital?"

"He was. For a day after he suffered the chest pains. Though they advised against it, he insisted he did not need their care."

"He's so damn stubborn," Raina muttered.

Dharr recognized that Raina was very much her father's daughter. "Yes, and it would help greatly if you could convince him to rest."

Her laugh was without mirth. "Short of chaining him to the bed, I doubt I could keep him there if he doesn't want to cooperate."

"I am hoping you can persuade him."

She stared at some focal point above Dharr's head for a few moments before saying, "School doesn't end until next month. I'd have to find someone to take my classes."

"Is that possible?"

Raina seemed to be running on automatic, her eyes unfocused, most likely from the unanticipated news. "Yes. And I would need to pack, of course. I should probably call Mother, but I can do that when I arrive in Azzril. Otherwise, she might try to talk me out of going."

"Then I assume you have decided to come with me?"

She frowned at him. "What choice do I have? If Papa needs me, then I have to be there for him."

Dharr was pleased—and surprised—she had not presented any real resistance. "We can leave in the morning. I have my private jet awaiting instructions for our return."

"I want to leave tonight."

Another unexpected revelation. "Would it not be best if you had a decent night's sleep?"

"It's a twenty-hour flight. I can sleep on the plane."

"If that is what you wish."

"It is." She pushed away from the counter. "I'll take a quick shower and then make a call to the school's headmaster. If you want something to drink, you'll find it in the fridge."

He greatly wanted to join her in the shower, another unwise idea. She rushed into the bathroom, this time closing the door, leaving Dharr alone to make his own calls from the cellular phone. After he'd arranged for the flight to leave tonight, he took the opportunity to look around while Raina prepared for the trip. She had several other oils on display aside from the one of the girl, but the painting set on an easel in the corner drew his attention. Although it was not complete, he had no trouble discerning it was a partially nude woman with long light brown hair staring out to sea, a man standing next to her, his face turned into her temple, one arm laid across her back and his hand resting at the top of her buttocks in a show of possession.

Dharr experienced an unexpected stab of jealousy that perhaps this man was Raina's lover. Perhaps they had stood near this very place, taking in the view after having made love. But he would not confront her with his suspicions. He'd had no reason to expect her to remain celibate. She had been free to do as she pleased with whomever she pleased. She still was.

Even though he had no plans to have Raina Kahlil as his wife, he could still imagine what it might be like to have her in his bed.

And those fantasies should remain as such—only fantasies. Yet he was about to embark on a twenty-hour journey with a woman who had undeniably captured his interest. A true test of his fortitude. He would not succumb to baser urges, even though one definite part of his anatomy might be telling him otherwise.

It was absolutely huge.

Raina had been expecting some kind of a smaller private jet, not an enormous hunk of flying metal with a 7 in its identifying number. But why was she so surprised? Dharr Halim wouldn't settle for halfway in his chosen mode of transportation or anything else he endeavored.

Still, she hated flying with a passion. In fact, she hadn't flown since the night she'd left Azzril for America. If it hadn't been for her father's illness, she would never have stepped on a plane again. But she did step onto this plane, immediately greeted by a steward dressed in a tuxedo. "Welcome, Miss Kahlil and Sheikh Halim. I will be available to tend to your needs."

Not exactly in the mood to be overly polite, Raina sent him a smile and a muttered, "Thanks."

"We will contact you when we are ready for dinner," Dharr said from behind her.

As Raina walked the plane's aisle, Dharr followed at a minimal distance, making her more nervous with every step they took. He'd always made her nervous, even when she'd been a girl—the kind of discomfort that stemmed from being in the presence of a man too magnetic for his own good. Too gorgeous to ignore with his unreadable dark eyes and a body that would make many a woman fall at his feet and kiss the expensive loafers he walked in. And in part, because she'd known from the time she was a child that he'd been chosen for her. She'd recognized his charisma long before she'd admitted to liking boys of any kind. But she'd been quick to deny she'd had a minor crush on him, even if she had.

But she couldn't allow any attraction to him at all. They were too, too different. Her mother and father had never worked through those differences, and their estrangement had almost destroyed Raina. She loved them both to excess, but she'd grown up as a pawn in their war of wills—until recently. Now she was on her own and she would make her own decisions. That did not include bending to her father's insistence that she marry Dharr Halim, in accordance with tradition. She had no desire to do anything with Dharr Halim.

Okay, that wasn't exactly true. The minute she'd discovered him standing on her deck, looking imposing and as breathtakingly handsome as he had the last time she'd seen him, she'd imagined doing a few things with him that didn't involve matrimony. More like consummation.

Two men in dark suits stood as she passed by an area that looked like a lounge with eight white seats, two facing two others on her left, the same on her right, televisions suspended above each group of chairs.

The men—bodyguards she presumed—offered her courteous smiles and nodded at Dharr as he moved around her and told them in Arabic, "We are not to be disturbed."

Raina was disturbed. Very disturbed. She didn't like the thought of being hidden away with a man whose every move showcased his sensuality, his power. But she followed him anyway when he glanced over his shoulder and said, "This way."

He paused to shrug off his coat and tossed it on one row of seats but left the white kaffiyeh, secured by the ornate gold and blue band indicating his royal status—the one thing that differentiated him from the rest of the occupants on the plane, setting him apart from most men Raina had known, aside from her father. It served as a symbol of prestige, wealth and all the things Raina had cast off since she'd gone to America as a teenager. She preferred keeping company with surfers and recreational sailors, common folk, not crowns or kaffiyehs.

Yet she couldn't help but notice the way Dharr's black slacks adhered to his really nice butt, the expanse of his wide shoulders and the breadth of his back covered in a white tailored dress shirt, the way he moved with a hint of cockiness as if he expected everyone to bow and scrape in his presence. Raina didn't do bowing or scraping or drooling even though her mouth was oddly starting to water.

Obviously she was hungry. That was it. She hadn't had dinner.

Dharr led her past a few other groupings of chairs and a spiral staircase. As they ascended, she grasped the rail tightly so she wouldn't slip and fall since she continued to secretly regard his rear-end. When they reached the top, he opened a door to reveal…a bed? A queen-size bed covered by an ivory satin spread, built-in cabinets positioned on either side of the bulkhead. A regular recreational vehicle with wings.

Raina stopped and stared at Dharr who was now facing her. "That's a bedroom." And that was a brilliant observation.

His half smile showed a glimpse of perfect white teeth.

"Yes, it has a bed, but it also has a sitting area and serves as my office. We will be afforded more privacy here."

More privacy was a problem, Raina decided. She didn't think she should get anywhere near a bed with Dynamic Dharr in the room, especially behind a closed door in a plane with no way out aside from an emergency exit. She refused to sit up all night with a bunch of bodyguards or ride on the wing for the majority of the trip if he got out of hand.

She was being silly. Dharr hadn't made any overtures other than taking her hand, and that had been a comforting gesture. He certainly hadn't indicated that he wanted to get her into bed. And why was that whole concept of getting into bed with him making her shaky and sweaty all at the same time?

That didn't matter. She could do this. She could go into Dharr Halim's traveling bedroom and keep her distance.

When she failed to move, he asked, "Are you coming?" in a low, dangerous voice. The image of him saying the same thing to her in the throes of passion vaulted into her brain and took away her breath.

She shifted the yellow nylon bag from one shoulder to the other, the bag Dharr had insisted on carrying but she hadn't let him. Right now it felt as if it were weighted with bricks, not the few things she'd thrown together for her brief stay.

She encouraged her feet to move forward, move toward the room, and once inside, she was relieved to find that to her left, a table and more seats did exist, along with a built-in desk.

After dropping her bag on the floor and nudging it beneath the edge of the bed with one foot, she perched on the mattress and tested it with a push of her palm. "This is comfy."

"Yes, it is. Very accommodating."

She looked up to see Dharr's eyes had turned jet-black, sending her off the mattress as if she'd been shot out of a rocket launcher.

He indicated the two side-by-side chairs opposite the bed. "We will need to be seated here for take-off. After the pilot gives the clearance, you will be free to do as you wish, and sit—or lie down—wherever you wish."

Sitting seemed to be the smartest thing to do.

On that thought, Raina occupied the seat away from the window. She despised take-offs and landings the most. Her father had recognized her fear of flying, the reason why he'd come to California instead of expecting her to make the long trip to Azzril. But tonight, she would have to face her fears in order to make sure her papa's illness wasn't serious. As frustrating as he could be at times, as unbendable, she would die if anything happened to him.

Dharr settled into the seat beside her without giving her a second glance. He smelled great, like a forest after a rain, clean and fresh and full of secrets to behold.

She stared at him for a moment, wondering if his hair was still as thick and dark as it had been all those years ago. "Is that necessary, your kaffiyeh?"

He looked insulted. "In business, yes. It commands respect."

"But you're not on business now."

"True." He raked the covering from his head and tossed it onto the table not far away, confirming that his hair was still as gorgeous. Then he turned his deadly grin on her. "Is there anything else you wish me to remove?"

Her skin threatened to slink off her body with the pleasant thought of him taking everything off. "Very funny."

"I'm glad I have amused you."

He wasn't amusing her at all. In fact, he was making her perspire even more with his toxic smile and his bedtime black eyes.

A voice came over the intercom announcing they'd been cleared for take-off, shattering the moment and startling Raina.

Dharr sent her a look of concern as he fastened his seat belt. "Are you afraid of flying, Raina?"

She didn't dare admit she was afraid of anything, even if she was. She stared straight ahead so he couldn't see that fear when the plane began to back away from the gate. "I'm not fond of planes. Obviously—"

"Raina—"

"...they were designed by men, if you consider their shape."

"Raina—"

"Giant phallic symbols with massive engines."

"Raina."

She shot a glance at Dharr. "What?"

"Fasten your seat belt."

Great. The only thing protecting her from getting tossed around like rag doll and she'd almost forgotten to put it on.

After she snapped her belt and secured it, she sat back and gripped the arms of the seat. The plane taxied toward the runway while Raina did her best to think positive thoughts, to no avail. She loathed feeling so out of control.

"I think I should cut holes in the floor and run to help this thing get off the ground," she muttered. "It's unnatural, expecting something so big to take you airborne."

Dharr leaned over, his warm breath wafting across her cheek. "Some say that size can be important when it comes to achieving greater heights."

She gave him a mock-serious look. "You haven't changed a bit, Dharr Halim. Always the tease. But it seems you've graduated from tormenting me about my bony knees to delivering questionable innuendo."

He raked a slow glance down her body. "And you have graduated from the bony stage. If you recall, you were the one who compared the plane to a phallic symbol. I was simply following your lead."

Before Raina could deliver a retort, the engines whined to life. She closed her eyes, bracing for the moment when the tube of steel raced down the narrow strip of asphalt and hurled them into the air, hopefully without incident.

The louder the engine roared and the faster the plane went, the harder Raina gripped the arm of the seat. "Come on, come on, come—"

Dharr's mouth covered hers, cutting off her nervous chant and her random thoughts of doom. Raina didn't remember this being a part of the in-flight safety instructions. Didn't remember ever getting this kind of service—service with a capital S. In fact, she didn't even remember her name.

He introduced his tongue slowly, concisely, in a feather-soft incursion between her parted lips. She felt light-headed, breathless, when he pulled her left hand out of its death grip on the seat's arm and twined his fingers with hers. She melted more and more into mindlessness with every foray of his sinful tongue. Her heart rate started climbing and climbing with the plane, but she wasn't concerned with the plane. She wasn't concerned about anything as the kiss continued, growing deeper, more insistent with each passing moment. She only cared about Dharr's mouth moving gently against hers. His scent, his taste, his skill.

Dharr finally pulled away and sent her another heat-inducing smile. "I believe we have successfully completed the take-off."

Raina leaned over to look out the window, seeing nothing but sky, the setting sun and wisps of clouds. She had no idea how long the kiss had lasted or why she'd even allowed it. And she was fighting mad that Dharr had taken advantage of her fear. "Why did you do that?"

"To bring your mind and body to another plane aside from this one."

She had to admit, he'd done that, and quite sufficiently. "That wasn't playing fair."

"I was not playing, Raina. I was very serious." If his expression was any indication, he was dead serious. Seriously seductive.

"I guess I should thank you," she murmured.

"You are welcome. And should you wish me to divert your attention again during our flight, please inform me."

Of all the shifty sheikhs. "Well, thanks so much for asking my permission this time."

He raised a dark brow. "This time?"

She sent him a sharp look. "The last time. We are not going to do this."

"I believe we already have." He touched her face and slid one finger over her cheek, slowly, methodically, hypnotically. "Anything else you require of me, you need only ask."

She required only one thing, his absence so she could keep a tight grip on her control. But since it didn't look as if he were going anywhere for the next twenty hours, she realized she would have to be strong. Otherwise, she might end up using that nearby bed for something other than sleeping.

No way, Jose. She would be damned if Dharr Halim, with all his blatant self-assurance and magnetic machismo, would be her ticket to the Mile-High Club.

Two

Raina Kahlil would make an excellent lover. Dharr had decided that the moment he'd spontaneously kissed her. A rather good beginning to their reintroduction—and a dangerous one at that. However, he had not been able to think of any other means to allay her fears, or so he'd tried to convince himself. Yet he had been successful with his distraction. He had also awakened his own libido, which would result in a long, hard journey back to Azzril.

Raina also put everything into eating, as well, he realized, as she consumed the cold vegetable sandwich without bothering to look up. Odd that she'd grown so silent since they'd become airborne. He never remembered her being prone to keeping her thoughts to herself, even when she had been a young girl. Especially then.

She pushed aside her empty plate and dabbed at her face with a napkin, drawing Dharr's attention to her full lips. "That was wonderful."

"I apologize for not having a hot meal, but we had little time to prepare."

"The sandwich was great."

He picked up the bottle of Bordeaux from the table and held it aloft. "Would you like more wine?"

"Considering the altitude, I'd probably get drunk if I had another."

He refilled her glass then set the bottle aside. "Perhaps you would relax if you had another."

"I *am* relaxed." She pushed the glass away, knocking it off balance.

Dharr grabbed it up before it tipped over, saving the beige carpet from scarlet stains. He could not save his smile from making an appearance. "Are you certain?"

"Yes. I'm just clumsy." She folded her hands before her on the table. "So tell me, Dharr, are you completely in control these days?"

"In control of what?" Certainly not of his carnal urges in her company.

"Are you running the country?"

General conversation. He would participate for the time being, as long as she didn't ask too many personal questions. "My parents are traveling now and I have taken over most of my father's duties, although he is still king."

"Has Azzril changed much?"

"We have expanded the university in Tomar as well as the hospital. We are developing more modern agricultural methods and aiding the poorer towns with their growth."

"Do you have any women?" He could tell she regretted the query when her gaze wandered away. "I meant any women in power."

Dharr sat back with wineglass in hand, greatly enjoying the

slight rise of color on cheeks. He wondered how she would look flushed all over. "Yes, doctors, legal representative, professors."

She finally brought her golden eyes back to his. "What about government positions?"

The positions he was currently pondering had nothing to do with politics. "Not presently, but it is only a matter of time. Are you interested?"

"Heck, no. I was just curious. My mother always complained that women had little power in Azzril."

At one time, that had been true. But Dharr had made great strides over the past ten years. "And your mother, is she well?"

Raina picked up the napkin, kneading it much like the family cook had kneaded the evening bread when he'd been a boy. "My mother's lonely. She's never dated anyone since she left Papa."

"As I understand it, she is still married to your father."

Raina twisted the napkin with a vengeance. "Technically, yes. Neither of them has even considered divorce. I think that's ridiculous. If they aren't going to live together, why not just end it so they can move on with their lives?"

Dharr noted a flash of pain in her eyes and knew that her parents' estrangement had not been easy on her. "Perhaps they are both too full of pride. And divorce is still frowned upon in Azzril."

"My mother's from America where divorce is as commonplace as cars on the Los Angeles freeways."

He rested his hand on hers when she released her death grip on the napkin. "And commitment is taken too lightly."

She pulled her hand from beneath his and shrugged. "If you can't live together peacefully, why prolong the agony?"

"I suppose in some ways you are right, but I see marriage as an agreement that can be mutually beneficial if kept in proper perspective."

"What benefit would that be?"

He took a drink of his wine then leveled his gaze on her. "I can think of many ways a man and woman can benefit from each other. Procreation, for one. The process of procreating is another."

She folded her arms beneath her breasts, looking defiant. "All the great sex and babies in the world can't help a bad relationship. Passion fades and if there's nothing left after that, then all you have is a piece of paper and hatred."

"If you do not give yourself over to emotions, then hate would not enter into it. Respect is more important."

"Then you're saying that love should be avoided at all costs?"

"Are you saying that you believe in something as frivolous as love?"

"I've never been in love with a man, but my love for my parents is very real. Don't you love yours?"

"Yes, but that is different."

"How so?"

"I know that my parents' love for me is without conditions."

Her smile was wan. "Oh, I see. Someone has broken your heart."

How could she know that? Was he being too transparent? "I simply do not feel that it's wise to give yourself over to intangible emotions."

Raina stood, her golden gaze fixed on his. "Being such a cynic must be very tiresome."

"Where are you going?" he asked as she moved from behind the table.

"To the little girls' room, then I'm going to get ready for bed, if that's okay with you, Sheikh Halim."

"I have no objection. That is why the bed has been provided."

She smiled a skeptic's smile. "Oh, I just bet you put that bed in here for sleeping."

"Why else?"

"Don't play dumb with me, Dharr. I know you've had women on this flying love machine before. A man like you wouldn't spend his adult life without a few lovers."

That he could not deny, but there had not been all that many, and none had been more than a means for gratification. Except one. "Have you, Raina?"

She pulled her bag from beneath the bed and slipped the strap over her shoulder. "Have I what?"

"Taken lovers?"

"That's none of your business." With a determined lift of her chin, she turned away and disappeared into the bathroom. He had to agree, it was not his concern. That did not prevent him from wondering if her defensiveness resulted from the fact she had taken several lovers, or perhaps none. He preferred to believe the latter, although he could not explain why. Could not explain the envy when considering another man had touched her. Perhaps he was only being protective, or a fool.

A few minutes later, she came out of the small bath wearing a sleeveless royal blue satin shift that barely touched the top of her thighs. Dharr swiveled the anchored chair away from the table to face her as she turned her back to him. He watched while she bent over to replace her bag beneath the bed, revealing sheer white panties, not lace this time, but still impacting Dharr's desire for her. She pulled back the covers, fluffed her pillow, stretched out on her back and pulled the sheet up to her waist.

"Are you coming to bed anytime soon?" she asked, failing to look at him.

"I did not know you were interested in having me in your bed."

She raised her head and scowled. "To sleep, Dharr. This bed is big enough for both of us. You stay on your side, I'll stay on mine, and we'll be fine and dandy."

Dharr leaned back in the chair and assessed her with a long glance over her body concealed by the sheet. "I assure you it would be most difficult for me to remain on my side of the bed, unless you erect a wall between us." Dharr was fighting a different kind of erection at the mere thought of lying next to her and eventually on top of her.

"Oh, so you're not strong enough to just sleep with a woman without *sleeping* with a woman?"

"Quite possibly I could with certain women, but not a woman such as yourself, especially since you are wearing very little clothing."

She lifted the sheet and peeked beneath it as if she had no memory of what she wore. "I'm adequately covered."

After dropping the sheet, she rolled to her side and faced him, her cheek resting on her arm partially tucked beneath the pillow. "If I were at home, I wouldn't have anything on. I don't like wearing clothes to bed."

Dharr experienced a definite rise in temperature and a rise below his belt. Yet he didn't bother hiding his current state of arousal by crossing his legs. In fact, he stretched his legs before him so she would know what she was doing to him. At least then he could say he'd given her substantial warning, even if not a verbal one. "I certainly understand, Raina. I do not favor clothes at bedtime either. If that makes you uncomfortable, I will stay in this chair."

She sent a direct look at his lap, then said, "Fine. Good night."

That was not what Dharr wanted at all. He'd wanted her to be more persistent, had hoped she would encourage him to join her. But her eyes drifted closed and it wasn't long before her face relaxed with sleep.

However, he was not relaxed nor would he be when plagued with the fantasy of stripping out of his clothing and crawling in beside her, waking her with the most intimate of kisses, with touches that would make her body beg for his consideration. He could give her pleasure, but he would have to be satisfied to leave it at that. And that would not be acceptable. Not unless he considered her as the woman who would remain at his side as future queen.

At Harvard, he'd thought he had found the woman he wanted to make his wife, only to learn that she could never accept his legacy or his culture. She had led him on a sensual adventure then closed the door on any future they might have had together, walking away without even a personal goodbye, only a letter that told him they could never be together permanently.

And he would have given everything up for her. Everything.

Even his heart. Never again.

Raina slowly returned to consciousness after drifting in and out of fitful sleep. Disoriented, she thought she was back in her childhood bed in Azzril, until she looked to her left and saw the rectangular windows revealing night sky and heard the hum of jet engines. Then she remembered. She wasn't fourteen; she was twenty-five. She was on a plane bound for a country that was only a distant memory, and the euphoria she'd experienced only moments before had been the result of a dream.

A dream involving her mother and father holding her hand as she walked between them in the streets of Tomar, suspended in a time before her mother had stolen away in the night to board a plane bound for the U.S., taking her daughter on a journey full of turbulent weather and equally turbulent emotions.

Raina's world had come apart on that dreadful flight, and she'd experienced real fear for the first time in her life, not only from the horrible trip but also from a total loss of security knowing she would be entering a strange land without her beloved father. Worse, she hadn't even told her papa goodbye.

"I see you have awakened."

She turned her face toward the deep, controlled voice that floated over her like a satin veil against sensitive skin. Light from the lamp attached to the desk spilled over him, providing more than adequate illumination for Raina to get the full effect of the picture he now presented. If she had paints and a canvas, she would immortalize him—a portrait of dark against light. A representation of overt sexuality and undeniable power.

He looked as proud and regal as if seated on a throne instead of a chair. As dangerous as if he were a thief of hearts assessing his next victim with eyes as black as a bottomless cavern. His soft, sensuous lips, surrounded by a shading of whiskers, contrasted with the sharp, angular lines of his cheeks, his solid jaw and the straight plane of his nose.

His arms rested on the chair's arms in casual indifference, his large hands curled over the ends, the right one sporting a gold and ruby signet ring on his little finger. His well-defined biceps conveyed his physical strength; his forearms laced with prominent veins and a fine covering of dark hair revealed his absolute maleness. As did his bare chest where a spattering of crisp, dark hair covered his pectorals and surrounded his pale brown nipples before tapering into a V pointing downward toward his ridged abdomen.

Raina visually followed the strip of hair below his navel to the waistband of the pajamas he now wore. But she didn't stop there though she recognized she should. Instead she homed in on the dark shading at his groin apparent through the thin, white muslin material.

She knew she should quit looking, knew that her curiosity could get her into trouble if she didn't. But she couldn't tear her eyes away from the prominent crest that indicated he was aroused. Very aroused. And so was Raina when she imagined holding intimate knowledge of that very male part of him in her hands, deep inside her body.

She finally forced her gaze back to the ceiling and kicked off the covers, bending her knees, causing her nightshirt to slide to the tops of her thighs. Before she'd seen him sitting there, watching her, she'd been comfortable, even chilly. But now… Now she was incredibly hot, from the crown of her head to the tips of her toes.

She heard the chair creak but didn't dare look at him, not after she'd shamelessly appraised him like a jeweler's patron searching for the perfect diamond. He was as fine and flawless as a twenty-carat stone featured front and center in the display case. Raina wished he were behind glass now so she wouldn't be so tempted to further examine him, or to touch him.

"How long have I been out?" she asked, her voice husky from sleep and a desire for him that made little sense.

"No more than two hours." His voice was no less deep, no less lethal.

She afforded him a quick glance. "Two hours? That's all?"

"Yes. Did you not find the bed to your liking?"

"It's very comfortable." Raina wasn't, not in the least. "It's kind of warm in here, though."

"Do you wish me to turn up the air?"

"That would be great." Although she doubted any amount of air would relieve the heat coursing through her body.

He rose from the chair and walked to the bed, reaching up to adjust the round vents above her head. Just seeing the tuft of dark hair underneath his arm made her shiver.

He stared down on her, his gaze roaming over her bare thighs covered in goose bumps before coming to rest on her satin-covered breasts that tightened from his perusal. "Are you too cold now?"

"No."

"Are there any more adjustments you wish me to make?"

He dropped his hand from the vents and brushed his knuckles over his groin, as if inviting her to do the same. With little effort, she could touch him there. Linger there to learn if he was as powerful as he looked. Clamping her knees closed in response to the damp wash of heat between her thighs, she turned her attention back to the ceiling and gave herself a good mental chastising.

Her reaction to him was outrageous. She didn't really know him. She wasn't even sure she still liked him. But she was only human—all too human—and this physical attraction, this chemistry, if left unabated could cause her a world of problems.

"I'm fine now," she said, although she didn't sound at all fine.

"Good. Please let me know if I can assist you further."

Oh, he could, in some terribly wicked ways. She needed to stop thinking about that, stop fantasizing about him. After all, she only had fifteen or so hours to go in his company. She could manage that without turning into some sex-crazed female need factory.

What a crock, she thought when she blurted, "You should come to bed," after he turned around to return to the chair.

He faced her again, looking provocative with the lamp's glow as a backdrop. Six feet two inches of potent prince. Darkness and light. "I would not wish to interrupt your sleep."

"And I don't want to be blamed when you can't walk tomorrow because you're too stiff." Raina wanted to bite her tongue off the minute the words left her mouth.

His eyes narrowed and his smile made another slow, sultry appearance. "You are very observant, Raina."

She rolled her eyes, affecting disgust, when in reality her

whole body felt as if he'd lit a match to it. "I meant stiff as in a sore neck." She scooted over, practically hugging the wall, and patted the pillow beside her. "Climb in, Dharr. You can be a good boy for one night."

"I could be very good, I assure you."

Realizing she was playing a perilous game of chance, Raina almost rescinded the offer. But before she could, Dharr turned his back and snaked his pajamas down his hips, revealing his bare bottom and the backs of his hair-covered thighs.

She bolted upright like a jack-in-the-box. "What are you doing?"

He regarded her over one shoulder as he crossed the area, his muscled buttocks flexing with each step he took toward the desk. "I've told you, I prefer to sleep in the nude."

"So do I, but in deference to you, I've left my clothes on."

He snapped off the light, sending the cabin into total darkness. "Feel free to remedy that situation. I will not see anything this time."

"What do you mean 'this time'?"

She could hear the floor rasp as he approached the bed, sensed his presence even before he spoke again. "At your house earlier, you left the bathroom door open while you changed."

"That was so I could hear you."

"Are you certain it was not so that I could see you? Because I did see you, Raina. In the open door. In the mirror's reflection. And I have suffered the effects all evening."

Actually she'd assumed that from his position at the bar he hadn't been able to see anything, and she hadn't considered anything beyond his sudden appearance. Yet the thought of him watching her undress brought back the utter need, the searing heat.

The mattress bent with his weight and although it was basically pitch dark, the limited light coming from the windows allowed her to make out his profile as he stretched out on his back, his hands laced behind his neck.

If she knew what was good for her, Raina would lower the flaps over the windows so she couldn't see any details. She would turn over and smash her mouth against the wall to keep from answering the urge to kiss him. Before she asked him to make good on his promise to be very good.

Instead she fell back against the bed, as inflexible as a steel beam, her hands rigid at her sides. No way on earth could she go to sleep like this. She flipped over onto her stomach and buried her face in the pillow, her gown now scrunched up beneath her belly. This was why she didn't wear anything to bed. She hated having to tug and pull and adjust fabric that had managed to knot beneath her or practically crawl up around her neck.

She considered taking off the nightgown. Why not? Dharr hadn't thought twice about removing his pajamas, and he had suggested she do that very thing. Besides, he couldn't see her, and she could leave her panties on. He hadn't moved so he could already be asleep. Still, that meant both of them would wake in the morning in bed together, without clothes and with only a few inches separating them. He might get the wrong idea. Or was it the right idea?

No. She couldn't allow him to make love to her. That was too risky, albeit very tempting. She had no intention of marrying him. No intention whatsoever of sleeping with him. If she did, he might expect more from her than she wanted to give. She didn't belong in Azzril anymore. She had a life in California. She couldn't compromise her plans, her freedom, by getting involved with the wrong man. A man very much like her father, set in his ways and strong in his beliefs. A man who had admitted he had no use for love in a relationship.

Then why did she sit up, cross her arms over her chest, slip the gown over her head and toss it onto the end of the bed? Why did she lay back, leaving the sheet at her feet? She had no explanation for her behavior, no reason to invite Dharr's attention. No rationale to be lying in a bed, practically naked, with a man who was more or less a stranger, worrying about whether or not he would touch her when she should be worrying about her father's health.

That was it. She was obviously on emotional overload, suffering from a lack of sensibility due to an abundance of concern. But from the beginning, she'd suspected Dharr hadn't been telling the complete truth about her father's condition. In fact, she was starting to wonder if the whole thing was a ploy to get her back home for a wedding—her wedding. Otherwise, if her papa had been in dire straits, someone would have called her. She could have made a few calls before she'd left Los Angeles to verify the information for herself.

Instead, she had agreed to get on a plane with Dharr Halim regardless of her suspicions, followed him on board without any coercion like a sheep following a shepherd. A seductive shepherd.

Reality hit her with the force of a sonic boom. Had she been waiting for Dharr Halim to show up on her doorstep? Is that why she'd been so eager to go with him? Would that explain why she'd had a number of boyfriends and a bevy of excuses for never making love with any of them? Her reasons had all seemed valid at the time. The dangers of indiscriminate sex in the form of sexually transmitted disease. Those boyfriends' lack of responsibility to anything aside from hedonistic pastimes, the next thrill. She'd been involved with men who'd been anything but safe and steady, committed. Mature.

Which begged the question—had she been saving herself for Dharr?

No. Her mind repelled that thought as she reached down for the sheet to cover herself. But before she could, Dharr's hand gripped her wrist. And if he dared to touch her, she wouldn't be able to resist him.

But he only drew the sheet up her body, as she'd intended to do.

"Turn to your side, facing the window," he commanded.

She readily complied, thinking that was probably wise. But when he fitted himself against her back and told her in a rough whisper to sleep, she didn't care about wisdom. Her attention was drawn to the feel of him against her—power and strength and heat. Scorching heat that seemed to flow through her, intense and unavoidable.

She highly doubted she would get any sleep this night. She also doubted that this foolish fascination with Dharr Halim would be gone in the morning.

A few hours before, Dharr had showered, dressed and joined his men in the main cabin downstairs to discuss business for a short while before returning to his quarters. At the moment he was seated in the chair near the bed while Raina still slept, unaware that he'd been watching her, captivated by her innocence, overwhelmed by his desire to make love with her.

He imagined in explicit detail exactly how he would begin—with his mouth trailing over her warm skin, lingering at her breasts, finding the heat between her thighs until she trembled with her own need. Then he would sink inside her, bringing her to a climax again…and again. He endeavored to keep that fantasy only that—a fantasy—for to do any more than imagine would test his honor. She was already testing his strength.

The captain's voice came over the intercom announcing the need to prepare for landing in London, forcing Dharr from his musings and startling Raina awake. She bolted upright, the sheet slipping to her waist. Her silky gold-brown hair veiled her breasts with the exception of one nipple peaking through a parting in her long locks.

Dharr shifted against the menace of another erection as he took in the sensual sight—until awareness dawned in her sleepy expression and she snatched the sheet back up to her chin.

"What's happening?" she asked in a grainy whisper.

Dharr considered showing her exactly what was happening to him but instead said, "We are about to land."

"In Azzril?"

"No. London to refuel. We will need to take our seats."

She glanced around the bed, lifting the sheet to look beneath it and giving Dharr another inadvertent view of her breasts. "Where's my gown?"

Dharr smiled and nodded toward the floor near the end of the bed. "It seems you are a very restless sleeper."

Concern replaced her frown and she gripped the sheet once more. "I didn't kick you out of bed, did I?"

In some ways, she had. "No."

"Do you mind handing it to me?"

He stood and approached the bed. "That is not necessary. You might wish to return to bed after we are on the ground. You might as well remain comfortable."

She inclined her head and sent him a coy look. "Are you suggesting I belt myself in naked?"

A prime suggestion at that. But the sound of the landing gear dropping spurred Dharr into action. Without thought, he leaned over and pulled the sheet from the mattress, tucked it securely around Raina and then scooped her from the bed. "We have little time to argue about your state of dress."

"Undress," she corrected. "And I can walk, Dharr."

Truthfully he wanted to feel her against him, at least for a few moments before he secured her into the seat. "You should save your energy."

She looked at him quizzically. "Save my energy for what?"

He considered several responses to that as he buckled himself in beside her. "For when you arrive in Azzril. You will need your strength to deal with your father."

"That's true. I might have to sit on him to make him be good."

Dharr considered asking her to sit on his lap so he could prove to her how good he could be before thrusting the hazardous thoughts away.

The plane rocked on its descent and Raina immediately gripped the edge of the seat. Determined to ease her distress, Dharr lifted the armrest between them, draped his arm around her and tipped her head against his shoulder.

"I'm really okay." She stiffened against him when the plane swayed again, belying her calm.

"It will be over soon," he assured her.

"Not soon enough," she said, her face turned into his neck.

Although he had thought not to repeat kissing her for his own sanity, Dharr decided doing so again might help her relax, even if it robbed him of his returning composure. On that thought, he tipped her chin up and pressed his lips to hers in a succession of soft, coaxing kisses. Without warning, she clasped his nape and pulled him closer, opening her mouth as if she regarded him as her lifeline.

Lost in her kiss, the gentle glide of her tongue against his, Dharr slid his hand down her back, taking the sheet with him as he guided his palm lower until he contacted the satin edging of her panties below the dip of her spine. How easy it would be to work his hand beneath the fabric. How easy it would be to keep going. To forget that anything existed beyond bringing her pleasure…

The plane bumped onto the runway, causing Dharr to pull

away from her mouth. Yet he could not quite find the will to remove his hand from her back, even after the plane taxied down the tarmac and came to a stop.

Raina stared up at him, eyes unfocused, lids heavy. "We're here," she murmured.

"Yes, we are," he said as slipped his palm beneath the satin to knead her buttocks without regard to caution.

"How long before...we're off again?"

Dharr feathered his fingertips over the smooth curves even knowing he must stop. The captain's voice announcing their arrival forced Dharr back into reality. Reluctantly he moved his hand away and set it in his lap. "We should be departing in less than an hour."

Raina collapsed back against the seat. "Do I have time to take a quick shower?"

The image of her naked and wet came to him clearly. "Certainly. If you are not quite ready when it's time to leave, I will ask for a short delay."

She smiled. "Oh, I'll let you know when I'm ready."

With that, she unbuckled the belt and slid from the seat, turning her back to him. The sheet gaped, revealing the slender path of her spine, the curve of her buttocks where he'd had his hand only moments before and above that, some sort of gold image embossed on the small of her back, something he had not noticed until that moment.

"What is that?" he asked.

She glanced over her shoulder and looked down. "It's a tattoo of a magic lamp." She raised her gaze to his. "Didn't you see it when you were spying on me at my house?"

"No." At that point, he'd been trying to avoiding anything that might have been deemed inappropriate, even though he had not been completely successful.

She faced him again. "You certainly had me fooled, considering you seemed to be bent on rubbing it a few minutes ago. I thought maybe you were making a wish."

Had he known, he would have wished for more strength, and a weaker libido.

Following a sultry look, Raina pulled a few toiletries from her bag and headed to the bathroom.

Dharr stared out the window, absently watching the activity on the tarmac below yet seeing only the image of Raina's body imprinted in his mind. He would like to see all of her, every fine fold, every soft crevice. How he would like to witness her face in the grip of a climax he had brought about.

Shifting against the building pressure, Dharr drew in a deep breath and made that wish for more fortitude—something he would need in the next few hours.

Three

Normally Raina wouldn't even attempt to wash her hair since it took so long to dry. But she wasn't feeling the least bit normal at the moment, the reason why she'd immersed herself completely beneath the shower spray.

How in the heck had she developed such a strong case of the hots for Dharr Halim? Why in the world had she let him touch her so intimately, kiss her so thoroughly? Of course, she had to concede that the depth of that kiss had been her fault. But the depth of her current need had been his. He was just too damn sexy for his own good—and hers.

She slicked her hand through her hair, washing away the remnants of conditioner, wishing she could wash away the fire sizzling through her body—from forehead to toes, gathering force between her legs. Definitely there.

After shutting off the faucet, Raina stepped outside the mini-shower onto the mat, fashioned a turban around her hair with one towel then dried off and wrapped up in another, knotting it between her breasts. Just then, the door opened to Dharr.

Raina sent him a not-so-nice look even though she had some really nice chills. "Do you mind giving me a little privacy?"

"Not at all." He stepped inside and closed the door behind him.

"Do you need something?" Raina asked.

His eyes burned black. "I thought perhaps I would shave since it seems we will be detained for a while longer."

Panic bit into Raina. "Is there something wrong with the plane?"

"Not the plane. The weather. Rain and heavy fog."

"Of course. It's London."

Raina stifled a gasp when Dharr unbuttoned his tailored shirt, slipped it off and hung it on a hook fastened to the door. She wanted to touch his broad bronzed chest, run her fingertips over the tensile ridges of masculine muscle, taste his nipples with her tongue. She gripped the edge of the towel at her thighs to keep from giving in to those urges.

As if unconcerned over her perusal, Dharr pulled out a razor and shaving cream from the cabinet. She watched as he smoothed the foam over his jaw with precision, recalling how good his hand had felt on her bottom. Imagining how good his hands would feel all over her extremely overheated body.

He studied her from the mirror's reflection. "Is there something you need from me?"

Yes, she did, but she didn't dare tell him exactly what she needed. "No. I'm just enjoying watching you shave. It reminds me of when I was a little girl. I used to stand in the bathroom while Papa shaved. He loved to give me a foamy moustache."

Taking Raina by surprise, Dharr reached back and streaked some of the cream across her upper lip. "Do you feel at home now?"

She couldn't stop her laughter as she pulled the towel from her hair and swiped the white foam away. "I feel a little silly since I'm no longer a girl."

His dark eyes went darker, hotter as he focused on her breasts barely concealed by the towel. "I have noticed."

Raina noticed how with only a look, he could make her dissolve into a she-devil. "I guess I'll go get dressed now."

"What a pity."

She slapped him with the towel across his very tight butt encased in form-fitting slacks. "You are still a relentless tease, Dharr Halim."

"And you are a great temptation, Raina Kahlil. Almost more than I can withstand."

"I find that hard to believe, a big strong man like you."

Their gazes remained fixed in the mirror's reflection for a long moment until Raina decided she best get out of there before she suggested they initiate Dharr's onboard miniscule boudoir—standing up against the wall.

"I'll see you later," she said, then worked her way behind him. The small space allowed for little room to maneuver and her breasts brushed across his broad back. Her nipples tightened into hard knots against the towel and Dharr nicked himself, creating a trickle of blood streaming down his chin.

"I'm sorry," Raina said as she grabbed for a tissue, reached around him and dabbed at the cut, her front pressed against his back.

"I can handle a slight injury." Without turning around, Dharr clasped her wrist, tossed aside the tissue and drew her palm down his chest, down his abdomen and lower until she contacted the hard crest straining against his slacks. "This is more difficult to ignore."

Raina's breath hitched as she fought the urge to explore him, to know the details even if the slacks provided a hindrance to really experience all that power. But before she gave into the impulse, he pulled her hand back up to his chest. "Now leave before I am tempted to put that to good use."

Stunned into silence, Raina hurried out of the bathroom, closed the door and leaned against it. Her legs trembled. Her whole body trembled. She wanted him with an all-consuming need that challenged wisdom. She wanted to know exactly what it would be like to make love with him.

But she really shouldn't, for that kind of intimacy might bring with it bared emotions. She didn't want to feel anything for him beyond friendship. She didn't want to get caught up in his sensual web and find herself entangled to the point she couldn't break free.

If she thought she could be assured that she could keep all emotion out of it, she wouldn't hesitate to cross the limits just so she could know. But then, maybe she was stronger than she thought. So was Dharr Halim. And she probably wouldn't be any match for his kind of strength.

Admittedly the sheikh was a fantasy man. Her fantasy man. Not until now had she realized how true that had been most of her life. During her secret, intimate imaginings, he had appeared more than once even though she'd tried to force the images away. Even though she'd been little more than a child when she'd seen him the last time, she'd never forgotten him. She'd never forgotten his smile, his aura, his sheer masculine beauty. Maybe it was time to make the fantasy reality. She knew he would treat her with care if they made love. She knew he would be the perfect man to be her first lover.

When this journey ended, they would go on living separate lives. And after she saw to her father's recovery, she would return to America with a few good memories—if Dharr Halim was willing to give her those, and more.

* * *

After the hour delay had turned into four, Dharr and Raina had dined together, talking in generalities about her life in California, his work on Azzril's economy and the changes they had both encountered over the years. All the while, Dharr had silently cursed himself for his weakness where Raina was concerned. He'd barely been able to concentrate on conversation due to his fascination with her mouth. She'd seemed totally unaware of the effect she had on him. However, after the warning he'd given her in the bathroom, she should have no doubt. And he'd had no shame in showing her, something he hoped he would not regret. Yet since she had boarded his plane, he had been quick to toss away common sense or courtesy, for that matter. He had to remember who she was—the daughter of his father's best friend, a woman who should be shown the utmost respect. A woman who held too much power over his attention at the moment. At any given moment.

Right then she sat on the bed, legs crossed, pencil and paper in hand, creating something he could not see from his vantage point in the chair. But he could see the fullness of her unencumbered breasts outlined in detail against the tight knit top, and that alone kept pulling his attention away from the newspaper he pretended to be reading.

The phone attached to the wall shrilled, sending him out of his chair to answer the summons. As suspected, it was the call he'd requested.

He held out the receiver and told Raina, "It is for you."

She looked up from her drawing and frowned. "Who is it?"

"Come and see."

She set the paper aside and slipped off the bed, the gauzy pants she now wore flowing with every step she took, accentuating her pleasing shape and her grace as she crossed to where Dharr was standing. She gave him another question-ing look before taking the receiver and saying, "Hello?"

When she smiled, Dharr felt her joy as keenly as if it were his own. "Papa? How are you?"

After reclaiming his seat, he tried not to eavesdrop on the conversation but was surprised to hear her converse with her father in fluent Arabic, as if she spoke it daily. At least he could be assured she would have no trouble communicating once they returned to Azzril. He, on the other hand, could have a great deal of trouble keeping his hands to himself even after they arrived in his country.

He continued to watch her, enthralled by the way she twined one lock of hair around her finger, her expressive eyes, her bouts of laughter.

"Yes, Sheikh Halim is taking good care of me, Papa," she said as she sent Dharr a brief look of appreciation. He would like to please her more before their travels ended, although he did not dare knowing that nothing more would exist be-tween them. And that was beginning to work on Dharr in ways he could not comprehend.

Granted, Raina Kahlil could be deemed a suitable candi-date for future queen considering her legacy. And she was beautiful. Intelligent. Young and vibrant. Any man would be honored to have her as his wife.

Yet Dharr acknowledged that Raina would be reluctant to consider settling into that role—unless he could somehow convince her that certain advantages did exist should they de-cide to adhere to the marriage terms. Then he promptly real-ized he was trying to convince himself of that very thing.

He rejected that notion altogether. Primal attraction was the only thing that existed between them at present, even if he found her to be interesting, and exciting beyond all bounds. He could not let down his guard and entertain anything but fondness for her knowing she would not stay with him. Knowing she had a life in America that would not include him.

Before she hung up the phone, Dharr moved onto the bed and picked up the drawing to find she had sketched a good likeness of him, including the scowl he had most surely been sporting.

"You weren't supposed to see that yet," she said from above him.

He regarded her over one shoulder. "You are very talented, but I do not believe I look this serious."

She sat down beside him. "Yes, you do. Most of the time. I'm assuming that stoic demeanor is in part because of your duty."

In part because of duty and in part because of his unanswered desire for her. "I do not take my responsibility lightly." The reason he could not act on that desire.

She balanced her heels on the edge of the bed and hugged her knees to her breasts. "I know. And thank you for the phone call."

Her closeness created another fire that burned low in his belly. "Is your father well?"

"Yes. And why didn't you tell me he was staying at the palace when he has a perfectly good mansion of his own?"

"He has limited company and very few servants. I felt it best he be attended to by my staff, including my physician."

"I appreciate your kindness more than you know."

Dharr appreciated every nuance of her beautiful face, every vibrant smile. "You are welcome. And my apologies for the delay in our journey."

She shrugged. "That's not your fault. You have no control over the weather."

"True, but I know you are anxious to see your father."

She collapsed back onto the bed, her hair forming a halo around her face. "If not for him, I wouldn't be so ready to leave. I don't mind this plane when it's not moving."

Dharr shifted where he could see her better. "Have you had a bad experience before?"

"Do you mean with flying?"

"Yes. Something that brought on your fear."

She stared at the low ceiling. "The night I left Azzril with my mother, it was stormy. The flight was bumpy all the way to the States. I was terrified."

Her tone more than proved that to Dharr, but he had other suspicions in terms of her fear. "And you were leaving your home."

Her gaze came to rest on his. "Yes. Leaving my papa and at the time, I really didn't know why."

"Did your mother not explain? Did she not comfort you?"

Raina sat again and clutched a pillow to her chest, as if she needed the security. "She was zoned out most of the trip and for weeks after that. At first she told me we were only in California temporarily, then she finally told me we wouldn't be back in Azzril."

The abject pain in her voice disturbed Dharr. "That must have been difficult for you."

She shrugged. "I managed. But my life's been a breeze compared to yours."

"In what way?"

"You're an only son, Dharr. You've been groomed to eventually rule a country, no questions asked."

"I have always accepted my duty and all that it entails."

She appeared doubtful. "But you went to college in the States. You must've enjoyed your freedom during that time. No responsibilities except making the grade."

Odd that she seemed to understand him so well. "I only had limited freedom. The press was relentless."

"That's true. I remember Mother showing me pictures of you in magazines and the newspapers. I especially recall a few times when I saw you keeping company with some socialite named Elizabeth something or other."

Dharr internally flinched over hearing the name. "I am surprised you would have been interested in my private life."

"Of course I was interested. She was on the arm of my presumed future husband." She smiled around her sarcasm. "Do you two still keep in touch?"

Dharr had no cause—or desire—to revisit the past. "I believe it would be best if we agree not to question each other over former relationships."

"Obviously dear Elizabeth is a touchy subject. But it's a deal. No talk about past loves."

"I never said that I loved her." Even though he had.

"Whatever you say, Sheikh Halim. You keep your secrets and I'll keep mine."

The only secrets Dharr wanted to know about Raina Kahlil had to do with her response if he made love with her. Even though she'd brought back the bitter memories, his focus was still on the woman he'd known as girl all those years ago. Even now he would gladly climb into the bed with her, divest them of clothing and learn her well. Yet honor prevented him from doing so.

Dharr rubbed his eyes in an attempt to erase the visions and when he opened them, he found Raina frowning.

"You look tired," she said. "Did you get any sleep at all?"

"Some."

After repositioning the pillow, she laid back and patted the place beside her. "Come here. We can take a nap while we're waiting for this heap to get off the ground again."

Every instinct Dharr owned shouted danger. "Perhaps that is not such a good idea."

"Come on, Dharr. We have on clothes. It's no big deal."

He was not that weak. He could lie down with her and do

nothing more, or so he hoped. "I suppose you are right." He stretched out on his back beside her, one arm lying rigid at his side, the other bent beneath his head in an effort not to touch her.

Yet Raina greatly complicated matters when she curled up close to his side and rested her cheek on his chest. Something deep within Dharr began to dissolve. The warmth that flowed through him had only partially to do with carnal cravings. Feelings he did not care to allow threatened to surface. Yet when she tipped her face up and whispered, "You smell great. You feel good, too," all his resistance fled as he drew her mouth to his.

Once more he gave in to his need for her, culminating in a kiss that began tenderly before turning deeper. Dharr framed her face in his palms, drawing on her heat, her essence. Their limbs became entwined as they explored each other with their hands, avoiding places that would send them effectively over the edge.

Then Raina slid her hands down his back to his buttocks and nudged him over until he was completely atop her. Though their clothes provided a substantial obstacle, the movement of Raina's hips beneath him created a friction that encouraged his desire despite his determination to keep his body at bay. Now only the true act of lovemaking could bring them closer.

As badly as Dharr wanted that very thing, he recognized the peril in continuing. In a matter of moments, he would not be able to stop. He would strip her clothes from her, remove his own clothes then take this interlude beyond the restrictions he'd purposely posed.

Mustering what little strength he had left, Dharr pushed away from Raina and sat on the edge of the bed, keeping his back to her. He could hear her ragged breathing that echoed his own then felt her hand on his back.

"Dharr, I think we should just give up."

He rested his elbows on his knees, lowered his head and streaked both hands over his face. "I do not understand what you are saying." A lie. He knew exactly what she was saying, and exactly what she wanted from him. He wanted it, as well, badly. But his head argued against that even though his body refused to listen.

She worked her way beside him and took his hand into hers. "We should give up pretending we don't want each other and just let whatever happens, happen."

He straightened and gathered all the arguments. "I would not want to dishonor you by making love with you without any commitment."

She smiled, a cynical one. "Dishonor me? This is not ancient times. We're both consenting adults."

"And you would be satisfied with only sex?"

"Yes, of course." Her tone sounded tentative, yet her expression appeared resolute. "I don't see why we can't just follow nature's lead. If we wanted to take a little pleasure in each other, why shouldn't we?"

She skimmed her fingertips up and down his arm, fueling his hunger for her once more when he imagined her hands beneath his slacks, doing the same.

For the sake of his own sanity, he bolted from the bed and faced her.

"I cannot forget who I am, Raina, or my responsibility. I promised your father I would see you safely to Azzril. He would not approve if I took advantage of this situation by allowing any more intimacy between us. I have already done enough."

She worked her way from the bed and stood before him, close enough to touch him. "I know all too well who you are, Dharr. But don't you ever wish you could forget for a while?

I know I do. I mean, I've been my mother's rock for ten years. I lived with her, supported her, basically baby-sat her until I moved out recently. For once I just want to let go. Do something I want to do."

"I cannot afford to do that."

She folded her arms across her chest and presented a look of defiance. "What not? Because you're supposed to be some superhuman without feelings or needs or desires? I know you have desires, Dharr. You've been playing games with me since we walked onto this plane. You stripped out of your clothes and crawled into bed with me last night. A few hours ago, you took my hand and you showed me how much you wanted me. You've been engaging in a tug-of-war and you're afraid to admit you're losing."

Dharr recognized the truth in her words even though he did not care for it. "I am a man, Raina, and I admit I have done things I should not have done. Yet I must stop before we go past the point of no return."

She smoothed a hand down his chest. "I think we've already gone past that point, Dharr. We went past it the first time you kissed me. You know it. And I know it, too."

He pressed his palm against her fingers, intending to take her hand away. Instead he held it against his pounding heart. "Again, it would not be fair to you. Since both of us do not intend to uphold our marriage contract, we would have no commitment to each other. If we are to make that clear to our fathers, then it would be unwise to continue on this path."

She moved closer, almost flush against him. "No one would have to know what goes on between us on this plane. After we're in Azzril, it would be our secret."

It was no secret he wanted her; that much Dharr could not deny. Yet he considered another pressing issue aside from the one beneath his slacks. "Even if I did decide to consider what you are saying, I have nothing on board to protect you from pregnancy."

She frowned. "That could be a problem since a child is something neither one of us needs."

Finally she was seeing the logic in what he was saying. "So now you understand the risk and why we cannot proceed."

Her smile appeared, slow and sultry. "We could if we didn't completely make love. There are other ways we could enjoy each other without the actual act. I'm sure you know more than a few."

He did and the temptation to show her was almost overwhelming. "You deserve much more, Raina."

She circled her arms around his neck. "We deserve to have this time together, Dharr. We deserve to lock out the world and forget about everything but each other. I dare you to be only the man, not the preeminent prince, for the next few hours we have together."

Framing her face in his palms, he tipped his forehead against hers. "You are testing my strength, Raina."

She pulled one of his hands to her breast. "I intend to do more than that to you."

Tossing all caution aside, Dharr claimed her mouth again in another heated exchange, fierce and fiery and in many ways, forbidden. He fondled her breast, tested her nipple with his fingertips through the thin material. He lowered the top's strap and left her mouth to kiss her shoulder, all the while warnings raging in his head. Yet he was helpless in her presence. The man wanted her without hesitation; the prince argued against the wisdom in that.

The man won out as he began to back her to the bed.

The rap on the door jolted Dharr from the erotic haze and sent him away from Raina. Storming to the entry on the heels of his frustration, he opened the door only enough to see the intruder, his senior staff member, Abid Raneer.

"What is it?" Dharr's tone sounded gruff and impatient despite his attempts at remaining calm.

Abid nodded. "Forgive the intrusion, but the captain wishes to speak with you, Sheikh Halim."

"I will be there in a moment."

Without another word, Dharr closed the door on his assistant and leaned back against it for support.

Raina was seated on the edge of the bed, her arms crossed over her breasts, which did nothing to quell Dharr's desire. "Is something wrong?"

Yes, Dharr decided. He was as hard as granite and that would not be easy to conceal. "I have been summoned downstairs. I will return as soon as possible."

"Okay."

When he made no move to leave, Raina asked, "Are you going?"

"I need a few more moments."

She sent her gaze to his distended fly, making matters worse. "I see."

And so would his men. "I would greatly appreciate your absence for a few moments. Perhaps you should retrieve a drink from the galley."

Her grin appeared, teasing and tempting. "You're going to leave me quivering with need? Hot for your body? Ready to jump all over you and tear off your clothes?"

Raina," he cautioned. "If you continue with that talk, I will be further delayed and you will have to wait longer for my return."

"Then you're going to consider what I'm proposing?" She sounded hopeful, and determined.

"We will discuss it as soon as I come back."

She smiled victoriously then pointed behind her. "I'll just go see what I can find in the fridge."

Dharr heard her soft laughter and the pad of her footsteps as she walked away. He willed his body to quiet, willed the return to restraint even though he recognized that when he walked back through the door, back to her, all restraint would be gone again.

Four

After ten minutes of staring at the ceiling, Raina decided that Dharr had reconsidered and caught another plane. If she hadn't recognized the total absence of logic, she might have panicked. She wasn't sure how she would continue this flight without him.

Of course she could do it. She didn't need his distractions, or at least she didn't want to need them. He'd already distracted her so much that she'd tossed away all her good sense for an opportunity that could prove to be very risky. But she'd never been afraid of taking chances; no need to begin now.

First, she had to have the man back, and she got her wish when the door opened and Dharr stepped into the room.

"What's going on?" she asked when she noted his stony expression.

"Nothing momentous," Dharr said as he closed the door behind him. "Only that we are about to take off again."

Raina only wanted to take off his clothes, and hers. Dharr seemed intent on preparing for departure when he sat in the designated seat. "Come. We will be leaving in a matter of moments."

Resigned that she had to do this, she took the seat next him for the familiar routine. She secured her seat belt, he fastened his own then wrapped his arm around her shoulder to pull her close to his side.

Raina couldn't deny the thrill of being next to him once more, hoping that after they got the journey underway again, he would be more accommodating. If she survived the take-off. She despised this part most of all. Dharr knew that well, evident by his soft lips trailing kisses along her jaw as the engines revved up and the plane reversed.

Raina risked a glance out the window to notice the rain still pounding the plastic pane. "Are you sure we should be leaving?" Her tone sounded high and wary.

"It is safe," Dharr whispered as he smoothed his palm up her bare arm. "You are in good hands."

Raina couldn't argue that point since Dharr's "good hands" breezing up the side of her breast had turned her insides into the consistency of oatmeal. But when the plane shook as they left the runway, even Dharr's caresses couldn't prevent the fear weighting her chest.

She buried her face into his neck and muttered, "I hate this. I hate being afraid."

With gentle fingertips, Dharr tipped her face up. "Look at me," he said, his tone commanding. "You have nothing to fear with me."

Oh, but she did. She feared the feelings he stirred within her, the urge to totally let go. She feared giving everything to him. Feared she wouldn't want to leave him when the time came to go back to her life, but not enough to put a halt to her plans even though he had yet to agree to her proposition.

"Take off your blouse," he whispered when the plane pitched as it banked to the right.

Her mouth dropped open from utter shock before awareness dawned and she leveled her gaze on his. "You've changed your mind." She posed the words as affirmation, not a question, because she could see surrender in his dark, dark eyes.

"You need distraction and I am going to give that to you."

Distraction she could definitely use but she hoped it wasn't temporary. "I'll take off mine if you take off yours."

"I see you are bent on bargaining with me for the remainder of this flight." Fortunately for Raina, he didn't sound angry. He did sound sexy as hell.

"That depends on how cooperative you're going to be from here on out."

He hinted at a smile while he released the buttons on his shirt. "That remains to be seen although I greatly question my wisdom."

"To heck with wisdom." Drawing in a deep breath, Raina crossed her arms, clasped the hem and pulled the top over her head. And now here they were, Dharr bare-chested and beautiful and she nude to the waist.

Once more he curled his arm over one shoulder, using his free hand to push her hair away and cup her breast lightly. "You are very tempting," he said. "Very beautiful."

Raina could barely draw a breath, much less manage a thank you. And her oxygen level decreased severely when he dipped his head and drew a nipple into the wet warmth of his expert mouth. She slid her hands into his hair and closed her eyes, the turbulent take-off all but forgotten, replaced by a host of sensations provoked by Dharr's soft suckling.

As he continued to mesmerize her, he traced the silver

loop at her navel with a leisurely fingertip, enticing and exciting her into mindlessness. Yet he didn't make even the slightest move to lower his hand. He simply continued to draw random designs on her belly above where the belt rested low on her lap, laving his tongue across her nipple a final time before working his way up her neck and to her ear.

"When we are cleared to leave these seats, do you know what I wish to do?" He spoke in a low whisper, his warm breath filtering over her neck.

"What?"

He traced the silver loops in her lobe with his tongue. "I am going to take you to the bed."

"To sleep?"

"To touch you. To learn every inch of you, if that is what you still want from me."

"Promise?"

"You may count on it."

Raina counted the seconds until he would make good on his promise. Waited for someone to tell them they could get out of the blasted seats.

When that didn't immediately happen, Dharr rested his hand on her thigh, rubbing his knuckles back and forth on the inside of her leg. Overcome with her own need to know how affected he might be, Raina slid her palm up his thigh and back down again, moving closer and closer to his groin each time.

"You are entering dangerous territory, Raina."

She grinned. "What's wrong with being a little dangerous?"

He brushed a kiss across her lips then pulled her hand back to his chest. "I am entitled to my turn first. Orders from the sheikh."

He prevented Raina from leveling any kind of come-back when he kissed her again, using his tongue like a feather while he slipped his hand between her thighs, applied a slight pressure there, bringing about a rush of wet heat. Raina was only slightly aware of the rocking plane as she concentrated on Dharr's distraction. His touch served as her only reality at the moment and one she never wanted to leave, at least not yet. Not until she experienced the limits of Dharr's skills, although she truly suspected there were no limits to what he would do to make a woman feel good. He was doing it to her now.

When Raina made a small sound of need, Dharr balanced on the threshold of madness. Yet he reminded himself that he did intend to take this slowly should they change their mind. And that was about as likely as either of them pursuing the marriage arrangement.

Dharr kissed her breasts again, then went back to her mouth, playing his tongue against hers in meaningful strokes, caressing her through the thin fabric of her pants, indicating what he would do to her body if given the chance to completely make love with her. And though that chance would not come on this plane, he would still give her the greatest pleasure she had ever known, or die trying.

The bell sounded and the fasten seat belt sign went out, causing Raina to tense, effectively interrupting their interlude.

Dharr took her hand into his and studied her flushed face. "Are you certain you want to continue this, Raina?"

She squeezed his hand tightly. "Yes. Unless you don't."

"I want it," he said. "Very unwise, I know, but this need I have for you makes very little sense."

She smiled. "Maybe we shouldn't worry about being sensible. After all, what else are we going to do to pass the time?"

The humor in her tone contrasted with Dharr's lack of mirth, yet he would always remember Raina's smile, no matter what the future held. "I suppose you are right, although most people would take that time to sleep."

She reached over and unfastened his seat belt, brushing her

fingertips across his increasing erection. "We're not most people, Dharr."

Dharr could not argue that point even though the debate in his mind continued over whether he should allow this tryst. Yet when Raina leaned over and whispered, "I believe our bed's waiting," all questions and concerns drifted away.

Standing, he held out his hand to her and she took it without hesitation. Once they made it to the bed, Dharr vowed to remain in command. Yet he could not resist kissing her without restraint. A long, deep kiss. A prelude to what would come.

Once they parted, Dharr could not discern who was more winded. He locked into Raina's golden eyes and told her, "We will take this slowly."

She frowned. "If we go too slowly, I'll go crazy."

"I plan for you to do that very thing."

"I'm looking forward to it."

"Now lie facedown on the bed."

She sent him a quizzing look. "May I ask why?"

He brushed her hair back from her breasts and leaned to take another brief taste. "You may ask, but you will have to wait and see. I will only say that if we are going to go forward with this, I intend to do it well."

"I'm going to hold you to that."

He drew a line down her jaw with a fingertip. "Trust me, Raina. I am not going to hurt you in any way. And anything that I do to you that you do not care for, you only need tell me and I will stop."

Her smile appeared, a bit shaky yet still a smile. "I trust you."

He wasn't certain he trusted himself to stop when necessary. "Good. Now on the bed."

When she reached for the drawstring on her pants, Dharr clasped her wrist. "Not yet. I will take care of that later."

"Okay, as long as you do."

While she climbed onto the bed onto her belly, Dharr set about lowering the shades on the windows and turning down all the lights except for the one above the bed that cast Raina in a sensual glow. He then opened one of the built-in cabinets and retrieved a bottle of massage oil.

After squeezing a few drops into his palm, Dharr sat on the edge of the bed, the bottle braced between his knees. He paused a moment to survey the golden lamp peeking from the waistband of Raina's pants, seriously doubting that the sultan knew his daughter had permanently marked her body, nor did he believe her father would approve. Dharr also recognized that her father would disapprove of what they were about to do.

Pushing those thoughts aside, he told her, "Pull your hair away from your back." Once she complied, he started the first part of the journey by spreading the oil across her shoulders.

"What is that heavenly smell?" she asked in a languid tone, her words muffled by the pillow where she'd buried her face. Eventually he would request that she watch what he was doing, but not quite yet.

"It is plumeria oil."

She lifted her head and looked back at him. "Massage oil, huh? And you tried to tell me you've never had a woman on board."

"The past shall be kept in the past, Raina." He bent and kissed her cheek. "What matters now are the hours we have together. Only us and no one else."

"You're right. I'm sorry." She laid her cheek back against the pillow. "Now carry on."

Exactly what Dharr planned to do. With calculated caresses, he worked his way down her back, curling his fingertips around her sides and using his thumbs to track the fine beads of her spine. When he reached the tattoo, he leaned down to kiss the spot before continuing his downward progress.

He slid his hands beneath her belly, tugging the drawstring to loosen the material and to provide access to all of her body. He smiled when she lifted her hips, allowing him to lower the pants slowly, taking her panties with them until he had them pushed to her thighs. The sight of her taut buttocks, the feel of her soft skin beneath his palms, only served to threaten his patience. But he refused to hurry this exploration, for both their sakes. Impatience could prove detrimental to his control. He could not allow that to happen.

Once more he dipped his head to apply a kiss, this time on each buttock then lightly flicked his tongue along the cleft. Raina's gasp brought his gaze back to her where he found her hands fisted tightly on the pillow.

After he worked the pants completely away and tossed them aside, he bracketed her hips and said, "Turn over."

She did as he asked, her breasts rising and falling in anticipation of what would come next. And what he planned for her would also prevent normal respiration, as soon as she was ready.

On that thought, Dharr propped two pillows beneath her shoulders then took the oil and placed a few more drops in his palm. He applied the liquid to her slender neck before working his way to the rise of her breasts.

"Watch, Raina," he whispered as he circled her nipples with his fingertips. The oil had created a fine satin sheen over her skin; his fondling had created a glaze in her eyes.

"That feels so good," she murmured, her voice low as if speaking took great effort.

Dharr paused to ply her lips with soft teasing kisses, pleased when each time they parted, Raina raised her head to seek his mouth once more.

"Do you wish to feel better?" he asked after pulling away

from her lips, suffering from the loss yet knowing he would eventually return there.

"By all means."

"Then you shall."

He skimmed his hands down her abdomen, spreading more of the floral oil in his wake before he paused to play with the silver ring in her navel. He found that jewelry quite intriguing. He found every inch of her intriguing, from her thick silky hair to her pink painted toenails.

Only then did he allow himself to study the shading between her thighs, knowing that in doing so, he would become excruciatingly hard at the sight, and he did. Yet his own needs would not take precedence over hers.

After applying more oil to his palm then setting the bottle on the floor, he bent her legs toward her hips. He sent his hand over her knee, down her well-toned calf and to her delicate ankle then did the same to her other leg. He moved almost to the end of the bed and nudged her thighs apart, leaving her open to his eyes.

When Raina laid her hand on her abdomen, for a fleeting moment he believed she might try to cover herself. Yet she didn't. She did continue to stare at him, expectancy in her expression, heat in her eyes.

He now faced a certain dilemma—would he use his hands or his mouth to give her pleasure? He would like nothing better than to test her with his tongue, an act that would be deemed one of the most intimate between a man and a woman. Perhaps he should avoid that level of intimacy. He had to remember that after they left the privacy of this plane, nothing else would come of this liaison.

He moved onto his knees between her legs and with both hands, pressed downward strokes from her navel toward her pubis, stimulating the blood flow to heighten her orgasm, as he had learned long ago. Lower and lower he traveled, through the shading of hair until he parted the soft pleats to reveal his ultimate goal. He swirled a fingertip round and round her swollen flesh, watching her face grow slack with every caress.

When Raina lifted her hips, encouraging him toward his mark, he quickened his pace, applied more pressure, knowing that she was coming closer to a climax. He guided one finger inside her to experience the waves of spasms, imagining her surrounding him yet knowing he must settle for only this.

A soft moan hissed out of her mouth and she bit her lower lip as he continued to touch her again and again, intent on giving her another release. But she grabbed his wrist and pulled him forward atop her before he could continue.

"Did I hurt you?" he asked, his voice hoarse from his current position between her legs. He would only have to lower his fly and shove down his briefs to thrust inside her.

"Do I look like I'm in pain?"

She looked beautiful in the aftermath of her fulfillment, but he was definitely in pain. "I want to touch you again."

"No." She worked her way from beneath him and nudged him aside. "Now it's my turn, Dharr."

As much as Dharr wanted her hands on him, he still feared a total loss of restraint, something he could not afford. Right now he was bordering on throwing caution to the wind to bury himself inside her. If she touched him, he would have to rely on solid sense to remind him why they could not end this interlude with true consummation. "That is not necessary. This time we have left I promised to dedicate solely to your pleasure."

Without regard to his words, she rolled onto her side to face him and reached for his fly to lower his zipper. "Yes, it is necessary. For me. Now take off your clothes so we'll be even, or I'll be glad to do it for you."

As far as Dharr was concerned, the odds were stacked against him, even more so when she stroked him through his briefs. Caution be damned, he would allow her to touch him, at least for a time. He would endeavor to hold back although that prospect seemed challenging. But he would face that when the time came.

Leaving the bed and her intoxicating touch, he removed his pants and briefs then stood before her, allowing her to see exactly how she had affected him. The increasing pressure between his legs only grew worse as her gaze traveled over his body.

She smiled and tapped one finger against her chin. "Well, you are certainly happy to see me."

He moved a step closer to the bed at his own peril. "Do you find everything to your liking?"

She continued to study him with a total lack of inhibition. "I would say you're definitely a ten."

A sudden surge of jealousy hurled through Dharr. "In comparison to whom?"

She rose to her knees before him and flattened her palms against his chest. "I'm not comparing you to anyone, Dharr. Remember, the past is in the past."

He did not appreciate having his words thrown back at him even though he admitted she was right. Still, the thought of another man making love to her only fueled his determination to prove himself. If he could not be her first, he would most certainly be her best.

Nudging Raina back onto the bed, Dharr stretched out to face her and gently rolled her taut nipple between his forefinger and thumb. "What would you have me do now? I am open to any request. Or perhaps you would wish me to choose."

She ran both hands down his chest, following the stream of hair before pausing at his abdomen. "I expect you to let me have my turn."

He gritted his teeth when she circled her fingertip around his navel. "Again, I am not certain that is wise."

"Wise or not, I'm going to do it. Now let me have some of that oil."

He hesitated a brief moment in recognition that if he gave into her whims, he could be in for heaven mixed with hell. But he would allow her the opportunity since he did not have the strength to fight her on the issue. He'd been in a steady state of arousal since their first encounter. He only hoped he could maintain some semblance of self-discipline.

Reaching behind him, he retrieved the bottle and squeezed a coin-sized dab into her open palm. "That's not very much," she said.

"A little goes a very long way." How very true. Being so close to her went a long way toward stealing Dharr's resolve to stay strong.

At first her touch was tentative, nothing more than a fingertip breezing down his length as she watched with fascination. She grew bolder with her discovery, yet somewhat hesitant at times, leading him to wonder if perhaps she had never touched a man this way before. He only wished that were true. Then she took him completely into her oil-slicked hands, her movements more deliberate—and deadly to Dharr.

Robbed of his will, he tossed the bottle of oil into the floor, not caring if he'd closed the lid. He only cared about Raina's tempered stroking and enthusiastic exploration. Other women had touched him this way yet not exactly this way, with such thoroughness and curiosity.

Tipping his forehead against hers, he lowered his eyes to watch her ministrations, knowing that by doing so he would only create more havoc on his resolve to allow this only for a while. A long breath hissed out from between his clenched teeth when she swirled one thumb over the sensitive tip several times.

With the last of his waning strength, he said, "Stop."

"No." She defied him not only verbally but also by quickening her pace.

He pulled her closer, his hips surging in time with her cadence. It was too much, yet not enough. "Not this way."

"There isn't another way."

Lost to her touch, he uttered the next thought that came to mind. "I want to be inside you."

"You know you can't," she said in a breathless whisper.

Dharr realized that all too well. Realized that in a matter of moments, self-control would desert him and he would have no choice than to let go completely. He'd been a fool to think he could begin to stop it, or Raina.

All sound disappeared save the rasp of his breath, or perhaps it was hers. He soon arrived at the place where coherent thought collided with sensation. Where logic retreated and primal instinct took over. He had no claim on his body, no power to fight the rush. The climax came with striking potency, bringing with it rigorous release, then welcome relief. And finally, awareness.

For only the second time in Dharr Halim's life, he was totally powerless—and completely enslaved—by a woman. And he realized she could hold the key to keeping him that way for the remainder of their journey, if not longer.

Raina left the shower and returned to the cabin, inhaling the pungent aroma of the exotic floral scents combined with sex lingering still, though she'd washed the remnants away from her skin. But she couldn't rid herself of the memory of Dharr's hands on her only a few hours before, or what she had done to him. Nor could she ignore that she only had an hour left before recollections of an incredible experience with a highly sensual man were all that remained.

She had no idea what he thought of her now. He had no idea that she'd never touched a man the way she'd touched him. True, she had seen her share of male anatomy in art classes when she'd painted nudes, and she'd dated several men who had attempted to persuade her into their beds or the back seat of their cars. Not one had ever tempted her enough to totally let go of all inhibitions—until Dharr Halim.

Tucking the towel securely between her breasts and tightening the ponytail high atop her head, Raina tiptoed past the bed where Dharr still slept. She had every intention of getting dressed before waking him, but she was drawn to the glorious scene laid out atop the rumpled sheets—one beautifully nude man lying on his stomach, one arm casually resting over his head, the other across the place she'd left minutes before.

His hair was sufficiently tousled—and sexy, but then so was the rest of his amazing body. From the hue of his cocoa-colored skin to the backs of his hair spattered thighs, he was undeniably gorgeous. And his butt—well, Raina couldn't find the words to express the splendor of that.

When he stirred slightly and turned his face toward her, she took a seat on the edge of the bed and laid a hand on his back. "Dharr, are you awake?"

He didn't respond or open his eyes so she stretched out beside him, lifting his arm and draping it over her middle. Raina assumed he was still asleep, allowing her the opportunity to look her fill a while longer. His dark lashes fanned out below his closed eyes and a shadow of whiskers surrounded his sensuous lips—lips that she wanted to kiss again and again and again. But as soon as they walked off this godforsaken plane, that wouldn't be possible. Everything that had happened between them to this point would have to be kept secret, and it couldn't happen again. Not if they wanted to keep up the pretense that they were only friends and not destined to marry, regardless of their fathers' wishes. Only she found herself wishing…

No. That was totally absurd. She and Dharr might be united by cultural heritage, but they lived two very different lives. She wouldn't be happy in Azzril, and he sure as heck wouldn't be traveling to California to see her. Half a world separated them by distance; a whole universe divided them in terms of their goals. It simply wouldn't work between them even if she inherently knew how well they worked in bed, albeit in a limited sense. She also knew that if protection from pregnancy had been readily available, she would have known everything—how it would have felt to have him inside her. Now she would probably never know.

Feeling somewhat melancholy, Raina resigned herself to what had to be and decided to dress. But she barely moved an inch before Dharr pulled her closer and buried his face in her exposed neck. He radiated heat like a potter's kiln and he still smelled like the oil she'd personally applied to his body.

Raina shivered from the sudden sexual awareness, the onslaught of an unfathomable need for him. Only him. Without saying a word, he lavished her neck with light kisses, abrading her skin with his beard though she really didn't feel it much. She did feel his hardness pressing against her pelvis, felt the damp heat between her thighs in response. In her logical mind, she recognized she should stop him before they went any further. In her heart of hearts, she didn't have the desire to do that. And when he flicked open the knotted terry cloth with one finger, any and all objections went the way of the towel he pulled from beneath her and tossed onto the ground.

His warm mouth closed over her nipple while he fondled her other breast with slightly callused fingertips. So attuned to what Dharr was doing to her, she was only mildly aware that he'd nudged her legs apart. But soon she became very aware that he had slid his hand down to guide his erection between her legs, much too close to the point of no return.

She needed to stop him, *had* to stop him *now*. But before she could articulate her concerns, he rolled off her and onto his back, one arm covering his eyes.

"Get dressed, Raina." His tone was harsh, authoritative.

"I will, but first we should—"

"Get dressed before I do something we both regret."

Raina only regretted that they hadn't been able to completely make love. As she snatched up the discarded towel, then her bag and returned to the bathroom, she couldn't stop the sudden sour mood.

For the next few days, she would go to bed alone until the time came for her to return home. She would not be able to enjoy his kisses, lose herself in his touch or to touch him. Would never know how it would be to have him fill her completely. Worse, they would walk around pretending that nothing had happened between them.

But something had happened to Raina, and it wasn't only about lovemaking or the lack thereof. She not only admired Dharr Halim, appreciated his kindness and his concern for her, his comforting embrace. She was starting to feel so much more.

For someone who had no designs on settling down with a sinfully seductive sheikh, she was certainly doing a good impression of a woman falling in love.

Five

As the plane made its final descent, Dharr did not dare to do anything more than hold Raina close to his side. As badly as he wanted to kiss her, he recognized he had already done too much. She had weakened him to the point that he had almost thrown away all caution.

At least she seemed more relaxed now despite the upcoming landing. Her hands rested in her lap as she stared straight ahead, seemingly lost deep in thought. He missed having her head resting against his shoulder, missed distracting her with his kisses. And he knew that once they returned to Azzril, he would miss much more than that.

The plane landed smoothly and in a matter of moments, they were cleared to leave their seats. In silence, Raina gathered her bag from beneath the bed and slipped the strap over her slender shoulder. Dharr almost asked if he could help her but knew he would be met with a resounding "no."

They walked to the door, still not speaking, until Raina faced him. "I guess this is it," she said.

Dharr slipped his hands in his pockets to keep from touching her. "Yes, it seems it is."

"We'll just pretend none of this ever happened."

"We will keep it our secret."

"What about your staff?" She glanced at the bed now in total disarray. "They're going to know something when they change the sheets."

"I trust they will remain silent. They are very loyal to me."

"That's good to know." She worked her bottom lip between her teeth several times before finally looking at him again. "Thanks, Dharr. I would never have made it through my return to flying without you."

"It has been my pleasure." The greatest of pleasures for Dharr.

She turned to the door. "I guess we should probably go now."

Before she could release the latch, Dharr rested his hands on her shoulders. "Wait."

After turning her around, he met her soft gold gaze, wariness in her eyes. "What is it?" she asked.

"One more kiss."

"I'm not sure we should."

He brought her hands to rest against his chest. "Only one, to seal our vow of secrecy."

"Okay. Just a little one."

"Of course."

Yet when he bent his head and touched his mouth to hers, as always she opened to him. Her lips were soft, pliant, welcoming. She drew his tongue into the heat of her mouth with gentle persuasion. They wrapped their arms around each other in a tight embrace, feeding each other, feasting on each other.

In another place, at another time, Dharr would notify the crew they would not be leaving soon. He would take her back to the bed and make love to her. Truly make love to her. But in one coherent moment, he realized that would not be possible.

With effort he pulled away from her lips yet kept his arms around her. "That should be sufficient."

Her ensuing smile was shaky. "And you have no concept of 'little.' But that's okay. At least it was memorable."

And so had been their time together, Dharr decided. He longed for more time with her, more touches, more talk. More of everything.

Aside from avoiding her completely while she was in his home, he was uncertain of how he could fight his attraction to her. But he knew he must, or risk certain emotional peril when she left him.

The city had changed, Raina thought as the armored sedan arrived at the highest point of the mountain road revealing, Tomar—the capital city—spread out in the valley below. Amber lights dotted the panorama, providing a breathtaking view. The ancient palace, situated at the gateway to the old village, remained the focal point. But a few high-rise buildings silhouetted against the night sky were scattered on the opposite end of town.

"Tomar's grown quite a bit," she told Dharr who had kept a fairly wide berth between them, physically and emotionally.

"Yes, it has. We have become much more modern."

Raina couldn't argue that point, nor could she argue she wasn't attuned to Dharr's every move, his scent and the taste of him still lingering on her lips.

Rolling down the window, she let the cool desert breeze blow across her face to try and erase all those little details, but to no avail. She could still feel his hands and his mouth on her skin, as if she were completely bared to him.

The vehicle bumped down the barely paved road, jolting

Raina against Dharr's shoulder. She should probably move away from him so as not to create any suspicion, but she found comfort in his touch, even if it was only minor. He didn't reach for her hand as he had on the plane, didn't tip her head against his shoulder, didn't even look as if he wanted to touch her. He continued to stare out the opposite window, totally detached.

Raina decided she might as well get used to it now, the physical and emotional distance. Dharr obviously was more than willing to uphold his hands-off promise. And that made Raina surprisingly disappointed and a little bit peeved.

She'd been nothing more than a readily available diversion. An easy means to pass the time. She meant nothing more to him than that, and she might as well accept it. But isn't that what she'd wanted, too? Yes, and she needed to remember that. She also needed to remember something else. "Could you remind me to call my mother in the morning?"

"That has already been done."

Raina didn't even try to hide her shock even though Dharr still refused to look at her. "You called her?"

"My assistant did, at my request, when we were grounded in London. I felt it best she not worry."

"Don't you think I should have been the one to tell her?"

Finally he glanced at her. "I thought it might be best coming from someone else."

"What exactly did your assistant say to her?"

"That I was escorting you to Azzril to see your father, and nothing more. In fact, he did not speak to her personally but he did reach a woman named Mona who promised to pass along the information."

Mona, the meddling maid. "I'm sure she was very thrilled to do that. I still think I should have called her personally."

"You can call her tomorrow."

Raina could but now that her mother knew exactly where she was, and with whom, it might be best to wait a day or two for her to calm down.

When they pulled up at the palace a few moments later, Raina couldn't get out of the vehicle quick enough, waving off the driver's offer of assistance with her lone bag. She didn't need his help, and she didn't need Dharr Halim.

The doors opened wide as they entered the ornate palace foyer—midnight blue tile with a white border, beige brick walls, black and white mosaic ceiling, two metal Egyptian sentries guarding the wide arched entry showcasing six white-marble stairs with a red-carpeted runner. And at the top of those stairs stood a lone woman dressed in dark clothing, small in stature with a big smile. Raina immediately recognized the endearing features, the salt-and-pepper low bun, the warm and welcoming expression of Badya, Raina's one-time nanny and faithful family employee.

"Welcome home, little one." Badya opened her arms to Raina who gladly accepted her embrace.

"It's so good to see you, Badya," she said after they parted. "What are you doing here?"

"Your father released most of his staff after you left."

The first round of surprising news and, Raina suspected, not the last. "I can't believe he would let you go."

Badya nodded toward Dharr who now stood beside Raina. "The royal family was kind enough to offer me a position as the house manager. I have enjoyed my time here very much although they do not work me very hard."

"She is too modest," Dharr said. "This household would fall down around our heads were it not for her."

"What else am I to do since there are no babies to tend?"

Raina smiled. "You certainly tended to me well, although I did manage to cause you more than a little trouble at times."

"No more than I could manage, *yáahil.*" Badya glanced at Dharr then lowered her eyes. "Forgive me. I should refer to you as Princess Kahlil now that you are no longer my charge."

Raina's mouth dropped open before she laughed. "I'm no princess, Badya. I'm just me, the *bint* who used to hang out with you in the kitchen, giving you lots of daily grief."

"Badya is correct," Dharr stated. "You are technically a princess while you are here."

Raina ventured a quick look his way. "But my father was exiled from Fareesa years ago."

"He is still a sultan, and you are still royalty."

"Half royalty," Raina corrected before she turned her attention back to Badya. "How is my father?"

"He is waiting for you," Badya said. "He insisted he would not sleep until he knew you were safe in Azzril."

Raina wanted to see him badly. But she wasn't sure she had the strength to endure any questions about Dharr should he decide to pose them, and she knew he would. "It's the middle of the night. Maybe I should wait until morning."

"He will not stand for that," Badya said firmly, then more quietly, "He has missed you very much and he will not retire until he has spoken with you."

"I will go with you," Dharr said. "Then we will retire to bed."

That sounded like a plan to Raina though she realized he'd meant separate beds. "After you," she said with a sweeping gesture toward the curving staircase leading to the upper floors.

Raina followed Dharr up the stairs, reminding her of two nights ago when she'd done the same in the plane. Only now she knew exactly what his butt looked like without the benefit of slacks.

Once they reached the corridor outside her father's suite,

Dharr turned to her. "If he asks questions about our trip, be brief."

"I know that, Dharr. If we're lucky, this visit will be brief."

"I would not count on it. He has not seen you in a while."

"I'll handle everything fine. You don't have to stay."

"I would prefer to see how he is doing."

The concern in Dharr's tone prompted Raina's latent fears. "Are you not telling me everything? Is he worse than you've been letting on?"

"I have told you everything. I am more concerned with you."

She folded her arms across her chest. "Oh, so you're worried I'm going to spill the beans and tell him we spent a good deal of time fooling around?"

"No. I am concerned that he might press you about our marriage arrangement. I do not want you to have to answer to that alone."

"How chivalrous of you. But again, I know how to handle my own father."

"I am certain you do. I am still going in with you."

Resigned Dharr wasn't going to give up, Raina rapped on the heavy door and waited for her father's "Come in," before she turned the knob.

She stepped inside to find her beloved papa lying on crisp white sheets contrasting with his navy pajamas, his head propped on two pillows, a book resting on his chest and his reading glasses and near-gray hair askew.

Raina propped her hands on her hips and looked mock-disapproving. "Now what are you doing up this time of night, oh stubborn sultan?"

He grinned and held out his arms. "You are here, safe and sound, my child."

"Yes, I'm definitely here."

"Come and let your old papa get a better look at you."

On sluggish legs, Raina walked to him, perched on the edge of the bed and gave him a lengthy hug. "You're not old, Papa. You'll never be old."

He slid his glasses to the top of his head. "I would like to believe that but I fear my physical condition is saying otherwise." When Raina straightened, her father turned his attention to Dharr who was standing near the door. "My thanks to the *shayx* for bringing my daughter to me."

Dharr nodded in response. "It was my pleasure to serve you, Sultan."

Raina laid a hand on his arm. "How are you really feeling?"

He scowled. "Well enough not to be in this bed. I am still in control of all my faculties." He leaned forward and sniffed. "What is that perfume you are wearing?"

Perfume? She didn't have on any perfume. Unless… The oil. And she just thought she'd washed it all off. "It's new. A nice floral scent, don't you think?"

"Ah, flowers. That suits my *záhra*."

"You're too kind, Papa, but I'm not a flower tonight. I am about to wilt."

He brushed a hand over her cheek. "You do look tired. Did you not sleep on the plane?"

Not hardly. "Yes, I did. Dharr was kind enough to provide his quarters for the duration."

He shot a quick glance at Dharr. "As best I can recall, only one bed exists."

Uh, oh. "Yes. I slept there. Dharr stayed up most of the trip." And that part wasn't a lie.

"Then you two have gotten to know each other better?"

A tremendous understatement. "Yes."

Again her father looked to Dharr. "Would you mind if I spoke to my daughter privately?"

Raina glanced over her shoulder to see Dharr nod. "I will

be outside when you are ready to retire to your room, Raina. Peace be upon you, Sultan."

"And peace be upon you, Sheikh Halim."

After Dharr left the room, Raina turned to find her father's face forming a mask of concern. "Is there something you wish to tell me, Raina?"

She balled her hands into tight fists in her lap. "Tell you?"

"Yes. I feel as if you are concealing something from me."

Darn his intuition. "I'm not, Papa. Everything is going well with work. My life is in order. I'm settling into my new—"

"I am referring to your relationship with Dharr."

Despite internal panic, Raina attempted a relaxed façade. "I promise you, we got along just fine. He's a very interesting man."

"And he treated you well?"

"Of course. Why would you think otherwise?"

"Because you are a beautiful woman and he is a hot-blooded male. And although I consider Dharr the closest thing to a son, if I discover that he treated you inappropriately, I would have to kill him."

Raina released a nervous laugh. "You have a grand imagination, Papa, as always."

"My only concern is for you. I expect Dharr to treat you with the greatest respect and withhold any serious affection, at least until you are married."

Here we go again. "I am not even going to discuss that marriage contract, Papa, because as I've told you before, I have no intention of going through with it."

"You should not be so quick to toss the idea away."

"I don't want to get married right now."

He looked hopeful. "But you have not completely ruled out the possibility in the future?"

Leaning over to kiss his cheek, she told him, "Good

night, Papa. I'm too tired to hash this out now, and you need your rest."

"I am fine." He laid a hand on his chest, contradicting his assertion.

"Are you okay?" Raina asked, her tone laced with worry.

"Again, I am fine. I am taking enough medications to make the most ill of men miraculously recover from any maladies."

"Are you sure?"

He patted her cheek. "I am sure. Now run along to bed. We will talk again tomorrow."

"Okay." Raina saw escape at hand when she reached the door until her father called her back. She faced him once more. "What is it now, Papa?"

"How is your mother?"

Raina's heart clutched when she saw the familiar sadness in his eyes. "She's doing okay. She's not very happy that I moved out."

"She is lonely. How well I understand that."

"It doesn't have to be that way for either one of you, if you'd both quit being so stubborn and admit you still have feelings for each other."

"It is too late for us to be happy," he said. "But it is not too late for you. Search long and hard for that happiness, my daughter. And once you find it, do not let it go."

"I'm happy with my life, Papa." Oddly she didn't sound all that convincing. And her father wasn't convinced. She could see it in his eyes.

"Now get some rest," she said. "I'll see you in the morning."

"I hope so," he murmured. "I would also like to see a grandchild before I pass on to the great unknown."

Without responding, Raina sent him a smile before she rushed out the door.

Dharr was leaning back against the opposite wall of the

corridor, arms folded across his broad chest, looking gorgeous despite his ruffled hair and rumpled shirt. "Shall I show you to your room now?"

"Yes. We need to talk."

Dharr led Raina down the hallway to a room three doors from her father's suite. After they entered the room, she was vaguely aware of the recessed U-shaped sofa beneath an arched overhang and the rich russet colors mixed with turquoise. But she was very aware of the four-poster, carved bed not far away, and that had nothing to do with her lack of sleep.

First and foremost, she had to tell Dharr about her conversation. "Close the door," she said, her tone more anxious than she would have liked.

"Perhaps that would not be a good idea."

"I don't want anyone to hear us."

"Hear us?"

She let go a frustrated sigh. "Talking, Dharr. I think you need to know what my father just said to me."

"As you wish." He closed the door then faced her again. "I am ready to listen now."

Raina wasn't certain how she should tell him, so she simply blurted, "He knows."

Dharr took a few steps forward. "Knows what?"

"He knows that something went on between us."

"How would he know this unless you told him?"

"I didn't say anything that even remotely hinted at our…you know."

"Extracurricular activities?"

She pointed. "Exactly. He obviously sensed something. Maybe it's the oil. He smelled it, you know. I swear I thought I washed it all off—"

"Raina."

"Obviously I didn't, not that I didn't try. But then it was on the sheets when—"

"Raina."

"This morning, when we went at it again. I knew I should have taken another shower—"

He clasped her shoulders, ending her senseless rambling. "He would have no way of knowing it was massage oil. Now precisely what did he say to you?"

"He said that if he learned that you were inappropriate with me, or something like that, he would kill you."

Dharr had the nerve to laugh. "He must be feeling better."

"He said you weren't allowed to touch me intimately."

He dropped his hands from her shoulders. "I see."

"Until we're married."

Any sign of humor disappeared from Dharr's expression. "Then he brought up the marriage arrangement."

"Yes, he did. And I refused to discuss it with him. Of course, he added a little drama by clutching his chest although he insists it's nothing. I'm beginning to believe he might be partially right. Until that point, he looked perfectly fine."

"Do you believe he is manipulating you with his illness?"

Raina wrung her hands over and over. "I honestly believe he probably has been sick. I also believe that now that I'm here, he's going to milk it for what it's worth, hoping to convince me to hook up with you permanently. That was apparent when he mentioned grandchildren."

Dharr paced the length of the room then back again. "All the more reason not to give him anything to be suspicious about."

"I know. It's probably best we don't even look at each other when we're together."

Dharr stopped and frowned. "That would seem rather unusual, do you not agree?"

"Probably so." She shrugged. "I'm sure everything will be fine. Regardless of what he believes might have happened between us, he has no proof. And he did say he considers you the son he never had."

"I am flattered."

"I suppose you should be, although considering what we've done, that seems a little incestuous."

Once more Dharr moved in closer to her. "I assure you that any thoughts I have entertained about you have not been brotherly."

Drawn in by his sultry expression and his mysterious eyes, Raina slipped her arms around his waist. "I would have to say the same about you. I've never thought of you as my brother."

"Raina, we should not be doing this," he said, yet he pulled her totally against him.

"We're not doing anything. It's just an innocent embrace between surrogate family members."

"What I am considering now would not be deemed innocent."

She gave him a coy look. "And what would that be?"

He responded by claiming her mouth in a not-at-all innocent kiss. It was hot. It was deep. It was intoxicating.

But after too short a while, in Raina's opinion, it ended. Dharr stepped back and clamped his hands behind his neck. "You need to sleep."

She needed him. Raina called herself the worst kind of fool—a woman too weak to resist a man who shouldn't interest her at all. But he did. Too much. "You're right. Now run along to your bedroom. By the way, where is your bedroom?"

He dropped his arms to his sides. "You are standing in it."

"You mean we're going to sleep in the same bed again?" She couldn't conceal the surprise, or the excitement, in her voice.

"No. I am taking the suite at the end of the hall. It is smaller than this one and smells of fresh paint. You will be more comfortable here."

Not without him in her bed, as badly as she hated to admit it. "I really don't think it's necessary to put you out of your room. I can take the smaller one. I'm used to the smell of paint."

"I insist. And this room is also closer to your father."

Raina wasn't so sure that was a good thing, especially if in some uncontrolled fit of lust, she might hold Dharr prisoner, bound with some well-placed bed sheets. "If you're sure."

"I am only sure of one thing, Raina." He reached out and touched her cheek. "I will miss not having you in my arms tonight."

With that, he headed out the door without further comment, leaving Raina alone with a total loss of composure.

Unless Dharr Halim took a sabbatical on the other side of the world, for Raina Kahlil, ignoring him would be impossible.

"Will you be escorting Miss Kahlil to the celebration tonight?"

Dharr looked up from the financial documents to Abid Raneer, standing before Dharr's desk, confused over the query. "What celebration?"

"The one commemorating the recent marriage of Ali Gebwa's daughter. Have you forgotten?"

Dharr tossed aside the papers and dashed a hand over his jaw. "Yes, I had forgotten. I suppose I should make an appearance considering he is a major investor in the museum project."

"And one of your father's loyal supporters."

"True."

"You did not answer my original question. Will you be taking Miss Kahlil?"

Dharr had not considered taking Raina to a public function. Yet if he did not, that would be considered inhospitable. "I will ask if she would like to attend."

"Very good, Sheikh Halim. I will inform the sultan since he has been inquiring."

Dharr should have suspected as much. "Does the sultan plan to leave his bed to attend?"

"No. He suggested his daughter go in his stead."

"Again, I will ask." Dharr leaned back in his chair. "Now tell me again what the sultan's wife said when she contacted you after receiving the message?"

"She told me to tell the princess not to do anything she might regret."

"And she gave no other indication as to what that means?"

"I presume it could have to do with you."

Dharr presumed the same and he hoped he did not live to regret what he and Raina had done. "Perhaps she is concerned that the princess might decide to remain in Azzril with her father."

"That could be true, but I'm certain she will not be the only one to speculate on your relationship with Princess Kahlil."

"I do not plan to give anyone any cause for speculation."

"I am afraid you already have."

Concern sat like a massive weight on Dharr's chest. "What do you mean?"

Raneer took the seat opposite Dharr and leaned forward. "Most of your men are loyal to you, but they are still men, and men do talk. I have heard some rumors about your journey with Miss Kahlil."

"Unfounded rumors." Dharr recognized he sounded too defensive, which made him appear guilty. In truth, he was.

"That quite possibly is true, but tonight with you serving as her escort, many will believe you have decided to take her as your bride in accordance with the betrothal."

"Then they would assume wrong. Neither I nor the princess have any intention of upholding the marriage contract."

"Should anyone ask, what do you wish me to say?"

"Simple. The palace has no comment on the sheikh's personal affairs, and leave it at that."

"I believe your father would object to that response."

Anger and lack of sleep began to take its toll on Dharr. "My father is not present and he has left me in charge, so I will handle matters as I see fit. Is that understood?"

As usual, Raneer looked unaffected by Dharr's show of temper. "That is quite clear."

A change of subject was definitely called for, Dharr decided. "Speaking of the king, have you heard from him or my mother?"

"They left implicit instructions that they not be disturbed once they boarded the yacht two weeks ago."

"I suppose that is to be expected since it is their anniversary trip." Even after forty years of marriage, his parents still acted as if they were newlyweds. Yet they had an abiding love for each other, something Dharr had found very rare in his experience. Something he dared not hope for.

Raneer stood. "Is that all, your grace?"

Dharr picked up the documents and pretended to study them once more. "Yes. I have work to do. Tell Badya to inform the princess of our evening outing. If she agrees to attend, then I expect her to be ready no later than 7 p.m. as I do not plan to stay long into the evening."

"I will."

Dharr sensed Raneer staring at him so he looked up. "Is there something else you require, Abid?"

"No. I would only like to say that the princess is a beautiful woman. A man could do much, much worse."

Dharr did not need the commentary, even if Raneer was his

closest aid. "Yes, she is beautiful, and she is a free spirit. Any man who would be foolish enough to fall for her would have to be willing to do things her way."

"Much like yourself, I see."

"You may go now," Dharr said through clenched teeth.

Raneer nodded. "As you wish."

When Dharr was again alone, he tipped his head back against the chair and closed his eyes, the image of Raina arriving with great clarity.

Yes, she was a free spirit, intelligent and full of life. Yes, she would make a man a fine wife—if the man was strong enough to hold her. Dharr did not consider himself to be that man for he had already failed once with another woman who was much the same.

Regardless, the fantasy of making love to Raina took flight again. Now if only he could leave it at that. Yet he admitted that he craved to have the beauty in his arms—in his bed— once more.

Six

She looked like the scruffy side of a camel's hump.

Raina stood before the mirror examining the bags beneath her eyes, all the while thinking she could not believe she'd slept until 5 p.m.

When the knock came at the door, her heart skipped several beats. She started to reach for her robe to cover herself in case it was Dharr, then reconsidered. What the heck? He'd definitely seen her in a whole lot less.

She strolled to the door, her pulse fluttering with excitement and anticipation, only to find Badya on the other side.

"I see you have finally awakened," Badya said as she hurried into the room carrying a tray full of food that she placed on the table in the corner.

"You should've gotten me up hours ago."

"I tried but I could not rouse you."

"You must not have tried very hard."

Badya brought out her familiar grimace, the one she'd always used on Raina when she wasn't too pleased. "I put away all your clothes and still you did not move. I then checked to see if you were breathing, which you were, so I assumed you needed your rest after the flight." She gestured toward the fare. "Now come have something to eat."

Raina walked to the table and wrinkled her nose, her stomach roiling in protest. "I'm not really all that hungry, but I will have some coffee."

After Badya poured her a cup, Raina took a sip and tasted cardamom, bringing back a host of memories from a long-ago time. "I'd forgotten how good this is," she said as she dropped down in one less-than-comfortable chair.

"You really should eat, *yáahil*. You need your strength."

Raina needed strength, all right. At least enough to keep her hands off Dharr. She bypassed the pungent stew and grabbed a pastry that melted like sugar in her mouth. "I remember these date bars, too," she said after she swallowed. "You're still the best cook in Azzril."

"You are kind, *yáahil*, but I no longer cook. It is my recipe, though."

Badya took the chair across from Raina and smiled. "So have you found Sheikh Halim to your liking?"

Raina nearly choked on the cookie. "If you mean do I think he's nice, he's okay."

"I would say by the way that you look at him, he would be more than that to you."

Raina reminded herself to stop eating until this conversation ended. "What do you mean?"

"Perhaps I should say the way you look at each other, as if you share a secret. Perhaps you are in love with him."

Raina rolled her tired eyes and even that took effort. "That's ridiculous. Why would you even think such a thing?"

"Because every woman in this country below the age of sixty is in love with him. You will see that tonight when he escorts you into the village for the celebration."

"What celebration?"

"Two days ago, your childhood friend, Fahra Gebwa married Gameel Attar. Though the couple has left for their wedding trip, the celebration continues."

Wonderful. Fahra had always been a little sneaky snob and Gameel, whose name meant "handsome" in Arabic, was about as attractive—inside and out—as a dried-up blowfish. Like she was really one to talk at the moment. "That's good. She can spend all his money while he establishes his very own harem."

"True, it is not a love match, but a solid match."

"I just pity the children."

Badya laughed. "You are as quarrelsome as always."

Raina stood and stretched. "Only when it comes to people I don't care for."

"And of course, the sheikh would not be among those people."

Was she being that obvious? If so, she needed to practice camouflaging her attraction to Dharr, and fast. She wasn't certain how well she could manage that in the near future, especially in a public forum. "I still don't want to attend the celebration. Besides, I need to visit with Papa."

"It is your father who has ordained it. You are to go in his place."

Great. Just great. First Papa wanted to kill Dharr and now he was throwing him into her path. "I don't have anything appropriate to wear."

Badya came to her feet, strode to the closet and pulled out a teal sleeveless top with beads dangling at the hem and the matching wraparound skirt. "This will do. I will bring you a shawl to cover yourself since the desert nights can be cool. Now go and bathe and I will help you ready yourself. You need to be downstairs by seven."

Raina grasped for the final excuse. "I need to wash my hair and it won't be dry by then."

"I will braid it as I did when you were a child."

So much for that protest. As usual, Badya had an answer for everything. "Fine, but I doubt I'm going to have any fun."

Badya sent her a wily grin. "I would think a certain prince would have something to say about that."

Dharr was uncertain what to say to the sultan when he answered his summons. He was, however, pleased to find that Idris was seated for the first time since his arrival at the palace from the hospital. "It is good to see you up and about, Idris."

The sultan answered with a smile. "Having my daughter home has renewed my strength." He indicated the settee near the chair, which he now occupied. "Come sit with me a while before you go."

After Dharr complied, he braced for a serious conversation, and he was not disappointed when Idris said, "My daughter is a jewel, and she will be treated as such. Am I clear on this point?"

Hiding his guilt behind a stern expression, Dharr replied, "I am wounded you do not trust me."

"I am a man, Dharr. And I know it is not easy to resist a beautiful woman such as my daughter."

How well Dharr knew that. "You may count on me to treat her with the greatest respect."

"Good. Now have you given any consideration to the betrothal?"

As suspected, Idris was stilling holding out hope that Dharr would marry his daughter. "Raina and I have not discussed that at length, although I do know she plans to return to the States in a few days."

"Then you must prevent her from doing so."

A feat Dharr dare not attempt to undertake. "She is her own person and free to do as she pleases. I would not impose any sanctions on her because of an agreement you made with my father years ago."

"A good agreement, I might add." Although his tone was somber, it was not all that severe.

"These are different times, Idris. We do not hold the same beliefs as your generation."

"And those former beliefs are not always unwise. Marriages agreed upon by arrangement are most always successful. Those brought about by emotions such as love at times do not survive."

Dharr's own words to Raina two days ago. Yet somehow they sounded callous and hollow coming from her father's mouth. "I suppose you are right, but again, we have not broached the subject."

Idris leaned forward and leveled a stern gaze on him. "You should, and soon. My daughter might surprise you."

As far as Dharr was concerned, she already had surprised him at every turn, yet that had nothing to do with the marriage they both adamantly opposed. Still, he would give Idris some hope to avoid any upset. "I will consider it."

At least the sultan looked pleased, even if Dharr had no plan to bring up the contract to Raina again. "Good. Give the Gabwa's my best this evening. And take care with my Raina."

The door creaked open and a soft feminine voice said, "Did someone call me?"

Dharr immediately stood and faced the entry, unprepared for the sight of Raina dressed in an aqua blouse and skirt, her hair pulled away from her forehead and plaited in a long braid, revealing her exquisite features.

"Papa, are you sure you should be sitting up?" she asked as she bypassed Dharr, bringing with her the citrus scent he had detected during their first encounter in California.

"I am quite capable of sitting," Idris said, followed by a grumble.

Raina did not try to conceal her concern. "As long as the doctor says it's okay, I guess it's okay."

Idris's features softened as he looked upon his only child. "You are worried for naught. The doctor says it would be good for me to move around for short periods of time."

When Raina leaned over to embrace her father, Dharr caught a glimpse of bare flesh at her back and the top of the lamp tattoo. He would most certainly be engaged in a battle not to touch her tonight—a battle that would not be easily won.

Raina straightened and frowned. "Are you sure you want me to go into the village? I mean, I just got here."

"Yes, you should go," Idris said. "You need to recapture what is good about this country."

"I know what's good, Papa. I still remember."

"And tonight you shall make more good memories." He sent her a smile and sighed. "You are truly a beauty. You look so very much like your mother."

Dharr could not agree more, even when Raina's frown deepened and she said, "Minus the blond hair and blue eyes."

Idris turned his attention to Dharr. "Is she not beautiful, Sheikh Halim?"

"Yes, she is." More beautiful to behold that most of the women Dharr had kept in his company in the past. "And we are late. The guards are waiting for us and the car is ready."

"Guards?" Raina said, disapproval in her tone.

Idris patted her hand that now rested on the edge of the

table. "You are with a future king, Raina. And though we live in a peaceful country, there are those who would like to see him fall."

Dharr felt as if he had already fallen, down the side of a sheer cliff, grasping for a hold on his emotions every time he looked at Raina.

Raina sent Dharr a quick glance before regarding her father again. "Okay, I guess we should go. Try to get some rest, Papa."

"All I do is rest, my child."

"And you should. Dharr and I will check on you when we return." She turned her head and gave Dharr her smile." It shouldn't be too late, right?"

If Dharr had his wish, their time together would take all night—in his bed. "We shall make it a short evening."

Idris waved a hand in dismissal. "Now run along, young people. Do not give me another thought. I will be soundly sleeping upon your return. Enjoy your evening together."

The sultan's emphasis on the word "together" was not lost on Dharr, and he doubted it would be on Raina, as well. Oddly, Idris kept sending Dharr veiled warnings about his treatment of Raina, yet he seemed determined to keep them together.

Dharr followed Raina to the door and when she turned the knob, he placed his palm on her back as if it were only natural. After dropping his hand, he risked a glance back at the sultan, expecting to find anger in the man's expression. Instead Idris sent Dharr a knowing smile.

Fortunately Idris Kahlil had no knowledge of how thoroughly Dharr had previously touched his daughter. No doubt, he saw through Dharr's carefully formulated façade, and he wondered if tonight, everyone else would, too. Including Raina Kahlil.

Raina was touched by Dharr's attentiveness as he took her hand and helped her from the black sedan parked on the outskirts of the ongoing celebration. At the end of the village proper, modern melded with ancient in the form of multilevel buildings—the core of the business district. She chose to ignore that aspect and concentrate on the place she'd always loved—the true heart of Tomar, rich in history that seemed to be suspended in time, even tonight.

Raina's memories of Azzril had been of a haven for tourists from various countries looking to experience Arabian culture. A Mecca for all peoples and religions. Under Dharr's father's reign, and his father's father before him, they had known for the most part peaceful coexistence within the boundaries, shielded and sheltered from the rest of the world by a range of mountains. Considering the current state of the world, she wondered how long that would continue to hold true. She prayed it did.

The path they now walked had been cordoned off for their arrival, the outskirts surrounded by countless guards. The piquant smell of native foods wafted over the area—most likely arusia, the favorite rice dish for celebrations. The scents brought back Raina's fond recollections of a simpler time, before her parents had gone their separate ways. Only then did she realize how much she had missed the atmosphere, the culture that had been a large part of her formative years.

As Dharr navigated the alley separating two small stone buildings, they came upon a blazing fire surrounded by several men dressed in traditional white *dishdashas,* the turban-like *muzzars* resting atop their heads. They quickly came to their feet and bowed at the waist, their eyes lowered as if Dharr were a god. Raina had to admit with his kaffiyeh secured by the gold and blue band, the flowing white robes also trimmed in gold, he could pass for an ethereal being—an earthbound angel—one with dark, dark eyes and a deadly seductive smile.

Dharr acknowledged the men with a polite greeting and nod before continuing on into the center of activity. The sheikh's presence became known little by little, apparent when several of the onlookers turned toward them, muttering amongst themselves. The men bowed reverently and Raina heard a few nervous giggles coming from a gathering of attractive young women wearing brightly-colored *kandouras*—full length gowns—and elaborate jewelry. As Badya had said, females revered him as much as males respected him. Raina knew him as the man, not the prince. Knew him intimately, as a matter of fact. That thought brought a sudden rise of heat to her face.

As Dharr began to mingle with his subjects, Raina hung back, wondering if somewhere in this crowd another woman, maybe several, might know him just as well. Logically, that was highly doubtful. Any woman granted access to a future king would be carefully screened and discreetly presented to him, a woman who would not be seen among the masses.

Raina couldn't quite wrap her mind around Dharr keeping time with courtesans. Of course, that didn't mean he hadn't met more than a few other prospects during his travels. She wouldn't begin to speculate on what he'd done during his Harvard days. And then there was the matter of *the* woman—maybe even that debutante Elizabeth—who at one time captured his heart and for whatever reason, turned him loose. Even though Dharr still hadn't made that admission, she believed its validity. Why else would he be so jaded when it came to love? Why else hadn't he married long before now?

Still, she couldn't imagine anyone who had earned his love actually releasing him. Obviously there was a story there, one she would probably never know. And worse, she would probably never know how he felt about her. Was it only sex for the sake of sex? Was she only one of many who'd experienced his skills as a lover only to be discarded later? It truly didn't matter. In a few days, she would be going home, as soon as she was assured her father was on his way to recovery. Home to California and the life she had made. Home, alone.

A round of collective sounds of approval came from the crowd when Dharr waved away a guard to allow a little girl into the protective circle. He knelt before the child and smiled, a softer side of Dharr Halim that Raina had never really witnessed until now.

Not exactly true. If she thought back on the days when she'd known him as only a family friend, she recalled the times he had treated her as if she might be special. In one instance, he'd sneaked her a few cookies after her parents had forbidden her from having them before dinner. He'd given her a few of his favorite books and had forgiven her when she'd kicked him in the shin—hard—after he'd tugged on her braids.

At that time, she had been eight and he sixteen, still a yucky boy in her opinion, at least back then. Now he was a man. A striking, enigmatic man.

He would make a great king. An exceptional father. A wonderful husband. But not to Raina Kahlil. Never her. She reserved the right to choose a man who could love her back, and that man wasn't Dharr Halim, even though in some ways she was beginning to wish it could be so.

She kept her attention focused on Dharr. He now sported a smile reserved for the angelic child presenting him with a red paper flower as she whispered something in his ear. Then suddenly he looked toward Raina and gave her that same smile, making her heart plunge to the pebbled path beneath her feet.

Dharr patted the little girl's cheek, straightened and started toward Raina. With each step he took in her direction, her pulse quickened in response.

Once he stood before her, he offered the flower. "From an admirer."

She took the paper creation and waved to the child who favored her with a toothy grin. But her attention soon turned to Dharr when he said, "Walk with me," and started up the path past the quaint shops lining the border of the commons area where the festivities continued.

As they strolled along at a leisurely pace, surrounded by a contingent of guards in front and behind them, Dharr spoke to her about the recent progress in modernizing Tomar.

When he told her that an art museum was also in the planning stages, Raina came to a stop and faced him. "I'm surprised you didn't say anything to me earlier," she said.

"I assumed you might not be interested."

Her eyes widened. "How could you say that knowing art is my life?"

"In California," he corrected. "Not in Azzril."

That stung Raina more than a little, but she could understand why he might believe that. "I'm interested in anything having to do with art. Do you already have any commitments in terms of collections?"

"I have my own collection I will donate, except for one particular piece."

When the cool breeze intensified, she tightened the shawl around her shoulders even though she wasn't at all cold. Thanks to Dharr's presence. "A very special piece, I take it?"

"Yes. A Modigliani."

One of her favorites. "Wow. I would love to see it sometime."

He leaned over and although they spoke in English, he lowered his voice and said, "It is hanging in my bedroom, over the fireplace. I am surprised you did not notice it."

She hadn't been coherent enough to notice much of anything in the massive bedroom. "You can show it to me later," she murmured, hoping her suggestive comment had gone unnoticed by the surrounding guards who were keeping a safe distance. Considering the return of the fire in Dharr's eyes, it hadn't been overlooked by him.

They started down the walkway once more, passing a shop where a gold lamp showcased behind glass caught Raina's eye. She stepped into the small store where a gray-bearded man stood behind the counter.

In Arabic, she inquired about the price of the incense burner and the shopkeeper informed her it was pure gold, and very pricey. Resigned that it wouldn't be in her budget, she turned away and nearly ran into Dharr head on.

"Do you want it?" he asked her in a sinfully deep voice.

She wanted him, even more than the lamp. "I can live without it."

"You should not have to live without it if it is what your heart desires."

Without waiting for her response, Dharr stepped up to the counter and requested it be wrapped up for Raina without even asking the price. However, she wasn't sure the man could even answer considering his shocked expression and his apparent need to bow several times to his prince.

Raina tugged on Dharr's sleeve to get his attention. "It's gold and I imagine very expensive."

"I can afford it."

"I know that, but you really don't have to do it."

"I could tell by your eyes that it captured your fancy."

"Maybe I should rub it and see if a genie pops out. Then it might be worth the price."

He leaned over once more and whispered, "I prefer to rub the other lamp you have in your possession."

While Raina fought a strong case of the shivers over the sensual suggestion, Dharr took the package from the man and handed it to her. "It is now yours," he said, then told the shopkeeper to send him the bill personally.

And just like that, Raina was holding a priceless lamp and a desperate longing for the prince who had presented it to her. But as they started away once more, she began to realize the extent of Dharr's true worth when he continued to pause now and then to acknowledge his people, taking careworn hands into his, patting the heads of children, as if he were as common as the rest. In reality, he was quite uncommon to Raina—a man who truly cared about something beyond finding a new way to get a quick rush. A man who didn't take his responsibility lightly.

Dharr stopped and turned his attention to the commons when a drum began to beat, announcing the *Razha,* a celebratory dance performed by men sporting swords and spouting poetry. Raina stood by him and took in the wonderful spectacle she remembered from her youth. The moderate wind continued to blow, but that didn't relieve the heat when Dharr twined his fingers through hers. The gesture surprised her even though he held their joined hands close to his body, the robes providing some measure of concealment.

Several fires dotted the area, illuminating the performers in an almost surreal haze. The strong scent of sandalwood *bokhur* wafted over the area from the incense shop behind them. The drumbeats picked up in tempo as the men began to leap in a frenzied free-for-all.

When Dharr stroked his thumb over her wrist, Raina experienced a bout of dizziness. She felt drunk even though not a drop of alcohol had touched her lips. Totally intoxicated by Dharr's touch alone. If only she could step in front of him, lean back against him, have his arms wrapped around her, then that would make the night almost perfect. Almost. She could think of one other thing that would definitely involve perfection—making love with Dharr.

When Raina swayed toward him, Dharr clasped his arm around her waist and held her to his side. "Are you not feeling well?"

"I'm just a little light-headed." Her voice was so soft he barely heard her.

He told her, "Wait here," took the flower and package from her then approached his most trusted guard. After handing him the items, Dharr voiced his concerns in English so as not to be understood by most of the onlookers, requesting a place he could take Miss Kahlil for a time until he discerned if they would need to leave sooner than planned.

After Dharr made his way back to Raina's side, the guard approached the nearby shopkeeper who gestured toward the back of his store. Again Dharr took Raina's hand and when it appeared no one was looking, he pulled her into the shop's interior.

"Where are we going?" she inquired.

"In here," he said as he opened the door at the end of the aisle, revealing a small storeroom lined with shelves and boxes.

Dharr guided Raina to the only open space and positioned her back against the wall. "This has been too much activity for you. I should have insisted you stay at the palace tonight. You should rest a while, and then we will go."

She sent him a sultry smile. "I'm having a wonderful time."

"You seemed as if you might faint."

"Not at all. I feel fine."

And she looked incredibly beautiful. The fullness of her mouth, the length of her slender neck, the golden glow of her eyes only served to heighten his arousal. She had totally captivated him from the moment she'd entered her father's room, and even more so as he'd witnessed the firelight washing over her when he'd accepted the gift from the child. He was still completely captive to her, yet he was also concerned over her health. "Are you certain you are feeling well enough to continue?"

A long breath drifted from her parted lips. "I admit, I was a little light-headed for a few moments, but I think it was a combination of several things. The fires. The dancers. The incense." She slipped her hands beneath his robes and rested them on his waist. "Being so close to you."

He braced one palm on the wall above her head and kept the other arm at his side to prevent touching her. "This is unwise, Raina."

She exhaled a ragged breath, her gaze trained on his. "I want to be with you again, Dharr. I'm tired of pretending that I don't want you."

So was he. "We have only had to maintain that pretense for less than a day."

"For me, an hour was too long."

"But we said—"

"I know what we said. And if you tell me now—right now—that you don't want me as much as I want you, then I'll keep up the front."

The words would not form in his mouth for if he should speak them, he would be telling a grave untruth. Yet instead of a verbal reply, he professed his absolute need for her with a kiss so deep she would have no doubt. With his hands roving up her back beneath her blouse. With a press of his pelvis against hers to remove any question from her mind as to how much he wanted her.

He slid his palms up her sides then back down to her waist, his knuckles brushing against the sash that with only a tug he could have unbound in a matter of seconds, sending her skirt down her thighs to the cement floor. He could send her underclothes to follow and lower his fly, concealing them with the fullness of his robes, and know how it would feel to finally be inside her.

No one would disturb them. No one would be the wiser.

Yet she deserved better than lovemaking against a pitted wall inside a crowded storeroom. She deserved time to reconsider before it was too late.

When she reached for his fly, Dharr clasped her wrist to halt her. "Again, I have nothing to protect you from pregnancy."

She gave him a beseeching look. "I know this sounds crazy, and maybe I am, but I need to touch you *now,* Dharr. I want you to touch me."

He wanted that more than the respect of his people at the moment. "Not now. Not this time."

"Then you don't want me." Disappointment resounded in her tone.

To reassure her, he kissed her again before saying the only truth he knew at that moment. "This time, I want to be inside you."

Her eyes took on a wildness, exciting Dharr beyond all bounds. "Then do it. Soon."

Dharr said goodbye to his wisdom, or perhaps he had done that the moment Raina had walked onto the plane and back into his life. Yet that no longer mattered. Before she left him, he would have her, as long as he knew she understood exactly what she was asking.

Holding her face in his palms, he studied her eyes, making certain he did not find any hesitation. He did not.

"I promise you, Raina, I will finish this. Tonight."

Yet somehow he knew this would be only the beginning.

Seven

In the darkened sedan, Dharr kept a decent space between them. To Raina, it seemed like a hundred miles, and so had their return to the palace.

He'd remained quiet, not uttering a word on the journey. Of course, she hadn't said anything, either, because for the life of her, she didn't know what to say. She couldn't explain why she *had* to be with him because she didn't understand it herself. But she didn't feel the need to apologize for her behavior because she wasn't at all sorry. At least not yet.

She certainly might be sorry should Dharr change his mind and not follow through on his promise. She was beginning to believe that very thing when he failed to look at her, even when she asked, "How much longer?"

"We are almost to the gates."

"Good. I wondered if maybe we were lost."

"No. We both know exactly where we are going."

Reaching across the seat, Dharr laid her open palm on his thigh, then slowly, slowly, drew it upward until she contacted the unmistakable ridge before he placed her hand back on the seat between them.

A subtle answer to her question, but very much an answer, and one that made her heartbeat increase at an alarming rate.

Moments later, the motorcade entered the massive iron gates and pulled up in front of the palace. Dharr left the sedan first, offering his hand to Raina, which she took without a second thought. She had no second thoughts at all, especially when Dharr stroked his thumb over her palm before releasing her once more.

By the time she walked through the heavy double doors, Raina wanted to sprint up the stairs, shedding her clothes on the way. Not a wonderful idea considering Badya was waiting for them by the black iron banister.

"Did the sheikh and the princess have a good time tonight?" Badya asked in a pleasant voice.

"Most certainly," Dharr said from behind Raina.

"Is my father still awake?" she asked, feeling somewhat guilty when Badya confirmed that he had been asleep for hours and said he would see Raina in the morning.

"I'm off to bed then," Raina said, her tone overly cheerful, something she was sure Badya had noticed.

"Have a restful sleep," Badya replied, giving Raina a subtle cautioning look, confirming her suspicions.

Once she started up the stairs, Raina didn't dare glance back at Dharr or her former nanny. Anticipation, exhilaration, brought heat to her cheeks that traveled down her throat and spiraled throughout her entire body. Not until they reached the bedroom door did she face Dharr.

He looked down the hall both ways, then said, "I will retire to my quarters until the final guard passes."

"But you'll be back?" Raina hated how unsure she sounded, and worse, almost desperate.

"You may depend on it." He took one more quick glance down the hall, leaned forward and grazed his palm down her bottom before brushing a gentle kiss over her lips. "Be waiting for me."

Oh, he didn't have to worry about that, and Raina would have told him so had he not strode away, tearing the kaffiyeh off as he headed to the end of the hall and his room.

Raina waited until he completely disappeared before she entered her own room. His room, actually, and she'd been very aware of that fact when she'd seen his clothes hanging next to hers, smelled his sultry scent in the bath suite, investigated all his colognes and shaving supplies like some silly smitten school girl.

But tonight, the girl wouldn't be present. The woman would, waiting with great eagerness for a man who could answer every one of her fantasies.

Quickly she stripped out of all her clothes, took her hair out of the braid, turned down the lights and sheets, then stretched out on her back to wait for Dharr's arrival. Only minimal illumination filtered into the sheer curtains from the guard lights in the center courtyard. The clock on the far wall ticked down, second by second, minute by minute, while Raina stared at the octagonal recessed ceiling, attempting to count the crisscrossed sky blue tiles overhead though she couldn't really see them well. She turned her attention to the stone fireplace across the room where Dharr's favored painting hung above the mantel. Even the priceless nude couldn't hold her attention for very long.

The waiting, watching, wanting was excruciating and when more time had passed, Raina wondered if Dharr had changed his mind. Then she heard the door open and close, the click of the lock and the footfalls coming nearer and nearer.

She turned her head and saw him standing by the bed, powerful and imposing as he meticulously removed his clothes until she wanted to squirm and tell him to hurry. Once he was completely nude, he tossed something onto the nightstand, condoms Raina assumed. At least tonight he was prepared.

But she wasn't exactly prepared for the rush that went straight to her head when the mattress gave with his weight. He took her into his arms and kissed her thoroughly, gliding his tongue in an erotic tempo that foretold what he would do to her body. After a time, he feathered kisses along her jaw, down her throat and the valley between her breasts before drawing a nipple into his mouth, circling his tongue round and round until Raina thought she might fall into the realm of full-blown insanity. Yet he didn't linger long before he skated his lips down her abdomen, bracing her hips in his large palms as if to hold her completely imprisoned.

Raina couldn't muster much more than a shaky breath, couldn't budge other than to rest her palms on his head. She certainly didn't have enough force to protest, not that she wanted to, even when he kept going until his mouth was firmly planted between her thighs, plying her with the ultimate, intimate kiss.

Such sweet tyranny, such an absolute possession, as if he were marking his territory with his capable mouth. The building pressure coiled tighter with every sweep of his tongue, every tug of his lips. She tried to delay the inevitable, locking her jaw tight while tuning into every wonderful sensation. Higher and higher he took her as he lifted her hips up to gain full advantage, tearing away any plans she had to prolong the experience. She climaxed with a violent shudder, then another until she feared she might never stop shaking.

He worked his lips back up her body to her mouth then kissed her lightly once, twice, before leaving her arms. She wanted to groan in protest until she realized what he was doing after she heard the sound of tearing paper. Still, he kept his palm curled between her thighs, teasing her into another frenzy while he tended to the protection.

Now was probably a good time to tell him he would be her first lover. But if she made the revelation, would he change his mind? He might, and if he did, she would surely die from frustration. For that reason, she opted to go with the flow and explain herself after the fact.

Once again he came back to her, hovered over her and ran his hands through her hair. "I must ask you again," he said, his voice a rough whisper. "Are you certain?"

Now she was truly frustrated. "Dharr, if you stop, I'll scream."

He brushed a kiss over her temple. "I suggest that you might scream before the night ends, but not because I will fail to see this through." He moved over her, dividing her legs with his muscular thigh. "And hopefully not because I cause you too much pain, although you will experience some this first time."

He knew. "I understand that."

"Then you have not been with another man."

Raina realized he'd been baiting her into the admission. "It's okay, Dharr. I want this."

"As do I, but—"

She pressed a fingertip against his lips to silence his concerns. "No more questions. No regrets. We've come this far, we can't turn back. I don't want to turn back."

Just when she thought he might reconsider, he eased into her, carefully, methodically, stretching her to accommodate him. He wasn't a small man by any means and she wasn't sure how she could take all of him, but he saw that she would with one sharp thrust.

Raina tried to muffle the gasp, without success. He stilled

and spoke to her in a voice as soft as the shadows, alternating between English and Arabic, telling her in gentle tones how good she felt surrounding him. How long he had wanted this, wanted her. Lulled by his words, Raina's body relaxed until he began to move inside her with careful strokes. He kissed her again, first her mouth then her breasts, rubbed against her, creating a delicious friction that had her bordering on another orgasm that threatened to match the first. He clasped her bottom, drawing her closer to him and using his fingertips to explore while he maintained a steady cadence. But soon the act took a frenzied turn as he picked up the pace, harder and faster, until Raina clung to his shoulders and without thought, raked her nails down his back.

She surrendered to the rippling climax, hung on to him and rode each surge. Dharr's back went rigid against her palms, his heart pounding against her breast, and an almost feral groan left his lips now resting at her ear. He remained still for a few moments, silent, then muttered a mild oath in Arabic.

"What's wrong?" she asked, hoping it had nothing to do with her, or what they'd just done, but fearing it did.

He rolled away from her and settled her against his side, her head resting on his shoulder. "It was over too quickly."

Raina relaxed with relief. "I'm not sure I could've stood much more."

He tensed. "Did I hurt you that badly?"

She released a soft laugh. "I meant it was almost too good, if you know what I mean."

"I suppose I do."

Now for the question foremost in her mind. "How did you know I'd never been with anyone?"

"I was not certain but I did have a few suspicions. Or perhaps it was only wishful thinking."

She raised her head and frowned at him. "Oh, so it's that 'I'm macho and I want to be the first' thing."

He stroked his fingertips up and down her arm in an enticing rhythm. "You are an extraordinary woman, Raina. I did not want to consider a man taking advantage of you, although I might fall into that category considering I took your virginity."

She playfully slapped at his chest. "Oh, come on, Dharr. It was my choice. My decision as to who and when. And I chose you."

"Why me, Raina?" He looked and sounded much too somber for such a special time.

How could she explain when she could only speculate? "Maybe it's because I knew you would treat me well. Maybe it's because I knew you would know what you're doing. I wanted my first experience to be with someone I trust." Someone she cared about much more than she should.

He touched his lips against her temple. "I hope you were not disappointed."

She rose above him and pushed a lock of dark hair away from his forehead. "Let me tell you how disappointed I was." She kissed his cheek then his lips. "When we can do it again?"

Even in the limited light, his smile knocked her heart for a loop. "You surprise me, Raina. For one so young, you have very strong appetites."

"I'm twenty-five, Dharr, not fifteen. And I've suppressed my appetites longer than most so I have a lot of catching up to do."

His smile disappeared. "After tonight, if we should continue our intimacy, we risk getting caught."

"Maybe that's why it's so exciting."

"Then you are saying you wish to continue this affair until you leave?"

Affair. There it was. The cold hard truth. But wasn't that

exactly what she'd wanted? Of course. Just a few stolen moments with a sexy, mystifying man who had no plans for
commitment. Grab whatever time she could have with him,
until the time came for her to return to California. And then
tell him goodbye for good, even if she would never forget him.

She forced a smile around the sudden ache in her heart.
"Well, considering our recent history, I'm not sure we're
going to be able to stop. So yes, I don't see why we shouldn't
enjoy each other while we have the time."

"We would have to be very discreet."

"I can do discreet." If her face—and heart—didn't give
her away.

She planted a kiss on his chest then raised her gaze to him
once more. "So do you think we might give it another go in
a little while?"

He didn't seem all that responsive to her request, apparent
in his guarded expression and his rigid frame. "You and I both
need to sleep tonight. It would be best if we do that, in separate beds."

She couldn't stand the thought of him leaving just yet.
"Stay a while, Dharr. Just a little while."

He brought her head to rest on his chest and held her
tightly. "I suppose I could stay for a time, at least until you
fall asleep."

Raina relaxed against him, reveling in his heat, his strength,
his embrace. Yet as she closed her eyes, she fought the sudden sting of unexpected tears. This should be the best night
of her life, and in many ways it was. But she also knew it
would be over too soon, and too few hours remained in Dharr
Halim's arms, and his life.

The first light of dawn streaming in from the window
brought Dharr completely awake. With Raina securely

swathed in his arms, he had fallen into a deep, restful sleep for the first time in months. Yet should anyone learn he was in her bed, the consequences would be great. Especially if her father became privy to that knowledge.

Working his arm from beneath her, Dharr sat on the edge of the feather mattress and forked both hands through his hair. He must leave her soon, yet he could not resist looking at her one more time. She rested on her belly, her face turned toward him, eyes closed. Her hair, crimped because of the braid she'd worn the evening before, flowed down her back in soft waves. The curve of her bottom and the length of her legs only served to heighten his morning arousal. If they were free to do as they pleased, he would make love to her again.

Impossible. He had already dishonored her in many ways by making love with her once. Considering his suspicion, he should have asked again if she'd been with another man, before they had reached the point of no return. He should have stopped even then. He was not that strong in her presence, had not been strong from the beginning.

Coming to his feet, he snatched his clothes from the floor and went into the bathroom to wash, dress and destroy the evidence of their lovemaking. If only he could be so sure that what they had done would not eventually destroy her good standing with her father, or Dharr's resolve to keep his emotions protected. In that regard, he could already be too late, for what he felt for her had begun to take a turn beyond mutual need and desire.

Yet he had little time today to ponder that. He had several meetings scheduled, beginning in only a few hours. For that reason, he took one last glance at Raina and forced himself to leave before he disregarded his duty.

As he walked the hall toward his room, Dharr immediately noticed Abid standing near the doorway, leaning against the wall, holding a newspaper in his hand. Obviously it was much later than Dharr had realized, and much too late to conceal exactly where he had spent the night. No doubt his assistant had seen him leave Raina's quarters. Of course, he could say he'd forgotten something in his room. Or he could say nothing at all since it was not Raneer's concern, and he could trust him not to ask any questions.

"Are you certain spending the evening with Miss Kahlil was wise, your grace?" Abid asked as Dharr approached, shattering all expectations.

Dharr pushed open the door without looking at him. "I had to retrieve something from my room."

"I see."

The suspicion in Abid's tone, though warranted, did not please Dharr. He turned on his assistant and gave him a steely look. "Why you are here so early in the morning?"

Abid offered the newspaper. "I thought you should see this immediately."

Dharr took the paper and understood all too well his assistant's concern when the front-page headline came into view. Yet the accompanying photograph was much more telling— and damning—a picture of the sheikh and the princess standing near the shop where they had taken shelter, his arm around her and her head resting on his shoulder.

For a long moment Dharr stared at the paper in stunned disbelief before leveling his gaze on Abid. "Do you know how this came to be?"

"I presume the press made this assumption from that photograph taken last evening."

Dharr slammed the paper down on the nearby desk. "I ordered you to keep the press away."

"We carried out that order as best we could. That photograph could have been taken by a local or a tourist, then sold for a substantial sum."

"Are we certain no one among the staff is responsible for this?"

"I have no way of knowing for certain."

After pacing the room for a few moments, Dharr walked to the window and stared out over the landscape. The sun had begun to rise on the city, normally his favorite time of day. Yet he dreaded what might come in the following hours.

"What did the article say about the princess?" he asked, keeping his back to Abid.

"Only that she has been living in America."

Dharr turned and faced his attaché again. "Has the sultan seen it?"

"Not as far as I know."

"Good."

"But he is quoted in the article."

"Quoted?"

"You both have his blessing on the union and he hopes you both get to know each other well."

Idris had no idea how well they knew each other, and if he did know, he would no doubt withdraw any blessings. And worse, Raina would soon learn of the news. He could not begin to speculate how she would react. "I would prefer to tell the princess about this myself."

Abid nodded. "I will make certain she comes to you when she awakens. How do you wish to respond?"

Collapsing into the chair near the foot of the bed, Dharr rubbed his unshaven chin. "I will consider that in the next few hours."

"I could demand a retraction."

"That would call more attention to the princess."

"And if we say nothing, more supposition will abound."

How well Dharr knew that to be true, yet he was too exhausted to consider anything other than taking a shower to ready for his day—and how he would break the news to Raina. After she discovered that the entire country, quite possibly many countries, had begun to assume she had returned to marry him, she would want to leave immediately. Even if not, she would probably withdraw from him, and that bothered Dharr on a deeper level than he cared to acknowledge.

"One more thing," Abid said in a serious tone. "I heard from the king this morning."

"And he said?"

"He will be cutting his trip short in order to return the night of the reception for the Doriana diplomats at the end of the week."

"Did he say why?" Dharr asked though he already had his suspicions.

"He mentioned he wanted to be present for the official announcement of your engagement."

Dharr did not bother to inquire how his father was already privy to the news. As it had always been, any information involving his activities traveled at lightning speed.

He stood and indicated the door. "You may go now, Abid. I will see you in the conference room within the hour."

Abid executed a slight bow. "As you wish, your grace." He turned but as he reached the door, faced Dharr again. "You may trust that what I witnessed this morning will go no further."

"I appreciate your loyalty."

Yet Dharr doubted Raina would appreciate any of the recent events, except perhaps what had happened between them last night. At least he hoped that would be the case, because it seemed it would probably be the last time.

Raina realized she didn't look at all different this morning. A flicker of heat radiated from the inside out as she stood in front of the bedroom mirror, combing out her damp hair in long strokes reminiscent of Dharr's touch. She both dreaded and longed to see him again. Dreaded it because she didn't want to find any regret in his eyes. Longed for it because she missed him more than she thought possible.

When the knock came at the door, she fumbled with and flipped the brush onto the dresser with a noisy clatter, nervous anticipation making it impossible to maintain a firm grip on anything, especially her composure. But when she opened the door to Badya again, anticipation turned to frustration.

Badya whisked past her carrying a full tray and sporting a cheery smile. "I have come with your breakfast, *yáahil.*"

The last thing Raina wanted was food even though she should be starving. But what she wanted right now was a little bit of privacy, or a lot more of Dharr.

Raina grabbed up the brush and resumed grooming without looking at Badya. "You're determined to fatten me up while I'm here, aren't you?"

"Yes. That is my job. To tend to your needs, as I have in the past. As soon as I change your linens, I will be out of your way."

Before she could protest, Raina heard Badya's gasp coming from the direction of the bed.

"Oh, Raina. What have you done?"

Raina gripped the brush and closed her eyes. She could imagine exactly what Badya was seeing—the obvious signs of first-time lovemaking marking the sheets, faint but discernible.

"Don't jump to conclusions, Badya. It was just a visit from the monthly curse."

"Or perhaps a visit from the sheikh. I am not a fool, *yáahil.*"

Raina turned to issue another rebuttal, only to find Badya staring at the condom packages on the nightstand. She had no recourse but to tell her former nanny the truth.

She leaned back against the dresser, gripping the robe tightly to her. "It's no big deal, Badya." Lie number one.

"Neither of us planned it." Lie number two. "I doubt it will happen again." Lie number three, or so Raina hoped, even now that she'd been caught.

Badya collapsed into the settee near the window. "It meant nothing more to you than that? Did your mother and I not teach you anything?"

No, but Dharr had. "This doesn't have anything to do with you or my mother. It was my decision, and it's done."

"In my day, you two would be forced to marry after such behavior."

"It is not your day and neither of us intend to marry."

Badya shook her head. "I am very disappointed in the sheikh. He should know better than to take advantage of an innocent."

This time Raina laughed. "I hate to tell you this, but it wasn't all his idea. Your little girl's grown up, Badya. She's a woman now." A woman who happened to be very enamored of a man who was the consummate lover.

"That might be true, but you are still my *bint*."

Raina pushed away from the bureau, walked to Badya, leaned down and hugged her neck. "I'll always be your little girl in a way. And I hope you won't say anything to anyone about this."

Badya laid a hand on her ample breasts. "I would never do such a thing, even though I would greatly like to give the sheikh a good scolding."

"That won't be necessary." Raina suspected he'd already scolded himself quite a bit on this morning after. Funny, she didn't feel like doing any such thing. She had no regrets whatsoever, only some fine memories of a fantastical experience.

After coming to her feet, Badya embraced Raina again. "I have much to do this morning, so I will leave you for now to dress, then return with fresh linens. Unless you require something else of me. Perhaps my advice on the virtue of being virtuous?"

Too late. "That's enough, Badya. It's done and nothing can change that."

Badya shook her head. "Yes, you are right. I only hope you do not suffer from your decision."

Suffering was not an appropriate word to describe Raina's mood. Euphoric would come much closer although she didn't dare tell that to her self-appointed guardian. "I want to see Papa. Is he awake?"

"Yes, but first the sheikh would like a word with you."

"Now?"

"Immediately." Badya gave her a quick once over. "Or at least after you dress appropriately, although I am certain he has seen you in much less."

Obviously the woman wasn't going to let it go. Normally Raina would toss out a blistering retort, but she knew that would be futile under the circumstance. "Did the sheikh say what he wanted with me?"

Badya clucked her tongue while Raina bit hers. "I can only imagine. But he did not say exactly."

"Did he seem at all upset?"

"Yes, and with good cause."

Reaching around Raina, Badya snatched the newspaper from the breakfast tray and held it up. "Congratulations, Princess Kahlil. It seems you are going to be the next queen of Azzril."

Eight

"The Sheikh Claims His *Bride'*? Oh, please."

Dharr glanced up from the museum blueprints to Raina standing in the entry of the conference room, the newspaper clutched in her raised fist. With her hair bound high atop her head, her golden eyes alight with anger, she looked so much like an adult version of the former hellion, he almost smiled. Almost. Though she had greatly matured, he could not trust that she would not attempt to wrestle him to the ground. However appealing that might be at the moment, it would definitely not be appropriate for the seriousness of the situation.

"Close the door," he told her as he stood and rounded the lengthy table.

After she obeyed, Raina strode across the room to stand before him. "Do you have any idea how much trouble this is going to cause us?"

Dharr's current trouble involved recovering enough of his will not to kiss her or release each button on the plain white blouse to touch his lips to the valley of her breasts. "I do not consider it all that troublesome." A small falsehood to assist in alleviating her concerns.

"Are you serious?" She shook out the paper and held it up in his face. "Nice picture, don't you think? And that headline. Priceless. Funny, no one asked me a thing about my *engagement*."

As she turned her back and began to walk the room, Dharr said, "Our betrothal has been common knowledge for many years."

When she spun on him with fury calling out from her eyes, Dharr realized he had said the wrong thing.

"Is that why you really brought me here?" she asked. "Are you plotting with my father to make sure that I uphold our ridiculous arrangement? Maybe that's what last night was all about, deflower the sultan's daughter and then she would have to marry you?"

Dharr tamped down his anger over the accusations, particularly the final one, knowing that her distress was speaking for her. "I assure you, I had nothing to do with this. The media has a way of skewing the truth to suit their insatiable appetite for sensational news. As I've told you before, I have no desire to marry now or in the near future. And in regard to our evening together, I believe that was mutual." As well as unforgettable despite his guilt.

She looked somewhat contrite. "I'm sorry. You're right. At least about last night. But if you didn't leak this information, then who did?"

"It is only speculation due to our appearance together last evening. Those who would wish it to be will believe it."

"My father, for one." She tossed the paper onto the table

behind him. "He thinks a *marriage* between us would be the best thing since the invention of crossword puzzles and electric razors. This will thrill him."

He weighed his options and chose to unveil his own supposition. "Your father could be in part responsible."

"He wouldn't do that," she said with conviction.

"Did you not read the entire article? He has been quoted."

She grabbed the newspaper again and skimmed it silently before saying, "I can't believe he would stoop so low as to use the press to further his own pipe dreams."

"Perhaps he was not entirely responsible, yet he did seem rather pleased to give his blessing."

Once more she tossed the paper aside. "I'm tempted to give him a good piece of my mind."

"I understand, but considering his condition, perhaps it would be best if we simply ignore it."

"And you think it will all go away, just like that?"

Dharr knew better yet he was unsure how to handle the situation to suit everyone involved. "We will neither substantiate nor deny the information. When you return to California, that will serve as confirmation we've chosen not to adhere to the arrangement." And that would be a day he would not necessarily welcome, for many reasons.

Raina rubbed her temples and lowered her eyes. "Maybe that would be the best way to handle it. Just ignore the whole thing and hope it goes away."

She walked to the window and pushed open the curtained doors to reveal the verandah and the view of the street below. "What is going on down there?"

Dharr moved behind her to find hordes of people gathered at the perimeter of the palace. Many were holding up signs of congratulations, a few were laying flowers on the ground at the iron fencing, others chanting Raina's name.

He knew the first signs of notoriety, and soon Raina would, too. "I believe those are your admirers."

She looked back at him. "Mine?"

He rested his hand at her waist, savoring the feel of bare flesh where the top did not quite meet her black slacks. "News travels quickly here. They want to pay homage to the woman they believe could be their future queen."

She turned her attention back to the crowd. "But they're wrong. I'm not queen material."

Dharr could definitely argue that point. "You're beautiful, Raina. The daughter of a sultan. A perfect prospect."

She released a mirthless laugh that died when several villagers began to point toward the window. The sound of applause and gleeful shouts filtered in through the closed doors.

"Oh, wonderful," she said. "They've spotted us."

"Perhaps you should go out and answer their summons."

Once more she regarded him, alarm reflecting in her gaze. "Alone? I can't do that. I'm not like you. I've never faced anything like this."

"I will go with you."

"Won't that put you in danger, out in the open without your guards?"

The only danger at present was his overwhelming craving for her that could not be denied. "I have addressed my people from this very spot. As soon as the guards are made aware, they will position themselves accordingly."

She frowned. "You're really serious about this?"

"Yes. But it is solely your decision."

She shrugged. "Oh, why not. Might be kind of fun at that. I don't want anyone to think I'm a snob."

Dharr reached around her and released the bronze latch to open the door. The moment they stepped out beneath the iron lattice overhang, a roar emanated from the masses, the likes of which he had never known. Resting his palm against her back, he guided Raina to the end of the balcony, leaving a few feet between them and the edge of the railing. The guards immediately formed a protective shield along the sidewalk and streets.

As he watched her reaction, Dharr witnessed Raina's transformation. The sun cast her features in a radiant glow, shadowing the hollows of her cheekbones and highlighting her heart-shaped face. Her soft, pink lips shimmered as she smiled and waved to the crowd, a portrait of eloquence and grace.

Several photographers snapped pictures, but Dharr knew they could not do justice to her splendor—a beauty that started within before rising to the surface.

If she were queen, she would be beloved. Venerated, as his mother had always been. The marked adoration in the faces of his people filled him with pride, as if he actually had a claim on her. As if he planned to have her as his wife, not only as his lover. That could never be. Raina deserved a man who was whole and able to commit his heart as well as his life to her. And he realized all too well she, too, would leave him in pursuit of her own life, even if he thought he could give what she needed.

The crowd began to chant, requesting them to kiss. Raina turned and held him captive with her sensual smile, dared him with her golden eyes. So caught up on the moment, he pressed his lips to hers but only briefly. Yet it proved to be enough to draw more approval from his subjects as well as impact his own composure.

Raina masked her surprise well, at least superficially. "We've really done it now," she said through another bright smile.

"I am only giving them what they want."

"You're leading them to believe that we're really engaged."

"We were definitely engaged last night, even if not in terms of our marriage arrangement. But I do remember being joined in a mutual endeavor that I greatly enjoyed."

She sent him a quelling look before turning back to the crowd. "Stop it or I'm going to jump you right here in front of the masses. Wouldn't that make for a nice front page photo?"

"I would not want to share you with anyone in that regard."

She rested a palm at her throat. "Why, Dharr, you sound almost possessive."

He did, and he not only sounded that way, he felt that way, as well. "As long as you are in my company, I plan to keep you all to myself."

She continued to wave. "Sounds interesting. Can we go back inside now?"

"Certainly."

After a final acknowledgment of his people, Dharr gestured toward the door and followed Raina inside. Once there, the underlying tension hung thick over them while they stood face to face in the middle of the room. As Raina walked into his arms, he claimed her supple mouth in another kiss. This time their joining could not be deemed innocent or brief. As always, they feasted on each other, hands roving over each other's backs and hips, until they were both winded and forced to draw a breath. They only parted for a short while until they resumed the kiss, deeper this time, more ardent.

Dharr spun Raina around and backed her against the wall, forming his body to hers so she would know how much he wanted her. She answered with a tremor as he worked the buttons on her blouse, parting it enough to slide his mouth down her neck to the rise of her breasts.

He lifted his head and sought her eyes. "I need to be here," he murmured as he pressed his palm between her thighs. "But not now. Tonight."

She gave him a pleading look. "I can't wait until tonight. I'll go nuts."

Dharr had already sufficiently arrived in that state of madness that he'd experienced in her presence more than once. It only worsened when Raina lowered her eyes and lowered the zipper on his slacks.

This could not be, he told himself over and over as she freed him, playing her fingertips over him until he relinquished all his control. He pulled the drawstring at her waist and shoved her pants down to her thighs then did the same to his own. Balanced on the brink of taking her right there, without regard to the consequences, a knock sounded at the door, forcing them apart.

"What do you want!" Dharr shouted as he fumbled to redo his fly while Raina swiftly readjusted her own clothing.

"I have a message for the princess, your grace."

Abid. His timing had been both bad and good. Bad because Dharr wanted Raina with a need so great he would again throw all caution aside. Good because the interruption had prevented that very thing.

"Come in" Dharr answered in a tone that indicated his frustration.

"Excuse me, your grace," Abid said as he stepped into the room, keeping his eyes lowered as if he knew exactly what he had interrupted. "Princess Kahlil, your mother wishes to speak with you."

"Where's the phone?" Raina asked, unease in her tone.

"She is not on the phone."

Dharr saw the panic begin to form in Raina's face as awareness dawned. "What do you mean she's not on the phone?"

"She is downstairs, waiting for you."

* * *

Raina walked into the elegant private parlor to find her mother standing in the middle of the room, her arms stiff at her sides and her face showing definite signs of disapproval. Regardless of her obvious distress, Carolyn Kahlil still had chic down to a fine art. Her appearance was immaculate, from her blonde bobbed hair to her neat beige pantsuit, even though she'd probably been traveling all night. Raina definitely couldn't say the same for herself. Apparently her mother had noticed since she raked her gaze over Raina's blouse and the gap created by buttons that had been missed in her haste to redress after the earlier interlude.

Raina gave her a quick hug that wasn't exactly returned. "What on earth are you doing here?" she asked, all she could manage around her shock over the surprise visit.

"I booked a flight the minute I received the message you were here." Her mother looked her up and down again, as if she could actually see the effects of Dharr's kiss and touch. "And I should be asking you exactly why you're here, although I could probably accurately guess."

Raina crossed her arms over her middle to cover the gap. "I'm here because Papa needs me. He's been sick. Didn't they tell you that?"

"Yes, they did. But are you sure he's ill?"

Raina did not have the energy to deal with her mother's familiar bitterness. "Yes, I'm sure. And if you don't believe me, go see him."

Carolyn reached behind her and ran one manicured hand over the back of the sofa behind her. "I plan to do that very thing. I definitely want to get to the bottom of this."

"The bottom of what?"

"I'm determined to find out exactly why he summoned you."

Anger began to simmer below the surface of Raina's attempts at a tranquil demeanor. "I've already told you, he's sick. That's the only reason, whether you want to believe it or not. And frankly, I don't care if you don't love him anymore, because I still do."

A flash of pain crossed her mother's face but she quickly recovered. "If you want me to believe your father asked you here only because of his health, then tell me what I've heard about your engagement to Dharr Halim isn't true."

Raina shifted her weight with a nervousness that had yet to subside. "You saw the article in the paper."

Carolyn twisted her watch round and round her slender wrist. "I happened to be heading through the terminal in London to catch another plane and I saw it on a television. I stopped and almost missed my flight."

Oh, great. "It's already made news worldwide?"

"Yes, Raina. Dharr Halim is known beyond Azzril. He's handsome and eligible and royalty. Announcement of his— or should I say *your* engagement—interests a large part of the world. I'm hoping you're going to say this is a misunderstanding, otherwise you'll be making the same mistakes I did."

It was a mistake, but Raina resented her mother's insistence on comparing everyone's life to her own. "Why do you think it would be such a mistake, Mother? You've always been highly critical of my choice in men. If you think about, I could do a whole lot worse than a prince."

"True, if I thought you were doing this because you want to and not because you're bending to your father's will and going ahead with the marriage arrangement. I know how persuasive Idris can be."

"How well I know. He persuaded you into his bed when you were only seventeen."

"Exactly. And we both know what happened after that."

"You made a huge mistake and got pregnant with me."

Carolyn looked wounded. "I've never said you were a mistake."

"Not in so many words, Mother. But at times I believed you resented getting pregnant and now you want to blame Papa, which I think is ridiculous considering it does take two to horizontally tango."

"That's not fair, Raina. I loved your father."

Loved. Past tense. "Fine. But do you really think I'm not smart enough to avoid making the same mistake with Dharr?"

At least Carolyn looked somewhat contrite. "Of course I think you're smarter than that. But I also think that Dharr Halim is as charismatic as your father, and that is very hard to resist."

As if Raina wasn't well aware of that. "I'm not you, Mom. And Dharr's not Papa."

"I'm only concerned about your welfare, Raina. Azzril is no longer your home, or mine. You'll never be accepted here."

You didn't see what I saw a few minutes ago, Raina almost said but decided to hold her tongue. "Look, Mother, you don't have to worry about me screwing up. I'm a grown woman and quite capable of making my own decisions."

"I hope you decide wisely, before it's too late."

Before she fell in love with Dharr, Raina decided. Sometimes she thought it might already be too late. "I need to see Papa now."

Carolyn pushed up her sleeves as if preparing for a fight. "So do I."

"Fine. I'll show you to his room. We can go together."

"No. I want to see him privately first."

"Why?"

"I need to talk to him about a few things."

Raina's concern drove her to grip her mother's shoulders as she gave her a hard look. "Only if you promise me you'll be kind to him. He's not well. He doesn't need any more stress."

"I promise, Raina." Carolyn brushed a kiss across her cheek then stepped back to gather her purse from one chair. "I'll be gracious."

Raina pointed a finger at her. "I'm going to hold you to it. He's on the second floor, third door to the left."

"Thank you, sweetheart. And don't look so worried. Nothing's going to happen. I'm not armed."

As she watched her mother scale the stairs leading to the upper floors, Raina wanted to run after her. At the very least, she wanted to listen outside the door. Instead, she headed toward the place where she'd often gone to find solace in her youth during their frequent visits at the palace. The place where she'd sat with Dharr all those years ago, nursing a huge crush that existed even now. In reality, it had developed into much more than a simple crush.

Regardless, she wasn't going to marry him. They'd both decided that was out of the question. Then why was the prospect so appealing?

Yes, she definitely needed a few moments alone to think, to consider exactly what she was feeling for Dharr and what she intended to do about it. Then she would go see if her mother and father had forgone the fireworks in exchange for a little civility. And that was about as likely as Dharr Halim falling head over heels in love with Raina Kahlil.

Even though she'd insisted on confronting her mother alone, Dharr worried when he sought Raina out an hour later, only to discover that no one seemed to know where she had gone. He had learned that Carolyn had sequestered herself away in Idris's room, without her daughter. Hopefully that would not end badly.

Right now Dharr's only concern was finding Raina. He could think of one place that she might be since he'd been assured she had not left the grounds. He began his search in the gardens behind the palace proper, walking the paths leading to the stone shelter that had provided him with privacy on more than one occasion. Raina's favorite hiding place when she'd been a girl. Several times he'd found her there in the distant past, staring off into space as if she'd had much on her young mind.

He came upon her there today, looking much the same as she had back then, only more mature, and much more troubled. She sat on the stone bench behind the copper wall forming a barrier to prying eyes, heels resting on the edge and her knees clutched tightly to her breasts.

She did not acknowledge him, even when he took a seat beside her. "Did it not go well with your mother?"

Without giving him even a passing glance, she released a sardonic laugh. "Oh, you could say that. Seems news of our engagement has reached across the universe. She saw the announcement on television in London."

Dharr had realized that after learning his father had already been made aware, a fact he would conceal from Raina for now. "You did inform her there is no truth to the rumors."

"Actually, no, I didn't."

"Why?"

She lowered her feet to the ground and shifted to face him. "Because I'm tired of people telling me what to do. On one hand, my father would absolutely love it if I married you. On the other, my mother would rather see me shackled than to have anything to do with royalty. As always, I'm caught in the middle between the two people I love most in the world. And I'm sick of it."

The turmoil in her expression sent Dharr closer to her to take her hands into his. "Where is your mother now?"

"She's still talking to my father privately, and that worries me. I hope she has enough sense to be nice to him. If she does anything to set him back on his recovery, I'll never forgive her."

"Do you honestly believe she will compromise his health?"

"I don't want to believe that but her presence alone might upset him. It's been a whole lot of years since they've been in the same room together."

Dharr acknowledged she needed a sounding board, and he would gladly accommodate her. "You have not recovered from their estrangement."

"No. I wonder if I ever will."

"Have you ever confronted your mother over her decision to leave Azzril?"

"Oh, yeah. Both alone and in front of a few counselors during my rebellious years. But I'm not only angry with her. I'm mad at my father, too."

"It is my understanding your mother left without telling him of her intent."

"Yes, she did. And he just let her go. He never even tried to talk with her after we left. Never tried to get her back. He didn't *fight* for her."

Dharr understood why Idris might not have done that. He knew all too well what it was like to have a woman leave with nothing more than a written missive, taking an integral part of you with her, leaving only an abyss that no one could fill. "Perhaps he believed it would have done no good."

"Maybe not, but he should have tried. If you care about someone, you try until you've exhausted all your options. You don't just let someone you love walk away without at least giving it your best effort. They're both responsible for ruining each other's lives."

"And in some ways, for ruining yours."

She lifted her chin. "No, not my life. I haven't let them do that."

The bravado in her tone sounded false to Dharr and perhaps she was right, but only partially. Her parents may not have ruined her life, but they had dealt her a blow from which she had yet to recover. He could relate to that type of misery.

Even though he wished to stay with her and offer more consolation, he had several tasks he had to complete before days' end. "I must leave. Two days from now, we will be having a reception for a group of European diplomats and I am involved in the planning."

"Really? What country?"

"A very small principality known as Doriana. Perhaps you've heard of it?"

"Yes, but I don't know a thing about it. Geography was never my strong suit."

"It is situated in the Pyrenees near France. The king is a good friend and former Harvard colleague."

Her expression brightened. "Will I get to meet him?"

"He will not be in attendance since his wife has recently given birth. But you will be my special guest at the reception."

She favored him with a smile. "You know that's only going to make matters worse if I show up. Then everyone's going to think we're definitely an item."

He kissed her cheek. "Let them think what they will. I have no cause to hide you away in seclusion."

She gave him a mock pout. "Well, darn. I was hoping we could enjoy a little seclusion after everyone goes to bed tonight. Finish what we almost did in the conference room before my mother came calling."

Dharr would like nothing better, but too much was now at stake. "I'm afraid that would not be wise considering we are all staying on the same floor."

"True, and why is that?"

"The rest of the palace bedrooms are undergoing renovations."

She toyed with the top button on his shirt. "That's too bad. Maybe we could find a nice spot under a drop cloth. Or maybe a corner in the attic."

Dharr began to feel the familiar sexual stirrings and did his best to quell them. "I have work to do."

"And I guess I need to go and make sure there hasn't been any bloodshed between my parents."

Dharr offered his hand, which she took without hesitation. Even though he knew better, he couldn't resist kissing her, long and hard.

Once they parted, Raina smiled again as she kept her arms circled around him. "Thanks for giving me something nice to remember. And thanks for letting me vent."

"My pleasure." And it was, more pleasure than he'd ever thought possible. "I suppose I will see you again tonight during dinner."

"And after dinner?" she asked hopefully.

He touched her cheek, hating what he needed to say, yet knowing it had to be said. "Raina, too many people know, or believe they know, what is going on between us. With your mother now on the premises, it would be best if we discontinue our intimacy."

She lowered her eyes before contacting his gaze again. "You're probably right. But it was nice while it lasted."

More than only nice, as far as Dharr was concerned. "I will never forget what we've shared."

"Neither will I, and if you change your mind, there's something you need to know about my mother. She can be totally oblivious when it comes to what's going on right under her nose."

* * *

"Tell me, Dharr. Exactly what have you been doing with my daughter?"

Raina nearly choked on the bite she'd forced down her throat. For the past two nights, her mother had remained rigid and silent, barely civil to anyone, including Dharr who had joined them. Unfortunately he hadn't joined Raina in her bed. Hadn't sought her out even to give her a quick kiss. And oh how she'd needed him after she'd walked on eggshells with both her parents. Obviously the shells had just been shattered.

When Dharr led off with, "Raina and I—"

"Don't think that's an appropriate question," Raina finished for him.

"I believe it is a very fitting question, my child," her father said. He'd been practically bedridden for days and now he was seated at the end of the table, fully dressed and looking as if he were holding court. Dharr had taken his place at the opposite end, leaving Raina and her mother positioned across from each other to face off, which they definitely were at the moment.

"I can't believe you're actually taking her side, Papa."

"He's not taking sides, Raina," Carolyn said. "He's asking questions, and so am I. We don't understand what's going on between the two of you."

Raina gritted her teeth. "And that's really not any of your concern considering we're both of legal age and free to do as we please."

Her mother's eyes widened. "Are you two sleeping together?"

Not nearly enough, Raina thought. But before she could issue a protest, her father jumped back into the fray. "I would certainly hope that is not the case," he said, his features as hard as the chair beneath Raina's bottom.

Dharr continued to watch the verbal volley and Raina wouldn't blame him a bit if he decided to leave. Right now she could use him as an ally, but she understood why he wouldn't want to dive into the interrogation. Too many thorns in this bed of familial nonbliss.

Raina stiffened her frame and her resolve not to buckle under pressure. "You both can think what you will, but I'm not going to tell you anything other than Dharr and I are friends." Very good friends. "And neither will he."

Her mother dabbed at her mouth with a pristine white cloth napkin, then pursed her lips in displeasure. "Your father and I believe otherwise, Raina. We've discussed this at length. And we have a right to know exactly how far this relationship has gone."

Raina drummed her fork on the table before dropping it with a *plunk* on her plate. "Obviously you've discussed me at *great* lengths without my knowledge. I tried to see Papa twice today only to be told by Badya that I wasn't welcome."

Idris reached to his right and patted Raina's hand. "That is not true, daughter. You are always welcome. Your mother and I simply needed to catch up on several issues."

Raina pulled her hand from the table and wrung the napkin resting in her lap. "And you spent all that time talking about me?"

Carolyn's gaze flitted away. "For the most part."

Her mother appeared to be blushing, something Raina had rarely witnessed. Odd, but then so was this entire gathering.

Her appetite completely gone, Raina tossed the napkin onto the table and posed the question foremost on her mind. "What else did you discuss?" She braced for the bitter word *divorce.*

Carolyn's eyes went wide. "That is none of your business."

"Oh, I see. My parents' conversation about me and Lord only knows what else is none of my business, but mine and Dharr's relationship is yours? Sorry, Mom, but that doesn't cut it anymore. And I'll make you a deal. If you stay out of my business, I'll stay out of yours. Agreed?"

Her papa rubbed his jaw, indicating his increasing discomfort. "Raina, we are only concerned about your welfare. We want to make certain that if the rumors of your engagement are valid, you both have thought over that decision carefully. We would not be pleased if you make a mistake you cannot rectify."

Now that beat everything she'd ever heard to this point in her twenty-five years. Raina raised both hands, palms forward. "Wait a minute. If I'm not mistaken, you're the one responsible for the marriage arrangement, Father dear. And if I recall, you're the one who for years has been telling me what a nice guy Dharr is. How I should really consider following tradition. How he would be my perfect mate. And then that quote in the newspaper. Now you're telling me you've changed your mind?"

"We're just being cautious," her mother said. "We want to make sure you don't rush into anything."

All the years of resentment crowded in on Raina, robbing her of the last remnants of patience. "Well, believe me, I promise that I'm not going to get pregnant, if that's what's worrying you. I also promise that if and when I decide to marry, I'm not going to run out on my husband then spend years living a lonely life in an apartment with only a cat as company. Or holed up in a dusty mansion alone, pretending everything's okay."

Idris slammed his hand down on the table, rattling the dishes and startling Raina out of her tirade. "That is enough, daughter. You should not speak to your parents in that manner, especially your mother."

Raina's mouth dropped open then shut until she finally recaptured her verbal skills and enough sense not to cuss a blue streak. "You're defending her? Have you forgotten she left you in the middle of the night taking your only daughter away from you?"

"Your father understands why that happened," Carolyn said. "We've talked about that."

"Oh, yeah? Would someone like to explain it to me?" Too angry to be reasonable, Raina pushed back from the table. "Never mind. I'm not sure I want to hear it."

"Raina, please sit back down," her mother said.

Idris stood but made no move to stop her. "Your mother and I ask that you visit with us a while longer."

She gripped the chair forcefully as she pushed it beneath the table. "Not tonight. I'm tired and I'm going to bed. But you two feel free to stay up and discuss my life further. Right now I just want to be left alone."

Before leaving the room, she sent Dharr a quick look of apology before leaving him with her parents, practically defenseless. However, she figured he was more than capable considering he was in charge of a whole country. And he would probably need every diplomatic skill he possessed.

Nine

What he'd lacked in diplomacy at dinner, he'd made up for in lies. Not exactly lies, Dharr decided, but an omission of the truth. Yet he'd felt compelled to defend Raina's honor even if he had angered her parents in the process. Even if he had not necessarily honored her.

Now alone in the conference room where he'd met with Raina two days ago, he debated whether to seek her out, or leave her to her solitude as she'd requested. Yet he knew if he did find her, exactly where that would lead—back into his bed. Back into her body. Back into oblivion.

He stood over the museum blueprints laid out on the table, yet he could not focus on anything other than his desire to be with her. To be close to her. To make love with her. Because of his demanding schedule, he'd resisted those urges for forty-eight hours, and his resistance was waning.

When the knock sounded, his irritation increased, until the door opened to the object of his distraction.

Raina entered wearing the same clothes she'd had on at dinner, a tailored pink sleeveless top held together by a zipper and white slacks that formed to the curve of her hips. That zipper had captured his attention all through dinner and he saw no end to his fascination with it, or with her.

"May I talk with you a minute?" she asked.

He straightened and shoved his hands deep into the pockets of his slacks to quell the urge to go to her and without hesitation, touch her everywhere. "Please. I'm afraid I'm making little progress in my work tonight."

She stepped forward to the table opposite him. "I want to apologize for leaving you to confront my family alone."

"I managed."

She brushed her hair from her shoulders. "What did they say to you after I ran out?"

"Basically the same questions they asked of you. The state of our relationship. Whether we had been intimate."

He could see the tension seeping into her face and her frame. "What did you tell them?"

"I told them that they should respect our privacy. We are both adults and what transpires between us is our concern. I also informed them that should we agree to be forthcoming with more information, we would do so if and when we are ready."

Now she looked pleased. "Did my father threaten you after that?"

"No, although I believe he was practicing restraint solely for the benefit of your mother."

"And they bought all that without any protest?"

"I did not give them the opportunity as I took my leave and retired here."

"Thanks for defending me. I hope that doesn't come back to bite you on the butt."

He considered requesting she not reference anatomy in

their conversation. "I will stand firm in my resolve." His resolve was not the only thing standing firm when she strolled around the table and came to his side.

"Is this the museum?" she asked.

Her proximity made it difficult for Dharr to concentrate. But at least they could now discuss a more pleasant subject aside from her parents' grilling. "Yes. What I've been working on for the past two days. These are preliminary blueprints." He indicated the drawings of the various halls. "Exhibits will go here and the foyer will feature sculpture. That leaves a large space to the west. I am still considering its use."

Raina bent and surveyed the plans, holding her long hair back with one hand. "That's easy. You take part of the space and you build classrooms." She pointed a slender finger. "And here, you have a gallery devoted to the local children's art."

"Children?"

She faced him, leaning a hip against the table. "Sure. You'll give them an outlet for their creativity, something to do to keep them off the streets after school. I would've killed for this kind of opportunity when I was younger. That would've saved Badya many a trip into the village looking for me when I'd escaped for a little adventure."

Dharr smiled with remembrance. "I recall you were often seen running through the streets, absent of shoes and covered in dirt, poor Badya chasing after you."

"It sure beat hanging out at the house all day with those boring tutors. A girl has to have a little adventure now and then."

Dharr greatly wanted to give her adventure now, with or without shoes. "This program you're proposing. I assume it would be free to all who participate."

"Of course. Not everyone has your money or means. I'm sure you can find volunteers to teach and a few benefactors to fund the supplies."

"Yes, I could." He came upon a spontaneous idea, one that he doubted she would consider, but at least he could try. "Perhaps you should think about returning here to teach."

She turned her attention back to the blueprints. "I couldn't do that. I already have a job, and it pays. Besides, that would leave my mother all by herself. As mad as she makes me sometimes, she still needs me."

And so do I. The thought vaulted into Dharr's brain so quickly it took him aback. He refused to recognize its validity for to do so would put him in emotional straits. "What about your father?"

"He's managed without us. I suspect he still will. In fact, I wouldn't be a bit surprised to learn he has a mistress somewhere. Maybe several."

"That is not so."

Her gaze snapped to his. "How do you know?"

"Even a man of your father's caliber could not be discreet enough without rumors reaching the palace. He has maintained a reputation beyond reproach. He has had no other women."

"If you say so, but I find it hard to believe he's been celibate for eleven years, if not longer. And I still can't believe he spent all day in a room with my mother and they're not fuming at each other. In fact, they seemed almost amiable at dinner."

"Perhaps they are considering reconciliation."

"My guess is they're finally discussing divorce."

No matter how hard she'd tried to disguise it, Dharr heard the pain in her voice. "I realize that would be very difficult for you."

She turned and leaned against the table then stared at the bookshelves behind him. "You know, I don't really care anymore. As long as they move forward with their lives. This whole limbo thing is ridiculous."

She did care, that much Dharr realized. If only he could think of something to console her. If only he could take her pain away.

Pushing away from the table, she walked to the glass doors where she'd made her first appearance as the prospective wife to the crown prince. "Come here and show me where the museum's going to be."

Dharr walked up behind her, careful not to touch her and in turn, crush his control. He pointed toward the base of the mountain silhouetted against the night sky. "Do you remember Almase?"

"Yes. The rocks shaped like diamonds, not far from the Minhat ruins." She regarded him over one shoulder. "That's a wonderful site. I used to play there as a child. But aren't you afraid you're going to destroy it during construction?"

"We have considered that carefully. The museum will be built adjacent to the formation. We'll use materials that will create the illusion that the structure blends into the mountain."

"That sounds wonderful."

So was she, in many, many ways. "It will be, once it is done. We are hoping to have the museum completed in eighteen months, which is why I need to finalize the plans."

She turned and rested her palms on his shoulders. "Take me there."

As much as he wanted to do that, the following day would be full of meetings and tours with the Doriana diplomats. "I am afraid my schedule will not allow that tomorrow. Perhaps the next day?"

"Tonight. Take me there now."

"It is late, Raina. And too dark to see much."

She slipped her arms around his waist. "Exactly."

"The desert is not always friendly after dark."

"I trust you'll protect me. Besides, Almase has had so

many visitors, I doubt any vipers or scorpions still hang out there." She stood on her tiptoes and gave him a soft kiss. "I'll make it worth your while."

At that moment, he would do anything for her. Anything, except put her in peril. "Your mother and father could be tracking our whereabouts."

"I know and that's why we can't go to our rooms. If they happen to find out we've left, we only have to say we went for a midnight drive. And that's if we care what they think, which I don't. I only care about being with you. It's been two days and it seems like twenty. I've missed you."

He had missed her, as well. Ached for her, in fact. "I am still questioning the wisdom in this plan."

Her smile was sultry, fueling a searing heat deep within Dharr. "Let's do something daring, Dharr Halim. Let's get out of here and leave all our responsibility to family behind. Let's make love in the desert."

He lowered his head and took her mouth, an overture to the pleasure he would surely give her in answer to her fantasy. "You are very difficult to refuse."

"Then don't refuse me."

Dharr left Raina at the bedroom door with a brief kiss and instructions to meet him on the first floor as soon as she'd changed. She made quick work of shrugging on her jeans and pulling on her sneakers. She wasn't quite so fast when she fumbled with the buttons on the oversize oxford shirt. On afterthought, she retrieved the condoms from the drawer where she'd hidden them away, a guarantee he wouldn't have any excuse not to follow through. It took all of ten minutes, tops, before she was sprinting down the stairs on the way to her late-night rendezvous.

She pulled up short when she found Dharr standing at the

bottom landing, wearing his own pair of faded jeans, an equally washed-out crimson Harvard T-shirt pulled tight against his chest and a pair of brown lace up hiking boots. His dark hair was ruffled, probably from his own haste to dress, and he looked as if he'd morphed from premiere prince to college man. The effect was so devastating on Raina's composure that she almost suggested they march back up the stairs to a bedroom so she could peel every article of clothing away from his killer body.

Instead she hopped down the final steps and said, "I'm ready."

"As am I."

Following a quick, chaste kiss, Dharr took her by the elbow and guided her through a labyrinth of hallways until they reached a door that opened to several concrete stairs leading downward. At the bottom, Dharr pounded out a code, opened another heavy door and led her into an underground concrete garage housing several vehicles.

Once there, they came upon two men chatting it up in the corner near the hood of one sedan. When they noticed Dharr, they immediately came to attention in a military stance. Dharr made his request in Arabic for the keys to a Jeep. Amused, Raina watched the men practically falling all over themselves to retrieve them from the safe recessed into the wall.

Dharr told Raina to follow him to a black and beige Jeep parked in the corner among more sedans. He opened the door for her then rounded the hood to position himself behind the wheel. In a matter of moments, they were racing through the garage to the exit where a solid steel gate rose like the entrance to a mystical cave, revealing the magical night.

They maneuvered the lengthy drive at a speed Raina decided was well beyond the limits of safety before Dharr stopped at the guard station to address the sentry, saying little more than they were going for a drive. The man did not look at all pleased when Dharr insisted he did not need an escort, nor did he want one. But at least the guard opened the gate without further argument aside from some under-the-breath mutterings Raina couldn't quite distinguish.

Soon they worked their way through the silent streets of Tomar at a fast clip until Dharr reached the place where pavement turned to dirt. Then he stopped the vehicle, put it in park and turned to Raina.

He reached over and sifted her hair through his fingertips without speaking.

"What are we waiting for?" Raina asked.

"Before the road becomes rough, I wanted to do this."

Cupping her jaw in his palm, he leaned over and kissed her deeply, providing a perfect lead up to what she hoped would come later. He broke the kiss, frowned then following a rough sigh, slapped his palm against the steering wheel. "We have to go back."

He'd changed his mind, exactly what Raina had feared. "Why?"

"I have forgotten something again."

Straightening her legs as far as they would go, she fished through her pocket, pulled out two condoms and dangled them from her fingertips. "Do you mean these?"

His smile formed slowly, seductively. "Then I suppose we are ready."

"You don't know the half of it."

He rested his hand on her thigh. "But I promise I will."

"Good. And before we head out again, can you take the top off?"

He grinned. "You wish me to undress you now?"

Raina laughed, prompted by his show of humor and a lightness of being so welcome after the tumultuous meeting with her family. "That's a thought, but I meant the top on the Jeep."

"Whatever you wish, I will gladly accommodate you." Before she could say more, Dharr slid from the seat and commenced unzipping and folding back the covering, revealing the inky sky. Looking upward, she took in the glorious sight, realizing she'd lived so long in the city, she'd forgotten how brilliant a host of stars could be. How the desert during the day could be unrelenting, but at night it took on a life of its own—mysterious and seductive, like the man whose company she craved.

Dharr returned to the driver's seat, put the Jeep in gear and took off. They scaled the bumpy scrap of road, climbing upward through the mountainous terrain, heading toward a heaven of their own making. Fifteen minutes later, they turned off the main road and stopped at a circular clearing facing the valley below. Dharr left the vehicle while Raina simply stared at the spattering of city lights, knowing that most everyone was preparing for sleep while she was wide awake and wired. The view was breathtaking, but then so was her escort as he held out his hand for her to take.

To Raina, he was an integral part of the panorama—dark, mystifying and somewhat dangerous. Not in the sense that he made her afraid, but he was a huge threat to her heart. He'd already won a good part of it. Tonight he might claim it all.

Guided by the light of the near-full moon, hand in hand they ascended a rock-strewn path, taking them higher into the elevations above Tomar. Although Raina hadn't been to this particular place in over a decade, she had no trouble recognizing the diamond-shaped rocks pointing upward and to her right, the base of the mountain known as Galal—majestic—and very fitting. But it couldn't compare to Dharr Halim, equally magnificent and strong. And all hers tonight.

Giddy could best describe her current mood. And drunk with the freedom of being there with him, alone, knowing that anything she asked of him, he would try to give to her. She planned to return the favor.

"Come with me over here," he told her, his voice low and controlled, toxic to her senses.

She followed him to one steep embankment where he released her then began to climb. At the top, once more he held out his hand to her. "You must see this view."

"What's on the other side?"

"Flat rock that leads to the cliff."

Raina didn't mind heights as long as she was in a protected environment, with the exception of airplanes. But she wasn't feeling too confident about standing on weather-worn stone where one false move could send her over the edge.

When she hesitated, Dharr said, "It is safe. I will not let you fall."

Oh, but she already had—for him.

Clasping his large hand, she allowed him to pull her up. He turned her around to face the valley, his arms wrapped firmly around her and his chin resting atop her head. "This is the place I would come when I wanted to escape. I would view the city laid out before me, knowing it served as a reminder of why I accept my duty without question. I have vowed to see it thrive."

"Azzril is very much a part of you."

"And you, Raina."

She shook her head. "Not anymore. Too many bad memories."

"More than the good?"

She couldn't lay claim to that. "I guess I do have quite a few good."

"Except for your parents' disagreements."

After thinking a moment, she said, "You know, I only heard them fight one time, not long before I left with my mother. Maybe that's why it all came as such a shock. Maybe they just didn't want me to know how miserable they both were, although for the life of me, I can't remember anything but their love for each other. I have no idea what changed, but I guess I'll never know."

He tightened his hold and whispered, "We will make our own memories tonight. Good ones to replace the bad. Beginning now."

Remaining behind her, Dharr began to work the buttons on Raina's shirt until he had the placket completely parted. He held it open, allowing the breeze to flow over her bare breasts, tightening her flesh from the cool draft of air. Yet Dharr warmed her with his palms, playing her gently, thoroughly, until she grew winded with the same helpless need for him.

But then he dropped his arms and left her with only a whispered, "Wait here."

Raina had no intention of going anywhere without him. She sat on the rock opposite the view to watch Dharr as he strode to the Jeep. He pulled out a blanket and came back to her, spreading the multicolored woven throw over the stone surface. Obviously he was more prepared than she'd thought.

She took his offered hand and he drew her up into his arms, against the solid wall of his chest. He held her for a long moment before he stepped back, pushed the blouse completely away from her shoulders then tugged his own shirt over his head. They discarded the rest of their clothing in haste, piling the shirts and jeans onto the blanket to provide more cushion. They embraced again, holding each other closely, exploring with their hands in places they had touched before, yet the intimacy took on a dreamlike quality.

In her mind's eyes, Raina could imagine how they would

appear from below—two lovers silhouetted against the night, insignificant compared to the imposing surroundings, yet important to each other, at least for now. She took the image and mentally filed it away, knowing that some day she would put it on canvas, immortalizing them both captured in this precious moment.

Dharr laid her down gently on the blanket then kissed her much the same—a meaningful kiss that soon turned evocative, exciting. He moved his warm lips to her neck, toying with her hair as he continued his downward journey to her breasts, drawing one nipple deep into his mouth, then the other. Lower he traveled, his lips drifting over her abdomen before coming to rest between her thighs, creating a barrage of thrilling sensations in Raina.

She slid her fingers through his thick hair while he continued to encourage her to completely let go, using his tongue and lips and hands, washing away all uncertainty of her feelings for him. The stars above her fell out of focus and the wind picked up, bringing with it a mélange of scents and sensations. Time seemed to suspend as her body trembled with impending climax until she could do nothing more than give in to its force. She felt weak, boneless, the ground beneath her unforgiving, yet she didn't care. She only cared about him.

Intent on proving exactly how much she cared, after Dharr worked his way up her body with more open mouth kisses, she nudged him onto his back and took the same path down his torso as he had with hers, tracking the trail of dark hair with her lips until she reached her goal. He hissed out a sharp breath when she took him into her mouth. A murmured word of pleasure followed, then her name drifting on the breeze with a reverence that made her heart ache with longing.

She remained unrelenting in her movements, even when he asked her to stop because he could no longer hold on. She didn't stop until he pleaded with her, then told her how greatly he needed to be inside her. Now.

She smiled as she took a condom and sheathed him, and he smiled back when she straddled his hips and guided him inside her. But his smile disappeared as she set the pace, slowly at first then more frantic. Watching his face grow taut, his eyes grow hazy, was magical, and admittedly powerful, knowing that she could take him exactly where he had taken her. He clasped her hips as his body surged up with his own climax, sending Raina remarkably over the edge again. She collapsed against his chest, gasping for air, grasping for a hold on her runaway emotions. She was totally lost when Dharr kissed her again with profound tenderness.

How could she want him so much? How could she be so completely consumed by a man that she honestly didn't care if she ever returned to reality? Or ever returned to California, for that matter.

Despite her need to be cautious, she craved being close to the fire he'd continually created in her. Only stolen moments, she tried to tell herself but quickly banished those thoughts. She would pretend it was forever, even if it was only for tonight.

Dharr Halim had always been pragmatic. Analyzing numbers, not emotions, had been his forte. He had an aptitude for finance, never feelings. He admired art yet he could never imagine putting paint to paper. And creating poetry had not once entered his mind...until now.

With Raina next to him, cast in the first signs of dawn, he felt as if he could quite possibly write a sonnet.

At the moment they were seated on the hood of the Jeep, the blanket their only cover, their arms providing shelter from the morning cold. For hours they had talked, then touched, culminating in more lovemaking as intense as the first. He'd made it his mission to know as much as he could about her, both body and mind. She had done the same. He had never known a more willing lover, and he had never revealed as much of himself to any woman. Yet one part of him she did not know—his heart.

He felt no need to open old injuries only to bleed some more. He chose to cherish this time with her without discussing past mistakes, realizing these moments could be their last.

"I guess we should go now," she said, both her tone and her eyes laden with regret.

"Yes, we should."

"Which means we have to get dressed."

"True."

"Unless we want to drive back to town naked, although I'm not sure that would be good for your image."

If he thought for a moment they could do that without discovery, he certainly would. He would touch her on their return until he had given her more pleasure, just so he could watch her face. "I suppose you are right."

Yet neither of them made a move other than toward each other, their lips uniting again in a kiss that had Dharr reconsidering his need to return to his responsibility.

"Dharr," Raina murmured against his mouth. "We really do need to leave now."

He reluctantly pulled away and groaned. "If we must."

"We must."

They gathered their clothes and dressed on opposite sides of the vehicle at Raina's insistence. A good idea, Dharr decided considering he was on the verge of making love to her again despite his pending duties.

They traveled back to the palace without speaking, their fingers entwined, resting on his thigh. In the garage, they walked past the guards who averted their eyes, as if he and Raina were invisible. Once they reentered the palace, Dharr maintained his distance until they reached the staircase leading to the upper floor. Absent of restraint, he grabbed Raina's hand and turned her into his arms before she could scale the first step.

He kissed her again, stroked her hair, held her close as if he could not have enough of her. Raina proved to have the most presence of mind when she broke the kiss and said, "Someone is going to see us."

He lowered his lips to her throat. "I do not care."

She bracketed his face and forced him to look at her. "You say that now, but you would care if my father happened down the stairs. He's an early riser."

Dharr pressed against her. "And so am I."

"You're incorrigible, too." She backed away from him and climbed the first two stairs without turning around. "I'll see you tonight."

When he started toward her, she pointed a finger. "Stay right there until I get a good head start."

He propped an elbow on the banister and smiled. "And if I do not?"

"Then I won't be responsible when I lose it and tackle you on the landing, tearing off your clothes while shouting 'Take me now,' which will undoubtedly wake the entire household."

With that, she spun and sprinted up the stairs, leaving Dharr to watch her until she disappeared.

He decided to return to his office before retiring to his room to change. If not, he would be tempted to join her in bed for the rest of the day. He had too much to accomplish to be distracted, but as he began to review his schedule, he could not banish the images of Raina—her face flushed with heat when he'd made love to her and again with cold in the morning light. A face he would welcome waking up to each and every morning.

To continue considering such a thing would prove to be unfavorable to his plans. He would not marry in the near future. Not until his father insisted it was time to produce an heir. Only then would he choose a woman who was like him. A woman who possessed a certain amount of independence. Who enjoyed art. Who had a passion for life and a propensity for adventure.

Dharr realized he had just described Raina Kahlil—a woman who would be gone in a matter of days.

After Raina left the shower and crawled beneath the covers to grab a few hours' sleep, someone knocked on the door. Since Badya never came around this time of morning, she suspected she knew who that someone might be.

She grabbed the handle and said, "You are one stubborn guy," only to find her mother, not the sheikh, standing on the other side.

Raina tugged on the hem of her gown and bit her lip almost hard enough to draw blood. "Why are you up so early, Mom?"

"I've been visiting with your father." Without an invitation, Carolyn pushed into the room then spun around. "Where were you last night?"

Oh, joy. "How do you know I wasn't right here?"

"Because I came up to say good-night and you weren't anywhere to be found."

"I went out for a drive."

"With Dharr?"

"Yeah. Sorry I missed my curfew."

Carolyn folded her arms in true disapproving-mother fashion. "What is really going on between the two of you?"

This was so ridiculous, and typical. "Mom, I've already told you, and so has Dharr, that what we might or might not do together is really no one's business but ours."

"I'm worried about you, Raina. I'm worried you're getting in too deep."

Raina had to admit her mother had valid concerns. "I'm mature enough to handle it, Mother."

"You keep telling me that, then you disappear in the middle of the night like some teenager with a man who might as well be a stranger."

"He's not a stranger. I've known him for years."

"Exactly *how* well do you know him now?"

Raina was way too weary to dance around the truth any longer. Hanging onto her last scrap of self-control, she calmly said, "We're lovers, Mother. Are you happy now?"

If she was at all shocked over the revelation, Carolyn hid it well. "Are you going to marry him?"

"That has not even entered my mind." Not more than once or twice.

"But you're in love with him, aren't you?"

"What makes you think that?" So much for trying to keep calm.

"As they say, it's written all over your face."

Raina turned around and began to aimlessly arrange her toiletries on the dresser. "What do *they* know?"

Her mother came up behind her and rested a hand on her shoulder. "I've seen that same look on my own face. You're burning for him."

Burning? Raina stared at her reflection in the mirror. Funny, she didn't look as if she were on fire, even though in Dharr's presence, that couldn't be more true.

She shook off her mother's hand and faced her. "Okay, I admit I do have feelings for him. But it doesn't matter. We agreed from the beginning this thing was only temporary. Neither of us wants a commitment." How incredibly false she sounded.

Her mother's expression turned sympathetic. "Oh, sweetheart. I'm sorry. I hate seeing your heart breaking."

"My heart is still intact." Even if she couldn't guarantee for how long.

Carolyn braced both hands on her hips. "I ought to give him a good tongue lashing for leading you on. I should tell your father and let him do it."

Alarms rang out in Raina's head. "Do not tell Papa a thing. He doesn't need to know. And you can't blame Dharr for this. We were both in it together."

"But you're the one who fell in love."

Too exhausted to continue, she said, "Mother, I need to sleep some before tonight's reception. Can we discuss this later?" Or never.

She patted Raina's cheek. "Okay. You get some sleep. If you want to talk, come and find me."

When her mother turned toward the door, Raina noticed something very odd about the normally well-groomed Carolyn Kahlil. The tag on her slacks was exposed, as were the seams. Her mother's pants were on wrong side out.

"One more thing, Mom."

Carolyn turned, one hand braced on the knob. "What?"

"Were you only visiting with Papa. Or were you *visiting* with Papa?"

Her hand dropped to her side. "I don't understand what you're asking."

Raina gestured toward her mother's slacks. "You're wearing the same clothes you had on at dinner last night and best I can recall, you had them on correctly during our meal. Obviously you've taken them off at some point."

She looked down, then back up again. "I…uh…"

"You and Papa had a little post-separation coitus?"

"We are still married, Raina."

True, but she didn't even want to think about her own mother and father having sex. No child ever did. Especially a child who'd suffered through their estrangement for years. "Did you even stop to consider his heart condition?"

"He doesn't have a heart condition, Raina. He has a hiatal hernia. He's had it for years. If he doesn't take his medicine, he has chest pains, especially when he insists on eating spicy foods, which he does. His tests were all normal."

Fury caused Raina to grip her hands in tight fists at her sides, her nails biting into her palms. "So this was all a ruse to get me back here. And he got you in the bargain, too."

"That wasn't what he intended. His doctors worried it might be more serious, and he worried he might not ever see you again. So please don't blame him."

Raina was almost rendered speechless. "Mother, you two slay me. For years you wouldn't give each other the time of day. Now you're making whoopee and ganging up on me. What gives?"

She paused for a moment, looking somewhat indecisive. "Sweetheart, your father and I wanted to tell you together, but I guess now is as good a time as any."

"What is it, Mom?" Raina sounded like the little girl again. That same little girl who listened to her mother all those years ago say they wouldn't be coming back to Azzril.

"I'm going to stay here. We've decided to try it again. We've realized we still love each other very much."

How many years had Raina longed to hear that? How many times had she prayed for that very thing? But now, she experienced the sting of resentment and the bite of more abandonment. "That's just great, Mother."

Carolyn looked as if she might cry, something she rarely did. "I thought you would be happy."

Raina traded her guilt over being so harsh for some honesty. "Eleven years ago, I would've been thrilled. Now all I can think about is the nights I stayed awake wanting to go home and wondering why you and Papa split. Have those reasons changed?"

"Honey, I left because I knew how much your father loved his country even after they exiled him for marrying me. I saw him agonizing over it for years. I thought that if I returned to America, he'd try to go back and make amends, which he didn't. There's something else, too."

Raina wasn't sure she had the stamina to hear it, but she might as well get it over with. "What else?"

"After I had you, I couldn't have more children. I wanted to give him a son, an heir, and that wasn't possible. But he told me yesterday he never wanted any of those things, only me. Pride has kept us apart, and love has brought us back together, this time for good."

"That's very poetic, Mother." Raina felt the rise of tears, the joy mixed with the sorrow. She was happy her parents had made amends, but now she would return to California alone. She would also never know that kind of commitment with the man she loved.

Feeling remorseful over her callousness, she hugged her mother and pulled back before she started to sob. "I'm happy for you, Mom. Truly I am. I'm going to miss you, though."

Her mother cupped her cheek. "Your father and I wish you would consider staying. If not permanently, at least for a while."

Stay and face Dharr knowing he would never love her. She couldn't do that. In fact, she didn't want to stay a minute longer, but she had promised Dharr she would be at the reception. She planned to keep that promise. Tomorrow morning she would make plans to leave. "I'll be fine. I have a good job. And now that I know you'll take care of Papa, I need to go home."

Home. Had California ever really been her true home? Not really.

"And you won't stay a few more days?" Carolyn asked.

She didn't want to dash her mother's hope, at least not now. "I'll think about it. But right now I really need some sleep."

"Okay, honey. I'll see you tonight."

Raina escorted her mother out, then tried one more time to go to bed, only to be halted by another knock on the door. If she thought it might be Dharr, she would run. Believing that to be impossible, she dragged her feet all the way to answer the summons.

She was glad she hadn't hurried when she found a strange woman with severe short black hair and overdone makeup standing on the other side of the threshold, a long black bag draped over one arm. "Princess Kahlil, especially selected for you."

Raina took the bag and envelope she offered, thanked her and after the woman left, hooked the hanger over the top of the door. She slit open the envelope and read the message penned in bold script.

A special gift for a special woman. A dress fit for a queen. Wear it for me tonight—Dharr

For a queen? Surely he didn't mean… No, she would not read more into this than it was—a thoughtful gesture from a thoughtful man. An incredible man with incredible taste, she decided as she unzipped the plastic and slid it from the garment. The floor-length sleeveless white satin gown, its high collar accentuated with gold braid, would be deemed simple and elegant, but gorgeous.

Raina held it against her and surveyed it in the mirror. She loved it. Tonight she would wear it for him, and hope that he would be responsible for taking it off. Maybe she *would* stay a couple more days.

But she wouldn't be worth anything if she didn't get some rest. Dark circles didn't go well with white satin.

As she finally settled into bed for a nap, she couldn't prevent the excitement and the glimmer of hope. Maybe tonight would be a turning point in hers and Dharr's relationship. Maybe tonight, when they were alone again, she would find the courage to tell him how she really felt. And maybe, just maybe, he might admit he had feelings for her, too.

Ten

When Raina appeared in the entry to the grand salon, Dharr could not put into words exactly how he felt. Mesmerized by her. Proud of her. Lost to her.

The dress fit her perfectly, as he'd known it would when he'd selected it from those the local boutique owner had brought to him. He'd had no difficulty judging which one would fit; he had memorized every inch of Raina's body both by touch and sight. Her hair was pulled up high, three braids woven with gold ribbon trailing from where it had been bound. She wore more makeup tonight, yet it did not mask her beauty even though he preferred the natural color of her lips. When they were alone again later, he would gladly remove the lipstick and the dress. If they had the opportunity to be alone.

As he visited with the Doriana contingency, he covertly watched Raina, her movements refined as she mingled with the guests on the arm of her father. He wondered what it would be like to have her on his arm, showing the world that she was his. But she would not be his, and he needed to remember that. He would do nothing to threaten her coveted freedom. He would not be left with his emotions in shambles again. He would not watch her walk away with his heart, though he wondered if perhaps she would take a part of it with her despite his determination not to love her.

When she moved closer, he gestured her over. She excused herself from the sultan and came to his side, smiling when he said, "Princess Kahlil, this Mr. Renaldo Chapeline, prime minister of Doriana."

The portly balding man bowed and kissed her hand. "*Enchanté*, Princess."

"It's very nice to meet you, as well, Prime Minister."

Chapeline released her hand and regarded Dharr. "You have made a fine choice for a bride, Sheikh Halim."

Dharr glanced at Raina to find her looking at him expectantly before addressing the prime minister again. "I am afraid that what you may have heard are only rumors. The princess and I do not plan to marry. She will be returning to California soon."

He saw something else in Raina's eyes, something he could not define when she added, "Yes, I'll be returning very soon. Now if you'll excuse me, I believe I see my mother summoning me."

Dharr watched her walk away, perplexed to see that her mother seemed preoccupied with the sultan and not at all interested in Raina's whereabouts, and even more confused when Raina stopped to converse with Raneer on her way to join her parents.

"She is a beauty, Sheikh Halim," Chapeline said, drawing Dharr's attention. "I am sorry to hear she is not the one for you."

Yet she could be the one, Dharr realized in that moment. Or would be were she not intent on returning home. He turned his back, refusing to look at her any longer, refusing to acknowledge the soul-deep pain threatening to surface. Refusing to accept that he would soon have to let her go.

Raina summoned her parents into the foyer and prepared for the fall-out. "I wanted to let you both know I'm leaving tonight."

"Tonight?" Her papa's face reflected unmistakable fury. "Have you totally taken leave of your senses?"

Yes, she had, on more than one occasion with Dharr. But she had full control of mental function at the moment. "I have to get back to work. If I leave now, I'll be recovered from the flight by Tuesday at the latest." Even if she wouldn't be quite recovered from her limited time with Dharr.

"That's silly, Raina," her mother said. "Waiting one more day isn't going to matter all that much. We've barely seen you since I've arrived."

No kidding. "I think that's because you and Papa have spent all your time together, and that's okay."

"This is our fault," Idris said. "We have not afforded you much courtesy because we have focused only on—"

"Getting reacquainted," Carolyn interrupted. "But if you stay, we promise we'll pay more attention to you."

"I'm not a child, Mother. I don't need your undivided attention." She offered an unsteady smile. "You both need to catch-up on all the time you've missed together. And I really am happy you've decided to make your marriage work." Finally, Raina thought, but discarded the bitterness for the sake of her family. She couldn't change what had been, but she could learn to embrace what would be—her parents' happiness—even if her own looked bleak.

Her mother's joy illuminated her expression. "We're so glad you're happy, sweetheart. But I still don't know how you're going to manage to get a flight on such notice. Not to mention you'll have to drive miles to the nearest commercial airport."

"I've taken care of that," Raina said. "Mr. Raneer told me that the king and queen are due to arrive within the hour. He also told me I could use the private plane. All he has to do is arrange for another pilot to take me back to California."

Her papa looked handsome in all his royal finery, but no less unhappy. "Then it appears that is settled and obviously we cannot change your mind."

"No, Papa, you can't. I think this is best for all concerned." Especially for Dharr. He'd been so adamant in telling the prime minister their engagement was only a rumor that it seemed no hope remained for a permanent relationship between them. Oddly that's what she'd wanted all along—nothing permanent. But now she wanted so much more. If she couldn't count on some kind of commitment in the future, then no future could exist between them.

Her mother pinned Raina with a knowing look. "Have you told the sheikh your plans?"

"I'll talk to him before I leave." Something she was definitely dreading.

Her papa said, "Then I am to presume there are no plans for you both to marry?"

As badly as Raina hated destroying her father's wishes, she couldn't give him false hope. "No. No plans. There never were. Dharr and I began as friends, and we'll part as friends." She prayed that would be the case. "I'm sure he'll find someone who will make a good queen." And that thought made Raina both angry and sad.

Ready to get the goodbyes finished, she hugged her mother

first, then her papa. "You both take care. Maybe I'll see you soon. You could have a second honeymoon in California."

Raina hated the sadness in her papa's eyes, hated even more that she'd put it there. "God speed, my *záhra.*"

"Take care, sweetheart. Call when you're back in California."

"I will."

Raina turned and rushed up the stairs, holding back her tears until she was safely in her room—Dharr's room. While she swiped furiously at her tearstained face, she meant to pull her clothes from the hangers in the closet but instead found herself staring at his clothes. Slowly she ran her fingers over one tailored jacket, then lifted the sleeve and held it against her damp cheek. How terribly silly she was. How incredibly foolish she'd been. And how very hard she had fallen in love like some fickle female who didn't know what was good for her.

One thing she did know to be true—she was good for Dharr. They were good for each other. But if he didn't love her, if he allowed her to walk out of his life for good, then that couldn't be at all true.

Only one way to find out.

For the next hour, Dharr went through the motions of playing the perfect host, fighting the urge to search Raina out until he could no longer fight. He scanned the room filled with guests yet she was nowhere to be found.

He signaled Raneer and took him to one side. "Have you any word on my parents' arrival?"

"Yes. They should be landing at the airstrip in the next half-hour. They hope to make an appearance before the guests disperse."

"Good. Have you seen the princess?"

"No, your grace. But I have spoken with her."

"I noticed. What was that about?"

"She made a request."

"What request?"

"For use of the plane for her return to America."

Dharr attempted to sound as nonchalant as possible though he highly doubted he'd completely hidden his concern. "Did she say when she will be returning?"

Abid tugged at his collar. "She says she must return immediately. Tonight."

Dharr's concern increased. "Has there been an emergency?"

"None that I am aware of."

"Where is she now?"

"As far as I know, in her quarters, packing."

Dharr pushed his way through the guests, muttering apologies as he went. As he ascended the stairs, a thousand questions hurled through his mind. Why was she leaving now? Was he somehow responsible for her departure? Had she intended to go without telling him goodbye?

He wanted answers. Now.

Without bothering to knock, Dharr barged into the room to find Raina seated on the edge of the bed, arranging her clothes in the bag she'd brought with her.

He raked the kaffiyeh from his head and tossed it onto the corner table. "What are you doing?"

She afforded him only a brief glance before going back to her packing, seemingly unaffected by his anger. "I would think that's obvious. I'm getting ready to leave."

"Why now?"

After zipping the bag with a vengeance, she came to her feet. "I have to go back to work. Besides, I'm not needed here anymore."

If she only knew how much he needed her. If he only had the strength to tell her. "And your father? Are you no longer concerned with his health?"

"It appears that he has a stomach problem, not a heart problem. My mother informed me of that this morning, as well as the fact she intends to stay and work on her marriage." She released a caustic laugh. "Imagine that. After eleven years, they're going to carry on as if nothing happened."

"I would think that would please you."

"In a way it does, in another it makes me angry considering all the time they've wasted. But it really doesn't matter what I think. My mother is staying here to take care of him, and I'm free to return to my life in California."

She desired her freedom, not him, something he'd known all along. Dharr's defenses took hold, surrounding his emotions in protective armor. "Apparently you have made up your mind."

"Yes, I have. And thank you for letting me wear the dress. I've hung it in the closet. And I left the lamp for you, a little something to remember me by."

He would need no reminders. Her memory was already deeply etched in his soul. "You need not return any of it. It is all yours. I have no use for it."

"I appreciate that, but I'm sure you'll find someone else who will wear the dress better than me. A true queen."

That would never be true for Dharr. He would never find anyone who could compare to her. Anyone who would make a better queen. A better lover. A better life partner.

Raina retrieved an envelope from the nightstand then handed it to him. "Here. I wrote down a few things I want you to know. You can read it now if you'd like."

Another letter, a different woman, a repeat of history. "I will read it after you are gone. I must return to my guests."

When he saw the disappointment in her eyes, he almost gave in. "Fine. Suit yourself then."

The shrill of the bedside phone caused Raina to jump and

she snatched it from its cradle. "Yes?" A moment of silence. "Great. I'll be down in a few minutes."

After she hung up, she told him, "Your parents are about to land, so I'm going to catch a ride to the airstrip in the car that's scheduled to pick them up."

"It could be some time before they ready the plane for departure."

"I don't mind waiting. But first, I'm going to say goodbye to Badya, then I'll be going."

"You are not concerned with traveling alone?"

Her smile threatened to break through his self-imposed fortress. "I'm sure it won't be quite as pleasant as my trip here, but I'm not afraid of flying anymore. Thanks to you."

A sudden spear of desperation hurled through Dharr. "Is there nothing I can say to convince you to stay?"

She hesitated for a moment before saying, "Obviously not. But there is something you can do for me. Kiss me goodbye."

He wanted to refuse her, to keep up the façade of indifference. Yet when she moved into his arms, he was lost to her again. He touched his lips to hers, memorizing her taste, the soft heat of her mouth, knowing those memories would haunt him for a long time. For a lifetime.

Raina pulled away first and slipped the bag's strap over her shoulder. "At least you have your room back now."

But he did not have her, and that only fueled his discontent. What a fool he had been. Still, he did not want to leave her with angry words. "I will miss your company."

"And I'll miss your teasing, I think. If you're ever in California, give me a call. I'd love to show you the beaches." She nodded toward the painting over the fireplace. "If you ever feel the need to ditch that masterpiece, think of me, okay?"

He would think of her often. Every day. Every night. "Will you return in the near future?"

"Maybe someday."

And perhaps someday he would be over her, although that did not seem likely. He considered voicing his feelings, considered telling her that he wanted her to stay, not for a few days but permanently. But if he remained silent, at least he would not have to hear that she wanted only her freedom. That she could not accept what he had to offer. That she could not accept him.

He touched her face once more. "Peace be with you, Raina."

"And with you, Dharr Halim."

Then she was out the door, leaving Dharr feeling utterly bereft.

He had no time to ponder what might have been. In a short while, he would need to be downstairs to welcome his parents home. In the meantime, he needed to return to his visitors. Duty took precedence over Raina's sudden departure and the letter still clutched in his hand. He would not read it until much later, when he was once again alone.

Still, he needed a few more moments to regroup, to recover from the blow, then he would return downstairs. Collapsing into the chair near the window, he kept staring at the envelope. Kept wondering what she had said in a letter that she could not say to him in person. They had talked about so many things. He thought she trusted him. He had learned to trust her.

Unable to ignore his need to know, he tore open the envelope, withdrew the paper and began to read.

Dear Dharr,

I've never been all that good at verbally expressing my feelings except through my art, but since I can't really draw you a picture, I decided to write down my thoughts.

My mother and father's decision was only part of the reason why I needed to leave. The other has to do with you. I never intended to feel anything for you. Never intended to make love with you. And I definitely never planned to fall in love with you.

But I do love you, Dharr. I only wish I knew who caused you such pain that you've given up on love. I wish I could be the woman who heals you. If you're reading this and you still let me go, then I know there is no hope for us. As I've said before, if you love someone, you fight with all that you have to keep them close. What better proof of true commitment.

Regardless of what you decide to do with this knowledge, I will still love you anyway, and always. Raina.

Dharr read the letter again, absorbing the words, a profound pain radiating from his pounding heart. She had presented him with the ultimate test, urging him to undertake a battle to win her back. He would walk through the fires of hell to do that very thing.

And he would, beginning now, before she walked onto the plane and out of his life.

Raina stared out the sedan's window, her eyes clouded with tears she tried so hard to keep to herself. After she was alone on the plane, then she would cry all the way to California.

The sun was beginning to set over the mountains, washing the terrain in gold and reminding her of the night before in Dharr's arms. At least she had that memory to see her through until she got over him. That could take years, or a lifetime.

For a minute she'd thought they'd entered some sort of dust storm, then she caught sight of the vehicle pulled alongside of the sedan and heard the blare of a horn. She sat up straight, fearing some highway bandit was trying to commandeer the car—until she recognized the driver.

What was Dharr doing there?

She had no time to question his unexpected appearance before the sedan pulled over and Dharr yanked open her door. "Come with me," he told her as he clasped her hand and tugged her from the seat.

She stood in stunned silence while he tossed her bag into the Jeep and told the driver in Arabic to retrieve his parents and tell them he would be detained indefinitely.

He held open the Jeep's door and said, "Get in."

On wooden legs, Raina complied and settled into the seat while Dharr got back behind the wheel and took off. He turned around in the middle of the road, pausing to allow a shepherd herding his sheep to cross the dirt thoroughfare. Then he was off again, leaving a blanket of dust in his wake.

"Dharr, the airport's the other way."

He kept his gaze trained on the road. "I know."

"Where are you taking me?"

He still refused to look at her. "You will see."

It didn't take too long for Raina to realize exactly where they were going when Dharr navigated the back roads up the mountain. They arrived at Almase in record time, thanks to Dharr's speed-demon driving. She had no idea why they were here but she hoped to find out soon. She wouldn't allow herself to hope for more than that.

Rounding the hood in a rush, Dharr opened her door and led her once more to the place where they had made love. He turned her toward the valley, his arms wrapped around her from behind. "Azzril is a part of you, Raina. You belong here. It is your true home."

"Sometimes I don't feel like I have a home anymore."

He turned her around to face him, his arms resting on her shoulders. "You do have a home here, with me."

Hope niggled at her heart. "With you?"

"Yes. You must stay."

"Why?"

"Because you are also a part of me now, as I am a part of you. We would both regret destroying that bond."

Her hope grew stronger but she wasn't quite ready to believe just yet. "Dharr, I'm not quite sure what you're saying."

He hesitated a moment, looking out over the valley before again turning his soulful eyes on her. "What I speak of now, I will not speak of again. There was a woman long ago, when I was at Harvard."

"Elizabeth?"

"Yes. I was young and she was different from any woman I had known. We were very different. She was also my first real lover. She could not accept my culture, or my responsibility. She wanted nothing more than her freedom. She told me so in letter then left without saying goodbye."

"And I did the same thing."

"No, you said goodbye, and you also said something she never did, that you love me."

"I do love you, but I'm still concerned because it appears you've never gotten over her."

"I suppose I have mourned the loss for ten years, shielding myself from that pain. Now I realize that my loss was only felt so intensely because of my age. That losing her was not so great a loss after all. Yet if I lost you, that would be a loss greater than any I have ever experienced, because I have come to recognize that the love I feel for you is the love felt by a man, not a boy, for a remarkable woman. I realize now I was simply waiting for you."

Raina swallowed a gasp. "You love me? Are you sure?"

He gently held her face in his strong hands, forcing her to look into his eyes. "In my life, there have been very few things of which I have been so certain. If you desire it, I will toss away my duty and position. I will give everything up for you. I will follow you wherever you wish me to go, as long as I am with you."

Although shadows played across his features, she could still see the sincerity in his dark eyes, and the love she had been searching for. "You don't have to give up anything, and neither do I. You're right, Azzril is my home. And as they say, home is where the heart is, and mine's definitely with you." This time "they" were absolutely right.

"Then you will stay?"

She slipped her arms around his waist and smiled. "Yes. Does this mean I'm going to be a kept woman?"

"I hope you will be my wife."

Her laugh sounded broken and shaky from another on-slaught of tears trying to make their presence known. "You mean adhere to that silly marriage contract. Where do I sign?"

His own smile faded into a frown as he thumbed one rogue drop from her cheek. "You need not sign anything beyond an official document proving our marriage. What will bind us is our love for each other and nothing more."

"I'm all for that. Does the offer still stand for me to teach art?"

"No."

Raina saw the first real problem in their relationship. "I've worked most of my life, Dharr. I don't intend to sit at the pal-ace and plan social events twenty-four seven."

"Nor do I want that from you. I do want you to be the di-rector in charge of the children's program at the museum. If you still wish to teach, that will be up to you."

She held him close, buried her face against his shoulder, let the tears fall. Unrestrained tears of joy, of love without bounds. He kissed those tears away, then kissed her lips with an aching tenderness. When they finally parted, he sent her another smile. "You will be a revered queen."

Standing on her tiptoes, she kissed his forehead, his cheeks, then his mouth. "Right now I want to be your revered lover, but I guess we really don't have time since you need to get back to your guests. And I need to break the news to my parents that I'm staying for good."

He began to release the buttons on her blouse. "We shall be fashionably late."

Raina returned the favor by working Dharr's buttons, as well. "What are our parents going to think?"

"Our fathers will be grateful, for when we return tonight, I will be escorting my future bride."

Raina had made a beautiful bride. Even though several hours had passed since the wedding, Dharr was still remembering the vision of her walking down the aisle on her father's arm. And following their vows, she had been on his arm, showing the world she was his.

At the moment, Dharr stood in the bedroom he now shared with his new wife, admiring the painting hanging over the fireplace—a man and a woman silhouetted against the desert night, the lights of the city providing the backdrop—replacing the nude he had sold to donate money for the children's program. Raina had completed the masterpiece in less than a months' time while deep into plans for the wedding. And Dharr had missed winning the wager by one week, though he did not care. As far as he was concerned, all three Harvard colleagues had won.

The celebration continued outside the palace, yet Dharr and Raina had excused themselves early. For the past hour, they had made up for time lost together due to their commitments, and their mothers' determination to keep them apart until the wedding. However, they had managed to sneak away a few times in the middle of the night, returning to their favorite place to explore…each other.

"Are you coming back to bed now? I really need a good naked man to warm me up."

Dharr turned to find Raina stretched out on the bed in a provocative pose, nude, a vision not easy to ignore. Yet when he glanced at the clock, he realized he would have to disregard his own need to return to her, at least for a while. "As much as I hate the thought of not coming back to bed, we are scheduled to make an appearance on the veranda in ten minutes."

Her golden gaze raked over his equally nude body. "I dare you to go out there like that."

When he started toward the glass doors, she bolted from the bed. "Dharr, I'm not serious."

He turned and laughed. "Some day you will learn not to dare me unless you expect me to follow through."

She grabbed for her dress laid out on the chair at the bedside and her underclothes from the floor where he had left them. "I'll keep that in mind."

Dharr put on his tuxedo and robes then the kaffiyeh while he watched her dress. He would take great pleasure in removing her clothing again, once he had performed his duty—introducing the future queen to the adoring subjects.

After they were presentable, he took her hand and led her to the entry to the balcony, but before they could proceed, she pulled him to a stop. "Are we going to have to do this every night?"

He grinned. "I certainly hope so. Several times if you are willing."

She frowned. "I meant make an appearance."

"Only tonight. And when we have our first child."

After adjusting his collar, she patted his chest. "You know, my father mentioned that tonight. He wants to know when we're going to give him that grandson, and I told him not to push his luck."

"I prefer not to share you for at least a year, maybe two."

She winked. "I won't argue with that. I'd like to keep you in bed for at least that long."

"And you will have no argument from me." Leaving one arm around her, Dharr gestured toward the doors. "Shall we address the masses now, Princess Halim, so we might return to bed soon?"

"Why of course, Sheikh Halim. The sooner, the better."

"Masses" proved to be an accurate assessment, Dharr realized when they stepped to the railing surrounding the veranda. Two guards emerged from the darkness and flanked them on both sides as the crowd began to cheer. He positioned Raina in front of him, his arms circled around her. She rested one palm on his joined hands and waved with the other while myriad cameras began to flash.

"Great. Now I'm blind," she murmured.

He leaned close to ear. "When we go back inside, we need only to be able to feel our way over each other's bodies."

"And hopefully we won't have some reporter climbing up the trellis to capture that on film."

"I fear we will always have a certain amount of media attention. It is all a part of the life."

"I know. I read the Los Angeles paper today. The article said, 'California Girl Catches A Sheikh.'" She looked back at him. "Do you feel like you've been caught?"

"I feel I have been blessed."

Without regard for their audience or the guards standing close by, without any prompting, he kissed her soundly, thoroughly, bringing about another resounding ovation.

Once they parted, Raina smiled. "You are so good at that."

"Are you prepared to go back inside for more?"

"You don't have to ask me twice."

After a final wave to their subjects, they returned to the room yet remained in each other's embrace.

"Now when are you going to take me on that honeymoon?" Raina asked as she tugged the kaffiyeh from his head and slid the robes from his shoulders.

He reached behind her to lower the zipper on the dress. "Do you still wish to go to California?"

"Yes. I want to show you the beach. Up close and personal." She released the buttons on his shirt. "Without clothes."

"Would you mind if we make another stop while we're in the States?"

"Where?"

"I am scheduled to meet with my Harvard roommates for our tenth reunion in the state of Oklahoma."

She smiled. "So you can all bemoan your loss over that ridiculous wager?"

"So we can celebrate the fact that we have gained much more than we have lost."

Her eyes misted. "If you keep saying things like that, I'm going to cry again. I almost ruined my wedding dress during the ceremony."

"I will remedy that now." He tugged the fabric from her shoulders, allowing the dress to fall in a pool of lace at her feet. "And I will kiss away your tears, but I will never stop proclaiming my love for you."

"I'm going to hold you to that."

"And I am going to hold you, all night. Every night."

She pulled him toward the bed. "What are we waiting for?"

In a rush, they divested each other of all their remaining clothes and he took her back down on the bed. Dharr chose to simply hold Raina for a time, savoring the feel of her body against his, knowing he would never tire of having her in his arms, or his life. They made love again, slowly at first, then gave in to the passion that had consumed them from the beginning.

In the aftermath, Raina rested her head on his chest, her long hair flowing over him like a silken veil. She was nothing like he remembered all those years before, yet she was better, an extraordinary woman in every sense, and she would always be his, as he would always be hers.

Epilogue

In the smoky confines of Sadler's Bar and Grill, three men of status gathered with their wives—the cowboy, the king and the prince—conducting a journey back into their pasts and freely discussing the prospects of their future. Rowdy revelry filtered into the private room, yet no photographers lurked in the shadows, no paparazzi waited to catch a candid photo. Nothing disturbed the camaraderie shared by long-time friends as they passed the hours in the obscure Oklahoma town.

With his arm draped over Raina's shoulder, Dharr watched with amusement as Marc DeLoria teased his wife, Kate, who was still on the phone speaking with their nanny tending their daughters back at Mitch Warner's ranch. Mitch's wife, Victoria, rested one arm across her belly swollen with child—two children, to be precise. Both girls.

Mitch took his wife's hand and asked, "Are you okay, babe?"

She shifted in her seat and grimaced. "I will be if these babies cooperate and make an on-time appearance."

"Which reminds me, Halim," Marc said. "When are you and Raina planning to have a baby?"

Kate snapped the phone closed and elbowed her husband, causing him to wince and drawing laughter from the women. "That's really none of your business, sweetheart."

"Yeah, it is," Mitch chimed in. "We already have a head start with fatherhood, so I think it's time Dharr takes the plunge."

He glanced at Raina then smiled. "We do not plan to have children for a year or two. We do plan to have quite a bit of practice."

This time Raina elbowed Dharr. "You are so bad."

"They're all bad boys," Tori said.

"But that can be *so good,*" Kate added with a smile.

Mitch lifted his cowboy hat, ran a hand through his hair and set the hat back into place. "You beat all I've ever seen, Dharr. You were the first to be officially engaged—"

"Betrothed," Dharr corrected.

"Whatever," Mitch said. "And you were the last one to marry. You're supposed to produce an heir, and now you're telling us you're not even planning to have a kid for two years?"

"That is correct." He tightened his hold around Raina's shoulders. "And when we do have our first child, no doubt it will be a son."

Mitch held out his hand. "Wanna bet?"

"A banner idea," Marc added. "I propose we wager that the first man to have a son—"

"Hold it right there, Marc," Kate said. "Knowing all of you, that means we'll end up with at least ten kids a piece if none of you are successful."

Mitch turned to his wife. "That's the point. The pleasure is all in the participation. Right, Tori?"

Tori gave her husband a smile, a cynical one. "I don't think now is the time to discuss having a son, honey."

Seeing an opportunity for diplomacy, Dharr lifted his cup of wine. "To our future children and to our wives, who have effectively brought us to our knees and thankfully ruined our wager."

Tori lifted her glass of soda. "I think we'll all drink to that, right girls?"

Both Kate and Raina readily agreed, holding their glasses high.

Marc raised his beer for the toast. "Here, here."

Mitch did the same. "To friendship, the future and three real fine women."

As the party continued with more tall-tales and stories of exaggerated acclaim, all three men conceded one thing. When it came to a remarkable woman, and falling in love, all bets were definitely off.

* * * * *

COMING SOON!

We really hope you enjoyed reading this book. If you're looking for more romance, be sure to head to the shops when new books are available on

Thursday
9th August

To see which titles are coming soon, please visit
millsandboon.co.uk

MILLS & BOON

LET'S TALK
Romance

For exclusive extracts, competitions
and special offers, find us online:

- facebook.com/millsandboon
- @millsandboonuk
- @millsandboon

Or get in touch on 0844 844 1351*

For all the latest titles coming soon, visit
millsandboon.co.uk/nextmonth

*Calls cost 7p per minute plus your phone company's price per minute access charge

Want even more
ROMANCE?

Join our bookclub today!

'Mills & Boon books, the perfect way to escape for an hour or so.'

Miss W. Dyer

'Excellent service, promptly delivered and very good subscription choices.'

Miss A. Pearson

'You get fantastic special offers and the chance to get books before they hit the shops'

Mrs V. Hall

Visit millsandbook.co.uk/Bookclub

and save on brand new books.

MILLS & BOON